Trouble Comes in Threes

Copyright © 2024 by Denise Grover Swank

All rights reserved.

No part of this book may be reproduced in any form or by any electronic or mechanical means, including information storage and retrieval systems, without written permission from the author, except for the use of brief quotations in a book review.

✵ Created with Vellum

Trouble Comes in Threes

Rose Gardner Investigations #8

Denise Grover Swank

*For everyone who wasn't ready to say goodbye.
Including me.*

Other Books By Denise Grover Swank

Rose Gardner Mystery

Rose Gardner Investigations and Neely Kate Mystery

Carly Moore Mystery

Maddie Baker Mystery

Magnolia Steele Mystery

Darling Investigations

Harper Adams Mystery
Probable Cause (short story)
Little Girl Vanished
Long Gone

Chapter One

"Aunt Rose! Wake up! How much longer?"

I was still half-asleep when a small hand gripped my shoulder and gave me a hard shake. "*Aunt Rose!*"

I hadn't slept very well the night before—the baby was teething and had woken me up twice—so I struggled to open my eyes. Still, I knew my nephew Mikey was beyond excited to play his first soccer game. He'd been counting the days, and since the game was scheduled for six p.m., it was down to hours. I felt sorry for Mrs. McCallan, his first-grade teacher, who would surely be asked to take over countdown duties. "Ask Uncle Joe."

Mikey crawled over me, nearly kneeing me in the stomach, and the bed shook behind me as he bounced onto the mattress between me and my husband Joe.

"Uncle Joe! How much longer?"

Joe, who had the patience of Job when it came to the kids, said, "At dinnertime."

"We're eating dinner during *the soccer game?*" Mikey asked incredulously.

"No." The bed shifted as Joe sat upright. "You're playing when we're *supposed* to be eating dinner. How about I take us all out to dinner afterward to celebrate you winning the game?"

"But Aunt Rose says there are no winners or losers," Mikey

said, as though Joe had lost all the sense in his head. "We just play for fun."

"Then everyone's a winner. All the more reason to celebrate," Joe said, and Mikey shrieked with laughter.

I rolled over to see Joe tickling his armpit, making him double over with giggles.

My heart swelled with love. I'd been raising my niece and nephew and had recently had Hope when we married. It wasn't every man who would not only willingly but joyfully walk into an instant family of four. Then again, he'd been around long before I'd taken in my sister's kids and become pregnant with Hope. He'd lived next door to Violet and the kids for a while, and they'd started calling him Uncle Joe way back then.

"Are you awake *now*, Aunt Rose?" Mikey asked when he saw me looking at him.

"Now I am," I said with a warm smile, then teased, "I *really* wish you were more excited about your first game."

"I *am* excited!" Mikey squealed. "I am!"

I gathered him in my arms and hugged him tightly with tears welling in my eyes. My sister should have been the one he gushed to about his upcoming game, but Violet had died three and a half years ago. Then, less than a year later, her husband was sent to prison for fifteen years, and he'd made Joe and me the kids' legal guardians. I considered every day with them a blessing, especially after he'd tried to keep them from me for a short period after my sister's death. But I suspected neither Mikey nor his sister Ashley remembered that, and I wasn't going to tell them.

"You're hugging me too tight, Aunt Rose," Mikey said, wiggling in my arms.

"I'm just trying to fill you with love before you go to school."

"I already have lots of love," he said, sitting back on his heels. He turned to Joe. "Don't I, Uncle Joe?"

"You sure do, buddy," Joe said, his voice tight as he reached for Mikey and hugged him too.

"Why's everybody so huggy today?" Mikey said, shrugging Joe off after a few seconds.

"It's a huggy kind of day," I said, the unshed tears stinging my eyes.

Mikey hopped off the bed and ran out the door, always in a hurry to get to where he was going.

"Go get ready for school," I called after him. "We'll be down to make breakfast in a few minutes."

After he left, Joe turned to face me, sorrow filling his eyes. "You're feelin' it too?"

I nodded, trying to keep my tears from falling. "Violet should be here, Joe. She should be the one he runs to with his excitement."

He turned to me and cupped my cheek, giving me a gentle kiss before pulling back and smiling at me lovingly. "I know, darlin', but she's not. So we'll just make sure he and Ashley feel her love through us."

I nodded, but the sad truth was Mikey didn't even remember his mother. He pretended he did when we talked about her or Ashley brought up a memory, but other than photos and the few videos Violet and Mike had taken of themselves and the kids, his memory of her was a blank. It felt extra sad because my own birth mother had died when I was two months old. I hadn't even known she'd existed until I was twenty-four, and the mother who'd raised me was murdered.

Lordy, that felt light years ago, but in truth, it had only been six.

"Gross," Ashley groaned in disgust behind Joe's back. "You're kissing again."

"Yeah," little Hope said. "Gross."

I wasn't surprised the two of them had come in together. Hope hero-worshiped her ten-year-old cousin, and I was thankful Ashley didn't seem to mind. Not all preteen girls would be thrilled to have their nearly three-year-old cousin hanging on their every word and following them like a shadow. There *were* times Ashley got tired of her, but usually only when she had friends over, and even then, she let Hope spend a little time with her and her friends before sending her away.

Joe sat back up, laughing. "Unfortunately, for me, I wasn't kissing her when you walked in, but thanks for the suggestion." He made a production of leaning over and giving me a big chaste kiss on the lips, and the girls squealed in protest, although I knew Hope was only protesting out of solidarity with Ashley. She always liked it when Joe kissed me.

I sat up and got a closer look at my daughter. "Hope, what are you wearing?" She had dressed in a pair of pink shorts that she'd outgrown months ago, paired with a brown turtleneck sweater.

Asley shook her head. "I told her she couldn't wear that to school," she said with the ancient wisdom of a near-ten-year-old.

I opened my mouth to tell Hope she should change, but Joe slid out of bed and scooped our daughter into his arms. She broke into a fit of giggles.

"I think you look beautiful just the way you are, princess," he said, then kissed her forehead.

"Joe," I said carefully. "Your daughter is wearing booty shorts."

He glanced down at her and pressed his lips together. "On second thought, while Daddy's so proud of you for dressing yourself, how about you and me go pick out something else to wear to preschool?"

"But I like this shiwt," she said, glancing down at her round tummy.

"You can keep the shirt," Joe said, "but how about we change your bottoms so your legs won't get cold? It's still March, baby girl. It's not summer yet."

"Good idea, Daddy," Hope said, then wrapped her arms around his neck as they headed down the hall to her room.

Ashley remained in the doorway with an anxious look on her face.

"Hey, Ash," I said softly. "Everything okay?"

She moved closer to the bed, standing next to Joe's side, twisting her hands in front of her.

"You can talk to me," I said encouragingly. "About anything."

She made a face. "I don't want Uncle Joe to be mad at me."

My brow shot up, and I patted the bed. She slid onto the mattress and kept her gaze in her lap. "Why on earth would Uncle Joe be mad, Ashy?"

She lowered her voice so I could barely hear her as she said, "I got in trouble at school yesterday."

I wouldn't have been more surprised if I'd heard the pope was converting to Judaism, but now that I thought about it, she'd been quieter than usual during dinner and bedtime the previous evening.

Joe had been the Fenton County Sheriff for less than a year, and since it was an elected position, sometimes he was forced to do some gladhanding. The night before, he'd attended a townhall meeting, leaving me to deal with four children on my own. Needless to say, the night had been chaotic, but I still felt terrible for not noticing that she'd been upset. "What happened, sweetie?"

She picked at the cuticle on her thumb. I could tell she'd been picking at it for a while because it was beginning to bleed. Goodness! She was so much like her mother! Violet used to do the same thing when our mother was on a rampage. You could tell when she was being extra mean because Violet would have multiple Band-Aids on her fingers and thumbs.

Also like her mother, Ashley was the perfect child at school. She never got in trouble. I couldn't imagine what she could have done. The only time Violet had ever gotten in trouble was when she'd tried to protect me. Was Mikey somehow involved?

I covered her hand with my own to stop her from picking at her skin. "Ashley, I promise you that if Uncle Joe gets upset, he'll quickly get over it. What happened?"

She tucked her chin to her chest, her tangled blond curls falling next to her face. She mumbled something unintelligible.

"I couldn't hear you, sweetie."

Tears fell from her eyes onto her lap. "I don't want to say it."

My heart began pounding, not because I believed she'd done something awful, but because something had deeply upset her. "How about you whisper it in my ear, okay? Then we'll figure out what to do about it."

Nodding as she lifted her face, she cupped her hand around my ear and whispered, "Oliver said my daddy was a dirty criminal who worked with a bad, bad man." She leaned back and looked up at me with tear-filled, cornflower-blue eyes. "My daddy's not a dirty criminal," she said defiantly, but then fear filled her eyes. "Is he?"

My heart stuttered. Ashley knew her father was in prison and had seen him only a handful of times because of Mike's insistence that the children stay away. He would be there until after she graduated from high school, and he hadn't wanted his kids to be burdened with his shame. Still, neither Joe nor I had emphasized that he was a criminal. "Ash, honey, people make mistakes. Your daddy made some big mistakes, just like I told you and Mikey."

Her chin quivered. "So he *is* a dirty criminal? Because Oliver said only dirty criminals go to jail."

My heart ached for her as I cupped her chin and stroked her cheek with my thumb, trying to soothe her. "No, sweetie, he's not a dirty criminal, but he *is* considered a criminal. It was very unkind of Oliver to say that to you." My anger blossomed, but I tried to keep it in check. Oliver was in Ashley's fourth-grade class. He'd picked on her from time to time since they'd started kindergarten, and while it was probably equally unkind for me to call a ten-year-old a shithead, if the shoe fit…

"Did he work for a bad, bad man?" she asked, eyes wide.

Her question made me pause. A lot of the information about what Mike had done wasn't necessarily made public, but that didn't mean there wasn't plenty of speculation. Most people speculated that Mike had been working for a local drug czar, Denny Carmichael, who was also incarcerated. But in truth, he'd been working for Hope's biological father, who was currently running a tavern in Lone County, Arkansas, about two hours away.

The ache inside my chest deepened.

I hadn't thought about James Malcolm in a good bit, but I saw him in Hope's eyes and her chin. The way she studied things that puzzled her and the way she didn't back down from a fight—although Joe attributed that to me.

Only a handful of people knew that James was Hope's biological father, and I intended to keep it that way. Joe might not share her DNA, but he'd been there since I'd found out I was pregnant. He'd held my hand, offering support during my pregnancy, and then carried at least half the load of caring for a newborn before we'd made our relationship official with a marriage license.

Joe Simmons was Hope's father in every way it counted, and I *did* count my blessings every day. But I hadn't forgotten that James had willingly sacrificed a relationship with his daughter to keep her safe. I was grateful for that too.

Ashley was waiting for an answer about whether her father had worked for a bad man, but I had no intention of touching that subject with a ten-foot pole. At least not on a Tuesday morning when we were already running late for school.

"Your daddy worked for a group of bad men," I said carefully, "but you don't need to worry about what he did right now. When you're older, we can talk about it…if you want."

She stared at me for a few seconds, then nodded. "Okay."

I forced a grim look. "So now that I know what Oliver said, tell me what happened after he said it."

"He said it in front of the entire class, and everyone started saying my daddy was a dirty criminal. Then he made fun of me when I started to cry, so I kicked him in the shin." Shame washed over her face.

She was worried Joe would be upset with her, but I suspected he was going to be secretly proud. In fact, he was likelier to be disappointed she hadn't kicked *both* shins.

I took her hand and cradled it in mine. "Two wrongs don't make a right, but I understand why you did what you did."

"Mrs. Pritchard wants to talk to you and Uncle Joe this morning before school."

I tried to keep from making a face. I had a busy morning, and I knew Joe had back-to-back meetings. "Did she send a note home?"

She nodded again. "It's in my backpack." Fresh tears slid down her cheeks. "I'm *really* sorry, Aunt Rose."

I pulled her into a hug, tucking her head under my chin. "Never be afraid to tell me when you're in trouble, Ash. You can tell Uncle Joe too. We'll always have your back."

"Thank you, Aunt Rose."

"Don't worry. I *will* be talking to Mrs. Pritchard about Oliver's behavior." I heard fussing across the hall, so I kissed the top of her head and dropped my hold. "We'll drop Hope and the baby off at preschool before I take you to school, okay?"

"But she wants to see Uncle Joe too."

"You let me worry about that. Uncle Joe has an important meeting he can't miss."

"I love you, Aunt Rose."

The fussing across the hall grew louder, followed by a sound that made me smile. "Momma!"

"I love you too, Ash." I kissed the top of her head again. "Now I need to go check on your cousin."

I slid out of bed and padded across the hall into the nursery to find my dark-haired, fifteen-month-old son standing in his crib. He smiled from ear to ear when he saw me. "Momma! Momma!"

"Did you have a good sleep, sweet Liam?" I asked as I lifted him out of bed and settled him on my hip. "How are your teethies doing?"

He opened his mouth and pointed to his teeth.

I grinned. "That's right. Those are your teeth. Do they still have an owie?"

His face morphed into an exaggerated frown. "Owie."

"I'm sorry." I carried him over to the changing table for a quick diaper change, then carried him downstairs, leaving him in his sleeper. I'd put him in his clothes for daycare after he ate because he hated bibs, and it wasn't uncommon for his clothing to get covered in his meal.

Joe was already scrambling eggs and making toast when we walked into the kitchen. After I settled Liam in his highchair, I walked over to Joe and gave him a kiss. "God bless you for starting breakfast."

He shot me a sexy grin. "You can make it up to me tonight."

I gave him another quick kiss. "That can be arranged, Sheriff Simmons."

He waggled his eyebrows. "I like it when you call me that. I have some plans in mind…" His voice had turned husky and trailed off.

Even now, in the midst of morning chaos, this man still made me tingle in all the right places. "Promises, promises," I whispered.

He released a laugh and swatted my bottom. "You go get ready," he said. "I've got this covered."

"You're still wearing your pajamas."

"My first meeting's at nine, and it won't take me long to get ready," he said, scrambling the eggs in a skillet. "We're good."

"Before I head up…" I lowered my voice. "We need to talk about something that happened to Ashley at school."

Turning serious, he glanced over his shoulder. She was standing next to the table, checking Mikey's backpack to make sure he'd put his homework in his take-home folder. I'd told her a million times she didn't have to do that, that it was my job, but she still liked to check. Another way she was like Violet.

"Is she okay?" Joe asked.

"Just shaken."

His worried eyes met mine. "Should I be concerned?"

"No, I don't think so, but I intend to talk to her teacher. I'll fill you in tonight."

He nodded, still frowning, obviously wanting to know more but trusting my judgment.

That trust had been hard earned, and I never wanted to give him cause to doubt me again.

Chapter Two

Weekday mornings were always a circus. I was planning a field workday with my company RBW Landscaping, which meant I didn't spend much time on my hair and makeup. My day would consist of digging and planting. Although, to be honest, I didn't spend much time getting ready on office days either. Putting on more than mascara and concealer and curling my hair wasn't worth the lost fifteen minutes of sleep.

After I threw on a pair of jeans and a light gray RBW T-shirt, I pulled my hair into a ponytail. Since I was meeting Mrs. Pritchard, I considered putting on mascara but decided against it. She could take me as I was.

After I brushed my teeth and swiped on some deodorant, I packed Liam's diaper bag and headed downstairs with an outfit to change him into.

Joe had already gotten everyone fed and was cleaning up the kitchen.

"You're the best," I said, giving him a kiss. "Are you riding with us to the game tonight?"

He took Liam's clothes from me and handed me a plate of eggs with a piece of toast. I sat at the table and started to shovel food into my mouth.

"We'll play it by ear. I might have to meet you there."

Mikey's face wrinkled with a frown. "Aren't you coming to my game, Uncle Joe?"

Joe set Liam on his lap and stripped him out of his sleeper. "Wild horses couldn't keep me away."

Mikey's eyes flew wide. "There's gonna be *wild horses* at my game?"

Joe laughed as he tugged a T-shirt over Liam's head. "Sorry, buddy. It's just an expression. There won't be any horses there. But *I'll* be there."

"Promise?"

"You bet."

"Is it my turn to bring snacks?"

"Nope." Joe said, now working on Liam's jeans. "That's in two weeks."

"We can't forget."

Joe laughed. "I doubt you'll let us."

"Uncle Joe and Aunt Rose are *responsible*, Mikey," Ashley said with a sigh. "They'll remember."

I was glad Ashley had more faith in me than I had. I suspected *she'd* be the one to remind us. But on the off chance she didn't, I'd already scheduled an alert on my phone.

I checked the time and stood, eating the rest of my eggs as I walked over to the sink. "It's supposed to be cooler today, so everybody get your jackets on and let's go!

Joe stood and put Liam on his hip, then picked up the diaper bag as I scooped Hope out of her chair and carried her out to my Suburban.

Ashley and Mikey were already climbing into their booster seats in the third row as I strapped Hope into her car seat. Just as I got her buckled, I realized I'd forgotten my own bag and Hope's. Joe was buckling in a wiggly Liam, so I hurried inside, grabbed both bags, and ran back outside, passing Joe on the way.

TROUBLE COMES IN THREES

"Have fun digging in the dirt," he said, giving me a quick kiss. He knew how much I loved planting.

"And you have fun with all your meetings."

"I knew the sheriff's position came with a ton of administrative stuff, but some days…"

"You're the best sheriff this county has had in a long, long time, Joe Simmons," I said, placing a hand on his chest and patting it. "You're doin' good, whether you can see it or not."

"Thanks, Rose. That means more to me than you know." Concern filled his eyes. "I know you were up with Liam a couple of times last night. Sorry I didn't help more."

"It was fine. You were beat, and I wasn't sleeping well anyway. Besides, you've taken plenty of turns."

"Did you have trouble sleeping because of your nightmares?"

I hesitated before answering. "Not last night, thank goodness."

He cupped my cheek. "You're safe, Rose. The kids are safe."

I wanted to believe him, but my nightmares of the literal nightmare we'd lived through three years ago had started up again a few weeks ago. They'd stoked my lingering fear that the Hardshaw crime group would reform and hunt me down for the role I'd played in their demise. I was even more terrified they'd hurt my kids.

Joe had assured me time and time again that we were safe and Hardshaw was gone for good. But my subconscious still didn't believe it.

"I know," I said with a soft smile, wishing I truly believed it.

"I'm lookin' forward to this weekend," he said with a sly smile.

"Me too," I said affectionately.

One of my favorite bands was coming to Little Rock on Friday night, and Joe had booked tickets and a room in a boutique hotel. Jed and Neely Kate had offered to watch the kids, so we were planning to leave work early on Friday and have dinner in Little Rock before the concert. We wouldn't be able to stay for long on Saturday—Mikey had a game at one—but we'd be able to sleep without interruption.

I said as much, and Joe gave me a wicked grin. "Maybe one interruption or two."

I laughed, lifting my brow. "Two? Someone's ambitious." We were lucky to get more than twenty minutes of sexy time at home.

He laughed too, then swatted my bottom and gave me a kiss.

I leaned back and looked up into his loving eyes for a second before giving his chest one last pat and jogging down the porch steps. After I tossed the bags into the passenger seat, I got in and started the car, taking a deep breath to settle down from the morning craziness. I was just about to back out of the driveway when Joe came outside carrying my thermal mug.

I rolled down the window, and he held it out to me. "I think you're gonna need your coffee."

I took it from him and sighed. "Is this ever gonna get easier?"

"Maybe when they've all graduated from high school," he said, grinning ear to ear. He loved every minute of the craziness. Most days, I did too, but today, I was worried about Ashley.

I dropped Liam and Hope off at the New Living Hope Revival Church daycare before rushing to take Ashley and Mikey to their elementary school.

It was the same school Violet and I had attended when we were little girls—where I'd been bullied mercilessly. It had been hard to come back for school performances with Violet when Ashley had started kindergarten, but I'd learned to deal with it. Still, walking in now with the kids pouring into the building caused my nerves to kick in. I couldn't stop the other kids from talking about her father, but I *could* expect her teacher to intervene on her behalf.

TROUBLE COMES IN THREES

After I dropped Mikey off in his classroom, Ashley grabbed my hand and squeezed. I glanced down at her and offered a reassuring smile as we walked down the hallway to Room 110.

Kids were entering Mrs. Pritchard's classroom, and she was standing at the front of the room, writing the date on the whiteboard.

I cleared my throat. "Mrs. Pritchard."

Ashley still clung to my hand as her teacher turned to face me with a disapproving glare. "Mrs. Simmons," she said, somehow looking down her nose at me, despite the fact I was a good fifteen feet from her. "I expected you to show up a half-hour ago."

This woman had been at West Side Elementary since I'd attended here, and while I'd never had her as a teacher, I'd known her to be strict. I'd almost requested a classroom reassignment for Ashley, but she seemed to thrive when firm rules were in place. In fact, I sometimes wondered if she floundered in the chaos at our farmhouse. I'd figured an enforced school environment might suit her. And I had to admit, other than a few incidents involving Oliver, Ashley had loved her fourth-grade year up until this point. But allowing children to taunt my niece over something—whether it be in or out of her control—was *not* acceptable, and I planned to make sure it didn't happen again.

I gave her a haughty look. "And I expect my kids to all go to bed without asking for a glass of water or wanting us to read the same My Little Pony book seventeen days in a row, but that rarely happens."

Her mouth dropped, and she stared at me in shock before she recovered, pinching her lips with condemnation. "Class is about to start, so this will have to wait until after school."

"No," I said, lifting my chin. "I'm here now, so we'll discuss it *now*."

"I'm afraid that's not possible," Mrs. Pritchard said.

"Then Ashley and I will be talking with the principal...*with* or *without* you, because I definitely have plenty to talk about with *him*." My hand tightened around Ashley's, and I led her out of the classroom toward the office.

"Mrs. Simmons," Mrs. Pritchard called after me. "Wait."

I stopped and turned to face her. She still looked angry, but she seemed to be trying to hide it.

There were fewer children in the hallway, but the ones who were there gaped at us before moving toward their respective classrooms.

Mrs. Pritchard stood in the doorway, glancing in the classroom. "Everyone start your morning work," she said. "I'll be back in a moment." She stepped into the hall. "This really should be handled after school."

"I'm here now, and I'm not going to have Ashley worrying herself to death over it all day long." I drew in a breath. "Ashley told me that Oliver said mean things about her father yesterday."

Her lips pressed into a thin line. "Oliver spoke the truth." Her brows lifted. "Or is her father not in prison?"

My belly burned with indignation. "I think I've heard enough. Come on, Ashley." I headed toward the office again, terrified of what I'd do to the woman if I was forced to face her a second longer.

"I don't want to get in trouble," Ashley whispered, giving me slight resistance.

"You won't, but hopefully Mrs. Pritchard will."

Ashley stopped in her tracks, bringing me to a halt. "I don't want her to get in trouble either."

"You let me worry about that."

I stomped into the office and demanded to speak to the principal, an older man who had been the principal when I'd attended over two decades before. He came out of his office a few minutes later and motioned for us to come in.

Ashley moved like she was on a death march, but I ushered her in, and we both sat on chairs in front of his desk. "Mr. Caldoni, thank you for seeing us so quickly."

"What seems to be the issue…" He glanced at Ashley, then back at me. "Mrs. Beauregard?"

So he knew Ashley. That was good. He had to know it was unusual for her to be caught up in drama. "It's Mrs. Simmons," I said. I was still legally Rose Gardner, but I let people call me by Joe's last name when it pertained to the kids. "Or Ms. Gardner. I'm Ashley's aunt. Her legal guardian."

His face went slack. "Oh. Right. I'd forgotten."

Ashley was still clinging to my hand, so I gave her another squeeze and a reassuring smile before I got down to business. "Mr. Caldoni, it has come to my attention that a boy in my niece's class has been harassing her and that her teacher, Mrs. Pritchard, did nothing to intervene. In fact, when I questioned her about it just a few moments ago, she seemed to condone the behavior by stating that the boy was speaking the truth."

Mr. Caldoni's jaw tightened as he turned to my niece and said kindly, "Ashley, why don't you tell me what happened?"

In a meek voice and with her gaze on her lap, Ashley repeated what she'd told me that morning, along with a few more details that made the whole situation even more unsavory. Oliver and some other children had tormented her for several minutes, and the only reason Mrs. Pritchard had eventually shut them down was because it had interrupted her lesson time. Oliver had resumed his harassment during recess, and Ashley had finally kicked him to make him stop.

When she finished, Mr. Caldoni lifted his gaze to meet mine. "Mrs. Simmons, we take bullying very seriously here."

Part of me wanted to say I wished he'd taken it seriously when I'd been Ashley's age, but this was about her, not me. Even so, I'd pull her out before I ever let anyone treat my niece the way I'd be treated at this school.

"I appreciate that, Mr. Caldoni," I said with a slight nod. "But apparently, Mrs. Pritchard doesn't have the same philosophy."

He folded his hands on the desk. "I'm sure this has been blown out of proportion."

"And I can assure you that it has not," I said firmly. "Ashley isn't prone to fanciful exaggerations. She believes in the facts. If she says this happened, then it did."

"I'll speak to Mrs. Pritchard after school."

"And I'm sure she'll deny it ever happened, or she'll dismiss it, the way she did a few minutes ago in the hallway, saying that he spoke the truth." I glanced over at Ashley and gave her another smile. "Ash, can you wait out in the other room for a moment? I need to speak to Mr. Caldoni alone."

"Okay," she said so quietly I barely heard her.

I waited until she walked out and the door clicked before facing him again. "Ashley's mother had a terrible illness that separated her from her mother for months before she came home and died. Then her father was arrested and incarcerated." I pointed to the door. "That little girl has been to hell and back and survived. I would like to consider West Side Elementary a safe place for her, but that was stolen from her yesterday, and she no longer feels safe here. Especially since her teacher has made it clear, she doesn't have her back."

He drew in a deep breath and let it out. "Mrs. Simmons, I know that Mrs. Pritchard can come across as harsh."

"Harsh is taking away recess when you don't have enough time to finish your in-class work. Allowing Ashley's classmates to harass her over something that she has absolutely no control over is Draconian."

He offered me a weak smile. "I will speak to Mrs. Pritchard."

"And, as I said, she'll deny the entire thing. You need to speak to some of the other children in the class to get the real story."

He stared at me for a moment. "Very well. I will."

My back stiffened. "When you confirm that my niece is telling an accurate account of what happened yesterday, what do you plan to do about it?"

"I can't discuss disciplining other students or faculty with you."

"I don't necessarily need to know the details," I said, "but I *do* need to know that this will be addressed, and a reoccurrence will not be tolerated."

"Of course. Of course," he said, patting his hands toward me. "I plan to get to the bottom of things."

"How can I leave my niece here, knowing you plan to send her back to the very place that hurt her yesterday before you address the issue?"

His face softened. "I understand your concern, Mrs. Simmons, and I am truly sorry Ashley was hurt yesterday. I *do* plan to address this, so it hopefully won't happen again, but until we have an actionable plan, either I or Ms. Klaas, the assistant principal, will sit in Mrs. Pritchard's classroom." He paused and lowered his voice. "You are not the first parent to notify me about what happened yesterday afternoon. In fact—" He gave me a soft smile, "—I'd planned to call you in a bit and discuss it with you."

I sat back in my seat. "Oh."

"I take the safety of our students personally," he said. "Both physically and emotionally." He held my gaze. "Attitudes about bullying have changed since you were a student here. I can assure you that I am full of regret for the way students were treated in the past."

I stared at him in shock. First, I was surprised he remembered I'd been a student here, especially since he'd called me Mrs. Beauregard. Second, I wondered if he was speaking in general or addressing me specifically.

"I'm glad to hear it," I finally choked out. "I will not stand by and let my niece's spirit be crushed when a teacher could have tried to stop it."

"That being said, children are often cruel," he said, sorrow in his eyes. "We can do everything in our power to stop it, but incidents happen."

"I understand that," I said, "but I expect the teacher to try to protect my niece."

"I agree. We're on the same page, Mrs. Simmons."

Some of the anger bled out of me. "Thank you."

"I can assure you, one of us from the administration will be observing the classroom for the next day or so. Ashley is in safe hands."

"Thank you," I repeated, on the verge of tears. "I *really* need for her to be okay."

"I understand."

I got up and found Ashley sitting in a chair in the receptionist area. I squatted in front of her and took her hand in mine. "Mr. Caldoni or Ms. Klaas will be in Mrs. Pritchard's classroom for the rest of the day, okay?"

She nodded, her eyes wide. "Am I in trouble for kicking Oliver?"

I cringed. Somehow in all of this, I'd forgotten about that.

"No," Mr. Caldoni said, following me out. "We'll consider having to deal with the situation at hand punishment enough."

"Thank you, Mr. Caldoni," she said, with tears in her eyes.

From my crouched position, I wrapped my arms around her and gave her a bear hug, holding her tight until she tried to wiggle free. I cupped her cheek in my hand and whispered, "I love you, Ashy. Never ever be afraid to come to me or Uncle Joe."

"Okay," she whispered back, a tear falling down her cheek.

"Do you want me to tell you if you're gonna have a good day?" I held her gaze so she'd understand what I was asking—whether she wanted me to try to see her day in a vision.

Ever since I was a small child, I'd had visions of the future. They used to be small things, like where someone's lost keys could be found or if someone's husband was having an affair. (Okay, maybe not small for the couple.) But the visions had always been spontaneous, and whatever I saw in my mind's eye blurted out of me when the vision was finished. I had no say in what came out of my mouth. More often than not, it got me into trouble.

The mother who'd raised me had believed I was possessed by a demon, and I'd spent a good portion of my childhood being locked in closets and beaten with wooden spoons. People around me had thought I was weird or crazy—hence, the bullying as a child.

But soon after my mother was murdered when I was twenty-four, I'd realized I could purposely try to have visions. Because I still blurted out whatever I saw, I sometimes had to talk my way out of humiliating or even dangerous situations, but I'd realized the futures I saw weren't inevitable. I could prevent bad things from happening by knowing about them beforehand. Using my gift had gotten me out of a lot of scrapes with criminals before Hope was born, but forcing visions of other people had started to feel like a major invasion of their privacy. I could ask a question of the universe and hope I saw the answer, but things didn't always go according to plan. Sometimes I saw embarrassing situations, and sometimes I saw things that were none of my business. So now, I always asked permission before forcing a vision.

She stared into my eyes and gave me a small nod, so I closed my eyes and asked the universe whether Ashley would have any trouble at school today.

I'd learned through experience that open-ended questions were risky. Visions went much better when I asked something specific, and I worried this question was too vague.

Suddenly, I was thrust into a vision, looking at my own face through Ashley's eyes.

"Did you have a good day?" Vision Rose asked.

I shrugged, unable to meet her gaze. "It was okay."

"Any trouble from the kids or Mrs. Pritchard?"

I shook my head, but a melancholy settled over me. "No."

The vision ended, and I opened my eyes. "You're gonna have an okay day," tumbled out of my mouth, and I held her gaze again. "Are you all right with an okay day? You can come to work with me today if you need a break."

"I have a math test," she whispered. "I don't want to miss it."

"I assure you, Mrs. Simmons," Mr. Caldoni said. "We'll take good care of her."

Which meant I had to take his word for it, but part of my heart was sitting in that chair, and it went against every instinct inside me to leave her.

"It's okay, Aunt Rose," Ashley said, sliding out of her seat and standing in front of me. "I want to stay."

"Okay," I said hesitantly as I stood. I still wanted to take her with me, but I knew I wouldn't always be around to fight her battles. Sometimes, she'd have to fight them herself.

But if she couldn't handle it, I'd be there behind her to fix it as much as I could.

"Come on, Ashley," Mr. Caldoni said. "We'll walk to class together."

I watched them head back to the hellhole that was Mrs. Pritchard's classroom and knew I had to trust I'd made the right decision.

Chapter Three

My business partner Bruce Wayne Decker was already at work with his crew when I pulled up to the Thatcher residence—not that I was surprised. He and his men usually got started around seven, and it was almost nine. They were all much faster and more efficient than I was at the physical aspect of the business, but RBW had come to life because I loved growing and planting.

I spent most days coming up with designs for clients, while Bruce Wayne handled the logistics of installing the designs I made with my best friend, and sister-in-law, Neely Kate. But sometimes my designs didn't work in the real world. Getting field experience helped me become a better designer…and Joe was right: I liked digging in the dirt.

Bruce Wayne waved as I walked over.

"Sorry I'm late," I said as I surveyed what they'd done so far. "I had to deal with an incident with Ashley at school."

"*Ashley?*" he asked in surprise. "What happened?"

Bruce Wayne, of all people, would understand. He'd had his run-ins with the law. In fact, I'd met him after being kicked off the jury when he was on trial for murder. I'd seen a vision that had proven his innocence, and since the prosecuting attorney had refused to believe me, I'd set out to clear his name.

I told Bruce Wayne everything, and he listened with a grim expression.

"Is she okay?" he asked when I'd finished.

"I'd like to say yes, but I'm not sure."

He nodded. "Unfortunately, what the kid said is true. Her father *is* in prison." He gave me a sidelong glance. "And he worked for a bad, bad man."

Pretty much everyone villainized James Malcolm—the "bad, bad man." Very few people realized what he had sacrificed for the county. Sacrificed for me and Hope. He'd lost everything, even his best friend Jed, and some days I struggled with the weight of my guilt.

But I couldn't contradict him. Bruce Wayne had never trusted James, and there was nothing I could say that would change his mind. I'd stopped trying long ago.

"I can't change what Ashley's father did or what happened to him," I said. "I just need to help her get through it."

"Unfortunately, I don't think you can stop it," he said with a frown. "Now that it has been brought up in front of her classmates, they aren't going to forget." He shifted his weight. "Maybe you should talk to Jonah about it."

"Good idea." A few years ago, Jonah, the pastor at New Living Hope Revival Church, had been my counselor for several months. He'd been a rock for me to lean on at a time when I'd desperately needed one. Besides, Ashley loved Jonah, and she might be more willing to open up to someone other than me or Joe.

He grinned. "I'm full of 'em."

"There's no denying that," I said emphatically. He'd come up with more than half of the ideas that had built up our landscaping business. And now that he had two kids of his own, he was even hungrier for success.

"Tell me where you want me," I said.

"A storm's supposed to roll in tomorrow afternoon—it might

even snow—so we're trying to get as much done today as we can."

"Snow?" I asked in surprise. We didn't usually get snow in mid-March, but then again, this was Southern Arkansas. The weather could change on you at the drop of a hat. "Okay, if you're wanting to get this job done quickly, that means I should work in a less critical area. Tell me what to do."

"That's where you're wrong. You can hold your own with the best of 'em." He sent me to work digging up an area where I'd designed a retaining wall. We needed to build a stable base before we started stacking the stones.

I got to work, and a few minutes later, Bruce Wayne, who was ripping out some bushes about ten feet from me, stared at the street and said in amazement, "Well, I'll be."

I glanced up and saw Neely Kate's car pulling up behind my Suburban and parking at the curb. Neely Kate got out and headed toward us in a pair of jeans and her bedazzled long-sleeved RBW Landscaping T-shirt.

"What's goin' on?" I asked as she approached.

"I thought I'd play in the dirt too," she said as she picked up a shovel and glanced around, refusing to make eye contact. In fact, her eyes looked puffy, like she'd been crying. "What are we doin'? Just digging up a mess?"

While this was hardly the first time Neely Kate had helped at a job site, she wasn't a fan of it. She'd told me once that she didn't need to try stacking a few stones in person to understand why something had gone wrong. "A pastry chef doesn't need to attend a wedding to see why her cake fell over when it's obvious a drunk bridesmaid tackled the groom after he'd screwed her the night before."

I'd nearly told her it wasn't the same thing, but for all of her bluster, she'd be the first one to show up at a job site if one of her designs didn't work. Plus, I knew for a fact that very thing had happened at her second cousin's wedding a year ago.

So why was she here? Based on the state of her eyes, now didn't seem the time to ask.

"We're prepping for a small retaining wall."

"Okay," she said with a sigh. "So I just dig?"

"Dig up over the spray-painted line," I said, gesturing to the orange line Bruce Wayne had already painted on the grass.

"Yeah, okay," she said absently.

I cast a worried look at my friend. Something was definitely wrong.

We started digging, and I hoped she'd confess what was bothering her while we worked. Neely Kate was a talker, and she usually wore her feelings on her chest like merit badges. Then again, I knew from experience that she was plenty capable of keeping secrets. She'd kept some deep, dark ones from me for years, and she'd only told me then because they'd risen up like ghouls in the night to haunt her.

After a few minutes, I asked, "Does Daisy still have a cold?" Neely Kate's daughter was about seven weeks younger than Hope, and they went to the same daycare. Since Daisy was Neely Kate's only child, she tended to be overprotective and got a lot more worried than I did over sniffles and skinned knees.

"Last weekend, she was blowing snot everywhere, but it seems to be getting better." She stopped digging and looked up at me. "Who knew kids had so many bodily secretions oozing out of 'em?"

"True," I said. "Thankfully, Liam seems to be over his. I'm just dealing with teething now. His molars are giving him fits."

Neely Kate glanced away, and more guilt washed through me. Neely Kate and Jed had adopted Daisy when she was a couple of days old because Neely Kate had been told she couldn't have children after a miscarriage several years ago. She loved Daisy more than life itself, but I knew some part of her wished she could still carry a baby in her own belly.

"Thankfully, that won't last long," Neely Kate said, pressing her foot on the edge of the shovel and shoving it into the dirt. A large thud sounded, and she took her foot off the shovel. "I hit something."

"A rock?" The ground here was full of them.

"No. Something else."

She dug up more dirt and exposed what looked like a piece of wood.

"It's probably a piece of two by four left behind from when they built the house," I said. Over the years, we'd found all kinds of things the builders left behind. Beer cans, wood, concrete. "Remember when Bruce Wayne found a toilet?"

"I do," she said, scooping out more dirt. "What's under here is a mystery." She gave me a grin. "Remember when we used to solve those?"

"That was ages ago, and definitely before we had kids."

She got quiet and dug out another pile of dirt. "Don't you miss it?" she asked, then looked up at me.

"Investigating?" I asked in surprise. I hadn't thought about those days in a long time.

But that wasn't exactly true.

I'd been thinking about James and Ashley and Mikey's dad… and having nightmares about Hardshaw coming back to seek their revenge. But Neely Kate didn't know about any of that. Not even the nightmares. I barely told Joe because speaking about it made me feel like I was giving Hardshaw more power over me. "What's in the water? First, some kid makes fun of Ashley about her daddy being in prison, and then you bring up investigating. It's not like we even got our PI licenses."

"Whoa!" she said, moving her shovel next to her and leaning on it. "What do you mean, some kid made fun of Ashley?"

I told her about my morning and my meeting at the school.

"At least they're taking it seriously," Neely Kate said as she dug more dirt off the piece of wood. I walked over to take a look. It was definitely bigger than a two-by-four. She'd exposed a section about a foot wide.

"Trust me. I'm going to follow up." I drew in a breath. "I can't imagine what Joe's gonna say when he finds out."

"He doesn't know?"

"She told me this morning, and you know how crazy our mornings are."

Her face went blank, and I tilted my head. "Okay, something's goin' on with you. Spill it."

She glanced over at Bruce Wayne and the three other workers. "I'll tell you over lunch because, fair warning, I'm not working out here this afternoon. I'm not a fan of perspiring."

I laughed. "There's a chance of snow tomorrow afternoon and evening, so I suspect it will be getting cooler, not warmer. And besides, no one told you to come out and dig with me."

"The office was too quiet."

Any other day, I would have accepted that statement at face value. Neely Kate was the most extraverted extravert I'd ever met, but I could see that something was bothering her. Had she and Jed had a fight? They didn't have them very often, but when they did, they were usually doozies. Still, she'd never been shy about telling me about their arguments, so it made me think it was something else.

I started digging with her, and within another minute, we'd uncovered more of the wood. Now that it was more exposed, it was obviously not a piece of construction wood. It appeared to be carved.

"It's a box," Neely Kate exclaimed in excitement.

I got down on my knees and started digging out dirt with my hands as I tried to uncover the sides. It was at least six inches tall, and once I exposed the bottom edge, I had Neely Kate pry it up with her shovel. Once one side was lifted, I reached in and tugged it out.

We both sat on the ground as I set the box in front of Neely

Kate. She brushed loose dirt from the carvings. An intricate tree was carved on top of the lid, and the sides were engraved with vines and flowers. There were curved wooden feet at the base, but one of them had broken off. The wood was damp, and it stunk a little, but the scent wasn't overpowering.

"What do you think it is?" she asked, holding it up to examine the sides.

"It looks like a jewelry box." I tried to open the top, but it didn't budge. I wiped some of the caked mud off the sides, looking for a keyhole, and finally found a small hole on one long side. "It needs a key. Do you see one in the hole?"

Neely Kate leaned over and scanned the small pit we'd just made. We both rummaged through the loose soil, but a couple of minutes of searching turned up nothing.

"What do we do with it?" Neely Kate asked.

"I don't think it belongs to the homeowners. They've owned the house only a few years." I grabbed my phone out of my back pocket and pulled up my camera app. "I'll take a photo and send it to them."

Still sitting on the ground with Neely Kate, I sent the photo in a text, telling them we'd dug it out of the spot where their retaining wall was going. Jill, the homeowner, called me right away, and I put her on speaker phone.

"What is it?" she asked in excitement.

"It looks like a jewelry box," I said, "but it's locked. Did you guys happen to bury it or know who might have?"

"Never seen it," she said, then hesitated. "But I don't feel right about taking it when it clearly belongs to someone else. The question is, who?"

"We can find out," Neely Kate offered enthusiastically.

I glanced up at her with wide eyes.

"You can?" Jill asked.

"Don't you want to know what's in it?" I asked.

"No," Jill said. "I'd rather return it to its rightful owner." She paused. "Do you really think you can find them?"

"Of course," Neely Kate said before I could stop her. "Piece of cake."

"Thank you," Jill said breathlessly. "Whatever it is, it looks important. I really want the true owner to have it. Of course," she added, "I wouldn't mind knowing what they found in it."

I started to ask her if she knew who had owned her house before she'd purchased it, but she said, "Oh, I've got to go. My client just walked in."

She hung up, and I put my phone in my lap, looking Neely Kate in the eyes. "What have you done?"

Her eyes shone with excitement. "I found us a case. I put it out into the universe, and it answered." She shook her head in amazement. "How crazy is *that*?"

"We don't do that anymore, Neely Kate," I protested. "We're landscapers. We have kids."

The sparkle in her eyes dimmed. "*You* have *kids*, Rose. I have one."

I reached over and took her hand. "You are an *amazing* mom, Neely Kate. That has nothing to do with the number of kids you have."

"What if I want more?"

I paused. "I'm sure Jed is open to adopting again."

She bit her bottom lip. "What if I don't want to adopt?"

"Oh, honey." She'd talked to multiple doctors about having a baby, but most had told her she had too much scarring, and that if she got pregnant, the chances of her losing the baby were high.

"Rose," she said, giving me a watery smile. "I'm pregnant."

Chapter Four

I stared at her in shock.

She chuckled, but it sounded strained. "If you don't close your mouth, a bug might fly in."

I shut my mouth and squeezed her hand. "How far along are you?"

"I'm not sure. I missed my period last month, but they've been spotty lately. I took the test this morning, and it popped up positive right away."

"But you haven't been feeling sick like the last time…" I let my words trail off. The last time was when she'd miscarried twins over four years ago. One had been an ectopic pregnancy, and she'd lost both babies.

"I know, but after I lost the twins, the doctor said I might have been so sick last time because I had double the hormones."

I nodded, scared to get excited for her until I knew all the facts. "What did Jed say?"

Her face fell. "I told him, and he said it was impossible. I showed him the stick, and he walked out the door and left for work."

"Wait. He just *left*?"

"Yep."

I stared at her in shock again, and she placed a finger under my chin, closing my mouth. When I regained my senses, I said, "That's not like Jed."

"I know, but he's definitely not happy."

"He's just in shock, Neely Kate. Give him a moment to get used to the idea."

"Is that how Joe reacted when you told him about Liam?"

She knew darn good and well that it wasn't. "You can't compare the two," I insisted. "We were *trying* to get pregnant. This is a surprise."

"Jed doesn't think it's a *good* surprise." Tears filled her eyes. "When Joe found out about Liam, he picked you up and spun you around. You told me yourself." A tear slipped down her cheek. "I wanted that too."

"He'll come around, NK. Just give him a minute."

She shook her head, more tears spilling out. "I'll *always* remember his reaction. He's spoiled it."

I leaned forward, pulling her into a hug, her chin resting on my right shoulder, and held her tight. I understood her disappointment. I could tell her that I'd felt the same way when I'd told James I was pregnant with Hope. Sure, it had been unplanned, and it was a shock, but I hadn't expected him to be so *angry*. And I hadn't expected him to strongly insist I get an abortion. I'd hoped he'd changed his mind and soften to the idea, but if anything, he'd only become more adamant that I couldn't keep the baby.

After Hope was born and she was kidnapped weeks later, I found out that while James had never wanted our daughter to be born, he would have moved heaven and earth to protect her. He'd given up his immunity deal with the government to make sure she and I were safe, and he'd also insisted that I deny his part in her DNA so no one would ever threaten her because of him. He'd wanted Joe to be her father. After some time, I'd realized that was the greatest gift he could have given her. Otherwise, she might be dealing with the same situation Ashley was dealing with now—only so much worse. Because James "Skeeter" Malcolm wasn't the lackey Mike Beauregard had been.

James truly was the bad, bad man.

"Are you having a tea party or digging out the base for the retaining wall?" Bruce Wayne called over with a laugh. Obviously, he couldn't see Neely Kate's tears.

Neely Kate pulled out of my embrace and wiped her cheeks with the back of her hand, smearing dirt under her right eye. "This is supposed to be a happy thing," she said with a sad smile.

"Then we'll celebrate with lunch," I said, reaching over and rubbing the dirt from her cheek with the back of my hand. "What would you like to have?"

"Would you think I was crazy if I said Chuck-N-Cluck? I've been craving their fried chicken and mashed potatoes."

I laughed. "I did say *anywhere*." And I happened to know it used to be her favorite fast-food restaurant. She'd moved on to a new chicken place in town—Let's Cluck a Deal—and hardly ever ate at Chuck-N-Cluck anymore. But sometimes there was comfort to be had in old things.

She set the carved box aside, and we finished digging the base for the retaining wall. I grabbed two stakes and some string to start leveling the ground, but Bruce Wayne shooed us away, saying it was time for the professionals to take over. I could have been offended—I'd built my share of retaining walls before—but I had to admit I was distracted. Better to let Bruce Wayne and his crew finish.

Neely Kate and I washed our hands as best we could with the garden hose. Then she picked up the box and carried it to the trunk of her car. "After lunch, I'll get started on the search."

"You never should have told Jill we'd find the owner," I said with a disapproving stare.

"Pleasssse," she said with a groan. "All it's gonna take is a call to the property department at the courthouse. I still know a few people there, and they'll give me a history of who's owned the house."

She had a point. She'd worked in the courthouse for years, and she had a knack for getting people to help her, including me.

"Fine," I said. "I suppose a few phone calls won't hurt." I snuck a glance at her, seeing how much she needed this. "Why don't you go to the office and ask the property department for the names, and I'll stop by Chuck-N-Cluck and get our order?"

She clapped her hands together with glee. "Perfect."

After she told me what she wanted, I got in my car. But instead of driving straight to Chuck-N-Cluck, I headed to Carlisle Automotive.

I needed to have a little chat with Jed.

HE DIDN'T SEEM SURPRISED TO SEE ME WHEN I WALKED THROUGH the open bay doors of the garage, but he didn't say anything either.

"Hey, Rose," Witt, Neely Kate's close cousin, said, poking his head up from under the hood of a car. He'd worked for Jed since they'd opened their doors to their first customers over four years ago. "You havin' car trouble?"

"Thankfully, no," I said, continuing to the back of the garage. "I just need to have a little chat with Jed."

Jed gave me a look that suggested he'd rather have a root canal, but he didn't protest as I headed to the breakroom and sat at the dining table. He followed me in, shutting the door behind himself, and gave me a petulant stare.

"Look," he finally said with a dramatic sigh. "I already know what you're gonna say."

"Do you?" I asked with raised brows. "What am I gonna say?"

"That I should have been happier when Neely Kate told me she was pregnant."

"Actually," I said, looking up at him. "That's *not* what I was gonna say."

His eyes widened, but then he quickly recovered. "So what *are* you here to say?"

"I was gonna say that you're entitled to your feelings, Jed. I understand it was a shock. Sure, your reaction was a huge disappointment to Neely Kate, and I wouldn't be lying if I said that I didn't wish you would have covered your reaction, but what's done is done." I leaned my elbow on the table and propped my chin on my hand. "But what I *don't* understand is why you didn't at least acknowledge her pregnancy? Why did you just walk out on her like that?"

He sat down across from me, dragging his hand through his hair. I didn't have the heart to tell him he now had a grease streak across his forehead. Unlike Neely Kate's dirt smear, I wasn't going to rub it off.

"Because," he said, looking like he wanted to cry, "she knows I didn't want her to get pregnant. She knew I wouldn't see this as happy news, but she chose to pretend otherwise."

"Jed," I said, leaning closer. "I know you're probably scared. The chances of her losing this baby are high. But don't you see this was at least a *little bit* of happy news? She's been trying to get pregnant for ages."

"Yeah, she has, but obviously she didn't tell you what the last two doctors said."

"What?" I asked in confusion.

He held my gaze. "They told her if she got pregnant, it could potentially kill her."

I stared at him in shock. "*What?*"

He sat back in his chair and crossed his arms over his chest. "I guess she *didn't* tell you that part."

"No."

"We haven't been using birth control because we never

thought we'd get pregnant." He shook his head. "Obviously, we were wrong."

"Jed, I had no idea."

"Yeah, I figured."

We sat in silence for a few seconds before I said, "What are we gonna do?"

"I don't know," he said with a sigh. "She's adamant that she's meant to have this baby, that it was a miracle she got pregnant. She's determined to see this through."

"Okay," I said, my mind scrambling. "She just found out. Maybe once she thinks about you and Daisy…" I stopped, because while she loved Jed and Daisy with her entire being, she would never, ever end this pregnancy unless she had another ectopic pregnancy. She'd been forced to end her first pregnancy years ago back in Oklahoma, and she still struggled with the guilt and pain of her loss.

He lifted one side of his mouth into a sad smile. "You just realized the truth."

My chest felt heavy. "Yeah."

His eyes welled with tears. "What am I gonna do, Rose? I love her so damn much. I can't live without her."

"You won't have to!" I assured him. "We'll do everything in our power to protect her. We'll put her in a plastic bubble if we have to." I thought about her digging at the Thatcher's this morning. There'd be no more physical labor until after this baby was born.

He nodded, not looking entirely convinced. Neely Kate wasn't a sitter. She was a doer, and we likely had at least seven months to go.

After a second, Jed made a face. "Would you…" He paused, rubbed his chin, and leaned forward. "Would you have a vision to make sure she's going to be okay?"

I hesitated. "If it were up to me, I'd have a vision in a heartbeat. But it's not my decision. It's Neely Kate's."

"But you can suggest it," he said, warming up to the idea. "And if you see her…"

"Die."

He nodded, tears welling in his eyes. "If you see her dead, then maybe she'll come to her senses."

Even then, I wasn't sure she'd do anything to end her pregnancy. She'd just try to find a way to avert the outcome.

"Let me think about it," I said, then held up my hand when he started to protest. "I can suggest it, but we both know Neely Kate's never been shy about asking me to have visions for her. If she wants me to have one, she'll ask herself."

"And she's not going to want to know," he said, sounding devastated.

"Like I said, it's her decision," I said. "I won't force it on her, and I'm not sure I should even suggest it. I suspect it might upset her."

He leaned his head back, staring at the ceiling as he released a groan.

"But there are other things we can do," I said, trying to sound more upbeat. "The first is to make an appointment with a doctor and see how far along she is. And make sure it's not an ectopic pregnancy. Years ago, she said the doctors told her she had a high chance of having another one."

"Yeah," he said, running both hands over his face. "That's good. A plan."

"Yeah," I agreed. "A plan." It sounded promising, but then again, we'd had plenty of plans back when we were trying to protect the county from criminal forces, and our plans had rarely worked.

Maybe a plan would work this time.

Right, and flying monkeys were gonna fly out of Jed's butt.

Chapter Five

I headed back to town, stopping by Chuck-N-Cluck to pick up our lunch before I drove to our office downtown.

When I walked in with the food, Neely Kate was at her desk with her phone against her ear and writing in a small notebook. The wooden box was on the side of her desk, all cleaned up, but it still gave off a slight musty odor.

"That's as far back as it goes?" she asked into the phone. After a moment, she said, "Okay, thank you, Phyllis! I owe you a cupcake." She hung up and set her phone on her desk. "I got a list of the homeowners."

I stopped next to her desk and pulled out the box with her fried chicken meal. "Do I want to know how many people have owned the Thatcher's house?"

"It's not that bad," she said, not wasting any time as she opened the box. She grabbed a chicken breast and took a big bite.

I carried the bag with my meal over to my desk and sat. "I've found that your definition of not that bad and mine are often *very* different."

"Fine," she said with a groan. "There have been six homeowners, but considering the house is nearly ninety years old, that's not bad."

"And one set of those six owners is the Thatchers?" I asked.

"Yep, so that leaves five homeowners to find," she said. "Easy peasy."

Against my better judgment, I decided to play along. The majority of the cases we'd investigated in the past had been at my friend's urging. I could see plain as day she needed the distraction.

But it was more than that…

I had to admit that something deep inside me needed this too.

Restlessness had been running through my blood. Maybe it was all this dredging up of my past, or maybe it was because my life seemed consumed with diapers and bedtime routines. And while I loved every single minute of it—I wouldn't trade my life for *anything*—there were moments when I needed more.

The need had been there for a while. I'd tried to ignore it, telling myself I was tired, and what I *really* needed was more sleep. But it had persisted—a yearning for something I couldn't explain.

"Okay," I said, looking her in the eyes. "We'll do this. Together."

She practically bounced out of her seat with excitement. "Really?"

"Yes, but we have to set some ground rules."

"Okay."

"First, we can't let our jobs slip. It's March, and we're starting to get busy. Bruce Wayne's got to keep his crew working, which means we can't fall behind."

"I'm good with that."

"Second—and this is important—if this gets dangerous, we stop."

"Of course," she said dismissively.

"No, I mean it. I've got four babies to think about, and you have two. We can't be putting ourselves in danger."

She grew serious. "You said two babies."

"That's right, which brings me to number three: you have to make an appointment to see the doctor."

Her face paled. "Rose, I'm scared."

I wheeled my chair closer to hers. "I know you are, and I'm scared *for you*, but this is gonna be a high-risk pregnancy, and you need to start your prenatal care right away. I'll only do this if you make an appointment."

Tears filled her eyes, but she nodded. "Will you go with me?"

"Of course!" I assured her. "That is, if Jed doesn't."

She looked away. "He won't." She was silent for a moment. "I'm not sure he's gonna forgive me for this."

"He will, Neely Kate. He's scared too."

Her gaze swiveled back to mine. "You talked to him."

I gave her a sassy smile. "*Someone* had to try to talk sense into the man."

She laughed, but then her smile fell. "He told you everything?"

"Not everything, but enough that I understand why he's scared." I considered bringing up his idea about me forcing a vision of her future, but decided now wasn't the time. She needed other information first.

Her lips pressed tight. She was silent for several moments before she said, "Can we not talk about it right now? I just want to enjoy my greasy chicken and track down who to talk to about the jewelry box."

"Sure," I said, "but you're making a doctor's appointment as soon as you finish eating. Then we'll start tackling this mystery."

Neely Kate kept her end of the bargain and got the first available appointment the next Tuesday morning. As soon as she hung up, she grabbed her paper with the homeowners' names and started searching for the first name on the list.

I took new photos of the box and uploaded one to an internet search engine to see if I could find a similar one. The search proved fruitless, not that I was surprised.

"I think this was hand carved," I said, examining it again. "Not mass produced. I'm guessing it would mean something to whoever owned it."

"But why would they bury it?" she asked.

"That seems to be the question," I said. "Maybe it was a time capsule. They were really into those around the bicentennial in the 1970s."

"Or maybe they killed someone and buried their heart like in that Edgar Allen Poe story."

I gave her a blank stare. "*Or*...maybe it was a teenage girl who broke up with a boy and buried the notes he wrote to her. We might never know. If we find the owners, they might choose to keep it to themselves."

"Oh my stars and garters!" she exclaimed. "You're right."

"It's a possibility. Do you still want to do this?"

She pursed her lips, considering it, and then let out a long breath. "Yeah. I do."

"Okay," I said because I still wanted to pursue this as well. "I've considered posting photos to Facebook and asking if anyone knows anything about it, but I'm afraid someone will fraudulently claim it." I looked up at her. "Which means I think we should stick to talking to previous homeowners, if possible. If we don't get anywhere with the homeowners, we can try the Facebook route as a last resort."

"I agree," she said, beaming. "Because I've just found the people who sold the house to the Thatchers."

"Do we know where they live?"

"No," she said, "but the wife's on Facebook. Lauren Abernathy. She works at Little Bo Peep's Boutique."

"That's the kids' clothes store in the new strip mall out by the nursery," I said. "We can go out there and check in with Maeve. I need to see if the plants for the Beetham job arrived today, and I want to see if she's still coming to Mikey's soccer game."

"We'll be there," Neely Kate said, then sobered. "At least Daisy and I will."

"Jed's gonna get used to the idea, Neely Kate. He just needs more time."

"Yeah. You're right." But she didn't sound totally convinced.

We wrapped up what we were doing, then went to check on a job site before we headed to the boutique.

"I've been wanting to check this place out," Neely Kate said when I pulled into the parking lot. "I hear they have some really cute girls' clothes."

Daisy was always dressed to the nines, often wearing sparkles and bows, while I was lucky to get Hope in clothes that matched—as evidenced by this morning's struggle. Once we walked in, I instantly knew I couldn't afford this place, even if Hope would be willing to wear ruffled skirts and headbands with bows.

I walked to the counter and smiled, suddenly realizing that I probably didn't look like I belonged. I had dirt stains on my jeans, and I was still wearing my work boots. Neely Kate hadn't gotten very dirty this morning and had changed into a pair of cute ankle boots.

"Hi," I said. "I'm looking for Lauren Abernathy."

The woman behind the counter looked worried. "I'm Lauren."

She looked like she'd lost weight since her Facebook profile picture had been taken, and all her recent public posts had been memes about how crappy men were. I was guessing a breakup.

"Hi, Lauren. I'm Rose Gardner, and this is Neely Kate Carlisle."

Neely Kate, shuffling through a rack of girl's toddler clothes, looked up and waved before turning back to her searching.

"We're landscapers," I continued, "and we're working at your previous home on Olive Drive."

Panic filled her eyes. "I told Roger not to pack that sewage pipe with concrete."

"What?" I asked in confusion, then shook my head. "No. That's not why we're here." Although I made a mental note to tell the Thatchers they might need to have their sewer pipe examined. "Today when we were digging, we found a wooden box buried on the side of the house. We were wondering if you knew anything about it."

Her eyes narrowed. "A wooden box? What's in it?"

"It's locked," I said, glancing back at Neely Kate, who had pulled a couple of items from the rack and hung the hangers from her other arm. I was surprised she wasn't front and center asking questions, but maybe the lure of the cute outfits was too strong. I turned back to face Lauren. "It's about a foot long, about half as wide, and it looks hand carved. At the current homeowner's request, we're trying to find out who might have buried it so we can return it to them. I'm guessing you don't know anything about it."

She shrugged. "I've never seen anything like that, let alone buried it."

"What about your husband?" I asked. "Could *he* have buried it?"

Her mouth pinched. "That would require the no-good lazy asshole to actually pick up a shovel."

"So that's a no?" Neely Kate called out from the clearance rack.

"That's *definitely* a no."

"I thought your husband covered the sewer line with concrete," Neely Kate said as she pulled a dress off the rack and examined it.

"As if," Lauren snorted. "His brother did all the work while Roger sat in a lawn chair in the yard, knocking back his beers." She shook her head. "Roger 'supervised.'" She used air quotes.

"Could Roger's brother have buried the box?"

She shook her head. "No way. There isn't a sentimental bone in that man's body."

"How long did you own the home?" I asked.

"About ten years."

"Do you have any kids who could have buried it?"

She shook her head. "We never had kids. Roger didn't want 'em."

"A neighbor or a friend?"

"Nope. I guarantee you that no one buried any kind of box in my yard when we lived there. But maybe the couple who lived there before us. I think they were the Elgers."

"Thank you for your time," I said.

Neely Kate walked up to the counter with several items of clothing and set them down, holding up two shirts. *Soccer* was spelled out across the front of each of them in red sequins. "I'm getting these for Ashley and Hope to wear to Mikey's game. I got one for Daisy too."

"You don't need to do that, Neely Kate," I said, feeling guilty, but I knew Ashley would love it. And Hope would wear hers because it matched Ashley's.

"Of course I don't," she said with a wave of dismissal, "but I can get my nieces things from time to time. And besides, they were on clearance."

"Well, thank you."

After she paid far more than I would have for six items, we headed back to the car. Still, I had no judgment. Neely Kate had always cared more about the way she looked than I did, and Ashley was more like her than me. More like Violet. This was a good reminder to pay attention to that. I wondered if I should have searched the clearance rack for something for Ashley. Violet had left some money to the kids, but I'd refused to use any of it for day-to-day purposes. I was saving it for their future college education. Maybe I needed to rethink that.

But not today.

There were only a few cars in the parking lot when we pulled up at the nursery I'd founded with my sister Violet. When Violet had gotten sick, Maeve took over managing the shop, and thankfully had stayed on. Maeve was behind the counter with her laptop open in front of her when we walked in, and her face lit up when she saw us. She was in her sixties but didn't look it. In fact, I was pretty sure she looked younger than she had when I'd first met her nearly six years ago.

I'd met Maeve through my then-boyfriend Mason Deveraux. She was a widow, and she'd been lonely in Little Rock. She'd moved to Henryetta to be closer to her only living child, but when Mason had moved back to Little Rock three years ago, she'd stayed in Fenton County to run the plant nursery. She'd told me she had more friends here than she had back in Little Rock, so it hadn't been a hard decision, especially since Mason was a workaholic. Besides, she and I had grown very close. She'd become the mother I'd always wished for, and my kids called her Nana Maeve.

I was incredibly lucky to have her in my life.

"What are you two up to today?" she asked, walking around the counter to greet us. She was wearing jeans and a flowy floral top with her Gardner Sisters Nursery apron over both.

"We dug up a box on a jobsite," Neely Kate said. "We're trying to find out who it belongs to."

Maeve grinned. "You girls are solving a mystery? It's been a while, hasn't it?"

"Too long," Neely Kate said.

"I thought I'd stop by and see if the Beetham's plants showed up today. Bruce Wayne will be starting their job in a couple of days."

"They delivered them about an hour ago. I think Anna's out back, looking over the order right now."

Anna was Bruce Wayne's wife, and he'd met her after she'd started working at the nursery several years ago.

I glanced at the wall clock. "If there's anything missing, can you have her call me? If the greenhouse gets the order wrong, we'll have time to get it fixed before Bruce Wayne's crew starts working."

She frowned. "Anna tells me there've been problems with some of Bruce Wayne's new hires."

While we liked to work year-round, there were times when we didn't have enough work, so it wasn't uncommon for some of the new guys to move on to more steady jobs. Which meant Bruce Wayne was always looking for new workers come early spring. "We only had one quit so far, so that's better than last year, but I know a couple of them aren't working out as well as he'd hoped."

"Good help is hard to find," Neely Kate said.

"That's true," Maeve said. "Anna's amazing, but the other people I hire don't seem to last long." She smiled. "Moving on to happier things. Is Mikey excited about his game tonight?"

I laughed. "If you'd call him waking us up at the crack of dawn and asking how many hours were left until his game excited, then yes."

She laughed. "I love that little boy. He goes through life excited about just about everything."

Warmth flooded my chest. Her description fit him to a tee. "He sure does."

"Well, tell him that Nana Maeve is definitely coming, even if I'm a few minutes late, but I'll have something special for him after the game." She winked. "And for the others too."

"They'll be excited, but you know they're excited just to see *you*. In fact, Joe said he's taking us all out to dinner after the game. Would you like to join us?" I turned to Neely Kate. "You, Jed, and Daisy are welcome too."

"I'd love to come," Maeve said. "And Mikey's gonna have his own cheering squad at the game."

She was right, and after my lonely, loveless childhood, it felt like a dream come true.

Chapter Six

After I dropped Neely Kate at the office so she could retrieve her car, I headed to the church to pick up the kids. Ashley and Mikey took a bus to the daycare after school, which made the pickup routine so much easier because I only had to make one stop. Today, I was especially relieved Ashley didn't have to stay at the school longer than necessary. I was anxious to hear how her day had gone and to see if it had changed from my vision.

I went to the elementary kids' area in the multipurpose room first. Some children were outside playing on the playground, but Ashley was sitting at a table with other kids who were working on homework. As if sensing I was there, she lifted her head. When she saw me, she jumped out of her seat and ran for me, throwing her arms around my waist.

This didn't match my vision.

My heart stopped. Had there been another incident?

I squatted and looked her in the eyes. "How did today go?"

She glanced away. "Okay."

"Really okay, or not really okay?"

She shrugged.

"Did Oliver say anything else?"

She shook her head but stayed quiet.

"What about Mrs. Pritchard?"

She shook her head again.

This part somewhat matched what I'd seen. Something had happened, but I could understand why she didn't want to talk about it right now. "How about we get the little kids and head home?"

She hugged me again and mumbled, "Okay."

I asked the daycare teacher to pull Mikey from the playground while I checked Hope and Liam out of their respective rooms.

Liam was thrilled to see me. When I picked him up off the floor mat, he wrapped his arms around my neck and hugged me tightly. My heart melted as he murmured, "Momma," and gave me wet kisses on the cheek.

After I grabbed his bag, we headed to the three-year-old room to get Hope. She and Daisy were playing in the kitchen, pretending to cook something at the stove. Daisy was wearing a pink tulle skirt, a pink long-sleeve T-shirt, and a pink headband with sparkles. She definitely took after her mother—while Hope was in her brown turtleneck and a pair of striped leggings. Daisy seemed more excited to see me than Hope, who ran to Ashley and gave her a hug.

"Is my mommy coming too, Aunt Rose?" Daisy asked in a sweet little voice.

"She'll be here any minute." I squatted next to her and tucked a blond strand of hair behind her ear. "We'll get to see you again tonight at Mikey's soccer game."

"Will Uncle Joe be there too?"

"Yep, and Nana Maeve too."

"Yay!" she exclaimed in glee, and Liam mimicked her, although I was pretty sure he didn't know what he was excited about.

I hurried the kids along to snag Mikey, and then we headed home, where I let Muffy out and got the kids going with their afternoon routine. Mikey didn't have any homework. While he and the little kids were playing in the living room, I found Ashley at the kitchen table and decided to take advantage of the alone time.

I sat next to her and folded my hands together on the table. "Did anyone bother you today?"

She kept her gaze on her math worksheet. "No."

"Was Mr. Caldoni or Ms. Klaas in your class all day?"

"Yeah, but everyone knew they were there because of me."

"Wrong." I leaned forward and placed my hand over hers. "They were there because Oliver and his friends said unkind things, and Mrs. Pritchard didn't stop them."

She glanced up at me. "But everyone thinks it's because of me."

I wrapped my arm around her back, and she leaned her head on my shoulder. "I'm so sorry, Ash. I wish I could make this better."

"I know, Aunt Rose. You tried."

"This will blow over soon. I promise. Okay?"

She looked up at me with teary eyes. "Okay."

Mikey shouted that Liam was slobbering all over his stuff, so I ran to the living room to see Liam practically French kissing Mikey's soccer ball.

Before we left for the game, I had everyone change—Mikey into his uniform of a red T-shirt with the soccer organization's name on the front, a pair of black shorts, and a long-sleeve black T-shirt underneath. The girls were excited to wear the shirts Aunt Neely Kate had gotten them, but Liam wasn't thrilled when I tugged a warmer shirt over his head. It was cool, and it would get even cooler outside as we came closer to sundown.

I packed extra snacks for the two littles, along with more diapers for Liam, then told everyone it was time to head out again.

"Can we bring Muffy, Momma?" Hope asked. Muffy sat next to her, giving me a pathetic look.

"No, sweet girl," I said, shoving a shoe back on Liam's foot. "No dogs allowed at the soccer game."

"But she's sad," Hope said in a small voice. "She misses us."

As though Muffy knew Hope was petitioning for her to come with us, she lay down with her chin on her paws, looking even more pathetic.

"I'd love to take her—"

Hope let out an excited squeal.

"—but we can't. We'll get kicked out if we bring her." I couldn't help thinking Hope had a point. Muffy thrived on being with her people and hated being alone for hours at a time. I'd left her alone far too often lately.

But there wasn't anything I could do about that at the moment, so I chased everyone but Muffy out the door, and we headed to the game.

I was exhausted by the time I pulled into the parking lot, but Joe was already there, thank goodness. The sight of him standing next to his patrol car in jeans and a long-sleeved T-shirt, his butt leaning against the hood, gave me butterflies. He looked even sexier than the day I'd met him nearly six years ago. A warm glow filled my chest as I parked, and it surged when he walked over to my door and opened it for me, then gave me a soft kiss. "You look frazzled."

"Rough day."

He cast a quick glance at Ashley and gave me a questioning look.

"That too, but there's something else I should probably tell you before Neely Kate and Jed show up."

His mouth turned down, and concern filled his eyes. "Should I be worried?"

"Yeah, maybe, but let's get the kids out first, and then I'll tell you."

Mikey had already unbuckled and was trying to crawl past Ashley, who was working on Hope's carseat straps.

"Move out of the way!" he exclaimed. "I've gotta get to my game!"

"Whoa," Joe said, moving to the passenger side. "You're early, buddy, and it's not nice to mow down your sister. Especially when she's helping Hope."

His bottom lip stuck out. "Sorry, Ash."

"It's okay," she muttered under her breath, clearly still holding a grudge.

I finished getting Liam unbuckled and moved to the back of the car to get the double stroller.

"I'll take care of that," Joe said. "Why don't you take Mikey over to his team? The girls and I will meet you on the sidelines."

With Liam on my hip, I got Mikey delivered to his coaches with plenty of time for warm-up practice. Ashley was steering the empty stroller, with Hope helping her push, while Joe carried three lawn chairs. He set up the chairs, and I sat in one with Liam in my lap. The girls saw Maeve walking from the parking lot and ran to greet her.

Joe leaned over and rested his arm along the back of my chair. "You have about twenty seconds to fill me in on whatever you can, darlin'."

I leaned closer, lowering my voice. "Neely Kate will likely kill me for telling you, but she's pregnant."

His face lit up with joy.

"Don't get too excited. I guess there's a potential health scare. Jed's none too happy about the situation, and Neely Kate's holding it against him." I figured it was better to ease him into the situation than to tell him outright her life was in danger. Although they hadn't grown up together, Joe and Neely Kate were half-siblings.

His body went rigid. "What kind of health scare, and how's he reacting?"

"I don't know exactly, and he's not talking much. He's scared."

"Is my sister in danger?" he asked, his face turning pale.

"I'm not sure, but I insisted she make a doctor's appointment as soon as possible. She's going on Tuesday morning."

"I thought she couldn't get pregnant."

"They thought so too, but apparently, a couple of the last doctors said it could be dangerous for her if she *did* get pregnant. She took the home test this morning, so she doesn't know how far along she is, only that the test was positive, and Jed wasn't excited because he's scared to lose her."

His mouth dropped open. "She could *die?*" he asked loudly enough that a couple a few feet away turned to stare at us.

Lordy, I'd screwed up. I hadn't meant to tell him that part, but he was an intelligent man. Of course, he'd read between the lines.

"Let's not think that way," I said in a whisper, shifting a squirming Liam on my lap. "She's gonna be fine. But you know Jed. He's overprotective of his girls."

He didn't respond. Instead, he gazed past me and got to his feet, reaching for the stadium chair slung over Maeve's shoulder. "Hey, Maeve, let me help you with that chair."

Each girl held one of her hands. Hope had to let go so Joe could get the stadium chair, but she grabbed it up again as soon as Maeve was free.

"Girls," Joe said. "Let Nana Maeve catch her breath. You've got the whole game to see her."

"And dinner too," I said. "I invited her to join us."

"Even better," Joe said, snatching up Hope. "I haven't seen my baby girl all day. Don't you want to spend time with your daddy?" He kissed her cheek, and a giggle burst out of her. But she soon got wiggly, so he set her down, and she ran back to Maeve to complain about me making Muffy stay home.

Joe reached over and covered my hand on my thigh with his. I offered him a warm smile.

"Joe," Maeve said, leaning closer. "What do you make of Rose's mystery box?"

He shot me an inquisitive look. "What mystery box?"

"Oh dear," Maeve said in alarm. "Was I not supposed to mention it?"

"No, you're fine," I said. "I hadn't gotten a chance to tell him about it yet. We're just now seeing each other today."

"What mystery box, Aunt Rose?" Ashley asked with interest.

I told them about digging up the box with Neely Kate and how the homeowner had asked us to find its owner. I pulled out my phone and let them see the photos I'd taken.

"What's in the box?" Ashley asked.

"It's locked up tight, so we're not sure, but Aunt Neely Kate is hoping the owner will let us see once we locate them."

"They need to share," Hope said with a pouty face. "Sharing is nice."

"Share," Liam parroted.

I gave Hope a grin. "Maybe we don't *want* to know what's in it. Maybe it's gross and stinky."

Hope giggled.

"Or maybe it's full of money," Ashley said. "Like a buried treasure."

I looked up at her. "Whatever we find, I'll be sure to tell you about any progress that we make."

"So you're investigatin' a case," Joe said quietly.

Grimacing, I turned to face him. "It's not like you're thinking."

"I'm thinking that you girls haven't investigated anything in years."

My heart dropped. "It's nothin' dangerous, Joe. I swear. I made Neely Kate promise that if it became even remotely dangerous, we'd stop." I held his gaze. "I have too much to lose to go risking my life over the contents of a box I don't even own."

"Agreed," he said with a forced smile. "You're right. Of course, you're right. It's a buried wooden box. How dangerous could finding the owner be?"

"Don't go jinxing us like that," I said.

Neely Kate and Jed showed up next with Daisy. The two of them still seemed distant, but Jed was clinging to her hand, and I took it as a good sign she hadn't shaken him off.

Joe jumped up and threw his arms around his sister, giving her a tight squeeze, and then—as though realizing what he'd done—he pulled back and held onto her upper arms. "Sorry. I didn't mean to hug you so tightly."

Neely Kate gave me a pointed stare. "You told him?"

"I had to," I said apologetically. "He's my husband."

She rolled her eyes, then looked over to see if Maeve had noticed. Thankfully, Daisy was just as excited to see Maeve as Hope had been, so she was preoccupied.

Joe started to lead Neely Kate over to his chair, as though she'd just had a hip replacement that morning.

"I'm perfectly capable of putting one foot in front of the other, Joe Simmons," she complained, pulling her arm from his grasp. She plopped down next to me and scanned the field. "Where's Mikey?"

"Out there," I said, pointing to the field. "They're warming up."

Jed gave Neely Kate an exasperated look, but Joe leaned in and said something. Then the two of them headed over toward the coaches.

Neely Kate reached for Liam, and he went to her, playing with the strands of her hair. He'd always been fascinated with her hair, and one night after we'd gone to bed, I'd teased Joe that Liam was going to have a thing for blonds.

"*I* only have a thing for one brunette," he'd said before proceeding to prove it.

"Have you told Jed about the box?" I asked. "Maeve let it slip to Joe."

"No." She cast me a sideways look. "How'd he take it?"

"I assured him that we'd back off if it got dangerous. He didn't seem too concerned."

She nodded. "Jed won't have a problem with it."

I suspected she was right. Jed liked to baby her, but he wouldn't interfere with this. Especially since she obviously needed it.

"Did you tell him you made the doctor's appointment?"

"Yeah," she said, watching Mikey kick a ball to another player. "He says he wants to come with me."

"That's good," I said insistently. When she didn't answer, I said, "I know his reaction this morning was disappointing, but you need to give him some grace with this."

"I know," she said with a sigh. "And I will, but I'm gonna make him sweat a little bit first."

The referee blew his whistle to start the game, but Joe and Jed stayed down by the coaches. The two little girls were busy playing with some Barbies that Daisy had brought, and Ashley moved closer to me and Neely Kate. I snagged her hand and tugged her to me. Relief flooded me when she sat sideways on my lap, resting the side of her head on my shoulder.

Maeve gave her a worried look. "Is Ashley getting Daisy's cold?"

"No, she's just feeling out of sorts," I said, rubbing Ashley's back. She stayed for a good five minutes on my lap, longer than I would have expected. She was ten going on thirty-five, and according to her, sitting on laps was for babies.

Neely Kate shot me a worried look, but there was nothing to say, so she rubbed Ashley's back too and kissed the back of her head. She might be facing trouble at school, but I vowed she'd never question whether she was loved. Thankfully, there were plenty of people in her life to prove it.

The teams were coed, and the kids tended to huddle up as they moved up and down the field. We all cheered when Mikey made a goal. We weren't supposed to keep score, but Mikey's team was the obvious winner.

After the game, Joe scooped Mikey up and put him on his shoulders, then brought him over to us.

The girls and Liam cheered as they approached, congratulating him on his goal, and Mikey grinned from ear to ear. Joe let him pick what he wanted for dinner, and he asked to go to Pizza Palace, a new place that had games and a play area for kids.

Since we didn't get to the restaurant until around seven, we didn't leave until nearly eight, which was the littles' bedtime. Once we had the kids clean and in pajamas, Joe told me to go take a moment for myself while he helped get their teeth brushed and read bedtime stories.

I kissed everyone good night and left him to it while I went down and made a cup of tea. After I put on a thick sweater, I took my tea and a blanket out to sit on the porch swing Joe had installed a couple of years ago. I needed a few minutes to decompress.

Joe found me about twenty minutes later. He was carrying his own mug. He lifted the edge of the blanket and sat next to me, tucking the blanket under his leg.

"How'd you know where to find me?" I asked, resting my head on his shoulder.

"This seems to be your favorite place lately."

"It's quiet out here."

"And it's noisy in there," he said, pushing off the porch with his feet to set the swing in motion. "I know it's been harder for you since I got elected sheriff. You're carrying a good portion of the load on your own. Would it be easier if we got someone to watch the kids at the house?" he asked quietly. "Or maybe someone to do some of the housework, like the mountains of laundry?"

"The housework sure, but someone to watch the kids here?" I considered it. "I suspect Hope and Liam would hate it. They love daycare, and Hope would really miss Daisy. Those two are inseparable." I took a breath, admitting something I'd been considering for a few weeks. "I'm wondering if maybe I should go part time."

He turned to me in surprise. "But you love what you do."

"I know," I said, feeling a lump in my throat. "But everything is just so crazy. Four kids is a lot."

"I know," he said, grabbing my free hand with his own. "Sometimes I wonder if I should have waited to run for sheriff until Liam was older. It was easier when I worked with you at the nursery and the landscaping business."

"Yeah, it was easier," I said. "But you weren't happy. Not really."

"I loved working with you and having a flexible schedule to help with the kids. I feel like I've dumped it all in your lap for my own happiness."

At times, I felt it had all been dumped on me too, but I'd never seen it as a selfish move on his part, which was why I'd never admitted it to him.

"You love being sheriff," I said. "And you're good at it. Not to mention the people love you. They *need* you."

"But you and the kids need me more."

"It's just growing pains," I said, sitting upright and turning to face him. "We're still feeling our way. But even if you were working with me, I'd still feel this way. I rush them off to school and daycare, then rush to get us all home. And we both know things are just going to get busier and crazier. Ashley loves her dance classes, and the older she gets, the more classes she'll be taking, and then there's Hope and Liam..." I took a breath. "I'm thinking about hiring another designer so I can pick Mikey and Ashley up when school gets out, then get Hope and Liam. But the tradeoff is, I'd be bringing home less money because I'd have to pay the designer."

"If it comes to that, we'll figure out the money part," he said. "Don't make your decision based on that."

I nodded, then took a sip of my now lukewarm tea. "I just feel like I'm missing so much of their little lives," I said past the lump in my throat.

"I know, I feel it too. If you want to go part time so you can be with them more, I'm all for it, but if you're doing it because of guilt for not being here, we'll figure out a way to make sure everyone's happy." He kissed my temple. "Including you, Rose."

"Thank you."

"Now tell me what's going on with Ashley."

I filled him in on our conversation that morning, my talk with the principal, and our discussion after school.

"She seemed okay tonight at the Pizza Palace," he said, tightening his hold on my arm.

"I know, but I think we took her mind off it. I'm hoping it will all just die down after a few days."

"How about I take her to school tomorrow?" he asked. "I'll take her to breakfast and see if she'll talk to me."

"She'll like that," I said. "But just remember she was worried you'd be upset."

"I hate that she thought that. I'll be sure to let her know I'll always have her back."

"Good." I snuggled into his side. "You're a great daddy."

"I have my own guilt," he said softly. "I feel guilty that I'm not home as much because my job is taking me away from all of you."

"We already discussed this," I said, wrapping an arm around his chest and tucking my hand under his arm. "I'm happy you ran for sheriff."

"I know, but still…I miss you and the kids."

"So let's plan a family weekend," I said. "No job stuff, just you, me, and the kids. Games and fun all weekend. Maybe we can go to the zoo in Little Rock for a day in a few weeks."

"I'd love that." He tilted his head down and kissed me with more passion than he would have in front of the kids. Heat flooded my veins.

"What do you say we continue this upstairs?" he murmured against my lips.

"I'd say that's the best idea you've come up with today."

Hours later, I woke up with a start, sitting upright in bed and gasping for breath. The room was pitch black, so I knew it was the middle of the night, but it took me a second to orient myself.

"Rose," Joe said, sounding anxious as he sat up and wrapped an arm around me. "What's wrong?"

I took a breath, trying to still my racing heart. "I don't know."

"What happened?"

"I don't know," I said, groggy from sleep. "I think I had a bad dream."

"You don't remember it?"

I closed my eyes and tried to remember what I'd dreamed of but only recalled fragmented pieces that made no sense. A warehouse with shelves stocked with cardboard boxes. A scream. Gunshots. A woman lying on the ground...

I'd had plenty of nightmares related to my Hardshaw fears, but none of them had been like this. They usually included bits and pieces of the past, combined with imagined confrontations. But even though they terrified me, they always felt like dreams. This had felt *real*—even if I could only remember fragments of it.

Even stranger, it had felt an awful lot like a vision. But I'd never had a vision while I was asleep before, so I quickly dismissed it.

I shook my head. "No. Nothing really to tell." I turned to face him. "Maybe I'm just anxious about Ashley."

"Yeah," he said absently. "That's probably it. It's about one-thirty. Do you want to try to go back to sleep?"

"Yeah." I lay down, and he tucked me into his side, his fingertips stroking my bare arm. I closed my eyes and tried to settle down, but now my mind was fixated on Ashley. And Hope. "Joe?"

"Yeah, darlin'?" he whispered against my hair.

"I keep thinking about Ashley, but also about Hope." I paused. "Joe, what if someone found out and…?"

His fingers stopped. "No one's gonna figure anything out," he said reassuringly as he cupped my arm and squeezed. "She looks plenty like you, and she's got brown eyes like me. No one's ever gonna question it."

"But I keep thinking about what would happen if someone did, and I'm not belittling what's happening to Ashley, but Hope…" My voice broke. "It would be so much worse, Joe."

He lifted my chin, and I could see outlines of his face in the dark. "It won't happen, Rose. I promise. But God forbid, if it did, we'd move somewhere far from here, where no one has ever heard the name Skeeter Malcolm, okay?"

"But your job and mine…"

"They're just jobs. We protect our kids. At all costs."

His voice was tight, and I, of all people, understood why.

His father, J.R. Simmons, had only cared about him in as much as he wanted his son to carry on the legacy of the Simmons name in both politics and business—and when Joe had balked, J.R. had schemed against him. He'd never once considered what his son wanted or needed.

The people who'd raised me hadn't been much more considerate. My father had left my mother after Violet was born because he'd been carrying on an affair with a woman named Dora Middleton. When Dora got pregnant with me, he moved in with her. She'd been killed in a car accident before I was two months old. He'd been lost without her and had taken me to his childless sister and husband. But my mother had used his grief to get him to return to Henryetta and reunite their family. She'd vowed to love me as her own daughter.

She'd lied.

She'd spend her life resenting me, and when I'd started having visions, she'd used that as an excuse to abuse me more openly.

And my father had let her.

Joe knew about my childhood, and I knew about his, and we'd both vowed our children would never feel unloved and that we'd support them in all things.

Even if we had to leave everything and everyone we loved to do it.

His body tensed. "Ashley and Mikey might not have our last name, but they are our children." He paused, his voice turning hard. "Which is why I plan on making my own visit to the school tomorrow."

I almost felt sorry for Mr. Caldoni.

His body softened, and he placed a kiss on my forehead. "Given everything you're worried about, it's no wonder you woke up," he said, his fingers resuming their meandering on my arm. "But with Hope, don't go borrowin' trouble, darlin'. We have plenty of our own."

Chapter Seven

I woke before the kids, so I took advantage of the quiet time to work on some designs in the sunroom off our bedroom. It had been my own baby nursery for those two short months before my birth mother's death, but I'd turned it into a home office. I loved working there in the mornings with my coffee while watching the sun come up. It gave me a great view of the barn and the horse pens, which had been vacant for a few years. If I started working part time, maybe we could house rescued horses again.

I wanted to get as much work done as I could before going into the office because I knew Neely Kate and I would be searching for the owner of the box, which was still in the back of my Suburban. There was a chance the box would belong to the next homeowner on the list, but I had to admit to myself that I hoped the search would take longer. The idea of working a case had grown on me, and Neely Kate and I were pretty good at it. Plus, it was something exciting to work on, even though the stakes were low.

My mind drifted to my dream. It had mostly faded, but I still heard screams in my head and remembered the sight and smell of blood. I tried to shake it off and focus on my work.

Liam began to fuss in his room a good half-hour before

everyone else was supposed to get up. Joe stirred, so I told him I had it and headed for Liam's room.

He was standing in his crib and broke into a broad smile when he saw me.

I shut the door behind me and picked him up, giving him a hug. "Don't you know it's still sleepy time?" I asked. But he hadn't woken up in the middle of the night, so I called it a win.

After I changed his diaper, I took him and my laptop downstairs. Muffy, who always slept with Hope, heard us and hopped off her bed, following us downstairs.

It was chilly outside, but Liam loved the outdoors, so I put on his jacket and shoes over his pajamas, and we went outside with Muffy, roaming over to the barn. I showed him where the horses used to be and then pointed across the field and told him that once upon a time, Daddy had lived on the other side.

Goodness, that seemed like so long ago.

My gaze landed on the barn, and I once again marveled at everything that had taken place there. All of that seemed like a lifetime ago too, and while I didn't miss the danger—especially now that I had children—I had to admit part of me craved the excitement.

I hoped the mystery box would help curb that yearning, but I feared it would only feed it.

I wasn't sure how long we'd been out there when Joe appeared at the back door, telling me he was cooking us breakfast. So I scooped Liam into my arms and carried him to the house, Muffy beating us to the door.

We started the morning chaos, but I was already dressed, which made things easier. Joe and Ashley left before I did so they'd have time to chat at breakfast. She'd seemed thrilled by the special attention, and I hoped she'd tell him about everything that was going on so he didn't have to hear about it secondhand.

I fed everyone the scrambled eggs and toast Joe had made. Thankfully, everyone ate and cooperated when I said it was time to go. Without Ashley to boss the little kids around, Mikey filled her role to some extent, beaming when I told him he was a good big brother.

Soon, I had three kids in my car, and we were on our way into town.

I said goodbye to Mikey in the carpool lane at the elementary school, then headed to the daycare to drop off Hope and Liam. On my way out, I ran into Jonah.

"Hey, Rose," he said, smiling from ear to ear. "I haven't seen you in a few weeks."

"Liam had a cold last week, so we kept everyone home from church," I said with a grimace.

He waved his hand. "You don't need a sanctuary to spend time with God."

"True enough." I started to walk past him, then stopped. "Say, Jonah, I know you don't officially have your counselor's license in Arkansas, but did you ever work with kids?"

His smile fell. "Is everything okay?"

I pulled him to the side of the hall and leaned in, keeping my voice low as I gave him a short recap of what was going on with Ashley.

"I think it might help her to talk to someone who isn't me or Joe." I shrugged. "Joe took her out to breakfast, so he might get through to her, but I think this is just the beginning of things." I drew in a breath. "I mean, there's no denying where her father is, but she's such a rule follower. I think she'll really feel the stigma of it."

"How about I pull her out of after-school care today for a chat?" he asked. "I can't officially be her counselor, but I can tell you if I think she needs to see someone."

"Thank you," I said, already feeling relieved.

"Kids can be so cruel."

I shook my head, my own memories flooding back. "Isn't that the truth?"

"How are *you* doing?" he asked, his gaze holding mine.

"Honestly, I've been feeling a bit frazzled since Joe's gone back to the sheriff's department, but we'll work it out." I rolled my eyes. "I mean, we aren't the only family with two working parents."

"If any two people can make it work, it's you two," he said. "But that doesn't mean you're not entitled to feel tired and frustrated. Just remember, there's no shame in asking for help."

My heart filled with warmth. "Thanks, Jonah." He'd always had a knack for helping me feel better about things.

As I drove to the office, my dream hung at the back of my mind like a tiny splinter stuck under my skin. It was still coming in fractured bits, and I was hopelessly trying to piece them together. It felt important.

I arrived at work before Neely Kate, so before I went in, I headed to the coffee shop a few doors down. I ordered my usual latte but told the cashier, "I can't remember Neely Kate's latest order."

"Got it here," the barista said, holding up a laminated paper square that had black marker drawn through words and new things added. "She makes changes all the time, but we try to keep her most current iteration. Right now, she's into a white chocolate mocha with three pumps of white mocha syrup and a pump of caramel made with almond milk.

I nodded. "Okay. I'll take one of those. Only make it a decaf."

"Neely Kate's giving up caffeine?" the barista said, shaking her head. "Won't she just fold up like a house of cards? She's like the Energizer Bunny, and I have a bet with Sebastian that she's fueled by caffeine and sugar."

"You're probably right," I said with a laugh. I should have realized they'd notice. "That's why I'm not telling her it's decaf."

He laughed and made the drinks, which I then carried to the office. Luck had it that Neely Kate had just arrived and was about to unlock the front door.

"Good morning," she said with a bright smile.

"Did you make up with Jed?" I asked as she inserted the key and turned the knob.

"We've reached a truce," she said with a smug expression, which I took to mean she'd told him how things were going to be, and he'd agreed to go along with it.

"I got a bit of design work done this morning before Liam woke up," I said. "In anticipation of using part of the day to track down homeowners."

"Good thinkin'," she said as she pushed the door open before grabbing the coffee cup I offered. Her brow lifted.

"Decaf," I said.

"How'd you explain that?"

"I told them you had too much energy, and I was trying to slow you down."

She laughed, and I was thankful she was in a better mood today. "I hope you don't mind, but last night, after we got Daisy to bed, I located the next homeowner on the list."

"That's great," I said. "What did you find out?"

"Lauren Abernathy was wrong. They weren't the Elgers. They were the Fredricksons. They currently live in a smaller home here in Henryetta. Bill works for the post office, and Margaret works at Walmart."

"I could always use more diapers," I said with a conspiratorial look.

"And I need more toilet paper. I've been peeing like every few hours."

"We don't know if she's working," I said. "Do you want to go by her house first?"

"Works for me."

"Okay, it's still early, so maybe we work for an hour or two, then we try to track down Margaret Fredrickson?"

"Deal."

I didn't realize Neely Kate had set a timer until it went off an hour and a half later. At least I'd finished the design I'd been working on that morning and started a new one.

By the time I got moving, Neely Kate had already shut down her computer and was grabbing her purse out of her desk drawer.

"I'm driving today," she said. "No offense, but I suspect your car's gonna smell like a locker room."

"No offense taken," I said, grabbing my purse and cell phone. "Because I can confirm it does, but I suspect it's likely more from the box than Mikey's soccer pads and cleats."

"We can put the box in the trunk of my car."

I grabbed it out of my SUV as she locked up the office. We got into her Lexus and headed to the address she'd preprogrammed into the map app on her phone. She parked at the curb and got out, heading to the front door of a house smaller than the Thatcher's. They must have downsized.

Neely Kate knocked on the door, but other than a barking dog inside, there was no sign of anyone home.

"I really *do* need diapers," I said.

"And I need toilet paper."

We headed to Walmart next, and when we walked through the entrance, I grabbed a cart. "Do you know what Margaret looks like?"

She pulled up her photos on her phone and showed me. "From what I can gather, she's in her forties, but she doesn't post her own photos much. One of her friends tagged her in this photo."

I leaned in closer to see a slightly overweight blond. "Okay. I guess we can just wander the store, and if we don't find her, we can ask someone."

"Sounds good."

I headed to the baby section. After I grabbed a large package of diapers, I checked out the little boy's clothes. It was getting warmer, and Liam needed a whole new wardrobe for when it got hot—which, knowing Arkansas weather, wouldn't be far off. I grabbed several pairs of shorts and T-shirts, while Neely Kate let her fingers run over some tiny baby clothes.

"Do you want to get something?" I asked. "I know you don't know if it's a boy or girl, but they have gender-neutral clothes."

She slowly pulled her hand back. "No. I don't want to jinx it." Her gaze shifted to the side, and her eyes lit up. "I think that's her."

I turned to where she was staring, and sure enough, a blond woman was stocking children's socks at a display.

Neely Kate left me in the dust as she hurried over, calling out, "Margaret? Margaret Fredrickson?"

The woman looked half-scared as Neely Kate charged toward her. "Yeah," she said hesitantly, then looked around her as though wanting witnesses if Neely Kate attacked her.

"Hi," Neely Kate said with a huge smile. "I'm Neely Kate Carlisle, and this here is Rose Gardner." She gestured to me. "We both work for RBW Landscaping." Then she added, "Rose is an owner."

"Oh," the woman said as recognition lit up her face. "I've heard of y'all, but I don't need any landscaping."

"Actually," Neely Kate said, "your bushes are overgrown, and your flower beds need to be redone."

I elbowed her in the side as a look of horror filled Margaret's eyes.

"What Neely Kate is trying to say," I said forcefully, "is that we're doing a job at your previous residence on Olive Street, and we dug up a box that doesn't belong to the homeowner. She's asked us to find out who buried it."

She gave me a blank look. "Why?"

I narrowed my eyes in confusion. "Why what?"

"Why are you trying to find them? If they buried it, then they obviously didn't want it anymore."

"Are you saying it's yours, and you don't want it?" Neely Kate asked. I couldn't tell if she was disappointed that we'd potentially crashed and burned or excited that we could finally open it ourselves.

"No, it's not mine. I'm just saying if the person buried it, they obviously didn't want it to be found." She made a face. "What if there's a dog buried inside it? People bury pets, you know."

I turned to Neely Kate in horror. I hadn't even considered it could contain a dead animal, but I quickly dismissed the idea.

"The box is too small for a dog," I said.

"Not a really tiny dog," Neely Kate said, holding up her hands and bringing them closer together. "They have like three-pound dogs now. Or maybe even dog ashes."

Margaret nodded and gave me an I-told-you-so look.

"Did you or your husband bury an animal while you lived there?" I asked.

She shook her head. "We didn't have any pets."

"Is there any way your husband could have buried something?"

She pursed her lips. "You say it's in a box?"

"A fancy carved box," Neely Kate said.

Margaret shook her head. "No. Bill's too cheap to bury something fancy. If he'd wanted to get rid of it, he would have sold it in a garage sale."

"What about your children?" Neely Kate asked. "Could they have buried something?"

"My kids were toddlers when we lived there. I think I would've remembered owning a fancy box, let alone one of them burying it."

"What about your neighbors?" I asked. I could tell she was getting annoyed with our questions, but I figured it wouldn't hurt to ask one more.

She snorted. "When we lived there, a feeble old man lived next door. I heard he died a few months after we moved out.

There's no way he would have been outside, burying a box in the dirt."

"Well, thank you for your time," I said, then handed her one of my business cards. "If you think of something that might help us find the owner, feel free to call or text me at this number."

She took the card and looked it over. I knew she wouldn't be calling. In fact, I suspected she'd be dumping the card into the nearest trash can as soon as we left, but it felt like the right thing to do.

We walked away, and once we were out of earshot, Neely Kate said, "What do you think?"

"I think she's telling the truth. I don't think the Fredricksons buried the box."

"No, I meant, do you think there's an animal inside?"

I stopped and turned to her. "It's not big enough, Neely Kate."

"So maybe it's not a dog," she conceded. "What if it's a hamster or a gerbil? One of those would definitely fit into that box."

Unfortunately, she was right.

"I mean, maybe we should take a moment to think this through," she said. "How would you feel if someone showed up at the office with a box that held the bones of your momma?"

"No one's showing up with the box holding my mother's remains. She's in a six-foot-long casket."

"You know what I mean. For all we know, it could hold the ashes of a *person*."

Crappy doodles. She *did* have a point.

I narrowed my eyes. "You just want to open the box."

She shrugged, trying to look innocent. "Given this new train of thought, it seems like the right thing to do."

I stabbed her shoulder with my finger. "If you want to call Jill Thatcher and ask her if she wants us to open the box to make sure there's not a dead animal inside, go ahead, but *I* won't be making that call."

She stuck her lip out and crossed her arms, then let out a sigh. "I guess you're right."

"So now we move on to the next person on the list. Did you look them up?"

"Not yet."

"So how about we finish shopping, then go to a restaurant and have a working brunch? Afterward, we can go to my consult at one, then talk to whoever we find next before your consult at three."

"Sounds good."

We headed to the checkout, and I cringed when I saw my total. I wasn't sure I could afford to go part time with four kids to clothe and feed, but I'd worry about that later.

Chapter Eight

The sky had turned ominously dark when we headed outside, so we decided to eat at Merrilee's Café since it was close to the office. After we ordered our food, Neely Kate pulled out the list of homeowners.

"George and Adolpha Whitlock are next on the list. They owned the home for about twenty years before the Fredricksons."

"Where does that put us time-wise?" I asked.

"Are you suggesting we might be going back far enough that the homeowners might be dead?" Neely Kate asked.

I cringed. "Well, that's a blunt way to say it, but yeah, given the house is nearly a hundred years old."

"The Fredricksons only owned the home for three years, so we're only back about fifteen years now."

I nodded. "We definitely need to look up the Whitlocks." I pulled out my phone.

We spent the next ten minutes looking up any combination of George and Adolpha Whitlock but came up with nothing. Neither of them was on social media under their real names, and even a simple internet search pulled up a big fat nothing.

The waitress brought our food, and Neely Kate set her phone down. "I'm going to text around and see if any of my contacts know them."

If any other person had said that, I might have suggested they were delusional, but Neely Kate had a vast array of sources, some through her large extended family and some through people she'd met since moving to Fenton County when she was a preteen.

When we finished, the air had turned colder, and it had started to rain.

We headed out to Neely Kate's car and drove to my one o'clock consultation. Neely Kate stayed in the car to work her magic searching for the Whitlocks, and I borrowed her umbrella to knock on the homeowner's door. She came outside with her own umbrella, and we walked around her yard while she told me what she wanted. I took multiple photos and notes on my phone, then sent the homeowner inside while I took measurements. I told her I'd have something to her within the week.

A half-hour later, I climbed back in the passenger seat to see Neely Kate beaming.

"You found something," I said as I strapped on my seatbelt.

"Sure did. Turns out Mr. Whitlock is dead, God rest his soul, but Mrs. Whitlock is at the Piney Rest Nursing Home."

I wrinkled my nose. "I always hated that name. It sounds more appropriate for a cemetery."

"True." She lifted her brow. "So you still wanna go over there before my three o'clock appointment?"

"Sure."

The nursing home had opened a couple of years prior, and despite its name, it had the reputation of being a well-run facility. After Neely Kate parked in the lot, we walked in through the entrance and stopped at the reception desk.

"Hi," Neely Kate said with a huge smile. "I'm Neely Kate, and this is my friend Rose. We're hoping to chat with Miss Adolpha. Adolpha Whitlock."

The receptionist's eyes lit up. "Oh, Miss Adolpha will love having the company. Her kids come see her, but not as often as she'd like, and she loves to chat with people." She leaned to the side and glanced into an open room to the side of us. "Miss Adolpha's over there in the great room, sitting with a new resident. She's the one in the green and white shirt."

We thanked the receptionist, headed into the great room, and stopped dead in our tracks when we saw who she was sitting next to.

It was my old neighbor and nemesis.

I couldn't stop my loud groan.

"What in the world is *Miss Mildred* doing here?" Neely Kate asked me under her breath.

I stayed rooted in my spot. "I knew she'd moved into a care facility a couple of months ago, but I had no idea it was this one."

Neely Kate shot me a mischievous smile. "You know Miss Mildred's gonna do everything in her power to keep Miss Adolpha from talking to you."

"I don't know," I said hopefully. "Sure, she doesn't like me much, but things have gotten better between us." Especially after we'd worked a case together.

Neely Kate let out a loud snort. "Then why did she leave Jonah's church and go back to the Baptist church?"

I clenched my teeth. "That wasn't my fault."

"Maybe not, but you know darn good and well she was blaming that Jell-O incident on *you*."

I crossed my arms over my chest. "Fine. You have a point. You take the lead."

I was nervous as I followed Neely Kate over to the two women who were sitting in front of the TV watching an episode of *Golden Girls*.

"You're crazy," Miss Mildred said with a sneer. "Sophia is eighty years old."

"No I'm not. My granddaughter told me the actress playing her was younger than some of the other actresses," the other woman said in a patient voice.

"Fake news!" Miss Mildred shouted.

Several of the other residents sitting around the room shot her dirty looks.

"Why, Miss Mildred," Neely Kate said cheerfully as she stopped next to them. I stayed a couple of steps behind. "Fancy meeting you here."

"Are you stalking me?" Miss Mildred demanded, looking like she was spoiling for a fight. Her white hair appeared to have been recently permed, and with her pale complexion, she looked a bit like a sun-deprived circus clown.

"We're not here to see you," Neely Kate said, still sounding gracious. "It just so happens we were lucky enough to run into you." She smiled at the elderly woman sitting next to Miss Mildred. "We're here to see Miss Adolpha."

"Me?" Miss Adolpha asked in surprise. Her face lit up with excitement.

"That's right," Neely Kate said. "Would it be okay if we sat down for a chat?"

"We were *talking*," Miss Mildred snapped, her eyes burning into me, making it obvious she still held a grudge.

"That's okay," Miss Adolpha said, waving a hand at her. "We can talk any old time."

Miss Mildred grabbed the cane next to her chair and used it to stand. "In that case, I'm not saving you a spot at yoga."

Neely Kate's eyes lit up. "Y'all have yoga here?"

"We've got all kinds of things here," Miss Adolpha said. "I should have moved in here years ago."

"The place wasn't here years ago," Miss Mildred said in a haughty tone, still struggling to get to her feet. Against my better judgment, I reached over to help her.

She swung her cane toward me, and I barely jumped out of the way in time.

"Mildred!" Miss Adolpha said in alarm.

Miss Mildred's face turned red as she struggled to regain her balance. "She nearly caused me to break my hip the last time she touched me!"

"That's an exaggeration," I said with a sigh. "You didn't fall."

"Well, if I had, I could have broken my hip."

"And I could have won the Powerball this morning if I'd bought a ticket," Neely Kate said. "And Rose could have woken up and looked like a movie star if she'd gotten more than five or six hours of sleep."

"Hey!" I protested.

She ignored me and continued, "You can't live your life with woulda, coulda, shouldas, Miss Mildred." Then, after a moment's hesitation, she added, "You're just a sore loser."

Miss Mildred's mouth dropped open wide enough we could see her bridge was missing in her back molars. "Well, I never!" she said, her eyes blazing.

Neely Kate propped a hand on her hip. "Had good manners? That's super obvious."

I stared at my best friend in shock. She wasn't usually this rude to people, not that Miss Mildred didn't deserve it, but she usually humored my old neighbor.

To my shock, the room burst into enthusiastic applause.

"You tell her!" an older man yelled from across the room.

"What did she say?" another woman with pink-tinged hair asked.

The woman next to her leaned in closer. "That pretty little thing just called Mildred a hippopotamus."

The pink-haired woman squinted at Miss Mildred. "I suppose her face kind of *does* look like a hippo."

Neely Kate turned to me and made a face that said *oops*, but merriment filled her eyes.

"Miss Mildred, why don't we take a stroll in the rose garden?" a younger woman in blue scrubs said as she hurried forward, arm outstretched.

Miss Mildred walked toward her and lifted her cane to smack

at her, but one of gentleman residents whom she passed grabbed the staff. "That'll be enough of that."

Miss Mildred looked like she wanted to spit carpet tacks at all of us, but instead, she let the aide lead her way. As they walked away, the aide turned back to Neely Kate and mouthed, "Thank you."

Neely Kate blushed when another round of cheers went up as Miss Mildred left the room.

Miss Mildred had always been rude and cantankerous but never violent. I couldn't help worrying about her a bit.

Miss Adolpha was already turning off the TV as Neely Kate dragged a chair over to sit across from her. The older woman stared at her with a mixture of fear and awe. My best friend shot me a look that said *maybe you should take this after all*.

I sat in the seat Miss Mildred had vacated and rested my hands on my knees. "We're really sorry about all of that. Miss Mildred used to live across the street from me when I was growing up, and she obviously doesn't care for me much."

Miss Adolpha seemed to shake off some of her stupor. "If Mildred had a quarrel with you, then I would guess that means you're a delightful girl."

I grinned. "I don't know about that, but I *do* know that Miss Mildred's go-to reaction is hostility. I think it's just a defense mechanism." I leaned closer. "Don't get me wrong. I'd still walk on the other side of the street to avoid her, but I think she's lonely."

"There are plenty of better ways to make friends," Miss Adolpha said, her knotted hands straightening the bottom of her shirt. "That's what I always told my students."

"You were a teacher?"

"For nearly forty years before I gave it up."

"Where did you teach?" Neely Kate asked.

A smile lit up her face. "Up in Magnolia. George and I used to live up that way. Then he got a job at Ingram's Manufacturing, and we moved to Henryetta shortly after we got married."

That seemed like a backward move. Most people moved away from Henryetta, not to it. "Did you and George have children?" I asked.

She smiled. "We had a mess of 'em." She tilted her head toward me. "Five. Two boys and three girls."

"And you raised them on that house on Olive Street?" Neely Kate asked in surprise.

Miss Adolpha's wrinkled forehead creased even more. "How did you know we lived on Olive Street?"

I drew a breath. "Miss Adolpha, Neely Kate and I are landscapers with RBW Landscaping, and we're currently doing a job at your former house on Olive Street."

Miss Adolpha looked confused but remained silent.

"We were digging to put in a small retaining wall, and Neely Kate and I uncovered a wooden box that had been buried there sometime in the past. It doesn't belong to the current homeowners, and they've asked us to locate the owners."

"Why would you go to that much trouble for a box?" the elderly woman asked.

"Because it's not just a cardboard box," Neely Kate said. "It's a beautiful carved, locked wooden box, and it had to mean something to the person who buried it. Mrs. Thatcher, the current homeowner, would love to see it returned to its rightful owner."

Neely Kate was far more driven to find the owner than Jill Thatcher, but I didn't see the point in correcting her.

"So you're here to see if it belongs to me?" she asked.

I nodded. "Yes. We've talked to the people who owned the house after you, and none of them know anything about it. We've been working backward, and you were next on the list."

Miss Adolpha glanced down at her lap, and after a few seconds, she gazed up. "So you found a box, and you're trying to discover who buried it."

"That's right," I said softly.

"I didn't bury a box, and I know George wouldn't have. He was much too practical for something like that."

"What about your kids?" Neely Kate asked.

"How big is the box?"

"A foot long and six inches tall." I held up my hands to show the approximate size as I spoke.

"I'm presuming it's heavy," she said.

"Somewhat."

She shook her head. "They were much too young to have done something like that. We moved when I was pregnant with Nate, my fourth child. David would have been about seven, so I don't see how he could have done it. Not to mention, I didn't have a fancy box for him or his two sisters to bury."

"What about a neighbor?" I asked.

She made a face. "It would seem odd for someone else to bury a box in our yard."

"It was on the side of the yard," Neely Kate said. "Between your old house and the neighbors on the right side when you're standing at the street, facing the house."

"The house next door was a rental house for some time, and a lot of people came and went," Miss Adolpha said. "But I do remember a family living there who had a couple of teenage girls, so I suppose it's possible."

"You said you moved when your children were small, but the property records show you still owned the property for several decades," Neely Kate said.

Miss Adolpha's gaze focused on the wall, like she was remembering days gone by. "Our family got too big to live there, so we moved to a bigger house and rented it out. We probably rented it for twenty or so years before we sold it."

"Do you have any idea how many renters you had?"

"I'd say five or six." She shrugged. "George took care of all that, so I don't remember."

"Do you happen to have a list of who might have rented from you?" Neely Kate asked.

Miss Adolpha hesitated. "No list. I remember a couple of names, but not all of them."

"Anything you have would be helpful," I said.

Her brow furrowed. "Of course, but it might take me a short bit to remember them." She smiled and tapped her temple with her index finger. "The memory's not what it used to be."

"Not a problem," Neely Kate said.

"I remember the Jacksons and the Kempners," she said after a moment, then pursed her lips together. "Sue Jackson, and her husband was Ron." Neely Kate nodded encouragingly as I wrote the names in a note on my phone. "And the Kempners were Billy and his wife Bobbie Jean." She gave us an apologetic look. "That's all I can remember, but if those names don't work out, I can ask my kids about it."

"This is a great place to start," Neely Kate said reassuringly.

I started to put down my phone when the familiar tingle of a vision began. I rarely had spontaneous visions these days, so I was taken by surprise when it engulfed me.

I was in a warehouse full of shelves lined with boxes. The light was dim, but I couldn't tell if it was nighttime or if the space was just poorly lit. Everything was hazy, as if engulfed in fog.

People were shouting. Gunshots rang out. Then I saw a woman lying on her side on the ground; her dark hair spilled around her on the floor. The blood seeping from her body began creating a large pool.

Then I was back at Piney Rest, staring into Miss Adolpha's face, murmuring, "I think she's dead."

The elderly woman's eyes widened. "Maxine is dead?" she cried out in alarm.

Obviously, I'd missed what she'd said about Maxine, whoever she was, but I was more concerned about what I'd just seen.

Neely Kate shot me a worried look and must have realized

what had happened because she said, "No, of course not. Rose probably meant..." Her voice trailed off, and I was surprised that Neely Kate was at a loss for words. I could count the number of times that had happened on one hand.

I was lost to come up with an explanation myself.

Years ago, I'd had multiple visions of people dying or dead. Shoot, I'd even seen myself dead more than a few times, but my life had been pleasantly violence free for nearly three years, so seeing a dead woman on the floor scared the wits out of me. Especially since what I'd seen just now matched the scattered memories I had of my dream.

I always had visions from the perspective of a person close to me, so had the vision been of Miss Adolpha or Neely Kate?

The answer was pretty clear.

"We need to go," I said, starting to get up, but my phone fell out of my lap to the floor.

Neely Kate gave me a wary look but quickly reached down and grabbed my phone. "Thank you so much for your help, Miss Adolpha," she said as she stood. "We'll be sure to let you know how all of this turns out."

Miss Adolpha kept her gaze on me. "Are you all right, dear?"

"I'm so sorry to run off like this," I said in a rush. Then I lied. "I forgot my daughter has a dentist appointment."

"Not to worry," the elderly woman said with a wave of her hand. "It was fun to get a little bit of excitement."

"We'll definitely be in touch," I said. Especially if the vision belonged to her. But how would Miss Adolpha end up in a warehouse with gunshots and a dead woman?

I snatched my purse and took off for the door. Neely Kate was a few seconds behind after she said her goodbyes.

Once we were outside, she grabbed my arm and pulled me to a halt. "What happened? Why are you running like your pants are on fire?"

"You shouldn't run if your pants are on fire," I said, sliding my free hand over my head. "You stop, drop, and roll."

"You would think that's common knowledge," she said dryly, "but I've seen some of my cousins do the opposite when they've caught on fire." She shook her head with a look of disgust.

"Your cousins…" I waved a hand. "Never mind. I had a vision."

"I figured," she said, her face turning solemn. "Of someone dead."

I nodded. "It wasn't very clear, like there was a haze over everything. I was in a warehouse. There were shouts and gunshots, and a woman was lying on the floor with blood running out of her." Tears filled my eyes. "I think she was dead."

Horror filled Neely Kate's eyes. "Who was she?"

Panic bloomed in my chest. "I don't know."

She hesitated, then asked in a shaky voice, "Do you think it was a vision of something I'm gonna see?"

"I don't know."

Her chest rose and fell as she started to work through what that might mean. "Rose, if it was a vison of something that's going to happen to me…"

"Then the dead woman was probably me," I said.

Chapter Nine

"We don't know that," she said insistently. "Did you see her face?"

"No. She was turned away, but even if she hadn't been, it was too fuzzy."

"What was she wearing?"

I closed my eyes as I tried to remember. "I don't know. Jeans, I think. Maybe a black shirt?"

"Lady in Black clothes?" she muttered under her breath.

The clothes I'd worn when I'd used that alter ego.

"I don't remember seeing a hat," I said. "And she wasn't wearing a dress."

"But at the end, you gave that up. The people who mattered knew you were her, and you stopped wearing the hat and the dress." She paused. "But sometimes you still wore black."

Had the dead woman been me?

"We're looking for the owner of a wooden box!" I cried out in dismay. "How could that get me killed?"

"Maybe there's something else going on," she said.

I dropped my hand. "You think there might be something dangerous in the box?"

"Maybe, but what if it has nothing to do with the box?"

"Okay..." She had a point. The box had been buried for who knew how long. Still, it wasn't like I was doing anything else liable to get me killed. "I don't see how it could be anything *but* the box. I haven't been involved in the criminal world for nearly three years, and when the Hardshaw Group was arrested and disbanded and James left, Dermot took over. Everything's been quiet ever since." I mulled it over a few seconds more. "The box is the only thing that makes sense."

She was silent as she turned to glance at her car. "We should open it. If whatever's in it is the cause of what happened to the woman you saw—"

"The *dead* woman I saw—"

"Then maybe it'll help us understand what we're dealing with."

I considered it. "No. We need to stop looking for the owner of the box."

"Rose," she said insistently. "We may not know what's inside that carved box, but we've opened a box nonetheless. *Pandora's* box. If this *is* related to the box, someone out there might know we're looking for the owners." She leaned closer and lowered her breath. "Just *knowing* about it might get us into trouble."

I took a step back, my heart beginning to race. "No. I can't do this again! When we did this stuff before, it was just me and Muffy. I was the only person I needed to worry about, Neely Kate. But I have *four kids*!" My panic began building. "I said nothing dangerous!"

"I know, Rose. I know," she said, reaching out to stroke my arm. "We'll stop."

Tears stung my eyes. "Thank you."

"But we still need to open the box. We need to know what's inside in case someone dangerous really is looking for it."

I took several breaths before I said, "Yeah. You're right."

She looked relieved. "We'll have to figure out how to get it open without damaging whatever's inside. Jed and Witt can probably do it."

"Okay," I said, feeling a sudden need to see and hug my kids. "Are you okay with doing that on your own? I want to take off early. I need to hold my babies."

"Yeah," she said, pulling me into a hug. "Of course." She squeezed me tightly, then released me. "I never meant to stir up any trouble, Rose. I swear."

"I know," I said insistently. "I never would have agreed to this if I'd thought it was dangerous."

"You have to know the last thing I want to do is put you in harm's way," Neely Kate said, her eyes glassy with unshed tears.

"I know," I said, offering her a half-smile. "This isn't on you, okay? You didn't do anything wrong, but now we need to stop."

I expected her to put up more of a fight, but we got inside her car and headed downtown to the office, both of us quiet for a few minutes.

"Do you want me to go to your consultation with you?" I asked. "If the vision was yours, then you're in danger too."

"No, I'm fine. I can do it on my own. We're going to put a stop to this, so we'll be fine."

"Okay," I said, feeling relieved. "I'll pick up the kids and work on the design for the earlier consultation at home."

"Work on it tomorrow," she said. "Enjoy the afternoon with the kids."

I started to protest, then I decided she was right. I was going to take them home and just be with them.

"Are you going to tell Joe?" she asked.

I drew in a breath. "I don't know." I hesitated. "I don't want to keep secrets from him, but I don't want to worry him. Besides, there's nothing he can do. It's just a vision." I turned to face her. "Are you going to tell Jed?"

"If you don't tell Joe, then no. But I don't want him hearing about it from Joe either."

"Let's see what's in the box, then decide."

"Okay." She shifted in her seat. "You're sure you don't want to come with me to open it?"

"No. Just tell me what you find."

"Okay."

She dropped me at the office, and I grabbed my stuff and headed to the daycare to pick up the kids. The elementary bus had just dropped off the older kids, so I grabbed Ashley and Mikey before they'd checked in and picked up the little kids. We stopped for ice cream cones and ate inside the restaurant while the windows became coated with drizzle. I tried to find out how Ashley's day had gone and get some details about her breakfast with Joe, but all she'd say was that she'd enjoyed spending one-on-one time with Joe, there'd been a substitute teacher, and the kids had been fine. I could tell there was more bothering her, but she was adamant about not talking about it, so I gave up, figuring I'd find out more about the breakfast part from Joe later. After we finished our ice cream—Liam, of course, was a sticky mess—and we headed home.

Ashley helped me make dinner—a chicken and noodle casserole—then she and Mikey worked on their homework while Hope, Liam, and Muffy played in the living room. Neely Kate still hadn't called to tell me what was inside the box, and it took everything in me not to call or text her. She probably hadn't had time to get to it yet.

Joe had texted while we were eating ice cream to say he'd be home around five-thirty, but he walked through the door a few minutes after six, right as the timer was going off for the casserole to come out of the oven. "Perfect timing," I said as I opened the door, pulled the casserole dish out, and set it on the stove burners.

He walked over with a sheepish look and gave me a kiss. "Sorry I'm late."

"It's okay. Did something come up?"

Grimacing, he shot a glance at the kids and lifted his brow.

He didn't want to talk about it in front of them.

"Should I be worried?" I whispered. My vision was fresh on my mind.

He kissed me again. "Nah, but..."

It wasn't something he wanted them to know about.

The kids were excited to see Joe, and he scooped them up one by one and showered them with kisses, then told them to wash their hands for dinner while he ran upstairs to change out of his uniform.

Hope and Liam were too little to take part fully, but we still liked to go around the table and talk about our days. Ashley was usually chatty, but tonight, she was subdued and told us a few facts about her day without saying anything of substance. Mikey made up for her lack of enthusiasm, telling us how he'd convinced his friends to play soccer at recess instead of kickball, but to his dismay, they'd had an indoor recess because of the rain. He followed up by telling Joe about getting ice cream before we came home.

"Was there some kind of celebration?" Joe asked.

"No!" Mikey exclaimed. "Aunt Rose said it was just because! She's the best!"

Joe gave me a warm smile before returning his attention to our nephew. "She sure is."

When it was Hope's turn, a huge grin lit up her face. "I colowed with mawkas and made lots of Ts."

"Ts?" Joe asked. "Like golf tees or iced tea?"

"No, silwy." She covered her mouth with a giggle. "The letta T. I colowed twees and tuwtles green. Miss Mandy let us use mawkas, Daddy!"

"Markers!" Joe exclaimed, pretending to be shocked. "You don't say!"

Ashley rolled her eyes, smiling despite herself, while Mike giggled.

"They was washable mawkas."

"Good thing. I'd hate for you to get marker on your favorite T-shirt," he said.

She looked down at her pink T-shirt with white, embroidered flowers. She'd worn it so many times; it was faded and had stains that wouldn't come out. But she loved it, so I still let her wear it. "How'd you know it's my favowite?"

"Because I'm your daddy, silly," Joe said, then leaned over and touched her nose with the tip of his finger.

"Everyone knows it's your favorite, Hopey," Mikey said good-naturedly. "You tell us all the time."

"Oh," she said, as though considering it.

"Anything else happen?" I asked, picking noodles off Liam's highchair tray and putting them back into his bowl.

"Only one mow thing," she said. "Cole thwew up on his shoes."

Joe and I exchanged looks, both of us offering silent prayers that Cole didn't have a contagious stomach bug.

"And one mow thing!" she exclaimed. "We ate ice cweam afta school."

"Mommy let you and Liam have ice cream too? It wasn't just for Mikey?"

"No, silwy," Hope said with a wide grin. "Mommy shawas."

"Yes, she sure does," he said, giving me a soft look I couldn't interpret.

Liam's turn was next, but he just crammed noodles into his mouth, so I told them that his paper from daycare had said he'd played with his friends, was a good napper, and ate all his lunch.

"Your turn, Uncle Joe," Mikey said enthusiastically.

"Oh, my day was boring," Joe said, shooting me a glance. "Lots of bor-ing paperwork."

Mikey must have bought the hard sell because his nose wrinkled before he swung his attention to me. "Did you dig up another box today, Aunt Rose?"

"Not today," I said with a dramatic sigh. "But I made a new

friend named Miss Adolpha. She lives in a place with lots of other older people. I thought maybe we could all drop by to see her sometime. I'm sure she'd love a visit from some sweet children."

"Sweet children? Where are you gonna find some of those?" Joe teased.

Mikey burst into laughter, and Hope and Liam joined him, mostly because he was laughing, which meant *something* had to be funny, even if the joke had gone over their heads. To my relief, Ashley cracked a smile.

"What were you doing at a nursing home?" Joe asked as he scooped more casserole onto his plate.

"She was one of the homeowners from the house where we dug up the box."

"Did she know anything about it, Aunt Rose?" Ashley asked.

"She didn't. She said her husband had passed a few years ago, and her kids were too young to bury it, so we hit a dead end."

Joe lifted his brow in surprise but didn't say anything.

"So what happens to the box?" Ashley asked.

"I told Neely Kate to open it and see what's inside."

"What was in it?" Mikey asked, his eyes bugging with excitement.

"What was in it?" Hope parroted, even though I was pretty sure she didn't have any idea what we were talking about.

"I don't know," I said, shrugging my shoulders in an exaggerated move. "She hasn't told me yet."

Joe's eyes widened. "You didn't open it with her?"

"Neely Kate's the one who's been eager to see what was inside," I said. "So I told her to go for it, and I took off early and took the kids for ice cream."

He studied me for a moment before shifting his focus to his casserole.

After we finished dinner and cleaned up the kitchen, we

played a game of Candyland at the kitchen table. I reveled in this moment of peace, even though Ashley was still too quiet. I tried not to let myself dwell on my vision.

I was still struggling with the fact that I'd seen part of the vision in my nightmare. It didn't make sense because my visions had never worked that way before. That suggested that perhaps it wasn't a vision of either Neely Kate or Mrs. Whitlock, which could be a good thing, but it also raised questions. Were my visions changing? If so, what did that mean?

After a couple of rounds of the game, we started on the bedtime routine, splitting our duties. All the kids piled into Ashley's bed so Joe could read them a story, and even though he'd told me I could have a moment to myself, I sat in a chair in the corner and thanked God once again for giving me this man to be my husband and the father of my children.

When he finished the story, he put Hope and Mikey to bed while I rocked Liam in his room for a few minutes.

After I got him down, I found Joe downstairs in the living room with the remote in his hand. "How about we watch some Netflix?"

I sat down next to him, took the remote from his hand, and placed it on the coffee table. "*Or* you could tell me the reason you were late."

He turned sideways on the sofa to face me. "There was a murder down in Pickle Junction."

My heart skipped a beat. "What happened?"

"There's still a lot under wraps, but a man was shot." His eyes narrowed. "Why are you freaked out, Rose? There've been murders since…" He paused. "Since everything."

He was right. There *had* been murders, but this one felt different, which was crazy, since I didn't know anything about it.

He was waiting for an answer, so I shrugged and snuggled up next to him. "Things just feel *off*."

He wrapped an arm around me. "How so, and does this have anything to do with you deciding to stop trying to find the owner of the box?"

I was close to telling him I'd had a vision, but I couldn't bring myself to do it. He'd worry, and obviously, it was a vision, which meant the only thing that could be done was to try to avoid the situation that might have caused it. So the fact I was letting the search for the box's owner go meant I should be safe.

"I think it had more to do with me wanting time with the kids." I placed my hand on his chest. "Do you think your investigation is going to interfere with our trip to Little Rock?"

He squeezed my arm. "No. I think we're still good. We've been planning this for months. I'll do whatever it takes to make it happen."

"Thanks, Joe, but I'll understand if it doesn't work out." Wanting to change the subject, I lifted my gaze to his. "How did this morning go with Ashley?"

He let out a sigh. "She wasn't very open about what was going on, but I assured her that I'm always there for her, and she never has to worry about telling me anything." He was silent for a moment. "It still kills me that she thought I was going to be mad at her."

"I know, but I don't think it had anything to do with you. Not really. She was hesitant to tell me too. I think it was shame holding her back, although I assured her that she had nothing to be ashamed about."

"I tried to tell her that," he said, his hand tightening on my arm. "I told her that her father is a good man who made a terrible mistake, and that he loves her and Mikey like crazy." He paused. "She brought up Violet."

My heart skipped a beat. I tried to talk about my sister with them as often as felt natural, but Ashley wasn't always open to it. "And?"

"She said she misses her, and sometimes she gets angry that she died."

"Oh, poor baby," I said, my heart breaking. Then I remembered that Jonah was supposed to talk to her after school. "Oh no! I screwed up."

"How in the world did you screw up?" he asked in disbelief.

"I was about to suggest that we have Jonah talk to her about Violet, but then I remembered she was supposed to talk to him this afternoon. I picked her up before she even checked into afterschool care."

"You know," he said softly, "I think ice cream and hanging out with you and the other kids was good for her. She can talk to Jonah tomorrow."

"Unless I pick them up early again."

He kicked his feet up onto the coffee table. "You ready to make the move to part time?"

"No, not yet. But leaving early a few days this week isn't exactly part time."

"True, but you can go part time if you want, Rose."

I drew in a breath. "I'm not sure I want to. I'd like to spend more time with the kids, but Ashley and Mikey are in school all day anyway." And if I were honest with myself, part of the reason I'd agreed to search for the owner of the box was because I was a little bored. Part time wasn't going to help with that. I wasn't like Violet, who had loved being a stay-at-home mom.

"And besides," I added, "if I did go part time, money would be tight, and it's already tight."

"And the sheriff's position in Fenton County doesn't pay all that much." I heard guilt in his voice.

"Stop," I said, lightly elbowing his side. "I have absolutely no regrets about you taking this job, Joe. We discussed it before you ran. I knew you'd have days with long hours."

"But I still feel like I'm shirking my responsibilities to you and the kids."

I shifted on the sofa to look up at him. "You're keeping the county safe, and that means more to me than you know." I held his gaze. "Was the murder in Pickle Junction a run-of-the-mill murder, or is it something to be worried about?"

"The truth?" he asked with a guarded gaze.

I nodded. "Always."

"I don't know yet."

Chapter Ten

Joe had to leave early the next morning to deal with the murder investigation, but getting the kids out the door went relatively well.

It wasn't until we were halfway into town that I realized I hadn't heard from Neely Kate about the box. I wasn't sure what that meant. Had she opened it and decided to continue investigating without me? Or had the contents been so boring, she hadn't bothered to let me know? Neither answer sounded quite right.

Daisy was at daycare when I dropped the kids off, so I wasn't surprised to see Neely Kate sitting at her desk when I walked into the office.

She glanced up and gave me a sheepish look. "I didn't open the box."

I stared at her in surprise. "What?"

She made a face. "Jed and I got into a huge fight, and he was the last person I wanted to ask for help."

"So do you still want to open it?"

"Of course, but I decided to see if you'd changed your mind about opening it with me."

I stared at her for a long moment. "Yeah," I finally said. "I want to open it with you. But how do you plan to get it open now?"

"I was thinking we could ask Bruce Wayne."

I grinned. "Brilliant idea."

"You're not worried it's going to jinx you or anything?" she asked.

"No." I cringed. "I'm kind of embarrassed about running off and leaving it with you yesterday."

"What? Why?" she barked, sitting upright. "Rose, *you* were the one dead in the vision!"

"First of all, we don't know it was me, and second, if it was, you were there in danger too."

"Did you change your mind and decide to tell Joe?"

"No," I said with a sheepish shrug.

She gave me a commiserating look. "I guess there was a whole lot of male nonsense going on last night." She obviously thought Joe and I had fought as well, and I was about to correct her when she said, "Do you want to force a vision to see if you can figure out whether the woman was you?"

Lordy, why hadn't I thought of that yesterday? "Yeah. That's a good idea." I walked over to her desk and grabbed her hand as I sat on the edge. Closing my eyes, I asked the universe if I was going to get shot in a warehouse with Neely Kate watching.

And got a big fat nothing.

I then asked the universe if I was the woman in the vision I'd had yesterday.

And got more nothing.

I opened my eyes and said, "Nothing."

She shook her head. "What does that mean?"

I grinned at her. "It wasn't me."

She grinned back at me, her eyes wide. "It wasn't you?"

"No."

"Then who was it?"

My sudden elation burst, and I sobered. "I don't know."

"So what do you want to do?"

I knew what she was really asking me. Did I want to save the person I'd seen in my vision?

I considered telling her about my dream two nights ago, but it seemed crazy now that I thought about it. I could only remember fragments of it, and the similarities were probably a coincidence. I'd already come off looking like a fool yesterday when I'd high-tailed it home. I'd look even sillier if I suggested I'd dreamed about the murder first.

"I need to have another one," I said. "The person who got shot might not have been me, but the vision was probably of your future, which means *you're* in danger, Neely Kate. I need to have another vision and ask about you, not me."

Her face paled, but she looked reluctant. "I don't know."

"Neely Kate!"

She took a breath and released it. "Okay, but don't be asking anything about my baby."

"I won't. I promise."

She held out her hand again. "Then okay."

I grasped her hand and closed my eyes, asking the universe to show me if Neely Kate was going to be in danger in a warehouse, adding the last part on at the last moment. If she had another ectopic pregnancy, she could very well be in danger, and I might see that moment instead.

But the universe showed me nothing.

I opened my eyes and shook my head.

"I wasn't in a warehouse?" she asked.

"No."

"Maybe we changed something," she said in confusion.

"Maybe. Or it could have been Miss Adolpha's vision."

"You're kidding."

"I know it seems weird, but…"

"We've seen weirder things," she finished, not looking happy about it.

Her statement made me reconsider my decision not to tell her about the dream. She was right—we'd seen more than our share of oddities.

"So what do you want to do?" she asked, interrupting my thoughts.

"Uh..." I was about to tell her about my nightmare, but maybe I'd just imagined the connection. The dream *had* been vague. Or maybe I was just hesitating because I didn't want to acknowledge that my visions might be changing. "We have to go back and see Miss Adolpha so we can figure out whether she's in danger."

She made a face. "I was afraid you were going to say that."

"You don't want to see Miss Adolpha again? She was a sweet elderly woman."

"I don't have a problem with Miss Adolpha. It's Miss *Mildred* I don't want to see again."

"Fair enough."

She drew in a deep breath. "I guess this means we won't be opening the box yet."

"Let's hold off until after we see Miss Adolpha. But then we have to come *right back* so I can work on my proposals. If we want to do more sleuthing, it will have to wait until this afternoon."

"Okay."

"And the only reason I'm suggesting we go see Miss Adolpha now is because I'm worried *she* might be in danger. Not because we're resuming our investigation."

"Which is the only reason I'm agreeing to go," she grumbled.

"I'll buy you coffee as an incentive," I said, heading for the door.

"I'd rather have a cupcake."

"Deal."

We locked the office and headed across the square to Dena's Cupcake Shop. Dena wasn't necessarily a fan of Neely Kate and me. She'd dated Joe at one point, and for a long time, she'd blamed me for "stealing" him from her. I could understand why it had looked like that from her point of view—Joe had moved in with me when I was a few months pregnant to help protect me and Hope and keep her parentage a secret. We hadn't gotten back together until later, although she didn't know that. Thankfully, her hostility had softened over the past few years.

When we walked through the doors, several people were already in line. In addition to cupcakes, Dena had started serving to-go breakfasts, which were popular with the courthouse employees.

We waited in line, and when it was our turn, she took one look at me and said, "What's going on with the murder down in Pickle Junction?"

Neely Kate stared at me, eyes wide and mouth gaping. "What murder in Pickle Junction?"

"Didn't tell your best friend, huh?" Dena said sarcastically. "What did we elect your husband for if there's just gonna be people murdering each other all over the county?"

"To be fair," I said, "it's one murder. I can't even remember the last time someone was killed."

"Last fall," Dena said in a know-it-all voice.

"Okay…" Neely Kate said, starting to get pissed. "That seems like pretty good stats to me."

"Of course you'd think so," Dena spat at her. "He's your brother." She shifted her attention back to me. "I heard it was drug-related."

So much for softening toward us.

I held up my hands in surrender. "I don't know the first thing about it, Dena, so don't be trying to get information out of me."

"Do you think I believe that you *really* don't know anything about it?"

"It's true," I said, trying not to sound defensive. "It's an official investigation. It sounds like you might know more than I do."

Neely Kate leaned closer to the counter. "What do you know?"

"Why don't you go ask your brother?" Dena snapped.

"His name was Harvey Smith," said the woman behind us. "He lived in Pickle Junction and worked for Jefferson Sanitation."

I spun around to face her. She looked young, probably in her twenties, and her eyes were bloodshot and swollen.

"You knew him?" I asked softly.

"He was *my* brother." Her gaze narrowed on me. "Is your husband really the sheriff?"

I nodded. "Yes. Joe Simmons is my husband."

"Do you know if he's gonna just mark it up as another junkie's death?"

"I promise you that he'll do a thorough investigation."

Dena snorted. "Like he kept his promise to me?"

"He didn't promise you a doggone thing, Dena," Neely Kate said. "You two dated for about two minutes, nearly four years ago. Can you just let it go? I thought you were with Mitch Castlebaum."

Dena lifted her chin. "We broke up."

Hence, her renewed campaign against us.

I turned my back on Dena and said, "Joe is a fair man, and he'll investigate your brother's death. I promise." I expected Dena to snort again, but she kept quiet this time. "Would you like Joe's phone number so you can call him and talk to him about the case?"

"Why would you do that?" she asked, her tone suspicious.

"Because he's fair, and he'll listen to you," I said, digging one of Joe's business cards from my purse. I held it toward her. "He has an open-door policy with the citizens of this county."

She took the card and looked it over before stuffing it into her jeans pocket. I was pretty sure she didn't plan on calling him.

"What's your name?" I asked softly.

Her eyes hardened, and I was sure she wasn't going to answer, but then she said, "Darlene. Darlene Smith."

"Well, Darlene, as soon as I leave here with some cupcakes, I'll send Joe a text and let him know to expect a call from you."

"Is this some kind of trap?"

"No, of course not," I said insistently. "I only want to help you. I promise."

She stared at me in amazement. "Why? You don't even know me."

"I know you're grieving, and you want answers. And Joe's the man to find them for you." I stepped aside. "Now, why don't you order whatever it was you came here for, and Neely Kate and I will order next."

She walked to the counter, and while she ordered her breakfast sandwich and coffee, Neely Kate leaned into my ear. "Why didn't you tell me there was a murder in Pickle Junction?" she hissed.

"I didn't think it was important."

"It's not like there have been a lot of murders around here lately."

We both knew she meant *not like there used to be*.

"And it's not like I know anything," I said under by breath. "I wasn't lying when I said it's an official investigation. Joe's not spilling any secrets. Besides, honestly, I forgot."

"But is it a coincidence that you're not seeing yourself dead anymore?" she whispered, so no one else could hear. "What if the murder prevented it from happening?"

"We don't know that it was me."

To my surprise, she didn't respond.

We ordered a baker's dozen cupcakes and a couple of coffees, one decaf, and while we waited, Neely Kate went to the bathroom. When she came out, the food and coffee were ready, so we headed to Piney Rest.

Miss Adolpha was in the Great Room when we arrived with the cupcakes, minus the one Neely Kate had eaten during the drive. Miss Adolpha stared at us in shock as we approached.

"You girls came back. Did you find the owner of the box already?"

"Not yet," I said cheerfully. "But we stopped by Dena's Cupcakes and thought you and your friends might like some."

Several of the women she was sitting with let out excited squeals as Neely Kate set the box in the middle of the table. "But Miss Adolpha gets first pick," she said.

Miss Adolpha opened the box and picked out a cupcake with pink frosting, then turned the box around to the other people at the table. They acted like piranhas, everyone snatching cupcakes all at once.

I stepped back, even though I wasn't close enough to get caught in the frenzy.

"I think those were a hit," Neely Kate said under her breath.

Miss Adolpha got to her feet, holding her uneaten cupcake in one hand and her footed walking cane in the other. "I'm glad you girls came back by. I found something you might be interested in."

I snuck a glance at Neely Kate, who shrugged as we started to follow Miss Adolpha down the hall.

"At least we haven't run into you know who," Neely Kate said.

I laughed. "She's not Voldemort."

"Says you."

Miss Adolpha walked into her room and started rummaging around in a fancy pink cardboard box on her bed. The lid lay next to it, and she'd set her cupcake on her bedside table.

"When I was going to sleep last night, I realized I had some photos of the house from when my kids were little. I thought it might help you."

Neely Kate made a face. "Actually, Miss Adolpha, we're not looking for—"

"That would be really helpful," I said.

Neely Kate's mouth dropped open.

I walked over to the bed and peered into the box. "Are those photos of your kids?"

A bittersweet smile twisted her lips. "Five kids kept us busy, but no matter where we lived, our home was full of love and laughter."

"And you worked as a teacher while they were growing up?" I asked.

She glanced over at me. "I did."

"I have four kids, and my husband just took a job that keeps him pretty busy sometimes. I work full time myself and—"

"It's a challenge," she finished sympathetically.

"It is. Sometimes I worry I'm missing too much of their lives. The oldest is ten, and the youngest is one, and we're just so busy. I worry that some of them aren't getting the attention they need."

"I stayed home a few years before my younger three were in school," she said. "It was a joy, but I felt isolated here in Henryetta. There's no right answer, Rose. Different people need different things. Just go with your heart. But enjoy them now because soon, they'll be raised and fly from the nest."

"If you don't mind me asking," Neely Kate asked, "where do your kids live now?"

"They all moved away. There's not much here in Henryetta careerwise, so…"

"I understand," I said.

Miss Adolpha sighed. "Most of them live up in Little Rock, and they pester me to move up there, but I've lived here most of my life. I'm not sure I could do it. I had a wide group of friends, and even though some have moved on both geographically and metaphorically, I still have activities that keep me busy. Even in here." She cleared her throat. "In any case, I know I have some photos of the house in here, and like I said, I thought they could help with your search."

Miss Adolpha started pulling out photos. She looked so happy to be showing them to us that we kept asking her questions.

They'd lived in two houses, and there were multiple photos of both. But something struck me when I looked at one of the front-view photos of the house on Olive Street.

"Neely Kate, look," I said, pointing to the corner where we found the box. "There's a bush here."

She took the photo from me. "Oh my stars and garters! You're right."

"Is that a problem?" Miss Adolpha asked.

"That's where we found the box," I said. "And the bush wasn't there when we started the landscaping project."

"Which means the box was buried sometime after the bush was removed," Neely Kate said, getting excited.

"Do you know when it was removed?" I asked.

Miss Adolpha rubbed her chin. "George removed it not long before we moved out."

"So it could have been one of the renters," Neely Kate said.

"Or one of the girls I mentioned yesterday. The girls next door," Miss Adolpha said. "I'd forgotten how close the two houses were to each other."

Neely Kate's smile faded. "Miss Adolpha, did anyone dangerous live in your rental house?"

Obviously, she was thinking about my vision.

"Dangerous?" she asked in surprise. She shook her head. "No. Of course not. George was very careful about who lived there."

"What about next door?" Neely Kate pressed.

The elderly woman released a nervous chuckle. "Do you think whatever's in the box is dangerous?"

"No, of course not," I assured her. "We're just gathering information."

"Trying to make sure we don't accidentally talk to someone who's unsavory," Neely Kate said, trying to sound nonchalant but not quite pulling it off.

Miss Adolpha seemed to consider it for a moment. "There might have been someone."

"Someone dangerous?" I asked in surprise.

Her lips pressed together. "Yes. George claimed a bunch of thugs had moved in next door. They had lots of very loud parties, and the man who lived there was arrested for assault a few times."

I took a second to absorb what she'd said. "Do you remember their names?"

She considered it for a few seconds. "No. I can't seem to recall. I'm sorry."

"Do you know when they might have lived there?" I asked.

"It was when the Kempners lived there. They were upset with all the ruckus and threatened to break the lease and move. But thankfully, the man got arrested for something or another, and it must have stuck because he didn't come back. The other people living there moved, and new people moved in soon after."

"Do you possibly have a timeframe?" I asked.

She drew in a breath as she closed her eyes. "I want to say that my son Greg was eleven or twelve. He mowed the Kempners' yard one summer after Bill Kempner broke his leg. George considered dropping him off and picking him up later, but he was worried about leaving him alone with the neighbors next door."

"And how old is David now?" Neely Kate asked.

"In his late forties. So that would have been about thirty years ago."

"That's very helpful," I said. "Thank you."

"Even if I don't know their names?"

"We have their address and an approximate time of his arrest," I said. "We can look up arrest records."

Her eyes lit up. "Well, aren't you girls clever!"

Only I wasn't feeling very clever. We'd come here to see if Miss Adolpha was the source of the vision, and we'd gotten sucked back into investigating.

I shot a glance to Neely Kate, and she gave me a look that suggested the thought had occurred to her too.

The aide from yesterday popped into the open doorway. "Miss Adolpha, it's almost time for your watercolor class."

"Thank you, Devin," the elderly woman said with a smile.

"Watercolor classes and yoga?" Neely Kate said in awe after the aide walked away. "I'm thinking about moving here."

Miss Adolpha laughed. "As I said, I should have moved in here sooner."

"Does Miss Mildred take watercolor classes?" I asked, unable to help myself.

She laughed. "No, thank goodness. She's more into the oil painting classes. She makes a lot of abstract art with red and black slashes across the canvas." She shuddered. "It's very violent."

"That sounds about right," Neely Kate muttered under her breath, but I couldn't help thinking that it didn't sound like her at all. Cranky, yes, but never violent. Not like yesterday.

But we still hadn't accomplished what we'd come here to do.

"Let me help you pick up the pictures," I said, reaching for the photos now spread across her bed. I purposely brushed her hand with mine and forced a vision, asking, *is Miss Adolpha in danger?*

My mind stayed completely blank.

I opened my eyes and shot a puzzled look at Neely Kate, who had to know what I was doing.

"Try again," she mouthed.

I rested a hand on the older woman's shoulder.

Does Miss Adolpha go to a warehouse?

Nothing.

Does Miss Adolpha see someone get hurt?

This time, an image appeared, bright and blinding after the darkness.

Miss Mildred was standing on a table, waving her cane and shouting, "You're not the boss of me!"

"Get down, you old fool," grumbled an elderly man with a beak-shaped nose. "You're messin' up our card game." He was sitting beside the table she was standing on, and sure enough, playing cards were scattered all around.

She leaned over to smack at him with her cane but lost her balance and toppled onto the man and then the floor.

The old man started bellowing, and Miss Mildred started screaming, "You broke my damn hip!"

Miss Adolpha's room came back into view, and I said, "Miss Mildred's gonna fall off a table."

"What?" Miss Adolpha said, giving me a strange look.

"You need to watch out for Miss Mildred," Neely Kate said with a laugh. "She's a wild one."

We finished packing up the photos, and we followed Miss Adolpha down the hall to the art room. After we gave her quick hugs and sent her off to her lesson, we moved down the hall a few feet out of view of the watercolor class.

"I take it you didn't see anything," she said under her breath. "Other than Miss Mildred falling off a table. I would have loved to have seen *that*."

"Neely Kate," I admonished.

"Okay, I don't. Not really. The question is, what do you want to do about your vision?"

"We can't warn Miss Mildred to stay off tables. She'd likely climb on top of one out of spite."

"True."

"I guess we let fate take its course," I said absently, wondering why the older woman had suddenly become so violent. "Do you know why Miss Mildred moved in here?"

"Because she's old?"

I shot her a look.

"I don't know," she said with a shrug. "She has a cane now. Maybe she was having trouble getting around. We know she doesn't have kids to help take care of her. She doesn't have anyone."

She was right, and there wasn't much I could do about that.

We headed for the front doors, but as we passed the great room, I saw Miss Mildred sitting by herself, staring at the wall with a blank expression.

Despite my good sense telling me this was a bad idea, I walked over to her.

"What are you doin'?" Neely Kate asked in a low, insistent voice.

"Give me a minute." Seconds later, I squatted in front of my nemesis and gave her a soft smile. "Hey, Miss Mildred."

She blinked as if coming back to reality, and it took her a moment to see who'd caught her attention. "What do *you* want?" she asked, with enough venom to make most people run for the exit.

I ignored it.

"I was thinking it's been a while since you've seen Violet's kids."

Her face hardened. "At least a year."

"Since you left the New Living Hope Revival Church," I said.

"You want to talk about *that*?" she spat out.

"No," I said softly. "I want to arrange for Ashley and Mikey to come see you."

"Why?" she asked, distrust in her eyes, while Neely Kate let out her own "*Why?*"

"Because Violet liked you," I said. "And I think you loved her like a daughter. It's obvious you care about her kids. So I thought you might like to see them. Mikey's getting so big." I paused. "Did you know he's on a soccer team? He had his first game a couple of nights ago."

"Did he score a goal?" she asked in a meeker voice than I'd ever heard her use.

"He did." I tilted my head. "How about I bring him by this weekend, and he can tell you all about it?"

Her chin quivered. "Ashley too?"

"Of course."

Miss Mildred looked like she was about to cry. Then her eyes hardened. "Why would you do that?"

"Because I know you miss them, and I think they miss you too. And because they need more reminders of Violet. I'd love it if you could tell Ashley some stories about her mother when she was her age. I think she really needs it." I stood. "We'll see you this weekend, Miss Mildred." Then I ignored the shock on Neely Kate's face and headed for the door, leaving her to follow.

As soon as we were in the parking lot, I wasn't surprised when she said, "What just happened?"

"She's lonely," I said, continuing to my Suburban.

"And that's her own fault," Neely Kate said insistently. "She pushes people away."

"I know," I said with a sigh as I walked to the driver's door, leaving Neely Kate standing behind the vehicle. I glanced at her as I grabbed the door handle. "But it still felt like it was the right thing to do."

I got inside, and she quickly walked around and climbed into the passenger seat.

"She's so violent, which isn't like her at all," I said. "I think she feels hopeless. She gave up her house and her life, and now she's here. No one comes to see her, and she obviously doesn't have any friends."

"And whose fault is that?" Neely Kate countered.

"I know. She's never been an easy woman to deal with—"

"You *think*?"

"But she loved Violet, and she loves Violet's kids. And I meant it when I said it would be good for them to have something to remind them of their mother."

"Is this because of what's going on with Ashley at school?"

I considered it. "Partly, but I'd be lying if I said I wasn't worried about Miss Mildred." I swung my gaze to Neely Kate. "In my vision, she was standing on a table, trying to hit an older man with her cane. She fell into his lap and then onto the floor. She said she thought she had broken her hip."

Her nose scrunched. "How in the world did you see that?"

"Nothing popped up when I tried to force a vision about Miss Adolpha in the warehouse, so I switched it up, asking if she saw anyone get hurt."

"And she had a front row seat to Miss Mildred's table dance?" she asked with an ornery grin.

I grimaced. "Yeah."

She was quiet for a moment. "So it wasn't Miss Adolpha's vision that showed you the dead woman?"

"I don't know," I admitted. "I'm guessing it must have been yours, but something changed it." I wondered again if I should tell her about the dream.

"The murder in Pickle Junction," she said.

I wanted to argue with her, but the idea didn't seem that farfetched.

"We need to find out more about that murder," she said with a hard edge in her voice.

I stared at her in disbelief. "What are you talking about?"

She turned in her seat to face me. "We need to find out why Harvey Smith was murdered because whatever he was doing put us in danger."

I shook my head. "That's insane."

Her brow lifted. "Is it?"

My heart sank because I was worried she might be right.

"Do you think Joe will give you any information?" she asked.

I shook my head. "No. He keeps that stuff pretty close to the vest, and if I tell him about the vision, he'll freak out. He's been under enough stress lately. I don't want to worry him."

She flopped back in her seat and drew in a deep breath. "Then how are we going to find out?"

"I know someone who might help," I said.

I only hoped he wouldn't ask a lot of questions.

Chapter Eleven

"Who?" Neely Kate asked. Her eyes widened as it dawned on her. "Randy."

I nodded. It had been a long time since I'd needed an inside source at the sheriff's department, but Randy Miller had been my friend for years, ever since he was assigned to watch over me after a man I'd put in jail had escaped and threatened to kill me. We hadn't seen each other much since Liam was born, and I couldn't help wondering if part of the reason he'd been more distant was because my husband was now his boss.

"But…" I said, "I only want to ask him to help us with the box."

"You're not gonna try to get some information about *the murder?*" she asked in dismay.

"In the past, he gave me information because he knew there was an outside crime organization trying to infiltrate the county, and I had sources that could help counter it. Now I'm just a nosy mom. I don't want to put him in that position, and I definitely don't want to go behind Joe's back."

Her lips twisted to the side. "I suppose that could work."

I grabbed my phone out of my pocket but hesitated. "What about Jed? He might know something about the murder. And he might be able to help us dig up more on the guy with the record who lived next door to Miss Adolpha's lodgers."

Her eyes narrowed to slits. "I'm not talking to that man about *anything*."

"What happened last night, anyway?"

"I don't want to talk about it."

"Okay...so Randy it is." I considered calling him, but he was likely on duty, so I texted instead.

> Hey, Randy, sorry to just text out of nowhere, but I'd love to get together and chat. Can you meet for lunch?

After I hit send, I sent another message.

> It's been too long since we caught up

I set my phone on the seat. "Done. I have no idea how long it'll take for him to get back to me, so maybe we should head back to the office and work on some designs. How'd your consult go yesterday afternoon?"

"Good. I think they're going to want some extensive work done—a patio, gazebo, and even a water garden. *And* they've agreed to let us take photos and post them on our website."

"That's amazing! I can't wait to see what you come up with." I'd put my car in reverse and had started backing out of the parking space when my phone rang.

"Randy got back to me fast," I said, reaching to answer my car's touch screen, but as I pressed accept, I realized the call was from my partner. "Hey, Bruce Wayne." I finished backing up and headed out of the parking lot. "What's up?"

"You got a minute or two you can spare to run over by the jobsite on Hampton?"

I cringed. "Oh no. Did the plants not arrive in time?"

"Yeah, the plants got in okay." He hesitated. "It's something else."

He sounded dead serious, and my heart fluttered. "Is this something I should be worried about?"

"Why don't you just get over here, and we'll talk about it then." With that, he hung up.

I shot an anxious glance at Neely Kate. "Do you know of any other potential problems with the Beetham house?"

She shook her head, looking perplexed. "None that I know about. What do you think it is?"

"I have no idea."

It took ten minutes to get there, and I was a ball of nerves as I parked at the curb and got out. Bruce Wayne's crew was working despite the very wet ground, but one of his men was sitting next to the house with his elbows on his knees, his hands cradling his face. His clothes were caked with dirt and grass stains.

My heart sank. Had someone gotten hurt?

It wouldn't be the first time. We had insurance, and workman's comp would cover medical stuff, but I was still worried when I walked over to them.

Bruce Wayne, standing by the man, looked up, his face sagging with relief as he walked a few feet closer to us. "Oh, good. You have NK with you."

"What's goin' on?" she asked, turning her attention to the man sitting on the grass. I didn't know the crew very well—his guys tended to keep to themselves—but I recognized most of them by sight, even the new ones, and hadn't seen this guy before.

"All right," Bruce Wayne said to the other workers, who had stopped to see what was going on. "Everyone get back to work. We're already running behind because we're short a guy. No need to make us further behind."

"You're down a guy?" I asked, glancing around.

"One of the new guys I hired a couple of weeks ago didn't show."

"That's been happening a lot lately," I said with a frown.

"True, but that's not why I called," Bruce Wayne said. He stared at me solemnly. "You don't have to do this."

My stomach twisted, and somehow I knew what he was going to say before he said it.

"Do what?" Neely Kate asked.

The man on the ground stared up at me, his face pale. Dark circles underscored his eyes. He looked terrified. "Are you the Lady in Black?"

Neely Kate gasped, but I moved closer and squatted in front of him, my heart pounding so hard against my ribs, I wondered if he could see it. "I used to be, but I haven't been her in a long time."

His chin quivered. "I need your help."

I squashed the panic billowing through me. I needed to focus. I needed to *think*. "I'm not sure I can help you, but if you tell me what the problem is, I'll see what I can do."

He hesitated, then glanced up at Bruce Wayne.

"You can trust her," Bruce Wayne said. "I wouldn't have called her if you couldn't."

I wasn't sure whether to thank Bruce Wayne or strangle him. Instead, I focused on the man in front of me. But when I looked beneath the dirt smeared across his face, I realized he wasn't a grown man. He was a teenager.

Crap.

I'd helped a kid several years before, and he'd looked just as scared. Mitchell now worked in Jed's garage, and I couldn't help feeling a tug on my heartstrings to help the boy in front of me.

I sat on the grass, cross-legged, and rested my elbows on my thighs. "What's your name?"

"Austin."

I nodded. "Hi, Austin. I'm Rose. How old are you?"

He looked insulted. "How old are *you*?"

"Twenty-nine. Thirty this fall," I said matter-of-factly,

unphased by his antagonism. He was scared, and scared people acted out. "I promise you I've helped people of all ages, even teenagers, and I've never turned someone who came to me for help into the police or the sheriff."

"But you're *married* to the sheriff," he said with a sneer. "I've seen pictures of you in the paper." He shot a dark look at Bruce Wayne. "You said she'd help me, but I didn't know she was the sheriff's wife."

"I said you could *trust* her," Bruce Wayne said in a no-nonsense tone, "and you better give her the respect she deserves or get the hell out of here."

"So she can turn me in as soon as I leave?" he demanded.

"What would I turn you in for?" I asked, sitting upright. "I don't even know what you've done."

"I didn't do anything. I swear!" he said in a panic.

"Okay, Austin," I said softly. "So why don't you tell me why you need help."

He took several deep breaths, looking like he was about to cry. "I saw something I shouldn't have, and now I think they're gonna kill me."

I tried to hide my surprise. "Austin," I said quietly. "What did you see?"

He glanced up at Neely Kate.

"You can trust her too," I said. "She's a master at secret keeping."

He drew in more breaths, and I could see he was trying to decide if he was going to tell us or bolt.

"How old are you, Austin?" I asked again, keeping my voice soft.

He dropped his chin to his chest. "Seventeen."

"Do your mother and father know you're okay?"

He didn't lift his gaze, but defiance rang through his voice. "They don't give a shit about me."

"Are you sure?"

"Yeah." He reached down and plucked grass blades. "I ain't seen my dad since I was eight, and my mom kicked me out a few months ago when I got into a fight with her new boyfriend."

"Where are you living?"

"Here and there. Mostly friend's couches. Sometimes in my car."

"So what did you see that scared you?"

He looked up. "I saw two men kill a guy."

I tried to hide any reaction to his announcement. "Did this happen down in Pickle Junction?"

He shook his head. "No, it was here in Henryetta."

My gaze darted to Neely Kate, who looked as concerned as I was. Did that mean there'd been *two* murders?

"When did you see this happen?" I asked.

"Last night. Around midnight." He lifted his hand into his lap and began to pick dry skin off the back of it. "There's a party spot on the north edge of town."

"The abandoned Adkins plant," I said.

He looked up at me in surprise. "You know about that place?"

"Please," Neely Kate muttered. "We were getting into trouble out there before you even considered it a party place."

He looked us over, and the expression on his face suggested he found us lacking. "No offense, but you two don't look much like partiers."

"That's because we're not," Neely Kate said in disgust. "We were out there for far more nefarious reasons."

She was right, but I didn't see any reason to confirm it. Then again, his respect seemed to grow a notch or two.

He tipped his head. "Back when Hardshaw was here?"

"You know about Hardshaw?" I asked. If he were seventeen, he would have been thirteen or fourteen when that was going on. Too young to know about such things.

"My daddy was part of Malcolm's crew. Then he defected to Dermot."

At least he hadn't aligned himself with Denny Carmichael, the psychotic drug lord.

"So why didn't you go to Dermot for help?" I asked.

His upper lip curled, and his face hardened. "Because my daddy worked for him, and I don't want nothing to do with my daddy."

"I thought your father took off when you were eight."

He tightened his jaw and glared at me. "Just because he ignored me doesn't mean he didn't stick around the county."

"Fair." But my respect for his father was nil. "Does your father still work for Dermot?"

"I don't know. I haven't talked to him in three years."

I didn't know much about how Dermot ran his organization, only that the county's crime rate had been at an all-time low. So either Dermot and his crew were super stealthy, or they'd found other sources of income.

"So how'd you know to look for me?" I asked.

"Because when I was a kid, I remember everyone talking about the Lady in Black." He cast me another disapproving look. "You don't look very badass." Then he added, "No offense."

Neely Kate propped her hands on her hips and pinned him with a dark gaze. "You do know that 'no offense' doesn't mean crap when you actually are being offensive, right?"

"That's okay," I said, keeping my gaze on Austin. "I'm a bit out of practice, but I'm hoping the help you need from me won't require bad-assery."

"That's where you're wrong," he said in a flat tone. "I need protection."

"So you need to go to the police," Neely Kate said, crossing her arms over her chest. "Has anyone found this poor person's body?"

"It was a man, and they buried him just last night, so I don't think so."

"You saw them do it?" I asked.

"Yep, they murdered him in a building, then buried him behind a parking lot."

Crap. Definitely two murders. Were they related, or was it a coincidence? It didn't feel coincidental, given there hadn't been a murder in Fenton County in about six months.

"How was it you saw them kill a man and didn't get caught?" Neely Kate asked.

"I've been sleeping out there, and my car wasn't in the parking lot. They thought the place was empty."

"So why are you worried if they didn't see you?" I asked.

"Because I was stupid and followed them out there and took pictures with my phone. I wasn't thinkin', and my flash went off, so I took off running."

"Why don't you start at the beginning," I suggested. "Was anyone else with you?"

"No, I was alone. I've been staying out there for the last week or so. I was curled up with my sleeping bag, and I heard banging sounds coming from the front. Then two men were shouting at this guy."

He paused, and when he didn't continue, I prodded, "Then what happened?"

"They started beating him up. Kicking and hitting him and shit. He was moaning and crying out, but he wasn't sayin' nothin', and then one of the guys shot 'im. The other guy was pissed, and I thought his buddy was gonna shoot *him*, but after he calmed down, he told the guy that he was gonna be the one to dig the hole."

When he stopped talking, I said, "And then what happened?"

"They loaded him into the back of their truck, drove to the trees behind the parking lot, and buried him back there."

"And you *followed* them?" Neely Kate asked in disbelief.

I had to agree with her on this one. We both knew the layout of the place well. There wasn't any cover in the parking lot. It would have been hard for him to pursue them without being seen. "If you didn't want to report this to the police, then why would you follow them?"

He lowered his face. "I never said I was smart."

That I agreed with. I wasn't buying that it was the complete reason, but I was willing to let it go for the moment to get more information.

Neely Kate, on the other hand, wasn't feeling as generous. She propped a hand on her hip. "So you saw the truck drive back there, and you decided to stroll out there and watch them dig a grave like it was a spectator sport?"

Anger washed over his face, but fear flickered in his eyes before he masked it. "I don't have to tell you shit! You're not the Lady in Black."

"The Lady in Black doesn't exist anymore," I said, keeping my voice neutral. "And you're lucky we're talking to you at all. So if you want our help, take a deep breath, get your temper under control, and tell us what we need to know, or go on your way."

"So you can turn me in?" he spat, getting more agitated.

I was still on the ground, eye level with him, and I could tell Bruce Wayne was worried I was in danger. I didn't think the kid would hurt me, but I also wasn't going to give him the opportunity.

I got to my feet. "I'm not sure why you came to me, Austin, but when I was the Lady, there were rules that the people I dealt with had to follow. They either treated me with respect or dealt with their issues on their own. No one's forcing you to stay here. I only know your first name, and as far as I can tell, you haven't committed any crime. You wouldn't be the first person to witness a murder and keep quiet, and you sure won't be the last. You sit here for a moment and consider your options while I talk to Bruce Wayne about business that actually makes me money."

Austin's eyes were narrowed to slits, and his hands were clenched at his sides, but he remained silent other than his heavy breathing.

I walked over to the curb, leaving Bruce Wayne and Neely Kate to follow, then turned to face them as we formed a loose huddle. "How did this come about, Bruce Wayne?"

He cringed. "I'm so sorry, Rose. The kid showed up, acting desperate and asking for the Lady in Black. I asked him why he came to me, and he said some other guy had told him I was a contact for Lady. He told me he'd witnessed a murder and needed protection." He shifted his weight and crossed his arms over his chest. "I never should have called you."

"No," I said, glancing at the kid. He was still sitting on the grass, his face buried in his hands. "You did the right thing. If someone's looking for Lady, I need to know. Do you buy that he knew about me from his father's involvement with Dermot?"

Bruce Wayne shrugged. "It's possible."

"It seems weird that some guy told him to come to you," Neely Kate said. "Who is this guy?"

"I don't know," Bruce Wayne admitted.

"Do you think it's a setup?" Neely Kate asked me.

I blinked in surprise. "A setup?"

"It just seems weird that this kid would show up nearly three years after everything went down, looking for Lady."

It felt like my nightmares about Hardshaw were coming to life, but I told myself to calm down. Hardshaw was dead and gone. It was just an ironic twist that this boy had shown up looking for Lady at around the same time as the murder in Pickle Junction.

"Agreed," Bruce Wayne said, "but then again, if he grew up hearing stories about the Lady in Black, he's probably blown her up to be some kind of superhero."

I snorted. "Superhero?"

He didn't crack a smile. "You faced down some pretty dangerous people and took charge of the county's criminal element."

"Plus, some of the stories have probably been exaggerated," Neely Kate said.

I looked her dead in the eyes. *"Thanks?"*

She shrugged.

"Besides, I never *successfully* took charge," I countered with more force than I'd intended. "I tried to unite the underworld to deal with Hardshaw and failed miserably."

"I'm sure others tell it differently," Bruce Wayne said. He toed the ground with the tip of his boot. "In fact, I know they do."

My eyes widened. *"What?"*

"I'm not surprised this kid came to you, but everything else is fishy," he said, lifting his gaze. "He shows up looking for help, then says he recognizes you as the sheriff's wife from the newspaper." His jaw tightened. "What seventeen-year-old kid reads the newspaper, let alone recognizes the wife of the sheriff from it? How many photos have there been of you in the paper as Joe's wife? One? Two?"

"Three," I said under my breath. *The Henryetta Gazette* had also written an article about our landscaping business last year, but that had been about me, not Joe. "So why's he really here?"

"I don't know," Bruce Wayne said. "But I'd like to find out."

"How do you plan on doing that?" Neely Kate asked.

Bruce Wayne shifted his attention to her. "I think we should call Jed."

We were silent as we let the full implications of his statement sink in.

My panic returned. "We don't do this anymore," I said in a hushed tone. "We don't solve murders and protect people."

Bruce Wayne's kind eyes looked into mine. He said, "What if this kid really is in trouble? I one hundred percent believe he's lying and withholding information, but I'm not willing to cut him loose either." His face grew grim. "What if something else is going on in the criminal underworld? What if you and the kids are in danger?"

Oh, Lordy. What if he was right?

"The vision," Neely Kate murmured, sounding scared.

"What vision?" Bruce Wayne asked with an anxious look.

I cringed. "I had a vision yesterday. It was in a warehouse, and there were gunshots and a woman on the floor with lots of blood around her."

"Whose vision was it?" he asked, looking panicked. "Neely Kate's?"

"I don't know," I admitted. "I don't think so. It just hit me out of the blue when we were at Piney Rest talking to a resident. At first, I thought the woman on the ground might be me—she had dark hair, but the vision was hazy, and I couldn't see her face. Then, when I tried to force a vision, asking if Neely Kate was going to be in a dangerous situation or if I was about to die, I got nothing. And it was the same with the elderly woman we were visiting yesterday when we dropped by to see her this morning. Honestly, we thought it had something to do with the box we dug up."

Neely Kate grabbed my hand. "Have a vision now."

"Okay." It was a good idea, especially in light of the current situation.

I squeezed her hand and closed my eyes.

Will Neely Kate be caught in gunfire?

Nothing.

Will I be hurt or killed by gunfire?

Nothing.

Will Austin bring danger to me, Neely Kate, Bruce Wayne, or our families?

A vision began to appear, but it was slow to come—something I'd learned meant that the future might still be unsure.

Vision Neely Kate was sitting at my kitchen table between Dermot and me. Dermot had a mug clutched in his right hand, and Vision Rose was looking at him intently. "Do you think this is going to be a problem?" she asked.

"I don't know," Dermot said.

The vision ended, and I opened my eyes. "Dermot doesn't know if it's going to be a problem."

"You didn't see yourself dead?" Neely Kate asked, her eyes wide with anxiety.

"No. I had to go through a lot of questions to get an answer, but the one that gave me a vision was when I asked if any of us or our families were in danger. The vision was Dermot sitting in my kitchen saying what I just blurted out." I filled them in on the rest.

"You weren't in danger in the vision?" Bruce Wayne asked.

"No." I ran a hand over my head as I studied the boy. "We need to take him to Dermot."

"Or we could just call the police," Neely Kate said.

"The Henryetta Police?" I asked in disbelief. They were as incompetent as ever, and a few of them still tried to pin things on me for old time's sake.

Bruce Wayne stared at the boy with a frown. "If it happened out at Adkins, then technically, it falls under the sheriff's jurisdiction."

I shook my head in frustration. He was right. "Dammit."

"Why don't you want to call Joe?" Neely Kate asked.

That was a question I was struggling to answer myself.

The most logical solution was to call Joe, but something was holding me back.

And that something scared the wits out of me.

Chapter Twelve

I slid my cell phone out of my pocket and pulled up my contacts. Once I found Dermot, I took a breath to think this through. Did I really want to travel down this road? I had four kids and a husband—a life I loved—to consider, but it worried me that this boy had come searching for Lady, and Dermot would probably be able to provide more answers than Joe.

The kid saw the phone in my hand and jumped to his feet. "No police!" he shouted.

The landscaping crew paused their work and cast questioning looks in our direction, but maybe we'd found good help after all because they resumed their tasks without any fanfare.

"She's not calling the police, you fool," Neely Kate called over to him in disgust.

He hesitated, then sat back down.

"Is he hungry or thirsty?" I asked Bruce Wayne. "Maybe giving him some food will help settle him down."

"I already gave him some water and my sandwich for lunch."

I offered him a smile of thanks, then placed the call.

The phone rang for a few seconds before a gruff voice said, "Rose?"

"Hey, Dermot," I said softly. "Long time, no talk."

"Yeah," he said, sounding sleepy, and I realized I'd probably woken him.

"Sorry to bother you so early." Only it wasn't that early. It was after ten a.m. "I have a situation here, and I'd appreciate your input."

He paused. "That sounds ominous."

"A teenager showed up at Bruce Wayne's worksite, asking for protection from the Lady in Black."

"Shit."

"Yeah."

"Are you offering it?" he asked.

Was I? Why was I even considering this? "I don't know yet. I need more answers, and some of his story seems a little too contrived."

"I see."

I wasn't sure what that answer meant. It had been several years since we'd worked together, and I no longer knew his tells. "You don't have to get involved in this, Dermot. I just thought…"

"That I'd want to know? I *definitely* want to know. You and your kids are important to me, and I don't like that someone is asking about Lady after all this time."

I wasn't surprised by his answer. Dermot had helped deliver Hope in the woods in a breach delivery while we'd been in the middle of a dangerous situation. I'd named him her godfather, and he used to check on her from time to time after everything had died down, but I hadn't talked to him in over a year.

"Where are you?" he asked.

"Still at the worksite."

"Send me an address. I'm gonna swing by and have a little chat with your new friend."

"Is that a good idea?" I asked. "Should we bring him to you?"

"Ab-sol-utely not," he barked. "You don't get in a vehicle with him. Not without protection." Then he added, "Is Jed involved?"

"He knows nothing about this, but he's also kept his nose out of Fenton County criminal business."

"Does Joe know?"

"He has absolutely no idea. About any of it." My guilt rose up like a mushroom cloud. I'd worked so hard to earn his trust and not keep secrets from him, and this was a doozy of a secret.

It all gave me a moment of pause. What was I doing? I needed to hang up, call Joe, and tell him about the vision and this kid showing up looking for the Lady in Black after witnessing a murder, yet I knew Austin would *never* talk to Joe.

What if something bigger really was going on in this county? What if Hardshaw *had* come back? Maybe Neely Kate was right, and all of this was a setup. Someone could be using Austin to get to me, and if that were the case, it would be far easier for Dermot to suss it out than Joe.

I needed to go with my gut and let Dermot handle it. Even if guilt was eating at my soul.

"What does that mean?" Dermot asked.

"I'll tell you once you get here."

"Okay. Text me the address," he said, then hung up.

"Dermot's on his way," I said as I typed the address into my phone.

He responded within seconds.

Be there in fifteen

I told them what he'd said, then shoved my phone into my pocket.

"He's coming *here*?" Neely Kate asked in surprise.

I was just as surprised as she was. In the past, we'd gone out of our way to not be publicly linked, just like James and I had done when I was helping him. But this was a quiet, upscale neighborhood. No one would know who Dermot was, nor would they find it strange that a bunch of people were congregating on a job site. The only way we'd find trouble was if some type of violence broke out, and I was going to do everything in my power to make sure that didn't happen.

"So what do we do with Junior while we wait?" Neely Kate asked. "And what's gonna stop him from running once Dermot shows up?"

"We could have him wait in my car," I said. "I have child locks on the back doors, which would make it harder for him to get out, but I'd have to remove a car seat."

"No," Bruce Wayne said. "Don't do that. He'll be just fine there. I'll give him the piece of cake Anna packed in my lunch."

He walked over, leaving Neely Kate and me next to the street. He picked up an insulated lunch bag and handed the kid a container and a fork. The boy took off the lid and dug into the cake like he hadn't eaten in a week.

"I believe the homeless part of his story," Neely Kate said as she studied him.

"Yeah, me too. But the other parts don't make sense."

"Do you think he saw a murder?"

Part of me wanted to panic, but I made myself concentrate on the facts. "I suppose that part would be easy enough to corroborate. If they buried a body behind the Adkins plant, it would be easy to find the spot. I'm guessing they probably changed their minds after they got caught, but there'd still be evidence of digging."

"But who's gonna check it out?" Neely Kate asked. "Joe's men or Dermot's?"

"Crappy doodles. I don't know." How had I gotten myself into this situation?

"We could make the kid call in an anonymous tip," she suggested.

"Yeah. Agreed."

"But that doesn't help us figure out what to do with him if the murderers really are after him," she said. "We both know the sheriff's department won't protect him. They'll take his statement and cut him loose."

"I know Joe would *want* to protect him, but there's not much in the budget for him to do more than have a deputy do drive-bys of his house."

"And he says he doesn't have a home," Neely Kate added.

"I know. Not to mention, if we bring Joe in without Austin's permission, there's a chance Austin'll clam up." I ran a hand over my head again. "I *really* want to call Joe, but we need to find out what's going on. I'm terrified Hardshaw's back, and Dermot's in a better position to confirm or deny it."

Neely Kate frowned. "Unfortunately, I think you're right."

Dermot arrived in ten minutes instead of fifteen, parking his shiny black pickup behind my Suburban.

Bruce Wayne was standing next to Austin, and while the boy looked nervous to see someone else show up—an imposing man to boot—he didn't look ready to bolt. Yet.

Dermot walked over to me and Neely Kate. He was tall and broad shouldered, and a scruff covered his lower face. He had a swagger that suggested he would match any bullshit tossed at him and raise the ante. I had to admit that if I hadn't known him, I would have been intimidated.

His mouth lifted into a grim smile. "Sorry to be seeing you again under these conditions."

"And I'm sorry to drag you into this, but when he mentioned Lady—"

"Don't apologize," he said. "If he invoked Lady, there might be something goin' on I'm not aware of, and I like to know everything that's goin' on in the county." He glanced over at the kid. "I take it that's him?"

"Yeah."

"Why's he scared?"

"He claims he saw a murder out at Adkins last night. He says he took a photo of them burying the body, but his flash went off. He took off, and now he's worried they're after him."

"His flash went off?" he asked, his voice heavy with a thick layer of skepticism.

"Yeah," I said. "Like I mentioned, some of his story doesn't make sense."

Dermot kept his gaze on the boy. "I'm gonna talk to him."

"Here?" Bruce Wayne asked in surprise. "In the open?"

Dermot glanced at me, brow raised. "Up to you."

The other alternative was for him to take the boy somewhere for a chat—not that he'd likely agree to go. Even if he did, I wasn't sure Dermot would want me tagging along. Shoot, I wasn't sure I *wanted* to tag along. But this was my mess, and I didn't think I should be passing it off to Dermot.

At least not yet.

"Let's try it here first." I held his gaze. "He came to me, which means I'm well and truly part of it. You'll question him with me present." As I finished my statement, I was surprised by my own directness.

The corner of his mouth ticked up. "I wouldn't expect anything less, Lady."

I cringed at the name, but I'd fully embraced her at one point. I couldn't be all that surprised that she was still a part of me all these years later.

The four of us walked over together, and Austin stared at Dermot with fear in his eyes. He got to his feet, his hands shaking at his sides.

"I'm Tim Dermot," Dermot said with a slight nod. "I hear you're in need of Lady's protection."

Austin's face reddened with fury. "Why'd you call *him*?"

His anger didn't faze me. "Because I've been out of this world too long, and if you really need help, then Dermot's the one who's going to provide it."

"What?" Austin said in a sneer. "I told you my daddy was part of his crew."

"Your father works for me?" Dermot said in surprise, then shot me a scowl.

"I didn't think it was pertinent for you to know," I said. "At least he didn't defect to Carmichael."

"That would have been short lived," Austin scoffed.

"You know about Denny Carmichael?" Dermot asked, assessing him.

The boy snorted. "Who doesn't?"

"Probably most of the county," Dermot shot back. "What's your father's name?"

Austin lifted his chin in defiance. "Oscar Cowan."

"He doesn't work for me anymore," Dermot said, his voice neutral. "We had a difference of opinion."

"Yeah, well, he's a piece of shit, so I'm not surprised," Austin said, trying to sound tough, but defeat filled his eyes. I wondered if Dermot saw it too, but then I realized, of course, he did. To succeed in his role, he needed to see everything.

Bruce Wayne's crew were making halfhearted attempts to look like they were being productive while staring at us, but I was pretty sure one of the guys had been removing a bush from its plastic container for the past ten minutes.

"So you saw a murder out at Adkins?" Dermot asked, keeping his voice low.

"*You told him?*" Austin shouted at me.

Dermot held up his hands, and his face turned dark and menacing. "I'm not sure if Lady's explained the rules, but you do not shout at her, and you *will* treat her with respect. Older, more badass men than you have followed those rules, so either you do the same, or we don't help you."

"Yeah, she already told me," he said, walking away a few paces, then back again. "What is she? A damn princess?"

"More like a queen," Dermot said. "And you'll treat her as such."

Neely Kate's eyes widened, but Bruce Wayne didn't look that surprised.

What stories had been spread about my involvement in their world?

"Am I supposed to call her Your Majesty?" Austin asked in a smartass tone.

Dermot took a step back and turned to me. "Cut him loose."

I had a moment of panic. We didn't know anything, and if my name was being tossed around, I needed to know what was being said, especially if Hardshaw or someone just as bad was out there. But I also trusted Dermot, one of the many reasons I'd called him, so I shoved my hands into my front pockets. "Okay. Good luck, Austin." Then I turned around and started to walk back toward my car, Dermot following behind me, slightly to my left.

"Wait!" Austin called after us. "I'll be good."

"Keep walkin'," Dermot said under his breath.

I took several more steps, almost reaching the curb, when Austin called out again, "*Please*, Lady. I need your help."

I stopped this time and turned to Dermot, saying low enough so Austin couldn't hear me, "I think he really saw something. Would he act so belligerent if he were here for nefarious reasons?"

"Possibly," Dermot replied in an undertone. "If he were smart, he wouldn't want to seem too eager."

Not the answer I wanted to hear. "So what do you think he's here for?"

"I'm not sure, but I'd like to find out."

I nodded. "So we try again?"

He crossed his arms over his chest and glanced at the white picket fence next door. "If he's here to tell us about a murder, I'd rather him not do in the Jones' front yard."

"The Beethams," I said, then realized I was being too literal. "So where do we take him?"

"Let's start out in my truck, and we'll move him somewhere else based on what he says."

I considered it for a moment.

"*Please!*" Austin called out.

"Okay," I said, still keeping my voice low. "But *I* want to question him first. Then you can have a shot at him."

He nodded. "Okay."

He took a step, but I grabbed his arm and pulled him to a halt. "Is there something going on in the underworld, Dermot?"

He stared into my face. "The truth?"

"Don't insult me by insinuating I'd want anything but."

Sympathy filled his eyes. "You've been gone a long time. You've kept your nose clean." He paused and leveled his gaze with mine. "You're married to the damn sheriff. Once you know this stuff, you can't unknow it, and you sure as hell can't tell Joe."

I rubbed my face with my hand as my heart sank. What was I doing? But Joe was certain there was nothing big going on in the county, and if I could find information that proved otherwise, it would help him too. Right?

It didn't ease my guilt, but it still felt important to learn everything I could.

"You can walk away from this and pretend like it never happened," Dermot said kindly.

"And you'll take care of it?" I asked with more attitude than I'd intended as I dropped my hand.

"There's nothing wrong with handing this off to me," he said. "You left this world, and with good cause. And if I'm honest, I don't want you back in it, not because I don't trust you but because you've got four kids. You and I both know that this world and families don't mix." A familiar pain filled his eyes when he talked about the family he'd lost because of his involvement in the underworld.

"Dermot." My heart broke for him, just like it did every time he mentioned his family, which I could count on one hand. He kept his cards close to the vest, always. He only let this side of him slip out for a few people, and I counted myself lucky that I was one of the ones he trusted.

He pulled back his shoulders. "That being said, you're a grown-ass woman who pretty much saved this county and a whole lot of lives. You're more than capable of dealing with this. The question is, why would you?"

He was right. I should just let him handle the situation with the boy and have him let me know if I should be worried. Before my mother died nearly six years ago, I would have handed it to him and thanked him profusely, but I wasn't that woman anymore.

I took care of my own messes.

"No," I said, hoping I didn't regret it but already knowing I probably would. "You don't need to tell me about what's going on in the criminal world, but I have to hear this boy out and find out who told him to come to Bruce Wayne to find me. And if he really *did* witness a murder, I need to figure out how to deal with that too."

He nodded. "Okay. Let's bring him to the truck."

We headed back to Austin, who was flanked by Neely Kate and Bruce Wayne. He looked like he was about to be sick. He might have an ulterior motive for being here, but he was obviously scared shitless.

"Austin," I said, stopping a few feet from him. "We need to ask you some questions before we can help you, but your belligerence isn't doing you any favors. So do you want my help or not?"

"I think so."

"Either you do or you don't, boy," Dermot barked. "Which one is it?"

Austin flinched. "I do."

"And you realize that you're not gonna give Lady any lip, or you're out on your ass—no second chances?" Dermot asked.

"Yeah."

"Okay," I said, trying to hide my fluttering nerves. "We'll go sit in Dermot's truck and find out exactly what happened."

"I already told you what happened," he countered, sounding panicked. "And if I get in that truck, I'm as good as dead."

"Dead?" Dermot asked with a short laugh. "Who do you think's gonna kill you?"

Austin gave him an anxious look.

"Me?" Dermot asked, then narrowed his eyes. "Do I have reason to kill you?"

"I don't think so."

"Do I have reason to have beef with you?" Dermot pushed, moving a step closer to him.

To his credit, Austin held his gaze, even as his body shook. "You do if you had that guy killed."

Dermot took a step back. "Then you're safe because the only murder I know anything about is the one in Pickle Junction two days ago. Come on." He turned his back and started sauntering toward the truck.

I stared after him, hoping I was hiding my shock. Not because Dermot knew about the Pickle Junction murder but because he'd said the murder had taken place two days ago. As far as I knew, the sheriff's office had only found out about it yesterday.

What the hell was I doing, jumping back into this world of secrets and half-truths? Of lying to Joe?

I took one look at Austin with tears welling in his eyes, and there was my answer. He was just a kid, and he was scared. What if Mikey or Liam needed help when they were teenagers, and Joe, our friends, and I weren't around to give it? I'd want someone to step up for them, and I wanted to step up for this boy too. I couldn't turn him away.

I put my hand on his shoulder. "It's okay. He'll treat you fairly."

"I came to you, not him," he said softly as a tear tracked down his cheek.

"I'm not in this world anymore," I said. "So he's our best resource if you still refuse to talk to the sheriff." When he didn't answer, I said, "I could call my husband Joe. I promise he'll be fair too."

He slowly shook his head as he said in a defeated tone, "I can't be talkin' to the sheriff."

"Then we'll talk to Dermot, and if you feel uncomfortable, you tell me, and we'll leave. Together."

His mouth dropped open. "You'd still help me?"

"You came to me for help, so I'll help you as long as you treat me respectfully. Okay?"

He wiped his nose with the back of his long sleeve. "Okay."

"I'm comin' too," Neely Kate said. I was surprised she'd remained silent this long.

"Neely Kate's part of this too," I said in a tone that didn't brook argument. He was smart enough to heed that tone.

I cast a quick glance at Bruce Wayne, but he shook his head. He'd played his role in this, and now he was done.

Smart man. I couldn't help thinking I should follow his lead.

The three of us walked to the truck together. Austin and I got in the back seat, and Neely Kate sat in the front passenger seat. Dermot was sitting in the driver's seat, shifting sideways to face the boy.

"Austin," I said gently, "tell us again what happened. Only this time, give us more detail."

He swallowed. "Okay."

"Start with the men coming into the building," I said. "What were you doing, and where were you?"

"Where was I in the building?" he asked in confusion.

"We know that building better than you'd think," Neely Kate said.

"I was in an office in the back."

We knew that office well, but I refrained from telling him that. "And where were the men when they shot the other guy?"

"In that big open area next to the office. They kind of trapped him there, I think. I was sleeping, and I heard shouting and a lot of banging. I think they were chasing him through the place and had him cornered in that area. I was scared one of them was gonna come into the office and find me."

"Did you see them shoot him or just hear it happen?"

He swallowed again, shaking a little. "I saw it. The door was cracked, so I watched through the slit. He was on his hands and knees, beggin' 'em to not kill him, but they kept asking him where the package was. He said he didn't have it. The one guy got pissed and shot him."

"And the other guy was upset he'd done it?" I asked, restating what he'd previously said.

"Yeah. Like upset enough that I thought he was gonna shoot that guy too."

"Did they try to help the guy they shot?" I asked.

He shook his head. "No. He got shot in the head, and it was pretty obvious he was dead." His face paled even more.

"Ever seen someone killed before, kid?" Dermot asked.

Austin shook his head. "No, sir."

"It's gonna stick in there for a while, but don't try to ignore it or shove it down. That's only gonna make it worse. When all of this is settled, I have someone you can talk to."

"Like a *shrink*?" Austin asked in dismay.

"A therapist," Dermot said, "and you can trust him."

Neely Kate gave me a surprised look, but I lifted my shoulders into a barely discernable shrug. Dermot was a nurse practitioner before he'd gone full time in the criminal world. I didn't know how the career change had taken place, but it stood to reason mental health would be important to him too.

"So after they shot him, what did they do?" Dermot asked.

"They argued for a bit, then decided to bury him out back. One of them drove his truck around to the big open windows on the west side of the building—they don't have any glass, so you can just climb in and out."

We were aware of that too.

"So they hauled him out the window into the truck?" I asked.

"Yeah." He swallowed. "Only they didn't have anything to wrap him in, and the second guy, who seemed to be in charge, made the guy who'd shot him carry the end with his head. He complained that he was getting blood and brains on his shirt and his new boots, but the other guy just said if he hadn't shot the one guy they needed to talk to, he wouldn't be gettin' blood and brains on his shoes. He'd be lucky if he didn't get worse from the big guy."

"Big guy?" Dermot asked.

"Yeah. I figured he was the guy in charge." He snuck a fearful glance at Dermot.

"You thought I was the big guy?" Dermot asked without accusation.

"Yeah."

"And now you believe that I'm not?"

Austin looked over at me, then nodded. "Yeah. Lady said I could trust you."

I was floored that he'd already given me such blanket trust.

"So what happened after they left?" Dermot asked.

"I heard their truck drive off, and after a minute or so, I crept out of the room and saw all the blood and…" He swallowed again. "*Stuff* and figured if the police found out that I'd been staying there, they might think I was the one who did it. So I figured if I found 'em, I could prove they'd killed the guy, and I wouldn't be charged with it."

"So why not go to the police?" I asked.

He snorted in disgust. "You think they're gonna believe me?"

"They would if there's a body," Neely Kate said.

He snorted again. "Goes to show what you know. They treat all teenagers from Pickle Junction like trash. I wasn't gonna take my chances."

"Let's go back to after they took the body out," I said. "How did you know they were gonna bury it behind the parking lot?"

"I didn't, but when I climbed out the window, I saw the lights from the truck in the back. So I kept low and headed back there. I was surprised that the guy who was the shooter was actually digging a grave."

"And you took photos of him doin' it?" Neely Kate asked.

He nodded.

"And the flash went off?" she asked. When he nodded again, she said, "Wouldn't video have been better?"

He hung his head. "Probably, but I wasn't thinkin' right."

"Obviously," Neely Kate said under her breath.

I shot her a look, and she shrugged as though to say, *I'm just stating the obvious.*

"Let's have a look at those photos," I said, holding out my hand.

"They ain't any good," Austin grumbled as he pulled his phone out of his pocket and entered a passcode. After a few swipes and taps, he handed it over. "I only have a few."

The first image was a blur of white light with black in the background. There were no discernable people. If you used your imagination, you could see trees on the sides, but they could as easily have been Bigfoot.

"That's the one with flash," he said. "The others are worse."

"Worse than that?" Neely Kate asked in disbelief as I lowered the phone so she and Dermot could see.

I swiped to the next photo, which was pitch black. The next five photos were exactly the same.

"Now you see why I used the flash," Austin said.

"I guess," Neely Kate said.

I swiped again, and a selfie of Austin and a little girl appeared. Both had wide smiles that made my heart swell.

Austin quickly reached over and took his phone back. "That's all I have."

"Was that your sister?" I asked. "You look like you're very close."

He nodded, but his silence was proof enough that he didn't want to talk about it. He was protecting her.

"So when they saw you, you took off running?" I asked.

"Yeah, they started shooting at me, but I took off running through weeds on the land next to the plant, and I kept low so he was shootin' blindly."

"Good thinkin'," Dermot said.

The boy seemed to bask in his praise.

"So after you got away, what did you do next?" I asked.

"I walked for a long time, then I called a guy I know from school. He told me I needed help from the Lady in Black and that I should find a guy named Bruce Wayne who worked for a landscaping company. So I looked it up on my phone, and someone posted on social media that the landscaping company was working on their house this week. I looked them up on the internet and found their address and started walking."

"The plant is at least ten miles north," I said.

He nodded. "I walked all night, stopping to sleep some when I found an empty shed."

We were all silent for a moment before Dermot asked, "Why do you think they know who you are?"

Austin looked up at him, terror on his face. "I went back to the building to get my stuff—it's all I've got—but when I got there, none of my stuff was there." He paused. "I'd left my car keys there, and they were gone, but worse, they took my wallet."

He swallowed hard. "They have my driver's license. They know who I am."

Chapter Thirteen

We were all silent for a moment before I said, "We need to call Joe."

The car erupted into chaos as all three of the people shut in with me protested.

"Look," I said, holding up my hands to get their attention. "Joe will find a way to protect him." This boy knew too much for him to do otherwise.

"So can I," Dermot said, his jaw tight.

"Joe needs to know anyway," I said insistently. "He has to find out who murdered that man and bring them to justice."

Austin shook his head, and defiance filled his eyes. "I ain't talkin' to no sheriff. That's why I came to you." He reached for the door handle.

"Okay, wait," I said in a rush. "I told you I'd help you, and lettin' you run off isn't helpin' you."

"I ain't talkin' to the sheriff," he repeated, tears filling his eyes.

"How many warrants you got out for you, kid?" Dermot asked.

He blinked. "How'd you…" His shoulders sank. "Two."

"What for?" Dermot asked.

"Domestic violence."

"Was the domestic violence with your stepdad?" I asked.

"He's not my stepdad!" he protested.

"Okay," I said softly. "Your mom's boyfriend."

"He was hitting my little sister." His eyes hardened. "So I made him stop."

"Surely the sheriff's deputy who responded to the call took that into account," I said.

He released a bitter laugh. "Not when the guy you hit is King Major Comfort."

"The mattress guy?" Neely Kate asked in disbelief. "The King of Comfort beats up little kids?"

Austin gestured to Neely Kate with a dry look. "See?"

"He lives in *Pickle Junction*?" Neely Kate asked. "His mattress store is in Magnolia."

The boy shrugged. "Sure, but his family lives in Pickle Junction, and he won't leave his precious *mommy*."

Neely Kate's mouth dropped open. *"He lives with his mom?"*

"No, he lives with *my* mom. But his mom doesn't live very far away." He made a face. "But he's famous, so the sheriff won't do anything to him."

"Famous," Dermot scoffed under his breath. "That's not even his real name. It's George Major White."

I wondered how Dermot knew his legal name, and what that implied.

"It should be Major Asshole," Austin said.

"Listen," I said to the teen, "I'll talk to Joe. I'm sure if he knows the circumstances, then—"

"The kid's got a point," Dermot said. "The deputies are biased against pretty much anyone in Pickle Junction. And the kid shouldn't need a special favor to get the sheriff's department to treat him fairly."

My cheeks burned because he had a point. "You're right."

"No sheriff," Austin said to me, pleading with his eyes.

"Okay," I said softly, already wondering how I could approach Joe about the deputies' behavior with Pickle Junction citizens.

"No sheriff." But it didn't mean I couldn't find a way to bring this to Joe's attention.

"Do you know anything about this package they were asking about?" Dermot asked. "You said they were shouting. What were they saying?"

Austin swallowed, his Adam's apple bobbing. "I think he took something. They were asking him where it was."

"Did they say what *it* was?" Dermot asked.

The boy shook his head.

"You're sure?"

"Yes, sir."

"And they took your wallet?" Dermot asked.

The boy's face flushed, and his gaze dropped to his lap. "Yes, sir."

"What address will they see on your license?"

"My mom's house."

"And you say Major Asshole lives there?" Dermot asked.

Austin cracked a smile, then sobered. "Yes, sir."

Dermot nodded, then pulled out his phone and started tapping on it. "What's your address, kid?"

His mouth dropped open, but he quickly closed it. "I ain't tellin' you that."

"You want those guys to show up and kidnap your little sister to make you turn yourself in?"

His face flushed as his jaw hardened. "So I let your guys take her instead?"

"I don't take kids," Dermot spat. "I have principles."

Austin's eyes filled with distrust. "You can't have too many if my daddy worked for you."

Dermot's anger faded. "You're right about your daddy. He was a piece of shit, and I kicked his ass to the curb years ago. I don't know what the asshole's doin' now, but it sure as hell ain't workin' for me."

Austin started to say something, then stopped.

"You've got two options, kid," Dermot said matter-of-factly. "You either come with me and let me protect you, or you do this on your own."

Austin's eyes widened. "I came to Lady."

"Lady's retired," Dermot said. "I'm your only option."

The boy turned to me with a pleading look.

"He's right," I said, feeling guilty for passing him off to Dermot, but there was no way I could bring him home and risk the safety of my kids. "I'm retired, but you can trust Dermot. He's protected me more times than I can count. He'll protect you too. Or you can talk to my husband." By now, I knew there was no way he'd willingly talk to Joe, but my loyalty to him was strong.

"And I'll protect your mom and sister too," Dermot said, ignoring my suggestion. "Once you give me the address, I'll send someone to watch the house and make sure no one hurts them."

And try to intercept them to find out what they were up to, but I kept that part to myself.

Austin lifted his chin and gave Dermot a hard stare. "Why would you help me?"

Dermot didn't say anything for a second, then said, "I've got my reasons."

"Like killin' me?" the teen asked. His shaking hands belied his bravado.

"I ain't gonna kill you, kid," Dermot said with a snort. He paused, and his tone softened. "You remind me of someone, and I wished I'd helped him. Maybe I consider this a do-over."

Austin's eyes widened, and Neely Kate snuck a look of surprise at me. I had no idea who he was talking about, but it was obvious he meant it.

"We can protect your sister from Major Asshole too," Dermot said. "But only if you cooperate."

I hoped he was bluffing about only helping his sister if the kid cooperated, but looking at Dermot's dark expression, I wasn't sure.

Austin reached for the door handle. "I'm out of here."

Turning toward me with a grim look, Dermot said, "I wonder what will happen to the kid if we don't help him."

I knew what he was asking. He wanted me to have a vision, and I had to admit it wasn't a bad idea.

Turning in my seat, I placed my hand on the boy's arm and asked, *What will happen to Austin when he leaves this car?* I plunged into darkness and heard heavy breathing—*my* heavy breathing—because in the vision, I was Austin. My eyes adjusted, and I realized I was running through trees while someone chased me.

"Give it up, kid," a man called out behind me. "You've got nowhere to go."

"I didn't see nothin'!" I said with a sob in Austin's voice. "I'll be quiet! I swear!"

"We know you met with the Lady in Black," the man shouted at me. "We want to know what you told her."

"I didn't tell her nothin'!" I shouted, then stumbled over a rut, falling face down. I put my hands out in front of me to break my fall, and a sharp pain shot through my left palm. Panicked, I started crawling, trying to get up on my feet, but something slammed into my back, sending me face down in the dirt.

"Just tell us what we want to know, and you'll be free to go," the man growled, his foot firmly planted on my back.

I tried to get up, but he put his weight on his foot, pushing me down hard enough that rocks and sticks jabbed me in the stomach and cheek.

"What did you tell her?" the man growled.

"Nothin'! I thought she'd be more badass, so I didn't tell her nothin'. I left."

"We have ways of making you talk, kid, so save yourself the trouble."

Terror swamped my head. "I told her you shot someone."

"Did you tell her who we are?"

"I don't *know* who you are!" I shouted through my tears.

"Good." Then there was a loud bang, a sharp pain in my back, and I was plunged into gray mist.

I burst out of the vision, panting as I said, "You don't know who they are."

Neely Kate stared into my face with terror in her eyes, while Austin grumbled, "I already told you I didn't know."

I turned to Dermot, and he gave me a slight nod. He and Neely Kate didn't know what I'd seen, but they'd been around for enough of my visions and their aftermath to understand I'd seen something bad.

"Let me see your phone," Dermot said, reaching his hand out to the kid.

"I ain't givin' you my phone," he snapped.

"Then get out and face those guys on your own," Dermot said.

Austin turned to me. "I came to you for help! Not him!"

"I already told you I can't help you, Austin," I said quietly. There was no way I was bringing him anywhere near my kids after what I'd just seen. "Dermot will protect you, I swear, but I need to know something before you go with him."

"What?" he spat.

"Who did you call this morning? Who told you to come to me?"

He shook his head. "I can't tell you."

"Then we can't help you," I bluffed, not surprised when Neely Kate gasped in surprise.

"What?" Austin screeched.

"Give me a name, and you and Dermot can head to whatever safe house he has lined up."

He slowly shook his head.

In the past, I might have accepted his answer in the hope that he'd tell me more once I'd proven he could trust me. But I wasn't the only one in danger now, and I'd do whatever I needed to do to protect my kids. Even if it meant sending Austin to his death. It made me nauseous to admit that, but I had no choice. I only hoped he wouldn't be stubborn enough to run.

"It's the only way we'll help you," I said. "I need a name."

Tears flooded his eyes. "I ain't no snitch."

"The person who told you might be in trouble too," I said insistently. "Dermot and his men can make sure your friend is okay." I shot Dermot a pointed stare, and he nodded.

"You think they might go after him?" the kid asked in alarm.

"Did you tell anyone else you were comin' to see me?"

"No, just Justin." His eyes widened when he realized he'd just blurted his friend's name.

"Justin who?" Dermot asked in a neutral tone.

"Don't hurt 'im," Austin pleaded.

"Let's get one thing straight, kid," Dermot said, his voice tight. "I'm not a bullshitter. My word is my bond. I won't hurt a kid. We just need to talk to him."

"Justin Purcell. He lives down the street from me."

Dermot nodded. "He at school today?"

"I guess so."

"Good," he said gruffly.

If Justin was at school, he was probably safe from whoever was after Austin.

"Need anything else, Lady?" Dermot asked, his gaze boring into mine.

I tried not to cringe at the title. "No, but I need a moment alone with Austin."

He turned to face Austin. "You better be minding your manners." Then he opened the door and got out, Neely Kate following suit.

Once they'd closed their doors, I gave Austin a reassuring smile. "You can trust Dermot. I promise."

His eyes turned glassy. "I'm scared. What if they go after my sister?"

"Dermot will protect her." I paused. "I would trust him to

protect my own children and actually have. He's your—and your sister's—safest option."

"Okay," he choked out.

He'd looked so tough when I'd found him sitting in the grass, but now he looked like a scared kid. I wrapped my arms around him and pulled him into a hug. His body went stiff, then softened.

"I'm glad you came to me. I may not be personally watching over you, but I'll be checking up on you," I whispered into his ear.

Then I released him and got out. I had him and his sister taken care of; now I had to take care of my own children.

Chapter Fourteen

I walked over to Dermot and Neely Kate, who were standing in the yard about ten feet from the truck.

"What did you see?" Dermot asked. He looked grim as I told him about my vision. "So someone's watchin' us," he said, glancing around.

"I don't think so," I said. "They didn't mention you. Only me."

"Or they were only interested in you," Neely Kate said.

"That doesn't make any sense," I countered. "Which is why I asked who suggested me. Did they find this Justin kid, and he told them he sent Austin to me?"

Dermot crossed his arms. "I don't like it."

"Neither do I," I muttered. "Nothing about it."

"I want to have someone watch you and the kids."

I started to protest that Joe could handle it, then stopped. There was no way he could have deputies posted on all of us, and he'd only do that if I told him what was going on.

Lordy. Was I really considering not telling him?

My stomach churned. We were in such a good place. We were supposed to be done with secrets.

Neely Kate seemed to read my mind. "Rose, honey…"

I gave her a tight smile. "I'm okay." I took a deep breath and turned to Dermot. "I take it you're gonna watch Austin's house and try to intercept the guys after him?"

His eyes hardened. "You know it."

I nodded, feeling slightly better. "They may only be interested in me because they figured Austin told me what he saw."

"Maybe," he said. "But I plan to find out."

"Are you takin' him to a safe house?" Neely Kate asked.

"Yeah. I just need to call one of my guys to meet us there." He leveled his gaze on me. "You doin' okay?"

"I'm fine."

"I'm still gonna put some guys on you."

My head spun, making me dizzy. "I'm not gonna fight you on it, Dermot."

"You gonna tell Joe?"

I swallowed, my stomach roiling. "I don't know yet."

He nodded. "Well, let me know if you do. That way I can give my guys a heads up."

He started to walk away, lifting his phone, but I called after him. "Dermot?"

He glanced over his shoulder at me.

"Thank you." My voice broke with emotion.

"Think nothin' of it." He pressed his screen and lifted his phone to his ear.

"What are you gonna do now?" Neely Kate asked.

I ran a hand over my head. "I don't know. I guess pretend like this didn't happen and trust Dermot's men to protect us."

"You wanna have another vision?"

It made sense. I suspected the vision of the dead woman came from Neely Kate, and we'd made some life-altering decisions. It could have stopped Neely Kate from getting in a dangerous situation, and the woman in my vision from getting shot.

I grabbed her hand and tried to force a vision, but I still couldn't conjure the dead woman.

"Nothin'," I said when I opened my eyes.

"Well, that's a good thing," Neely Kate said with a forced smile. "We changed things."

"Yeah," I agreed. "Looks like we did." But I still wasn't satisfied the threat was gone.

"I'm hungry. Let's say we get lunch."

I checked my phone and saw I had missed a text from Randy.

Rose, great to hear from you! I'd love to get together. Want to meet at Merrilee's at noon?

How could I have forgotten I'd asked him to meet for lunch? I told Neely Kate what he said.

"Then I guess we have a lunch date," she said, her eyes bright. "So what do you say we go back to the office and get some work done first?"

"Yeah," I said, feeling unsettled. I wasn't sure how much work I'd be able to get done, but it was worth a try. "Let me talk to Bruce Wayne first."

He was cutting the plastic container from the root ball of a bush when I walked over. He looked up at me and straightened, leaving the plant on the ground. "Dermot gonna handle it?"

"Yeah." I glanced back at the boy in Dermot's truck. "Has there been chatter about me in the criminal underworld?"

"I'm ignorant to anything goin' on in that world. I've tried to keep my nose clean." His eyes bore into mine.

I knew what he wasn't saying. Not since he'd married Anna and started building his family.

"It just seems so random that Austin asked for me."

"I agree, but surely Dermot is looking into it."

"Yeah." I drew a breath, my mind racing. "I have to wonder if the murder in Pickle Junction has anything to do with the murder Austin witnessed. We haven't had many murders around here lately, so I find it hard to believe the two aren't connected."

"That seems like a job for Joe," Bruce Wayne said with a hint of warning in his voice.

"Yeah," I said absently. "You're right."

"You're not gonna let this go, are you?"

I held his gaze. "I have to protect my family."

"And you can do that by letting Joe and Dermot take care of it."

I knew that was what I *should* do, but I'd spent the first twenty-four years of my life doing what I was told and letting other people handle everything in my life. Six years ago, I'd decided I was done with that. I wasn't about to slip now. "Since when do I let other people do my dirty work?"

He made a face. "I was afraid you'd say something like that." He toed the ground, then looked up at me again. "Just be careful, Rose."

"I'd never put my kids at risk, but what if they're already in danger because of my past? I need to do whatever it takes to protect them."

"Without Joe?"

That was the part that got to me. Joe. I desperately wanted to confide in him, but Dermot was better suited to find out whether something was going on in the criminal underworld. And if I told Joe everything, I'd have to admit that Dermot had some of his men protecting our family, which would never fly. I just hoped Dermot would find out something quickly. "I need more information before I tell him. Dermot's men are going to keep watch over me and the kids. They'll likely be more help than the deputies."

He made another face that suggested he thought so too.

"Just be careful," he repeated.

Neely Kate and I didn't speak as we drove back to the office. I was too busy running everything through my head, and I suspected she was doing the same.

When I sat at my desk, I pulled up a design on my computer

and tried to work, but it was hard to focus on which type of flowering bush to put on the south side of a house when I knew murderers were actively interested in the Lady in Black.

Neely Kate nibbled on crackers while staring at her computer screen.

"It's going to be okay," she said after a few moments.

"I hope so," I said, still staring blankly at the screen.

The front door opened with a jingle of the bell on the doorknob, and I was surprised to see Jed walking in wearing jeans and his Carlisle Motors shirt. Jed rarely took off from work at lunch time. He was a family man, through and through, so he often took short lunches so he could finish up by five. The look on his face suggested this wasn't going to be a friendly chat.

"What are you doin' here?" Neely Kate asked as she swiveled her chair to face him.

"Why am I hearing from Dermot about you two getting involved with a witness to a murder?"

I cringed, but Neely Kate was more in the hot seat then I was in this instance.

She gave him a defiant glare. "I'm not speakin' to you, Jed Carlisle. Hence, I didn't tell you what's goin' on."

"This is serious, Neely Kate!" he shouted, his face flushing, but I could see the fear flashing in his eyes.

"Dermot has it covered," she said sweetly. "There was nothin' to tell. Besides, the kid was lookin' for Rose, not me."

He swung his attention to me. "What does Joe make of this?"

Oh boy. "He doesn't know yet," I said.

"What do you mean he doesn't know?" Jed's voice boomed through the office.

"It seems pretty self-explanatory to me," I said, my brows shooting up. "Besides, Dermot's got men watchin' me and the kids, so what's Joe supposed to do?"

He started to say something, then stopped.

"Exactly. Dermot's lookin' into it, and when there's something to actually tell Joe that won't just make him worry, I'll tell him."

"He has a right to know, Rose," Jed protested, then turned to his wife. "Just like *I* had a right to know."

"I'll tell him," I said. "I swear. But there's no point in calling him right now. The kids and I are safe, and he's busy trying to solve a murder. The boy refused to talk to Joe—and trust me I tried to convince him many times—"

"She did," Neely Kate said, nodding her head. "*Many* times."

"—so I figured it would be better to get Dermot involved than to just cut the kid loose." I finished.

He pressed his lips together and stared at me.

"Do you honestly think I'd be stubborn enough to put my children in danger?" I demanded.

His face softened. "No."

"Then trust me, Jed," I said just before the alarm on my phone went off, telling me it was time to walk over to the restaurant and meet Randy. I grabbed my purse and stood. "Now, if you'll excuse me, I need to leave for a meeting."

Jed shot a glance to Neely Kate, then me. "What kind of meeting?"

"Good Lord, Jed!" Neely Kate hollered. "She's a grown woman capable of making her own appointments."

He didn't look convinced, so I said, "I'm meeting Randy Miller, who happens to be a deputy sheriff, at Merrilee's." I gave him a smug look. "Can't get much safer than that." Then I walked past him to the door.

I expected Neely Kate to get up and follow, but she stayed seated.

"I'll try to knock out this design before my two o'clock meeting," Neely Kate said. "Jed can get me something for lunch."

I gave her a sympathetic smile, although I supposed I should have given it to Jed since he was still in whatever doghouse Neely Kate had put him in the night before.

Merilee's was directly across the square from my office. When I walked through the door to the restaurant, Randy was already seated at a two-top table in the back. He was wearing his uniform, and he lifted his hand in greeting. He looked relaxed and settled. He'd come a long way from the young deputy I'd met nearly six years ago. I headed back and slipped into the empty chair across from him. Two glasses of water were already on the table.

"I'm so glad you could meet me!" I said, meaning it. "I haven't seen you in months."

He shot me a grin. "You and Joe have had your hands full."

I swiped at a drop of water on the table. "Especially since Joe became sheriff."

The waitress walked over, her ponytail swishing against her neck. "Hey, Rose. What's it gonna be today?"

I ordered a club sandwich with tomato soup, and Randy ordered a burger and fries.

"So what's new in your life?" I asked Randy as the waitress walked away. "You look happy. Dating anyone?"

He chuckled as his gaze dropped to the table. "I've started seeing someone, but it's too soon to know if it's anything."

"Anyone I know?" I asked playfully.

"Nah, I don't think so. She's from up by Magnolia."

"How'd you meet? A dating app?"

He laughed. "Now you sound like Neely Kate."

I shrugged with a grin. "I guess she's rubbed off on me."

He laughed. "I pulled her over for a broken taillight."

"And she agreed to go out with you?" I asked with a snort.

His face flushed slightly. "I let her off with a warning."

"Well, I hope she's lovely," I said. "You deserve someone wonderful."

The pink of his cheeks turned more crimson. "I don't know about that." He shifted, obviously uncomfortable with the topic at hand, and said, "I hear Mikey's playin' soccer."

I told him about Mikey's game and then told him about the situation Ashley was dealing with at school.

He frowned. "I hate that for her. She's a sensitive kid, so I know how hard that must be for her."

"We've both told her and Mikey that their daddy made a mistake—a bad one—and that he's sorry. But we thought they were too young to know the full details."

"You've changed your mind?"

"No... maybe?"

Randy sat back in his seat. "I wish I was wise enough to give you advice, but I *do* know that keepin' secrets from kids never ends well. They always seem to find out."

My blood ran cold. I knew he was talking in general, but my mind naturally turned to Hope. All it would take was one of those trendy at-home genetics tests, and she'd find out that Joe wasn't her biological father. But would she find out who'd helped conceive her?

Well, that was trouble for another day.

"So you think I should tell her?"

"That's a decision for you and Joe to make, but if she's curious enough, she'll find the answers—with or without you."

I started to respond, but the waitress brought our food.

When she left, Randy said, "Just think about it."

"It's good advice," I said with a soft smile. "You're gonna make a great dad one day."

He blushed again. "We'll see."

I picked up half of my sandwich as I shifted the conversation. "Do things seem to be falling into place at the sheriff's department since Joe took over?"

Randy picked up the ketchup bottle at the end of the table, put some on top of his burger, and then added some to his plate next to his fries. "The transition wasn't that rough, to be honest. Sure, there were some guys who were difficult, but Joe was already their boss before he quit a few years ago. He slipped in pretty effortlessly." He hesitated. "Does Joe think differently?"

"No." I took a bite, then set my sandwich down as I chewed. "I think he expects too much from himself."

"He wants to do a good job and be a good leader. And he truly wants to clean up crime in the county."

"Seems like putting Denny Carmichael away helped with that," I said.

He considered it for a moment. "I suppose you're right. The feds took care of busting Carmichael and his gang. After he and Malcolm were arrested, the crime rate went down."

I decided to bring up Austin's accusation. "Have you heard anything about deputies treating teenagers from Pickle Junction differently?"

His eyes narrowed. "How so?"

"Like being less understanding." I shrugged. "Presuming the worst."

He pinned me with his gaze. "What brought this on?"

I knew he'd want to know what prompted my question. I should have already come up with a plan.

He set down his burger. "Is this your roundabout way of trying to get more information about the murder from yesterday?"

"No." I hesitated, trying to figure out how to word this. "I recently spoke to someone whom I encouraged to contact the sheriff's department, but he refused, saying he wouldn't be treated fairly."

His brow furrowed. "I see."

"This person was with someone else, and they both agreed he shouldn't contact the sheriff."

"And they wouldn't contact us because they thought they'd be treated unfairly?"

"Yes."

He was silent for a moment as he picked up a fry. "And has this person been treated unfairly before?"

"Yes, which made them even more reluctant to contact y'all."

"Do you know why they wanted to contact us this time?"

"Yes, but I'm not at liberty to say what it was, so don't ask."

"I see," he said with a nod. "Was it serious?"

I swallowed. "Yes."

"Can *you* report it?"

"It's all hearsay, so I'm not sure what good it would do."

He leaned his head over the table and lowered his voice. "I could unofficially look into it."

I shook my head. "While I appreciate the offer, I was sworn to secrecy."

He ate his fry, then picked up another. "This person is from Pickle Junction?"

"Yes." His question made me nervous.

"Does this have anything to do with the murder down there?"

"Not that I know of, but I can't rule it out."

Randy swore under his breath. "Why won't you tell Joe?"

"I haven't seen him since I came by this information."

"And how did you come by it?"

I slowly shook my head. "I can't tell you."

His face paled. "Are you mixed up in the criminal element?"

"No," I said firmly. "I am *not*. I have four kids to think about."

"Then how did you come by this information?"

"I didn't go lookin' for it," I said in exasperation. "It just came to me."

He started to say something, then stopped for a moment before ending with, "You need to tell Joe."

"And I will, but right now, I'm more concerned that this person is terrified to talk to the sheriff's department about what they know."

Frustration wrinkled brow. "Did you tell them your husband is the damn sheriff?"

"Of course I did," I said with a huff. "Trust me, it didn't persuade them to trust him."

"But they trusted *you*?"

I sat back in my seat and gave him a dark look. "What's that supposed to mean?"

"Did this person specifically search you out?"

"Why would they do that?" I hedged.

"It just seems strange that you came by this information the day after a murder took place."

"Look, Randy," I said with a sigh. "I'm just trying to work my landscaping job while raising four kids. I don't have time to be doing any underground criminal shenanigans."

He didn't look convinced.

I decided there was no way of being subtle now, so I might as well go for direct. "Things seem to have been quiet since Carmichael and his men were arrested and incarcerated. Do you think someone new has moved into the county?"

"Because of a single murder?" he asked, watching me carefully.

"Maybe I'm being paranoid, but I don't want to live through that hell again. Especially not as a mother."

His gaze softened. "I haven't heard anything about a new group moving into the county." He made a face and glanced around the room, then turned back to me, lowering his voice. "If it makes you feel any better, I think the murder in Pickle Junction was a drug deal gone wrong. But you didn't hear that from me."

Darlene Smith said she was worried the sheriff's deputies would chalk her brother's death up to another dead junkie. It stood to reason the murder Austin had witnessed was drug related too. Maybe the package the killers were looking for contained drugs. "Thank you, Randy. Truly."

"Joe would never let any harm come to you and the kids. And neither would his deputies. You and the kids are safe."

I wanted to take him at his word, but I couldn't help worrying there was something brewing that no one in the county had picked up on yet.

But I didn't want him to think I'd asked him to lunch to get information out of him about the murder, so I spent the rest of our meal telling him about the box Neely Kate and I had dug up and how we were trying to locate the owners.

"One of the older neighbors said it could have been buried by the people who lived next door, but she thinks the old neighbor had been arrested. We definitely want to steer clear of someone dangerous." I paused. "Do you think you could find out who it was if I give you the address and the approximate year the arrest might have happened?"

He narrowed his eyes. "Why don't you ask Joe?"

"Joe has bigger fish to fry with his murder investigation, but he knows we're looking for the owners, if that's what you're worried about."

"And you think I have more time?" he asked, deadpan.

Cringing, I said, "I didn't mean it like that, Randy."

He laughed. "I know you didn't, but I couldn't resist teasing you. Just tell me what you know, and I'll look into it."

"Thanks."

He tilted his head and studied me. "Did this Pickle Junction information come to you from your search for the owner of the box?"

"No. It's completely separate."

He nodded. "Just be careful, Rose."

"Trust me, I plan to."

I hoped those weren't famous last words.

Chapter Fifteen

After I told him what I knew, I paid for both lunches—much to his protest—and headed back to the office. Neely Kate sat alone at her desk, deep in concentration as she stared at her computer screen.

"Jed left?" I said as I closed the front door behind me.

"Yep," she said briskly, popping the P.

"You two still haven't made up?"

She shot me a glare. "Not after what he did."

"Maybe I'd be more sympathetic to your cause if I knew what he'd done."

"You're supposed to be sympathetic to my cause because I'm your best friend."

"Of course I am," I said, sitting in my office chair and swiveling it to face her. "But I could commiserate with you more if I knew what *awful* thing he'd done."

Her brow lifted as she shot me a look. "You're picking up on my devious tricks for getting information."

I grinned. "When you're in close proximity to the master, it would be stupid not to learn her ways."

She laughed, then sighed. "I don't want to talk about that, but I *do* want to know how lunch with Randy went. Did he agree to look into the neighbor who was arrested?"

"Yeah. He did. He also told me that they think the murder in Pickle Junction was drug related."

Her eyes widened. "He told you that?"

"He only told me after I admitted I was worried another organized crime group might be moving into the county. He said it to reassure me."

"I guess that fits with what the sister told us about him being a junkie."

"I thought the same thing," I said.

Her forehead creased. "Wait. Are you really worried someone else is moving into the county?"

"I don't know." I shrugged, trying to play it off. "Maybe. I'm probably just being paranoid." I paused, then voiced my biggest fear. "What if the Hardshaw Group has reorganized and wants to pick up where they left off?"

"Taking over the county?" she asked, her brow furrowed with worry.

And taking care of me, but I didn't voice that concern out loud. "I'm just being paranoid," I said as I turned back to my computer.

"Dermot would tell us if he thought they were back. He would know that you'd need to be prepared."

"I know." I pulled up the design I'd been trying to work on before lunch. "I told you. I'm being paranoid."

"That's understandable," she said softly, sounding lost in thought. I knew she was probably thinking about her half-sister Kate, who'd kidnapped Hope and tried to kill me. Even so, she'd had a massive soft spot for Neely Kate, her younger, secret sister. Neely Kate had known full well her sister was evil, but she'd been dealing with plenty of conflicting emotions.

Neely Kate popped up in her seat, plastering a bright smile on her face. "You know what would cheer us up?"

I gave her a leery glance. "What?"

"Opening the box."

I started to protest, but it wasn't the worst idea. It would be a good distraction, if nothing else.

She mistook my silence for disagreement and added, "Now that we're kind of looking into it again, I figure we should open it and make sure whatever's inside is safe."

"Good idea," I said with a smile. "How do you propose we do it?"

Beaming, she opened her desk filing drawer and pulled out the box. After setting it on her desk, she pulled out a screwdriver and a mini crowbar. "These oughta do it."

"I see you're prepared," I said with a chuckle.

"I may not have been a Girl Scout, but…"

"Did you bring those from home or run down to the lumber store?"

"Lumber store. Jed practically has his tools alphabetized. He'd notice if I took them, and I didn't feel like explaining." She shrugged. "Besides, it's not a bad idea to keep tools here at the office."

"True."

Laughing, I rolled my chair over the hardwood floor to her desk. "Let's try to damage it as little as possible." I leaned over to take a better look at the small keyhole. "Maybe we can pick the lock."

"Already tried it," Neely Kate said, picking up the screwdriver. "Using all kinds of things. Didn't work."

She slid the flathead screwdriver tip into the thin crack above the keyhole and pushed down on it. The crack of splintering wood filled the room, but the lid still didn't open.

"Let's try the crowbar," she said. "I got the crack wide enough to get it in there.

I did as she said, slipping the crowbar deep into the crack and then lifting. The wood cracked again. Although the lock broke, the lid stayed intact.

Neely Kate lifted it so we could both peer inside the red velvet-lined box.

"There's a necklace," I said, noticing a heart-shaped locket on top.

"And a ring," Neely Kate said, shuffling several envelopes to the side to pick it up.

"An engagement ring," I said in surprise as I took the solitaire diamond ring from her.

"It looks like it's about a quarter carat," Neely Kate said as I handed it back to her.

"What's inside the locket?" I asked as I picked it up and pried it open. It was empty. "Nothing."

"Let's check the envelopes," Neely Kate said as she picked up the greeting card-sized envelopes, handing one to me and keeping the other two. I opened mine first, and Neely Kate leaned in close so we could read it together.

It was a generic birthday card that said *Happy Birthday* and had an image of a cartoon cake with candles. The message inside said, *I hope you have a special day*! A short-handwritten note was to the left of it: *You looked beautiful in your blue dress last night. I hope you'll wear it when we go out next week.*

J

"An initial," Neely Kate said. "That's not helpful."

"Let's see what's in the other envelopes."

Neely Kate opened the second one, noting that nothing was written on the outside. This was just a generic off-white card without any design or writing. There were only two lines written inside.

Meet me in the park at ten. I wouldn't ask if it weren't important.

J

"Oh, ominous," Neely Kate said, handing the note to me. I looked it over, not finding anything else helpful while she opened the other envelope.

It was a similar off-white notecard, but this one had a longer message inside. She read it out loud.

S,

First, you know I love you. I'd do anything for you, but we both know this will never work. Not with your father and my mother. Not if we stay here.

I'm going away, because I think it will be easier that way, for both of us. Less temptation. I'm going to work with my Uncle Eddie in Montana. He's short a ranch hand, and I could use the physical labor. I'd ask you to come with me, but you've made it clear your life is here.

Mine can't be.

I love you, and I'm sure I always will. I wanted to marry you, S. This is the ring I bought for you, and if you change your mind, put it on and come find me in Montana. My sister can tell you how to find me.

If you choose not to come, then I hope you have a happy life.

Love always,

J

"Oh my stars and garters," Neely Kate said, dabbing the corner of her eye. "That's so sad."

"So it probably *was* one of the girls in the house next door," I said. "I guess we wait for Randy to get back to me with a name."

Neely Kate nodded, then let out a sigh. "It's just so sad."

"I know, but maybe when we give it back to S, we'll find out that she's with J and they got their happily-ever-after, despite losing the ring."

"I hope so," she said wistfully.

"Me too."

Neely Kate put the box on the corner of her desk, and we both got back to work.

I actually got some work done over the next hour before Neely Kate announced she was packing up to go to her consultation.

"You still want us to babysit tonight?" she asked as she got to her feet.

"Oh crap," I said with a frown. "I don't know. I asked Joe if we'd need to cancel since he's dealin' with the murder investigation, and he assured me we were still goin'. But we didn't talk about it this morning, and I haven't heard from him. Maybe he forgot."

"I doubt he's forgotten. Maybe he lost track of time." She made a face. "I'm askin' because of the stuff with Austin and the Lady in Black. I wondered if you'd be comfortable leaving the kids."

"I trust you and Jed to take care of the kids."

The look on Neely Kate's face told me she knew I was talking about more than feeding them dinner and putting them to bed at a decent hour. She offered me a warm smile. "So why don't you call him and find out what he's thinkin'? And even if you decide not to go to Little Rock, you two should at least go out to dinner." She cocked her head to the side. "Daisy's been lookin' forward to staying at your house for weeks. She'll understand if she can't spend the night, but at least let us watch the kids for a little while."

"Even if we don't go anywhere, you, Jed, and Daisy can come over for dinner. And she can definitely spend the night. Hope will love it. But I'll talk to Joe, then let you know."

"Sounds good." Neely Kate gave me a wave as she walked out the door.

I pulled out my cell phone and sent Joe a text.

Got time for a quick chat?

I could have asked him about tonight in a text, but I wanted to hear his voice. He knew I'd been looking forward to this concert for months, and I knew he wouldn't want to disappoint me. But if he felt like he needed to stick around Fenton County, I wasn't going to hold him to our plans. There would be other concerts and getaways. Besides, I wasn't sure I wanted to leave the kids, given everything else going on.

He called seconds later. "What's up?"

"How's your day goin'?"

He hesitated, then said, "I'm keeping busy. How about you?"

Even if I decided to tell him about Austin looking for the Lady in Black, I sure wasn't going to do it on a phone call. Still, I had to tell him something. "I just got back from having lunch with Randy."

"Oh?" I heard the suspicion in his tone, but I couldn't say I blamed him. It did seem coincidental given the murder investigation he was working on.

"You didn't tell me he was dating someone," I said, trying to throw him off.

"*I* didn't know he had a girlfriend," he said with a laugh. "But I don't believe for a minute that was why you asked him out to lunch."

"Maybe *he* invited *me*." After a couple of moments of silence, I said, "I asked him for some help with our mystery box investigation."

"What kind of help?"

I told him about asking Randy to look up the criminal record.

"Why didn't you ask *me*?"

"Because you're busy with a murder investigation. You don't need to be lookin' up arrest records from decades ago."

"I would have helped you, Rose," he said, sounding hurt.

"I know, but you've got enough on your plate." I took a breath. "Which leads me to the reason I asked if you had time for a chat. Given what you're dealing with, I hate to ask about tonight's plans."

"I haven't forgotten the concert," he said, his voice thick with defeat. "I was hoping we could still go, but something came up about an hour ago, and now I'm not sure I can get away."

My heart skipped a beat. "What happened?" Had they discovered the victim of the murder that Austin had witnessed?

"You don't need to be worried, Rose."

"Does it have to do with the murder you're investigating?"

"You know I can't tell you anything about that," he said, then added wryly, "And my deputies can't either."

"I already told you that I met with Randy to ask him for help with the box," I said, not that I blamed him for thinking otherwise. "But I have a right to know *something* if that's why our plans are changing."

"I'm sorry, Rose. I really, truly am."

I knew he was, but I still couldn't stop myself from saying, "That our plans are being cancelled or because you won't tell me?"

"Both, darlin'."

"I don't understand all the secrecy. I mean, sure, I understand why you didn't tell me about the murder, but at least you told me one had occurred. Now you're giving me absolutely nothing."

"I know, and I'm sorry."

"Should I be worried?" I asked. "Are the kids and I safe?"

"Of course you're safe," he said in confusion, then added in a softer voice, "You're worried about Hardshaw."

"You *know* I live with that fear."

"It's not them, I swear."

"Then what is it? Something must have come up if you're cancelling now and not earlier."

"You have to swear you won't tell anyone else what I'm about to tell you. Not even Neely Kate."

"She's not even here at the office. I wasn't going to see her until she and Jed came over later."

"There was another murder."

My blood went cold, but I was also overcome with relief. I hadn't felt right keeping something as huge as a murder from Joe. "Is it related to the one in Pickle Junction?"

"We're not sure yet, but that's part of the reason I need to stick around." He paused. "I'm really sorry. I know how much you were looking forward to going."

"That's okay," I said, alternating between relief that I wasn't leaving the kids overnight and disappointment that Joe and I weren't getting the alone time we'd been coveting. But on top of that was the anxiety that something bigger was happening in Fenton County and the Lady in Black was, like it or not, being drawn back into it. "I understand."

"I know you do, which only makes me feel worse."

My head was swimming with anxiety. Something about this murder had to be bothering Joe for him to be so tightlipped about it. Then again, someone getting shot in the head was serious business. Still, this wasn't Hardshaw or any other organized crime group. The most likely answer was a drug dealer was pissed at his underlings. "There's no need to feel guilty, Joe. I wouldn't feel right leaving the kids knowing there's a murderer on the loose."

"Jed might be offended that you're insinuating you don't trust him to protect our kids," he teased.

"You know I don't mean it like that."

"I know," he said more somberly. "And you don't need to worry. I don't think there's a dangerous criminal on the loose. I suspect this was some kind of feud over drugs, and even though we don't know much about the second murder, my gut tells me it's related." He hesitated. "I'll make it up to you. I promise."

"I know you will. Do you think you'll be home for dinner?"

He hesitated. "I'll try."

But in the short time he'd been sheriff, I'd learned that we shouldn't wait for him. "It's fine. Neely Kate said Daisy was excited to come over, so I'll still have them and Jed come over for dinner."

"I'm really sorry, Rose."

"You don't have to keep saying that," I insisted. "What you're doing is important."

"I love you," he said softly. "You're the best wife a man could have."

"I love you too. And don't forget you said that the next time you're pissed at me."

He laughed. "I won't."

Famous last words, but I was planning to hold him to them whenever he found out about Austin and everything else.

Chapter Sixteen

I gave Jed and Neely Kate the option to stay home for the night, but they insisted on coming over. He'd planned on grilling hamburgers and hot dogs for the kids, so we stuck with the plan. I suspected part of it was that Jed was worried about me and the kids, but he had no reason to be worried, given Dermot had some men in a car watching the house from the field to the north of our property.

Jed tried to pry more information out of Neely Kate and me, but we insisted we'd told him everything we knew.

"Why don't you call Dermot and get the scoop from him?" I suggested while I watched Liam toddle around the back yard with Muffy. Neely Kate and I were lounging in lawn chairs with margaritas—Neely Kate's drink a virgin—while Jed worked the grill. It was still cool, so we were all bundled up in jackets. Hope and Daisy were chasing dandelion seeds while Mikey tried to teach Liam how to kick a soccer ball. Ashley half-heartedly swung on the swing set Joe and Jed had installed several years ago.

"I already called him."

I turned to look up at him. "And? Does he have new information?"

"You're supposed to be stayin' out of it," Jed grunted as he flipped a burger.

"I got dragged into this, and now Dermot has men watching my family. Like it or not, I'm involved."

He sighed. "You know what I mean."

"I do," I said, my anxiety rising. "But I need to know if someone is coming for me or my kids."

Jed put the spatula on the side of the grill before he walked over to me and squatted, holding my gaze. "You and the kids are safe. I'm here. Dermot's men are watching from several angles."

"Several?" I asked in surprise. "I know about the guys to the north."

"There are also a couple of guys in the field to the south."

I was really slipping. "Oh."

He put his hand over mine. "You're safe."

"I'm safe with protection, but is anyone out to get me, Jed?"

His face turned grim. "I don't know yet."

I nodded. "Which means Dermot doesn't know yet." But he had to be worried if he'd posted multiple men near my property.

"He'll let me know as soon as he does."

"Excuse me?" I said, sitting upright. "He'll let *you* know?"

"The less contact between you two, the better."

He was right, and I knew it, but it still irked me. I wasn't the stupid naive woman I'd been before my mother's murder, content to let other people run my life. If I let Jed be the go-between, it felt like I was slipping back into that girl. Still, my husband was the sheriff, and if word got out that Joe's wife had been conversing with the alleged head of the county crime world, it wouldn't look good.

Setting my glass on the table between Neely Kate and me, I got up and walked over to Liam and played with him and Mikey until the burgers were done.

After I got the kids inside to wash their hands, Neely Kate and I carried the side dishes we'd made outside to the large outdoor table. The kids were excited to be eating outside, even if it was chilly, but the adults were quieter than usual. Thankfully, the only one who seemed to notice was Ashley. She gave us all funny looks but didn't call attention to it.

Jed wanted to stay until Joe showed up, but I insisted he take his family home, assuring him I had a security system, heavy duty locks, and a shotgun locked up in Joe's gun cabinet should I need it, not to mention my bodyguards outside. Part of me was worried Joe would notice them, but Jed had assured me they were well out of sight. Given I hadn't noticed all of them myself, I suspected he was right.

"Besides," I said. "Joe's gonna think it's weird if you're here so late. He'll be suspicious."

"As he should be. You need to tell him," Jed said.

"I know, but we'll see how tired he is when he gets home. If he's exhausted, I'll tell him tomorrow morning."

He searched my face but finally said, "Okay."

Daisy and Hope were upset they couldn't have a sleepover, but in light of everything going on, we mutually agreed it would be better if we had a sleepover another night.

I got the kids bathed and put to bed, but after I tucked Liam in, I stopped in Ashley's doorway and peered into the darkness. "Ash? You still awake?"

"Yes," she whispered.

I walked in and sat on the edge of the bed, leaving the hallway door open to let some light in.

"How were things at school today?" I asked.

"Okay."

"Did those kids say anything else about your dad?"

"Yeah, but it's no big deal."

"Would you like to know more about why your dad is in prison?" I asked gently.

My eyes had adjusted to the darkness, registering the surprise on her face. "You would tell me?"

"If that's what you want. Someone pointed out to me that kids discover the truth of secrets, and I'd rather you hear it from me and Joe instead of searching for things online."

"I've already searched online," she said quietly.

"Oh." I wasn't sure why I was surprised. She was a smart, resourceful girl. Of course she had. "What did you find out?"

Her voice broke. "That he's a murderer."

"He never killed anyone, Ashley. It's important you know that."

"But the paper said he helped someone get killed."

I started to protest, then stopped. "I'd like to believe he didn't know that would happen, because I do know he's a wonderful father and he was in a desperate situation."

"When me and Mikey were kidnapped?"

"Yes."

She stared up at me. "But you're the one who came and got us."

"Yes."

"Why didn't Daddy?"

We'd never really discussed their kidnapping, and she'd sure never asked these questions before. I decided she deserved the truth.

"A woman told me she knew where you were and took me to you."

"But there wasn't anyone with you when you found us."

"Once she showed me where you were, she left."

She didn't respond, but I knew she was mulling over what I'd told her.

"Why did she tell *you*?" she asked. "Why didn't she tell Daddy?"

"She didn't know where he was, but she knew I was at the nursery. She found me there and took me to find you." I was glossing over some parts, but that was basically what had happened.

"Daddy didn't save us," she said, her voice breaking again.

"He wanted to. I think he was trying in his own way, but my way worked first."

She sat up, threw her arms around me, and started to cry. I held her tightly and stroked her head as she sobbed into my shoulder.

"I'm so sorry, Ashley," I said. "I'm so sorry you've had to go through so much at such a young age. It's not fair."

"Life's not fair," she said, her voice muffled.

"I know, but I can still feel sorry that you've had to endure it."

She leaned back and looked up at me. Her tear-streaked face broke my heart. "You protected me when my dad didn't."

"I love you and Mikey as much as I love Hope and Liam. I would do *anything* to protect and save you. You *have* to know that."

"I do."

I cupped her cheek and kissed her forehead. "The kids at school will forget this soon enough and move on to tormenting someone else."

Her eyes hardened. "I think you're right, Aunt Rose."

I wasn't sure what her response implied, but I couldn't help thinking she had a plan to move them along faster. I started to tell her that encouraging them to be mean to another victim was unkind, but Ashley would never bully anyone else, which could only mean she had another plan for Oliver.

"Whatever you do, just don't hurt anyone who doesn't deserve it," I said. "And make sure no one else becomes collateral damage."

"What does that mean?"

"Just don't let anyone else get hurt."

"Like Dad?" she asked, her voice low.

She'd always called him daddy, so hearing the switch made my heart hurt. "Yes, like your dad."

"I won't, Aunt Rose. I swear it."

"I know you won't." I gave her a tight hug, kissed her forehead, and tucked her in.

As I stood to walk away, she said, "I love you, Aunt Rose."

"I love you too. I love you *so* much."

I walked out of her room, cracking the door, then headed downstairs to make a cup of tea while I waited for Joe. By the time I sat down on the sofa with my tea, I realized it was close to ten p.m.

What was taking him so long?

I turned on the TV and started watching a movie, but I was exhausted and quickly fell asleep.

I WAS IN THE WAREHOUSE WITH A MAN I DIDN'T RECOGNIZE. He looked to be in his forties and had dark hair and eyes. He was wearing a silky pink button-down shirt and a pair of black pants. He barked orders at people who scurried around doing as they were told, and when he was done, he turned to me and snarled, "This is all your fault."

My heart raced. He grabbed my arm and pulled me toward a doorway, but I resisted.

"Come on, Selena," he grunted, giving me a vicious pull that made my teeth clatter. "I don't have time for your bullshit games."

"Don't kill her!" I pled through sobs. "I'm begging you! *Please* don't kill her."

He stopped and gave me a hard look, then dragged me to the back corner of the warehouse, where a woman with long dark hair was sitting on the ground, her hands tied behind her back. She looked up at me, and I realized she was the woman from my previous vision. Her eyes were hazel, and her dark hair hung loose in tangles. Pieces of it were stuck to her face. She shot me a worried glance before glaring up at the man next to me. "Let her go."

He laughed. "You're both so concerned about each other it's kind of sweet." Then, without warning, he pulled out a gun and shot her in the forehead. She fell backward, blood spilling out onto the concrete floor.

I screamed and screamed, then my eyes flew open, and I realized it had been a dream. I was sitting upright on the sofa, actually screaming. I wasn't surprised to find Ashley at the bottom of the staircase, terror filling her eyes as she gaped at me. Muffy, who had gone to bed with Hope, was sitting on the staircase next to Ashley's feet.

"Aunt Rose, are you okay?"

I shook my head to orient myself. "Did I wake you?"

She slowly nodded.

"I'm sorry," I said as I reached toward her. I would have gotten up and gone to her, but I felt shaky and nauseated.

She didn't hesitate to come to me. I tugged her down to the sofa, wrapping an arm around her back and pulling her tightly to my side. Muffy jumped up onto the sofa and curled up in my lap. I stroked her head with my free hand.

"I'm sorry I woke you. I guess I had a nightmare." But was it just a nightmare? The woman who'd been murdered was the same person from my visions of the warehouse *and* my dream two nights before, only the vision had expanded and changed. The murdered woman had been in a different part of the warehouse this time, and she'd been shot while she was sitting down.

"*You* had a bad dream?" she asked, incredulous.

"Grown-ups have bad dreams sometimes," I said softly, leaning back into the cushions and bringing her with me. Little did she know I had plenty of them.

She snuggled into me. "It must have been really scary."

"It was." More than she knew. I had no idea who Selena was, and I'd never seen that man before. Was he part of a new crime group moving into Fenton County? Was he responsible for the two recent murders? The woman who'd been murdered looked so familiar, but I didn't think I'd ever seen her before. An overwhelming sense of relief that the body I'd seen definitely wasn't mine took over, but an undercurrent of anxiety still ran through my blood. While I didn't know the woman, everything in me screamed that I needed to save her.

My mind was racing. I'd obviously had a vision for a woman named Selena, but I was completely alone in the living room. How had that happened? Not to mention, I'd been *asleep*. Again.

"I heard you say, 'she got shot.'" Ashley said.

My mouth dropped open, but I quickly shut it as I glanced down at her. "I said that?"

"You were screaming, and then you shouted that, then you screamed some more."

I didn't have time to react to that because the deadbolt turned on the front door and glanced over to see an exhausted looking Joe walking in.

"Hey," he said, glancing at Ashley in surprise. "What are *you* doin' up?"

"Aunt Rose had a bad dream."

Joe's gaze turned to me as his forehead furrowed with concern.

"It's nothing," I said, even though it was definitely something. "I fell asleep on the sofa, and Ashley heard me and came down."

"She was screaming," Ashley said solemnly.

Joe's eyes narrowed as he walked over and sat on the coffee table in front of us. He took my hand. "You okay, darlin'?"

I gave him a weak smile. I knew what he was thinking. He assumed the two murders had stirred up my Hardshaw nightmares. "I'm fine. You're home late. What time is it?"

He cringed. "Almost eleven." He turned his attention to Ashley. "You ready to go back to bed?"

She twisted at the waist to look up at me. "Are you okay?"

I gave her a reassuring smile. "I'm fine. Really. I'm sorry I woke you."

"It's okay," she said, but she didn't seem convinced that I was all right. She turned back to Joe. "Will you tuck me in, Uncle Joe?"

"You know it," he said, but shot me a worried look.

I mouthed, *I'm fine*, then scooped Muffy into my arms and grabbed my mug with my free hand as I stood. "I'm going to take my mug to the kitchen, then go upstairs to bed."

"Okay." Joe pulled Ashley to her feet and guided her up the staircase, glancing back at me as I walked into the kitchen. After I poured out the half-full mug, I put it in the dishwasher, turned it on, and let Muffy out the back door to do her business. I stood on the porch and watched her, wondering if Dermot's men were still out in the fields. My dream had shaken me to the core. But while I wished I could write it off as another nightmare, there was no denying it had been a vision. It had all the earmarks of one. I'd felt the tingling in my head, and it had been crystal clear, not muddled like a dream. Ashley said I blurted out what I saw. What I didn't understand was how I'd had it. It made no sense, yet there was no denying it was too close to the vision I'd had at Piney Rest to be dismissed.

"I thought you were going to bed," Joe said, walking up behind me. He slipped his arms around my waist, pulling my back to his chest and placing a kiss on my neck.

His embrace made me feel protected and safe, and I covered his arms with my own. "I realized Muffy hadn't been outside since Jed and Neely Kate went home."

"Did Daisy spend the night?" he asked quietly.

"No, Jed and Neely Kate decided to take her home."

He was silent for a moment before he said, "Was your nightmare because of the recent murders?"

"Honestly, I don't know. It was the same nightmare I had a couple of nights ago, but this one was expanded." I paused. "It wasn't just a nightmare, Joe."

He stilled, then asked, "What was it?"

I turned in his arms and placed my hands on his shoulders as I looked up at him. "I had a vision yesterday, the morning after my first nightmare, and they were the same."

His eyes narrowed. "Wait. You're telling me the vision was identical to your nightmare?"

"I only remembered bits and pieces of the first nightmare, but yes. And the same is true of my nightmare tonight."

"Who was your vision of?"

"That's just it. I thought it was from Neely Kate, or possibly Miss Adolpha, the elderly woman we spoke to about the box, but when I tried to recreate it, I came up with nothing. And tonight… well, I was alone."

He looked troubled as he studied me. "What was the vision?"

"A woman was murdered in a warehouse. I didn't see her face clearly in the first dream or vision, so for a while I thought she might be me, especially when I thought the vision was attached to Neely Kate'"

"Rose." Joe lifted his hands to my upper arms, sounding agonized as he said my name.

"I thought maybe I saw my death because we were poking around about the box, so I told Neely Kate we couldn't look for the owners anymore. I tried to force the same vision, but nothing happened, so I figured maybe that had fixed it, but my dream tonight confirmed it wasn't me who was murdered. It was someone else."

His hands tightened on my arms. "Do you know who she was?"

"No. I saw the man who murdered her, but I've never seen him before in real life. The woman I was seeing the vision through was named Selena, but I don't know any Selenas. I have no idea who the murdered woman was."

He pulled me into a tight hug as Muffy bounded up the porch steps, jumping up on Joe's legs and begging for attention.

"Just a minute, Muff," he said burying his face into my hair.

"I'm fine, Joe. The woman wasn't me."

"Did you recognize where this took place?"

I shook my head. "No. It was a big warehouse, and in one section there were tall shelves with boxes. A good portion of it was empty. The woman who was murdered was in the back corner. The man was pissed at her and Selena, and he told Selena it was her own fault. Selena begged him not to murder the woman, but that seemed to piss him off more, so he dragged Selena back to where the woman was and shot her in the forehead."

He gasped. "That had to be terrifying."

I didn't respond since the answer was obvious.

"Let's get you inside," he said as he dropped his hands and wrapped an arm around my back, ushering me through the back door, then holding the door open for Muffy to follow.

Joe walked over to a kitchen cabinet and reached for a glass. "What did Neely Kate think of the vision?" He filled up the glass with water, keeping his back to me.

"She was just as puzzled about it as I was, and equally confused as to why I couldn't reproduce it."

He turned to face me and lifted the glass to his mouth for a sip. When he lowered it, he said, "Why didn't you tell me about this last night?"

"Because you were tied up with the murder, and I couldn't reproduce it after we agreed to stop looking for the box's owner. I figured the vision was a non-issue."

"But you're still lookin' for the owners of the box?"

"Only because I couldn't reproduce the vision. And the only thing we've done since the vision is ask Randy to look into the homeowner with an arrest record who lived next door. Besides, we opened the box this afternoon, and there wasn't much in it. A ring, a necklace, and some love letters."

He made a sympathetic face and set the glass on the counter. "Is there any chance it wasn't a vision?" I started to protest, but he held up a hand and took a step toward me. "Hear me out. You've never had a vision in your sleep and never of people you weren't next to. I know how worried you are about everything going on, and your concern that Hardshaw has regrouped and is coming back to the county. Maybe you just manifested the vision."

I stared at him in disbelief. "Are you seriously suggesting I *imagined* it?"

"No..." He ran a hand over his head and groaned. "I don't know. You have to admit this is unlike anything you've ever experienced before."

"I know what a vison is, Joe," I snapped. "I've had them my entire life."

"I know. I know." He started to pace. "I'm not tryin' to accuse you of not knowin' your own mind—"

"It feels an awful lot like you are."

He stopped and turned to face me. "I'm just tryin' to make sense of it." When I didn't say anything, he added, "Look, I'm exhausted." He gave me a pleading look. "I'm sorry."

I nodded, not able to bring myself to say it was okay. Joe was one of the first people outside my family whom I'd told about my visions. While I understood *why* he was trying to dismiss my experience, it still hurt my feelings that he of all people didn't understand. The visions weren't in my imagination. They had a feel to them that was undeniable, and I always blurted out what I saw. It had been a vision, no doubt about it. It was the dreams that were so similar to the vision that confused me. I'd witnessed a woman being murdered, and I had no idea who she was or how to stop it. I'd hoped Joe would help me figure it out, not accuse me of letting my imagination run wild.

"Rose..." He walked toward me and pulled me into a tight hug. "I'm sorry. Truly. I believe you. I guess I'm just scared about what it means."

"So am I."

He tilted my head back and stared into my eyes. "We'll figure this out, okay?"

"I don't know *how* we'll figure this out. I don't know whose vision I'm having, and I have no idea how to find out."

He cupped my cheek. "Randy's working tomorrow. How about I have him look for this Selena." He made a face. "I don't suppose you saw what she looked like?"

"No."

"That's okay, but you got a good look at the man who shot the woman and the woman herself?"

"Yeah."

He looked deep in thought before he said, "How about I ask our sketch artist to come out and draw what you saw."

"How are we gonna explain *that*?"

"Don't you worry about that. I'll offer to pay him off the books, and he'll just draw what you tell him to, okay?"

"Okay." It sounded like a step in the right direction. At least we were doing something about it, which made me feel slightly better.

He tilted my head up higher and searched my face. "You didn't see yourself or anyone else you knew?"

"No."

He hesitated, then asked, "Not even Dermot?"

My heart skipped a beat. "Why are you asking about Dermot?"

"I know you two are friends. I know y'all don't talk much anymore, but if there's anything shady goin' on in the county, he would probably know about it."

Something about the way he said *shady* made me believe Dermot had been on his mind today. "You think he's involved in the two murders?" I asked, incredulously.

His body tensed. "My gut says no, but I can't rule it out."

My heart skipped a beat. *Was* Dermot responsible for the murders? Why hadn't I thought of that before calling him about Austin? But he'd seemed genuinely surprised by Austin's story. He was also a man with morals, after a fashion, and I had a hard time believing he'd condone killing someone in cold blood like the murder Austin had witnessed. Then again, one of the men had said the "big guy" would be pissed...

"Rose?" Joe said, sounding concerned. "You look pale."

I blinked, trying to focus on what Joe hadn't said. "Obviously you think there's some bigger force a play if you're considering Dermot a suspect."

"I haven't made a connection, but it's too big of a coincidence for two people to be murdered in such a similar fashion is such a short time period."

"How were they killed?"

He frowned. "You know I can't be tellin' you that."

"I just witnessed a woman murdered in cold blood by a man who reeked of evil. I think I have a right to know if what I saw is part of this."

He took a step back and ran his hand over his head. "We have no idea if they were related."

"Where did you find the second body?"

"We haven't released that information to the public yet."

"I'm not the public, Joe," I said with plenty of heat.

"It wasn't in a warehouse, and it wasn't a woman, okay? They are likely unrelated."

"I need you to tell me where the body was found, Joe. It's important."

His face fell, and he studied me more closely. "You know something."

"I know plenty of things," I said, lifting my chin. "You'll have to be more specific."

"You know something about the murders."

"I'm not sure I do, but I do know *something*."

"Why don't you stop playing games and tell me what you know?" he asked with a grunt of frustration.

I crossed my arms over chest. "If you're gonna get an attitude with me, then maybe I won't tell you anything."

He shot me a look of exasperation. "Do you know how it's gonna look if it turns out you know something that could have helped this investigation and you didn't *tell me*?"

I dropped my arms to my sides. I seemed to have lost all reason and replaced it with pure panic. "You're more worried about how it's going to look then about the *safety of your wife and kids?*"

His face paled. "What does that mean?"

Crap. Why had I let my anger get the best of me? I took a deep breath to settle my nerves, but the woman's murder kept replaying in my head, and I was finding it hard to think straight. "This morning, someone showed up on a job site and told Bruce Wayne he was lookin' for the Lady in Black."

Joe's eyes widened. *"What?"*

"He'd witnessed a crime and wanted Lady's help. Bruce Wayne called me, and Neely Kate and I went over to talk to the guy. I tried to convince him to talk to you, but he freaked out and threatened to leave. He doesn't trust the sheriff's deputies. He says he's been mistreated by them before."

Joe's eyes hardened. "So he's got a record."

"First of all, he's a child," I snapped. "He's seventeen."

"That is *not* a child, Rose."

Ignoring him, I continued, "He has a charge of domestic violence against his stepfather, who was hurting him and his little sister. But of course, the deputies believed his stepfather."

"How do you know he wasn't lying to convince you to help him?"

"Because Dermot confirmed that teens in Pickle Junction aren't treated fairly."

His eyes widened. "So you *have* been talking to Dermot." It sounded more like an accusation than a question.

"I called Dermot because I told the boy I couldn't help him." When Joe didn't say anything, I added, "I couldn't very well bring him here like in the old days. We've got a house full of kids."

"Why is this boy hiding from my department?" he asked with a hard edge to his voice.

"I never said he was hiding from the sheriff's department. He saw something and now he's scared the people he witnessed will hunt him down and kill him, and I know it's true because he started to leave, and I forced a vison and saw him murdered."

"Did he witness one of the murders?"

Did I admit what I knew? Joe would try to track him down, and that would *not* go well. My reputation as Lady would become worthless. Then again, I wasn't the Lady in Black anymore, so why did I care? Nevertheless, it still mattered to me, and I realized I'd told Joe too much.

Joe took several breaths, his hands clenched at his sides, before he looked me in the eyes and asked with a tight jaw, "Have you reprised your Lady in Black role?"

I gasped. "You think I'd do that?"

"I don't know, Rose," he shot back angrily. "Would you? You took a meeting with Dermot today."

"Dermot is my friend, and you damn well know it!" I shot back. "He saved my life and the life of your daughter upstairs, so you be careful how you talk about him!"

"I'm bringing him in to question him about these murders tomorrow," he said. "And then, come to find out, you had a rendezvous with him today."

"A *rendezvous*?" I demanded in an undertone, worried our argument would wake the kids. "Are you kidding me right now? I told you someone showed up for the first time in nearly three years, wanting to see the Lady in Black, and the first thing you're doing is accusin' me of running around behind your back playing dress up?"

"We both know you weren't dressin' up at the end!" he shouted, his face red.

I gasped and took a step back. "I think we need to stop this discussion before either one of us says something we can't take back."

His jaw worked, but he didn't say anything.

I strode past him and up the stairs, peeking in on Ashley. She was on her side, facing the door.

"Why is Uncle Joe mad, Aunt Rose?" she asked in a small voice.

My level of anger at Joe ratcheted up multiple levels. She was already upset about my nightmare, and now she'd heard us arguing. "He's not mad at me, honey. He's just tired and cranky."

"But I heard him yelling at you. Is he mad that you had a bad dream?"

"No of course not, silly," I said, walking into the room and leaning over to tuck her in. "Grown-ups yell, and sometimes for no good reason."

"But Uncle Joe doesn't yell very much."

"I know, but like I said he's really tired and he had a hard day. Don't worry. I'm okay, and he'll feel better in the morning."

"Are you sure?" she asked sounding scared.

"Of course. Uncle Joe loves us, and he'd feel awful knowing he upset you."

"Okay. I love you, Aunt Rose."

"I love you too."

I left her room and shot a glare down the stairs, which was pointless since I could still hear Joe clanking around in the kitchen. I checked on the other kids, who were all sound asleep in their beds. Muffy had rejoined Hope, curled up on her bed, which meant she'd probably made a beeline for the stairs as soon as she heard us arguing.

As I got ready for bed, I mulled over how our discussion had gone. I could admit that he had a right to be upset that I hadn't told him sooner about Austin asking for Lady, but he'd gone too far when he'd accused me of purposely reprising my Lady in Black role.

I was so mad that angry tears streaked my face, but I brushed them away and climbed into bed. I tried to settle down, but all I could see was the face of the woman on the floor in the warehouse, and the hole that had appeared in her forehead before she collapsed to the floor. How was I going to find out who she was? Something inside me screamed that I *had* to save her.

Was I putting my family at risk by trying?

Chapter Seventeen

Liam woke me shortly after sunrise. Joe wasn't next to me, and it was obvious he'd never come to bed.

I crossed the hall and found my son standing in his crib, reaching for me. I scooped him up and showered him with kisses, then changed his diaper, telling him that Mommy was going to spend all day with him. He tried to repeat what I had said and blew raspberries at me. Obviously finding himself hilarious, he broke into giggles, which made me laugh too. My heart was still heavy after my conversation with Joe, but it was hard to be sullen when Liam's smile lit up my heart.

I carried him downstairs and found Joe sound asleep, sitting upright on the sofa. His head was leaned back against the top of the cushion, and his feet were outstretched on the coffee table. It looked like he hadn't intentionally slept down here, which made me feel slightly better.

"Dada," Liam mumbled softly, reaching toward Joe, but I carried him into the kitchen, whispering that Daddy had been working really hard, and we needed to let him sleep. I poured some Cheerios into a plastic bowl, grabbed a throw from the end of the love seat, then took Liam out the back door and around to the front porch. We sat on the porch swing, and I covered us in the throw to ward off the morning chill while Liam babbled about the birds and who knew what else while he ate his cereal. I smiled and repeated what he had said, and he grinned up at me. My heart melted into a pile of goo. I loved this boy with my entire being, and I couldn't help being worried that I'd somehow put him in danger. We could never truly escape our past, and maybe mine was catching up to me.

I'd been hoping Dermot would get to the bottom of what was going on, but now I couldn't help wondering if he'd had something to do with it. My only comfort was that Jed wouldn't be talking to Dermot if he thought he was responsible, and he sure wouldn't have let his men watch over us. Even so, I was in a real pickle.

What was I going to do?

A short while later, the front door opened, and a bleary-eyed Joe appeared, carrying two steaming mugs.

"I noticed you hadn't made any coffee and figured you might need some," he said with a sheepish look, handing me one of the mugs as an obvious peace offering.

I accepted it and took a sip. "How'd you know we were out here?"

"I heard Liam."

I cringed. "Sorry, I was trying to let you sleep. We should have stayed in the back."

"No, it was a delightful sound to wake up to, given everything I've been dealing with over the last few days."

Liam reached toward Joe. "Dada!"

Joe took a big pull of his steaming coffee, then winced as he set it on the ledge of the porch railing and picked up his son. Liam giggled as Joe hefted him up onto his chest and reclaimed his coffee cup.

Joe glanced at the spot Liam had vacated and gave me a questioning look.

I moved the blanket, and Joe sat beside me, settling Liam on his lap. I handed Liam his plastic bowl.

"I'm sorry," I said. "I overreacted last night when you questioned my dreams and my vision. You were tired, and you were just trying to understand."

"*I'm* sorry too. I was out of line last night," Joe said softly. "I never should have questioned your vision. I think it just scared the shit out of me, and dismissing it was the only way I could deal with it. I'm not typically a head-in-the-sand sort of guy, but apparently I was last night. I'm sorry."

"Thank you."

He turned with sympathy in his eyes. "How long has it been since you've seen someone die in a vision?"

"Since Hardshaw."

He nodded, then grimaced. "This must have freaked you out, and I just blew it off. I'm really sorry, Rose. You needed my support, and instead, I insinuated it was your imagination."

I leaned into him, resting my temple against his shoulder. "I understand why you were worried. I forgive you."

"I'm still going to have Randy look into who the Selena woman could be, and I'm going to call the sketch artist. I'll help you try to figure out who your vision was about."

"Thank you, but we both know looking for Selena in—I'm presuming missing person reports—will likely be a bust."

"But it's still worth a try," he countered.

I nodded. "Yeah, it's worth a try. Hopefully the sketch of the man will help."

"Agreed." He took another sip from his mug, then said, "It was especially out of line for me to accuse you of running around as the Lady in Black. I know you would never do anything to put yourself or our kids in danger. You've proven that time and time again. My only excuse is that I was tired and scared someone was seeking out Lady, not that it's any excuse at all."

"You're human, Joe, and *far* from perfect."

He laughed. "Thanks, I think."

"I'm far from perfect too. I should have told you about the boy showing up sooner, but I felt caught in the middle. I wasn't sure how to approach it."

"Because he wouldn't let you call me."

"Yeah. I tried every which way to Sunday to get him to tell you, but he kept threatening to run off, and even though I know I should tell you everything he told me, I still feel this weird loyalty to Lady." When he didn't protest, I continued. "This boy came to me because he thought I could protect him, and reaching out to me may have saved his life." I shook my head. "I'm not suggesting I *actually* saved his life, but he was scared, and when he felt he had no one to turn to, he came to me. He walked for miles to get to Bruce Wayne's jobsite to find me. I guess I couldn't help but think that if I handed him over to you, no one would ever trust Lady again."

"But she doesn't exist, Rose," he said insistently. "You let her go years ago."

"I know, but he thought of Lady as a safe refuge. How do I destroy that? Especially if something sinister is moving back into the county."

"But we don't know that something sinister is moving back into the county, and can't you see that by letting this boy come to you, others might do the same? Then you put yourself and the kids in danger because people seeking sanctuary are running from people who might try to get to them through you."

"I know, Joe. I know. And I'm torn up and confused about the whole thing. I just want to help people."

"There has to be another way, Rose. It's too dangerous to keep this up."

I knew he was right, but I couldn't stand the thought of people coming to harm when I could have helped them. "We don't know that anyone else will come to me. This kid asked his friend for help, and it was his friend who suggested he call Lady."

"I don't like that people are still talkin' about her," Joe said, his voice tight.

"I was surprised by it too, but I didn't waste any time calling Dermot, and he came and took the boy to a safe house."

His eyes narrowed. "You sure you can trust him?"

"Yes," I said. Even though I was having doubts about his involvement in this mess, I knew in my heart that he'd never hurt me. "I'd trust him with my life, and you know it. Three years ago, you trusted him too."

"We're in different positions now. I'm representing the law. He's on the other side."

"I'm not going to debate that with you," I said, wishing he'd understand. "But I needed help, and once again, Dermot showed up to give it to me."

"You could have called me. You *should* have called me."

I looked him in the eye, my heart aching that we were still disagreeing over this. "And you know why I couldn't. Perhaps you should be more worried that a kid witnessed a crime and was too scared to tell the authorities, and instead took a risk and asked to see someone who hasn't been around in nearly three years."

He did a double take, then started to say something when the screen door pushed open and a bleary-eyed Hope wandered out with Muffy on her heels. "I was looking for you, Momma and Daddy," she said in an accusatory tone.

Muffy took off for the front yard to do her business.

Joe took another long pull of coffee, then set it on the floor before he reached out to her. "Sorry if we scared you, sweet pea."

"I wasn't scawad," she said, waddling over to him. "I was lost."

"You weren't lost, silly," he said as he pulled her up to sit between us. "You were exactly where you were supposed to be."

"But I lost *you*," she said, sticking out her bottom lip.

"I'm sorry if we scared you," I said, tucking the blanket around her legs. "How did you know where to find us?"

"I heawd you and Daddy talkin'." She glanced over at Liam, outrage in her eyes. "Liam, you ate bweakfast without me?"

"He just had some Cheerios," I said. "I haven't made breakfast yet."

"Do we have school today?" she asked, leaning her head into my side. I couldn't resist leaning over and inhaling her sweet scent.

"Not today. We get to spend the whole day together."

"Can I play with Daisy?"

"You play with Daisy every day," Joe said. "Today you get to spend the whole day with Mommy."

"But you'll probably see her at Mikey's soccer game," I said, then glanced over her head at Joe. "He has a game at one."

Joe looked devastated. "I don't think I'll be able to make it."

Two homicides within forty-eight hours meant that for the safety of the county, the job obviously had to come first for him today, but after our fight, the whole Lady thing, and now my vision and dreams, I wanted to be selfish and tell him I needed him. But I wouldn't because he could help me best by catching the murderers, and I wasn't about to make him feel even guiltier than he already did.

"Joe," I said, placing my hand on his arm. "Mikey will understand."

He turned to me. "But will you?"

"Of course. You're protecting us too. How could I be upset?"

Ashley walked out the front door, shooting a wary glance at Joe. She walked over to me and sat on my free side, wrapping her arms around my waist. "Why's everyone outside? It's cold."

"Liam woke up early, so I brought him outside to see the birds and bunnies. What are *you* doing up so early?"

"I heard you and Uncle Joe talking." She gave Joe another look that he didn't notice as she tightened her arms around me.

She was here to protect me. It made me love her even more than I already did, which I hadn't thought possible, but it also made me sad.

I squeezed her back. "I was thinking about making waffles or French toast for breakfast. Any votes?"

"Waffles," Hope said.

"Waffs," Liam repeated.

"Liam always says what Hope or Mikey says," Ashley groused.

"You want French toast?" I asked, looking down at her.

She shrugged, not meeting my gaze. "I don't know."

"Joe, your vote can make this a tie," I said.

He made a face. "I'm not sure I'll be here for breakfast. I have to head into the station for an eight o'clock meeting."

"Oh," I said, trying not to let my disappointment bleed through.

"But before I go, Rose, you and I need to finish our discussion," he said pointedly.

Ashley's arms tightened around me.

"It's okay, Ash," I said as I kissed the top of her head. "Why don't we go inside, and you and the littles can watch TV."

She glanced over at Joe and reluctantly said, "Okay."

We all headed inside, and I gave Ashley the remote to pick something on TV. Joe trailed me into the kitchen.

"What's up with Ashley? You think she's still spooked by your nightmare?"

"That, and she's upset that she heard you shouting in the kitchen last night."

He ran a hand over his head. "Shit."

"Exactly."

"She thinks I would hurt you?" he asked in disbelief.

"I'm sure she knows you would never do that, but who knows what kinds of fights she heard between Violet and Mike before they split up—twice. I've assured her that married people argue sometimes, but maybe you should do some damage control before you go."

"Yeah," he said absently, staring into the living room from the kitchen doorway. "I will." He turned back to me as I pulled out a mixing bowl and whisk and set them on the counter. "But before I talk to her, I need to know what that kid witnessed, Rose."

"And I told you that I can't tell you." But I did need to find out where the second body had been found. There was no way I could ask him without giving him more details. Not that Joe would have told me anyway. I'd have to find out through a different source.

"That means you're withholding evidence, Rose," he said in frustration.

"*I* didn't witness *anything*," I said, brushing past him to get the flour from a cabinet on the other side. "What I'd tell you is hearsay."

"Anything is better than nothing. It's called *a lead*."

I shot him a glare. "No need to get snippy with me, *Sheriff Simmons*. And I'm not telling you anything without this kid's permission. It's his story to tell, not mine."

"It has something to do with one of these murders, doesn't it?"

"I'm not at liberty to say."

"Dammit, Rose!" he grunted in frustration, then flinched when he realized Ashley was standing in the doorway.

"Hope is thirsty, Aunt Rose," she said, seeming to shrink into herself. "I was going to get her some juice."

"Ashley," Joe started, but she turned and left the room before he could finish.

"Dammit!" he grunted again under his breath. "Now she thinks I'm some kind of monster."

"She's just not used to us arguing." I was still irritated with him, but I hated that Ashley had seen more of his irritation than mine. "We need to let her know that just because we're arguing doesn't mean we don't love each other."

"Yeah," he said, looking defeated. "That sounds like a good idea."

"Joe." I walked over to him and placed my hands on his chest, staring up at him with a soft smile. "I'm doing the best I can here, and I know you are too. I'll see what I can do about getting this boy to talk to you, okay? He needs to fully trust me first."

"Which means you'll be talkin' to Dermot," he said, crestfallen.

"I know that bothers you since you're bringing him for an interview."

"If word got out…"

"Then I'll find another way around it. What if I can get the kid to give me permission to tell you what he saw if I leave his name out of it. Will that work?"

"It's not ideal, but if that's the best we can do…"

"I might have another way to talk to him without going through Dermot, and no, I can't tell you what it is. I need you to trust me. Can you do that?" I figured Jed could play go-between.

He stared down at me. "I trust you."

I lifted up onto my tiptoes and kissed him hard. He wrapped his arm around the small of my back, pulling me close as he kissed me back. Then he leaned his forehead against mine and whispered, "I hate it when we fight."

"Me too," I whispered back.

Pulling away with a sigh, he glanced at the clock on the wall. "I need to get ready. Otherwise, I'm gonna be late to my meeting."

I took his hand in mine and tugged him into the living room. Ashley was sitting on the sofa between Hope and Liam. "Ashley, can Uncle Joe and I talk to you for a moment?"

She glanced over at Joe, her gaze hardening, but she nodded.

"Maybe let's come into the kitchen for a moment," I said. "Hope, will you watch your little brother and make sure he doesn't get into trouble?"

"Okay, Momma," Hope said, nodding at me with large, round eyes that made it clear she took her responsibility gravely.

Ashley followed us into the kitchen, and I gestured for her to sit at the table while Joe and I took chairs next to each other. I placed our linked hands on the table.

"Ash," I said gently, "I know you're upset with Uncle Joe right now, but I want you to know that grownups have arguments, especially married people."

"But you and Uncle Joe don't fight."

"We do," Joe said, "but we don't argue very often, and when we have in the past, we've tried hard to make sure that you kids never saw or heard us. I got careless."

Tears filled her eyes. "Why are you so mad at Aunt Rose?"

He gave me a questioning look, then turned back to face her. "It's grown-up stuff that doesn't have anything to do with you or any of the other kids."

"Are you gonna get divorced?"

"What?" Joe asked in surprise. "No."

"Definitely not," I assured her. "Joe and I love each other very, very much. You love Mikey, but sometimes you fight, right?" When she nodded, I said, "See? It's just like that. We're not getting a divorce. We're just disagreeing about a few things, but we'll work it out."

"Do you feel better?" Joe asked.

She nodded. "Yeah, but I still don't like it when you yell."

"I don't like it when I yell either," Joe said. "So I'll try my hardest not to yell anymore."

"Okay," she said.

He turned to me. "My vote is French toast—same as Ashley. So now, it's a tie."

"I've already decided to make both," I said. "So everyone wins. Now you better go get ready for work, or you're gonna be late."

He leaned over, kissed me, then stared into my eyes. "The luckiest day of my life was the day you married me." I snorted, and he turned serious. "I'm sorry I'm leaving you with all of this."

"We'll be fine. Go save the world."

He kissed me again, then got up and hugged Ashley, but as they walked out of the kitchen together, I couldn't help feeling that I was on the brink of losing something dear to me. I just didn't know what.

Chapter Eighteen

Jed, Neely Kate, and Daisy arrived at the soccer game ten minutes before it started. Hope hugged her cousin, acting like she hadn't seen her for weeks. I'd texted Jed that morning, asking if he could arrange for me to talk to Austin. I was hoping he'd have news for me.

We set up our lawn chairs away from the other parents. Hope and Daisy started picking clover flowers about ten feet away, while Ashley tied them together to make bracelets, necklaces, and crowns. It was Liam's naptime, so he sat on my lap and snuggled against me as he fought sleep.

Once we were settled, Neely Kate turned to me with an accusatory look. "Why didn't you tell me there was another murder?"

I shook my head in confusion. "What are you talking about? You were there when Austin told us about it."

Her eyes narrowed, then widened as she gasped. "Wait. You don't know?"

My stomach twisted. "Know what?"

"Rose, there was *another* murder yesterday."

My vision tunneled, and I held Liam tighter. "One that's different than the one that Austin saw?"

Neely Kate nodded.

I felt like I was going to be sick. "Was it a woman?" Joe had told me it wasn't, but what if he'd only said that to make me feel better? What if the dream had come to me *as it happened*?

"No, a man." She narrowed her eyes. "Why did you ask if it was a woman?" Her eyes widened. "Oh. Your vision."

I shot a look at Jed, but he didn't look surprised, which meant Neely Kate must have told him. I'd tell them both about my dreams later. "How do you know it's not the same murder as the one Austin saw? They could have moved the body if they found him somewhere other than Adkins."

"Because Austin saw the guy shot in the head," Jed said. "The guy they found was shot in the back."

I took several breaths, trying to ground myself. The vision I'd had of Austin popped into my head. "It wasn't Austin's friend, was it? I think they shot Austin in the back in my vision." I knew they would have told me differently, had it been Austin.

"No," Jed assured me. "Dermot picked the kid up, and he's hangin' out with Austin at a safe house."

"Did Dermot learn anything else about the murder?" When I realized that wasn't specific enough, I added, "I mean the one Austin witnessed, but I guess I should expand that to any of them."

Jed frowned. "No. He hasn't learned a thing, and I don't like it."

My stomach lurched. "Do you think Dermot had anything to do with the murders?"

"I don't have any proof that he did," Jed said pointedly.

Which meant he wasn't ruling it out. "Do you think Austin and his friend are safe with him?"

"Yes," he grunted. "They wouldn't be there if I thought otherwise."

I had to trust that Jed was right. "Have you heard back about me talking to him? Even if it's on the phone?"

"I haven't heard back yet, but I'll let you know as soon as I do."

"Thank you."

"Joe didn't tell you there was another murder?" Neely Kate asked me with a frown.

"He told me he was workin' on a murder investigation, but I figured it was for the one Austin witnessed." I made a face. "Two murders within a day or two is a lot. But three…?" I shuddered.

"I take it Dermot talked to Austin's friend, Justin?" I asked. "Did he say how he knew about Bruce Wayne being a source to find Lady? That shouldn't be common knowledge."

"He's been oddly quiet about that," Jed said. "Part of the reason Dermot has him hanging out with Austin is because he wants to keep an eye on them. He thinks Austin knows more than he's lettin' on. He's hoping the kid will start to trust him and share more."

"I take it someone checked for a freshly dug grave out at Adkins?"

"Dermot did," Jed said. "And I did too. There was evidence of digging, but no body."

"If Dermot thinks the kid is holding information back, then how do we know he was telling the truth about how the guy was shot? Maybe the investigation Joe is working on *is* the one Austin saw."

And maybe it was wishful thinking on my part, just like Joe had done last night.

Jed shook his head. "We checked out the warehouse too. There was blood on the floor, Rose." He grimaced. "And a few pieces of—" He stopped when Hope and Daisy ran straight to us.

I swallowed bile. I knew that he was about to say pieces of brain matter, proof that Austin had seen the guy take a headshot.

"Mommy, Mommy!" Hope cried out with excitement. "Look, I'm a princess! Ashy made me a crown."

Sure enough, she was decked out with a clover flower crown, along with multiple necklaces, bracelets, and rings. Daisy was adorned in just as many.

"Am I pretty, Momma?" Daisy asked Neely Kate, standing serenely in front of her.

"You're absolutely beautiful," Neely Kate said, beaming. She absently placed her hand on her belly.

A quick glance at Jed proved he'd seen it too.

The game started, and the girls stuck around while we cheered for Mikey. Thankfully, Liam, who had been born into a noisy household and was used to chaos, slept right through it. Mikey scored another goal, and after he ran over to us, glowing from it, I suggested we get ice cream before we headed home.

"That sounds good," Jed said, picking up Daisy. "What do you say, Daisy? Want ice cream too?"

I gave Jed a pointed look. It wasn't unusual for the Carlisle family to hang out with us, but I suspected Jed and Neely Kate planned to spend the entire day with me and the kids.

I wasn't wrong.

After we got ice cream, we headed back to the farm. The sky started spitting rain on the way home, so Neely Kate and I decided we'd rope the kids into making sugar cookies. We'd mixed the dough and had just put it in the fridge when a knock landed at the front door.

Jed was sitting at the kitchen table, and his head jerked up. He stood and looked me in the eye. "I'll get it."

I didn't argue with him. My stomach was in knots as he headed for the front door. The farmhouse was out of the way, and we didn't get many unannounced visitors.

A few seconds later, Jed was standing in the kitchen doorway with a grim look. "I have a guy on your front porch who claims he's a sketch artist. He says he's here to make a couple of drawings."

"Oh!" I exclaimed, dusting flour off my hands. "Joe said he was going to send one out, but I didn't think it would happen so fast." I started to walk past him, but Jed blocked my path.

His gaze pierced mine. "Why do you need a sketch artist?"

"It's a long story, which I'll share with you after he leaves." I brushed past him and went to the door.

"Sorry Jed made you wait outside," I said, stepping aside so the artist could come in. "I forgot to tell him you were coming."

"I'm Tony Baskins, the sketch artist for the sheriff's department. Your husband asked me to drop by to make some drawings for you." He shot a glance at Jed, who stood a few feet away, his arms crossed over his chest. "But I can come back if this is a bad time."

"No, it's a perfect time," I said, eager to get images of the man in my vision so Joe could hopefully find out who he was. I was less hopeful a sketch of the woman would help, but it was worth a shot. "How about we go into the dining room, and Jed can stay in the kitchen?"

The kids were excited to have a visitor, so they followed us. Tony sat at the side of the table, while I sat at the head. He pulled out a large iPad and an electronic pencil, as well as several books.

"Sheriff Simmons said you have two people for me to draw?" he asked as he pulled up a form on his tablet.

"That's correct," I said, feeling uneasy. The kids were beyond curious why a strange man was sitting with me in the dining room, let alone why he was drawing people, and they weren't shy about asking questions. Thankfully, Tony kept his answers vague. Then again, I suspected Joe hadn't told him much. Neely Kate stood behind them, giving me a questioning look.

"Neely Kate, why don't you and the kids finish the cookies?"

"Not a chance," she said, plopping down in a chair on the other side of the table from Tony, with Liam on her lap. "It's not every day you get to see a sketch artist at work."

The kids all took seats too, except for Mikey, who stood behind Tony and watched him in awe.

"I've never met a real artist before," he gushed.

"I'm sure Tony doesn't need an audience," I said. "We don't want to distract him."

"I don't mind if they stay," Tony said. "If they get distracting, I'll let you know."

Neely Kate gave me a smug grin, and I knew I'd have a lot of explaining to do once Tony left.

Tony turned his attention back to me. "First, I'll have you to describe the first person as best you can, any details you can remember, then I'll have you go through the books and pick out features that remind you of them."

"We can start with the man," I said. "He had black hair and dark eyes. Heavy eyebrows."

"That's good," Tony said, typing on his pad's detachable keyboard. "What else do you remember?"

"He had a pointy chin and sharp cheekbones. And he had a light mustache, not thick, and no beard."

Neely Kate gave Jed, who was still in the doorway, leaning against the doorframe, a piercing look. We didn't know anyone who fit that description.

I continued giving Tony details, such as the man's widow's peak hairline and deep-set eyes. Then he had me go through his books and pick out features.

The little girls and Ashley got bored and went into the living room to watch TV. Mikey stayed behind Tony's shoulder, observing in fascination, and Neely Kate remained in her chair, holding Liam, who was busy eating cheerios out of a bowl.

After I picked out enough photos to satisfy Tony, he began sketching on his tablet, pausing to show me the face width and length, the length of the nose, and the width of his eyes until I was satisfied with his result.

I shuddered as I stared at the cold eyes on the tablet. He'd definitely gotten the dark stare right.

"Okay," Tony said. "Onto the next."

"The second one is a woman," I said. And we repeated the same process we'd been through with the first sketch.

Tony started drawing her, and when he finished, Mikey gasped.

"She looks like you, Aunt Rose!"

I took a longer look at the face on the screen, and it hit me that he was right. I'd thought she looked familiar, and now that he'd pointed it out, there was no denying that she strongly resembled me. We had different chins and hairlines, but we shared the same eyes and nose.

To my surprise, Tony didn't ask any follow-up questions. Instead, he began to pack up his things. "If you give me your email address, I'll send a copy of each of these to you and Sheriff Simmons."

I gave him the information and followed him to the door. "Thank you again, Tony. Do I need to pay you now, or will you settle up with Joe?"

"He's already taken care of it, ma'am," he said with a head bob, then studied me. "Joe said this was personal, but if you need me to send these sketches to a detective, be sure to let me know. You don't have to wait for your husband to do it. Especially since he has his hands full with both murders."

"Thanks again, Tony," I said. "I'll be sure to let you know if I need help."

I shut the door behind him, and Tony hadn't even had a chance to go down the steps before Neely Kate pounced on me.

"What was that all about?"

I cast a glance at the girls, who were on the sofa, totally engrossed in the children's show on the television, while Ashley read a book on the love seat. I knew I should redirect them to do something else, but better to keep them occupied while I explained everything to Neely Kate and Jed.

"That was so cool, Aunt Rose!" Mikey exclaimed. "I want to draw people when I grow up!"

"You could practice by drawing your sisters and your

cousins," Jed said from next to the love seat. "How about I get you some paper to practice on."

Mikey jumped up and down. "Okay!"

"There's some printer paper in Joe's office," I said, motioning to the French doors on the far living room wall. "And also some pencils."

Jed and Mikey headed for the office, while Neely Kate followed me back into the kitchen.

"What was that all about?" she demanded in a hushed tone.

"Let's wait until Jed comes in so I don't have to repeat it."

Jed appeared in the doorway a few moments later, wearing a somber expression. "What haven't you told us, Rose? Has someone been poking around the farm? And why does that woman look like you?"

"No one's been here," I assured him. "It was from my vision."

"The one of you *dying*?" Neely Kate whispered.

"I had another vision last night, but I had it while I was asleep, and no one was around." I filled them in on what had happened and what I'd seen, along with the first dream vision I'd had.

Neely Kate's forehead wrinkled. "You had dream visions of yourself?"

"No, I'm certain it wasn't me. Plus, I heard her speak, and she was definitely someone else."

"Someone who looks like you?" Jed pressed.

"Apparently," I said, taking a seat at the kitchen table. "But this is the first time I've ever had a vision of someone who wasn't close to me, so I have no idea how I had it."

"And you're sure it wasn't just a garden variety nightmare?" Jed asked.

"Joe suggested the same thing, but I'll tell you what I told him. No. Besides, it was too similar to the vision I had at Piney Rest. I know it was a vision."

Jed nodded. "Okay. I believe you."

I sighed in relief that I didn't have to convince him. "Joe sent the sketch artist over because he figured he could run the faces through whatever system he uses to see if anything comes up."

"We need to run all of this by Dermot."

"Are you sure?" I asked.

"What's that mean?" Neely Kate asked in confusion.

I hesitated before saying, "If he had something to do with the murders…"

"We don't know that he did," Jed insisted. "And he might recognize the people you just described. Especially the man."

He had a point. "Agreed." I got up and grabbed my phone off the counter and saw the email from Tony. "I'll text him the images."

Dermot, I had a vision with these two people in it. The man murdered the woman. Do either of them look familiar? Also, have you ever heard of a woman named Selena?

I sent the text, uploaded the images, and pressed send.

He responded about thirty seconds later. *I have questions.*

I relayed his message to Jed and Neely Kate.

"I think he needs to come over," I said, not sure it was a good idea even though I suggested it. Especially since Joe was planning to bring him in for questioning that very day.

Jed pressed his lips into a firm line. "We could meet him somewhere."

"And what do we do with the kids?" I asked. "Because we both know Neely Kate won't agree to be left behind, nor should she. She's part of this." I ran my hand over my head. "We could ask Maeve to watch them, but she'll wonder what we're up to, and I don't want to lie."

"Not to mention, I don't want her to be alone with the kids," Jed said. "Not without protection."

"Maeve is out," Neely Kate said, then pushed out sigh. "And I'll stay with the kids."

"No," I said. "When we questioned Austin, I had a vision of

Dermot sitting at my kitchen table. I say we invite him here and ask him to be discreet." I turned to Jed for his reaction.

He took a moment, then nodded. "Okay. Make it happen."

This seems like an in-person conversation. Can you discreetly come over?

He answered within seconds. *Give me a half-hour*

Chapter Nineteen

I glanced at the dirty dishes and messy counter. "He'll be here in a half-hour. Maybe we can finish the cookies before he comes."

I called the kids back into the kitchen, and the girls were excited to resume the cookie making after Neely Kate pulled the dough from the fridge. Mikey was still drawing everyone, although he was disappointed that his drawings didn't look like Tony's.

"Tony didn't just draw people perfectly from the beginning," I said. "He had to practice a lot. Plus, he probably took art classes."

"Can I take art classes too?" he asked enthusiastically.

"Sure," I said, worried about how much they would cost and whether we could afford them. But he was so excited; I couldn't tell him no. I'd find a way to make it happen.

We had the last batch of cookies in the oven, and the kids had gone back into the living room when there was a knock at the back door.

Jed walked over and let Dermot in.

"I hear you had a visitor from the sheriff's department this afternoon," he said without greeting. Dark circles underscored his eyes. He looked exhausted.

"That's where the sketches came from," I said with a frown.

"Are you okay? Maybe you should go home and rest. You look tired."

"There's no rest with these murder investigations goin' on," he said, then gave me a pointed look. "Not to mention, I spent three hours at the sheriff's station this morning, answering a shit ton of questions."

"A detective hauled you in?" Jed asked.

"Nope, the sheriff himself."

I felt guilty for not warning Dermot, but I also felt loyal to Joe. If I was going to ride this line again, I had to be careful about what I shared with both of them.

"Do they really think you had something to do with any of this?" Neely Kate asked.

"I don't know," Dermot said, taking a seat at the end of the table.

"Did you?" I asked him with a hard stare.

He stared back, his eyes cold. "Which murder are you referring to?"

"Any of them."

His brow lifted, and he continued to stare at me long enough that I could feel Jed tense next to me. "No. Why? Do you think I might have?" he finally asked.

"You seemed to know something about the first murder when you showed up to talk to Austin."

"I knew who'd been murdered and that it was over drugs, but I didn't kill him," he said in a deadly tone. "Any other questions or concerns?"

I considered making him swear to it, but it seemed like I'd be pushing the boundaries of our friendship too far. "No."

"Good," Dermot said, his posture softening as he turned to Neely Kate. "The trip to the sheriff's station was a fishing expedition. I think he was trying to find out if I knew anything. Got any coffee?"

"I started a pot earlier," Jed said, then grabbed a mug and

poured him a cup, setting it in front of him. "Tell us what you *do* know."

"I don't know what the hell's goin' on. Don't even know where the body of the second murder victim was moved—only that it was." He glanced over at Jed. "My gut tells me this isn't a random string of murders, though. There's something deeper goin' on. Something I can't put together."

"We keep hearin' drugs," Jed said. "The question is, where are they from?"

"Agreed. I have some guys tryin' to find the first victim's friends. Maybe they know something."

"You don't know who was supplying them?" Jed asked, his words tinged with disbelief.

"No," he grunted, obviously not happy about it.

"We're talking about Harvey Smith's friends?" I asked. "Neely Kate and I met his sister at Dena's bakery."

"You know his sister?" Dermot asked, his brow lifted.

"I wouldn't say we *know* her," I amended. "We just met her, so she's more of an acquaintance, but she might be willing to talk to us."

"That would be helpful," Dermot said. "Because while I know about most of the drug running around the county, I don't know shit about the two known murder victims."

"You think someone's movin' in on your territory?" Jed asked.

"That's what I'd like to find out."

My stomach twisted into knots. "Harvey's sister's name is Darlene Smith, and I gave her Joe's business card, telling her to call." I made a face. "I never asked him if she did."

"Think she'd be willing to talk to you?" Dermot asked quietly.

Dammit. I didn't want to get back into investigating murders, but what if this was connected to my visions after all? What if I could save the woman whose murder I'd witnessed?

"I think she would," Neely Kate said softly, obviously understanding the seriousness of what Dermot was suggesting. Three years ago, she would have jumped at the chance to interview Darlene. She was more cautious now, but she was still very much herself. "Darlene was eager for the sheriff's department to look into who murdered Harvey. If she's not happy with their progress, I suspect she'll talk to us, if for no other reason than Rose has Joe's ear. And I'll let her know that I'm Joe's sister. Double our chances—and hers."

"What do you know about the second murder victim?" I asked Dermot.

"His name is Noah Parker. Best I can figure, he didn't know Harvey Smith."

"Where did he work?"

"Nimble's Lumberyard."

"Darlene said her brother worked for Jefferson Sanitation," Neely Kate said.

Dermot nodded. "We already looked into a possible connection. Jefferson doesn't pick up the trash at the lumberyard or Noah's house."

"So we need to find out what else they could have in common," I said. Talking to Darlene couldn't be that bad. I'd follow up and make sure she contacted Joe. But I wasn't sure Joe would agree with that strategy, especially after our argument last night and this morning.

Dermot turned to me. "Now tell me where you came across those two people in the sketches."

I told him about my visions, ending by telling him that I didn't know a Selena and had never seen either one of the people in the sketches.

"You think the vision might be tied to these murders?" he asked once I'd finished.

"The timing is right," I said. "Or it could be related to the box we dug up, but that seems unlikely."

"What box?"

Neely Kate and I told him about the box and our search for the person who buried it.

"What's in it?" Dermot asked.

"We opened it yesterday and didn't find much," I said. "An empty locket, a quarter-carat diamond engagement ring, and a few cards with a note from who we presume was a guy telling a girl he was going away because their families didn't approve."

"You got it here?"

I started to shake my head, but Neely Kate piped up. "It's in my car."

"Let's take a look."

Jed retrieved the box, and he and Dermot examined the contents for a few moments.

Dermot picked up the ring and examined it. "I doubt this was the reason for your vision. Can't see someone killing over this."

"People have killed for far stupider reasons," Jed grumbled. "But I don't see that happening in this case. Unless it's personal, it's not big enough for the effort."

Dermot picked up the cards and read them, reading the longer note out loud.

"Initials," he said when he finished. "Not very helpful."

"Maybe, maybe not," I said. "We met with several previous homeowners, and one thinks the box could have been buried by a teenage girl who lived in the house next door. Her father was supposedly arrested, so maybe he forbade her from seeing this boy."

"Or J's mother could have forbidden him from seeing S," Jed said. "He mentioned that her father and his mother wouldn't approve."

"But Miss Adolpha said the dad went to jail." Neely Kate said. "And then everyone in the house moved out. She could have gone to him then."

"Maybe she did," Jed suggested.

"You think she'd leave the ring?" Dermot said in disbelief.

"Unless she didn't bury it," I said. "What if someone else did, trying to break them up?"

"It's all so sad," Neely Kate said, walking over to Jed and putting her hand on his shoulder. He covered her hand with his.

We all stared into the box for a moment until I broke the silence. "I asked my friend Randy to see if he could find anyone with a criminal record listed at the house next door. I haven't heard from him yet."

"So if we find out his identity, then we could find the daughter," Jed said.

"Daughters," Neely Kate said. "Plural."

"Since Randy hasn't gotten back to you, I'll look into it," Jed said. "Now, about Darlene Smith." He hesitated, then held Neely Kate's gaze. "I'm not sure it's a good idea."

She propped a hand on her hip and shot him a glare. "Why the heck not?"

"What if Harvey Smith's murderer is watchin' his sister? Do you really want to be seen with her?"

"What if we meet her in public?" I suggested. "We met her by chance at the bakery. Maybe we could not-so-accidentally run into her somewhere else."

Jed crossed his arms over his chest. "Like where?"

"I don't know," I said. "Maybe we could arrange to meet her at the grocery store. I usually do my shopping on Saturday, but I didn't get a chance to go today."

"I don't like it," Jed said. "And I know Joe wouldn't."

"Joe wouldn't like me grocery shoppin'?" I asked in mock disbelief.

"You know damn good and well why he wouldn't like it."

I pushed out a heavy sigh. "You know I need to do this, Jed. You're just being stubborn."

"You call wantin' to protect you stubborn?"

"If she didn't call Joe, then she's not gonna talk to the police," I countered. "And you darn well know it. If we can find out something to help catch the killers…"

"It's not your job, Rose," Jed countered. "Not anymore."

"I know. But I've seen that woman in my vison murdered twice now. Three times if you take into account my first dream. It might not have anything to do with the murders, but it seems far too coincidental. Not to mention, I feel something deep inside…" I placed my palm over my chest. "There's this urgency to save the woman in my vision. I can't explain it, but it's like I know her, even if I don't." I took a breath. "On the off chance my vision *is* related—and even if it isn't—Darlene might be able to help us figure out what ties Harvey and Noah together. And if we can figure that out, then maybe we can identify the third murder victim." I paused. "Surely his family has filed a missing person's report."

Dermot snorted. "Not necessarily. If he was a hardcore drug addict, there's a chance his family wrote him off years ago. And his friends wouldn't report it."

All the more reason for me to help if I could.

"How about I bring someone with me when I meet her?" I asked. "You could come with me, Jed."

He didn't say no, which I took as a good sign.

"You're presuming she's gonna agree to talk to you," Dermot said.

"True," Neely Kate said. "She might not, especially if you're super weird about it."

"All I can do is try," I said, then turned to Dermot. "What do you think? You've been suspiciously quiet about my plan to talk to Darlene."

He leaned back in his chair and rubbed his chin before shifting his gaze to Jed. "I'm gonna have to agree with Rose on this one. The risk is minimal if Darlene agrees to meet her in public, and we could learn some valuable information. Perhaps keep anyone else from gettin' murdered."

Jed grumbled under his breath, then said, "Fine. But Neely Kate's not goin'."

"Why not?" she protested.

"Someone has to watch the kids," he grunted, then turned his attention back to me. "When's Joe gonna be home tonight?"

"I have no idea. I haven't talked to him all day."

"Well, it might not work out today anyway," Jed said. "It's nearly six. Unless she doesn't have a social life and likes to grocery shop on Saturday night."

Crap. He had a point.

"I could ask her to meet me tomorrow," I said. "I really do need to go grocery shopping. If Joe's home, I'll just leave him with the kids."

"And then I can go too," Neely Kate said.

Jed shot her a dark look.

"We still need to figure out how to contact her," Dermot said.

"I already got her contact info," Neely Kate piped up.

"What?" I asked in shock. "Why didn't you say so earlier?"

She shot Jed a look, then made a face at me.

"How did you get her information?" Jed asked.

Neely Kate propped her hands on her hips. "At Dena's. I saw her head to the restroom at Dena's while Rose was waiting on our order, so I followed her." She tilted her head toward Jed. "So can we go meet with her *now*?"

"No," Jed grunted.

Neely Kate grumbled as she opened her phone and texted me the contact information.

"Will she think it's weird that I'm contacting her when you're the one who convinced her to give you the information?" I asked.

Neely Kate shook her head. "I think it's fine as long as you don't give it to Joe or one of the other deputies."

"How'd you get her to give you her number anyway?" I asked.

Her cheeks flushed, and she gave me a sheepish look. "I told her we used to investigate crimes, and if the sheriff's department didn't find out what happened to her brother, then we might be able to help her. And I may have mentioned that you knew what you were doing because you'd helped bring down the Hardshaw Group. In fact, I'm surprised she hasn't reached out to us yet."

I could have admonished her for putting us out there like that, but it would probably be hypocritical since we seemed to be doing the very thing she'd told Darlene we used to do.

"I'm going to text her," I said. "If she doesn't respond, then maybe Neely Kate can call. I'm presuming you gave her your number?"

"I gave her a business card with both our numbers."

"A landscaping card or one of those sparkly cards you used to carry around in your purse?" Jed asked with a hard edge to his voice.

Before we'd had kids and gotten married, Neely Kate had wanted us to open a private investigation firm together. She'd wanted to call it Sparkle Investigations and had even ordered business cards. I'd nixed the name, but I'd been open to becoming PIs. We'd even worked some cases with a grumpy PI as our mentor.

Funny how things had changed so quickly soon after that.

"A landscaping business card," she said, her chin lifted high. "If you must know."

I picked up my phone, entered her number, and composed a text.

Darlene, this is Rose Gardner. Neely Kate gave me your contact information. I'd like to talk to you about your brother. Neely Kate and I are looking into a possible connection between your brother and the latest murder victim. Would you be able to meet me somewhere public, like a restaurant or the grocery store?

I pressed send, then set the phone on the table like it was covered in a deadly virus. My gut told me I needed to talk to her, but it still felt like sneaking behind Joe's back. "Now we wait."

Except we didn't have to wait long. She texted back within seconds.

Are you gonna tell your husband? Neely Kate said if I talked to y'all it would be confidential, but...

I glanced up at Neely Kate and read the text to everyone. She moved behind me and stared down at my phone as I answered.

I won't tell him if you don't want me to, but I promise he'll be understanding

She responded immediately.

You have to keep it to yourselves

I was slightly ashamed of how quickly I typed and sent: *Okay*

She didn't respond for nearly half a minute, and I thought she'd decided it wasn't worth the risk, but then a text popped up on my screen.

Just tell me when you can meet me and where

Then she sent: *Neely Kate has to be there too, or no deal*

Neely Kate let out a grunt of triumph as I looked up at Jed. "She says Neely Kate has to be there, or she's not meeting me."

Jed narrowed his eyes at his wife. "What did you two do?"

"Not a dog-gone thing," she snapped. "And look how hypocritical you're bein'. You'd let Rose go but not me?"

He started to say something, then wisely clamped his mouth shut. He seemed to be doing a lot of that lately.

"When's the meetup?" Dermot asked.

I texted: *When and where?*

I need some milk and bread, so tomorrow at the Piggly Wiggly at 2. But if I see any sign of your husband the sheriff or any other police officer, I ain't saying a word

My heart sunk as I sent: *My husband and his coworkers will be clueless. I promise*

I hated that I meant it.

Chapter Twenty

Dermot left a few minutes later, telling us he'd be at the grocery store before two to help protect me and Neely Kate in case something went awry. But before he walked out the door, I asked him when I could talk to Austin.

He paused with his hand on the doorknob and glanced back at me. "He doesn't want to talk to you."

I couldn't hide my shock. "Why?"

"No offense, but your husband calling me into the station made the kid scared of you." He walked out the door before I could say anything more on the subject.

"Do you believe that, Jed?" I asked, turning to face him.

He made a face. "I can see how it would scare him off."

"But he knew I was Joe's wife after he got to the jobsite and still stuck around."

"He might have people in his ear advising him to steer clear of you," Jed said. He added, "Or Dermot might be trying to protect you."

"He's never lied to me before," I countered.

Jed didn't answer.

We sat at the kitchen table in silence for several seconds before I looked at the clock on the oven and realized it was dinnertime. We hadn't figured out who was going to watch the kids or how I was going to explain going grocery shopping with Neely Kate if Joe was home.

"I need to make dinner," I said, getting out of my chair. "I'm surprised the kids aren't already in here complaining that they're hungry."

I jinxed myself—or Mikey heard me—because he came in seconds later, saying his tummy was rumbling.

I gave all the kids some cheese sticks while I started boiling water to make spaghetti.

"Neely Kate, Jed. Are y'all staying for dinner?"

"We're not leaving until Joe comes home," Jed said in a tone that convinced me it was pointless to argue with him.

"Fine by me," I said.

"I don't like that Dermot doesn't know any more than he did yesterday," Jed commented. "He's either keeping things from us, or he's lost control of his territory."

I didn't like the implications of either of those suggestions. "I don't like it either," I confessed. "But maybe Neely Kate and I will find out something useful from Darlene."

They both helped me put together a quick dinner, then Neely Kate watched over Mikey and Ashley as they got ready for bed. I took the three younger kids to my bathroom to bathe in my clawfoot tub. After I got them washed, I sat on the floor next to the tub while they played in the water. Daisy was excited to take a bath with her cousins, and even more so that she got to wear a pair of Hope's pajamas. They'd been in the tub playing for about fifteen minutes when Joe appeared in the bathroom doorway.

"Hey," he said softly.

I twisted to look up at him. He looked exhausted and defeated, and I couldn't help wondering if it was partly because we'd been at odds. I also suspected he wasn't feeling great about his investigation. I felt guilty for not telling him what I knew from Austin, but I still didn't feel right telling him without

Austin's permission, and I couldn't get it if he wouldn't even talk to me.

"Daddy!" Hope shouted, splashing water.

"Uncle Joe!" Daisy called out, while Liam excitedly patted the bath water, shooting it everywhere. "Dada!"

Joe laughed and walked over, squatting next to me as he addressed the kids. "No need to be painting the walls and the floor with water in your excitement."

"We missed you, Daddy," Hope said with an exaggerated pout.

Liam mumbled something in an attempt to mimic his sister, but it came out as gibberish.

"Sorry I'm late," he said to me, then gave me a gentle kiss on the lips. "What can I do to help?"

"You look exhausted," I said. "Have you eaten?"

"Not yet."

"Go grab the plate out of the fridge and heat it up. It's nothing fancy. Just spaghetti with meat sauce."

"I'm sure it's delicious," he said, then reached for Hope's hand and examined it, plastering an exaggerated frown on his face. "What happened to your fingers, Hopey? They look like they've been replaced with prunes."

"That's silly, Daddy," she said through giggles.

Daisy held up her hands. "Do I have prunes, Uncle Joe?"

"The pruniest," he said with a grin.

Liam held up his hands and mumbled something unintelligible.

Joe grabbed one of his hands. "You've got prunes too, and they look delicious." He pretended to eat Liam's fingers, and all three kids burst into a fit of giggles.

My heart overflowed with joy.

Joe glanced over at me. "I take it they're ready to get out?"

"We were just killing time. They're ready."

"Then how about you go rest and let me finish in here? You've been dealing with them all day. Let me take a turn."

"How about we do it together?"

Joe took Liam to his room to put on a diaper and his pajamas, while I got the girls out and into their pajamas. I took the girls downstairs and found Jed and Neely Kate in the kitchen with Ashley and Mikey, eating the cookies we'd finished baking earlier.

"Have you said anything to Joe?" Neely Kate asked, trying to keep her voice down, but Mikey heard her.

"About the artist guy?" he asked excitedly.

"That's right!" Neely Kate told him, but the look she gave me confirmed that wasn't what she'd meant.

"I haven't had a chance to tell him anything," I said, ushering the girls into chairs at the table, then grabbing them each a cookie. "We've had our hands full."

"Told me about what?" Joe asked as he walked in with Liam on his hip.

"There was an artist here, Uncle Joe!" Mikey exclaimed. "He drew people! I want to be an artist too, and Aunt Rose says I can take art lessons! He let me watch him work!"

"That's so exciting!" Joe proclaimed as he walked to the fridge and pulled out an aluminum foil-covered plate. "I wish I could have been here to see him. I bet it was really cool."

"It was, Uncle Joe! You also missed my soccer game." He made a face. "But I didn't make a goal this time."

Joe took off the foil and popped his plate into the microwave. "I really wish I could have been there, Mikey. And you don't have to score a goal every game. Sometimes you have to let the other kids score them too."

Mikey made a face. "Yeah, I guess so."

I handed the little girls their cookies, then walked over to Joe to take Liam, but instead he pulled me into his other side, holding me close and kissing the top of my head.

"Were you working *all day*, Uncle Joe?" Ashley asked as she took a tiny nibble of her cookie.

"I was," he said, sounding as exhausted as he looked.

"Do you have to work tomorrow?" Mikey asked.

Joe was silent for several seconds, so I peered up at him. He gave me an apologetic look before he said, "Yeah. I'm afraid so."

I wrapped my arm across his abdomen and gave him a tight squeeze to let him know I wasn't upset.

"That's so much work!" Mikey said.

"It is," Joe admitted. The microwave dinged, and he released his hold on me to turn toward it. "But it's important, so it has to be done."

"Go sit," I said. "I'll get it."

Joe did as I said, settling Liam on one leg after he sat at the head of the table. "I'm surprised you two are here so late," he said to Jed and Neely Kate.

"We came over after the game," Neely Kate said, "and then it turned into an all-day thing."

"I see," Joe said as I set the plate and a fork in front of him, then grabbed a glass of water. Liam reached for the spaghetti, but Joe moved his plate to the side. I would have taken the baby from him, but I could tell he needed to hold Liam, and that worried the stuffing out of me.

Joe wasn't just feeling guilty for being gone all day.

He was concerned.

Jed must have caught on too because he started giving Joe a play-by-play of the soccer game, much to Mikey's delight. Then Mikey took over and told him a detailed recap of Tony's process of drawing the two people.

"Who are they, Aunt Rose?" Mikey asked me.

"Just two people I saw," I said.

Ashley lifted her gaze and stared into my eyes. "In your nightmare?"

My lips parted in shock, and I wasn't sure what to say, but Neely Kate intervened. "We made cookies too, which the kids are sampling now."

"They's so good, Daddy," Hope said, holding her cookie toward him. "Do you want a bite?"

I was pretty sure Joe didn't want to mix sugar cookies with the big bite of spaghetti and meat sauce he'd just taken, but he took one anyway and made mmm sounds.

Hope beamed. "We helped make the cookies, Daddy."

"I could tell," Joe said, swallowing his food, then reaching for a glass of water and taking a big gulp. "It was full of extra love."

"I helped too, Uncle Joe," Daisy said.

"And I could taste your part too," Joe teased. "The really, *really* sweet part."

Both girls giggled.

While Joe finished his dinner, the kids all told him about their day, with Hope and Daisy repeating parts of what Ashley, Mikey, and each other had said. But he listened patiently, even though I could tell he wanted nothing more than to stretch out on our bed and go to sleep.

When he finished his plate, I got him a cookie, and he quizzed the girls on which parts they'd played in the cookie-making process.

Ashley was quiet, and I was worried about her. I knew I'd spooked her with my nightmare the night before, and now she'd caught on that I'd had sketches made of two people I'd seen in my dreams. Normal people didn't do that.

Joe shoved the last bite of cookie into his mouth and announced it was time for everyone to brush their teeth and go to bed.

The older kids complained that Joe had just gotten home, and they hadn't seen him all day, but I told them he was tired, and they could see him sometime tomorrow.

At least I hoped.

Jed announced it was time for his family to go home, and Daisy started to cry, begging to spend the night with Hope.

I glanced over at Joe to get his take. He was worried, but was he worried about our safety or the fact he had two homicides on his hands?

"I'm fine with it if you two are comfortable," Joe said, holding Jed's gaze.

That made me feel better. Joe would never encourage them to leave their daughter if he thought we might be in danger. The real question was whether Jed felt comfortable leaving her.

"Are you goin' to church tomorrow?" Jed asked.

I hadn't even thought about church, but that was our typical Sunday morning routine, so it made sense to go. Even if I would be handling all the kids on my own.

"Yeah. Are you wanting to pick up Daisy there?"

"That seems like a lot for you to deal with," said Neely Kate.

"We'll be fine," I said. We had a spare car seat for when Daisy was with us. "But if you two are getting a child-free night, you should leave immediately and take advantage of it."

Neely Kate gave Jed a dry look. "I suppose that depends on him."

Jed gave her a frown that suggested they were still in the middle of a disagreement. Maybe they'd be able to resolve it if they weren't tiptoeing around Daisy.

"Before I head to the office, I can help Rose and get the kids loaded in the car to head to church," Joe offered.

Jed relented, and he and Neely Kate kissed Daisy goodnight. She gave them gentle hugs and kisses, then ran upstairs so she and Hope could brush their teeth together.

Neely Kate motioned to the stairs. "They're gonna need supervision."

I laughed. "Really? This is my first time putting children to bed."

She cringed. "Sorry. Habit."

I gave her a playful grin. "Go. We're good. Enjoy your kid-free night, and we'll see you tomorrow."

We got them out the door and oversaw the children's teeth

brushing. I took Liam into his room and began to rock him under the low lamp light. He seemed especially clingy tonight, and I wanted to give him some extra attention.

Joe found me and said from the doorway, "I'm gonna take a quick shower. Meet you in our room when you're done?"

I smiled up at him. "Sounds like a plan."

I rocked Liam about ten minutes longer, then put him to bed. Next, I checked on all the kids, ending with Ashley. She was still awake, and she gave me an extra-long hug.

"Were they the people from your nightmare, Aunt Rose? You didn't answer earlier."

I could have lied but decided she deserved the truth. "Yes."

"But it was just a dream," she said. "Not a vision."

"I know, but Uncle Joe thought it was a good idea anyway." I paused. "I know it's been a while since I've asked..." I paused again. "Have you had any signs of having visions?"

"No," she said quietly. "But you said Mommy didn't have them either."

"You're right. She didn't. And I got mine when I was younger than you, but I didn't really have help with them. I had to figure them out on my own. If you get them, I don't want you to be alone with them like I was."

"Will Hope or Liam have visions?"

That was a question I'd been asking myself since I was pregnant with Hope. But so far, she hadn't shown any signs of having visions. I hoped she didn't. Liam either. Sometimes my visions were a blessing, but mostly, they were a curse.

"Did *your* mommy have visions?" Ashley asked.

I hadn't been prepared to have a conversation about visions, but Joe could wait a few more minutes. "No, she didn't, but my grandmother did. They used to call her the Oracle of Lafayette County."

"She didn't help you?"

"My daddy was older when he had me, and his mother was

older when she had him and Aunt Bessie, so she died before your mommy and I were born."

"Oh."

We were quiet for several seconds. I was about to get up and tell her goodnight when she said, "Do you see lots of bad things?"

While she knew I had visions, I didn't talk about them much, but I wasn't surprised she was pressing me, given the situation. "No, Ash. I mostly see good things."

"But you *do* see bad things," she pushed.

"Yes, sometimes I see bad things."

"Do the bad things scare you?"

"Sometimes," I admitted. "But I can stop the bad things from happening if I try hard enough."

"And you saw something really bad last night?"

I hesitated. "Yes. I don't understand how, but I think I had a vision in my sleep. You're right. Uncle Joe had Mr. Tony come over so we could try to figure out who the people are and try to stop it from happening."

"Someone got hurt?"

I hesitated again before telling her the truth. "Yes."

She shuddered. "I'm glad I don't have visions."

"Me too."

I leaned over to kiss her goodnight, but she said, "Why did that woman look like you?"

"I don't know," I said, sitting back up. "But I promise that she wasn't me."

"She looked a little bit like Mommy too," Ashley said quietly.

I considered that for a moment, then nodded. "Yeah, you're right."

"Hope and I look a bit alike," she said. "People sometimes think we're sisters, but we're cousins. Could she be your cousin?"

I stared at her in surprise. I hadn't considered that she might actually be related to me. "I don't *have* any cousins. Aunt Bessie and Uncle Albert didn't have kids, and my momma didn't have any sisters or brothers." But what about second cousins? I didn't know much about either side of my family tree. Maybe it was worth looking into.

"You don't need to worry about my visions, okay?" I said softly as I kissed her forehead. "I've got it under control."

"Okay, Aunt Rose," she said in a tone that suggested I hadn't been very convincing.

More guilt. If I hadn't woken her up with my dream, then she wouldn't be worried now. But at least she didn't seem to be concerned about my argument with Joe anymore.

I headed back to my room, ready to climb into bed with Joe and tell him all the things I hadn't been able to tell him with the kids around, but when I walked in, I found him lying on the bed in sweatpants and a T-shirt with his eyes closed, fast asleep.

The bathroom light was still on, so I brushed my teeth and got ready for bed. He was still asleep when I got into bed, releasing a soft snore, so I snuggled up next to him.

Maybe this was a blessing in disguise. I didn't want to lie to him, and this way, I wouldn't have to.

Then again, not telling him was a lie of omission.

I'd deal with that tomorrow.

Chapter Twenty-One

Joe was called into work before the sun rose. It was a short, clipped call that resulted in him getting up and throwing on his uniform.

"What's goin' on?" I asked, sitting up in bed while he went into the bathroom.

"Don't worry about it, darlin'."

I followed him into the bathroom. "Don't do that, Joe," I said, disappointment heavy in my voice. "I'm not a child. Tell me what's goin' on."

He turned at the waist to face me as he brushed his teeth, then spat toothpaste into the sink. "I can't, Rose. I'm in full media lockdown."

"I'm not media, Joe."

He pushed out a sigh and started brushing again. "I know," he said with his toothbrush in his mouth.

I crossed my arms over my chest. "I'm not going to tell anyone. I didn't tell Neely Kate about the second murder, and I suspect she's still holding a grudge because she had to find out from someone else."

He spat again, then rinsed his toothbrush under running water and rinsed out his mouth. When he stood upright, he turned sideways and leaned his hip against the counter. "There was another murder."

My stomach dropped. "What happened?"

"Someone was shot." He paused. "In the head. But it wasn't a woman, Rose," he said quickly, moving toward me and gripping my upper arms lightly. "It was a man. Someone found him in the woods by Schute Creek."

Nausea struck me again. "Someone shot him in the woods?"

"I don't know yet. The forensic team's on their way, and I want to meet them there."

"Did you ask Randy to try to find the guy in my vision?"

"He put out some feelers, but so far, nothing," Joe said.

"Ashley brought up something I hadn't considered," I said. "She said the woman looked a little bit like Violet too. She wondered if the woman could be a cousin, but I told her I don't have any cousins."

His face went slack. "You told Ashley about your vision?"

My mouth dropped open. "You think I would do that?"

"How does she know about the woman?"

I took a step back out of his reach. "She's a very bright girl," I said in an icy tone. "She asked me if the people that Tony drew were from my nightmare. Mikey was the one who noticed a resemblance to me. And when I checked on Ash, she mentioned the way people sometimes think she and Hope are sisters." I took another step back. "So to answer your question, Joe. *No*, I didn't tell her anything about my nightmare or vision. She just put it together."

He closed his eyes and ran a hand through his hair, making it stick up everywhere. "I'm sorry. I'm just tired. I don't know why my question came out the way it did."

I walked over and wrapped him up in a forward-facing hug, resting my cheek on his chest. "I know. I'm sorry that I got so defensive. I'm just worried. And scared." I glanced up at him.

"Three murders in as many days." I couldn't get the saying *trouble comes in threes* out of my head.

He frowned. "I know, and we're no closer to solving the first two than we were when we discovered the first body."

"Did Harvey Smith's sister get ahold of you?"

He pulled away and narrowed his eyes. "How do you know Harvey Smith's sister?" His eyes widened. "How do you even know his name? We haven't released it to the public yet."

"Neely Kate and I met her at Dena's Bakery. Dena was talking about the first murder, and Darlene was in line behind us. She mentioned her brother was the victim."

His eyes darkened. "Is that so?"

"You think I'm lyin'?" I whisper-shouted.

"It's just awfully strange that the sister of one of the murder victims just happened to be behind you in line and chose to volunteer the information that her brother was killed."

"I can't help if you find it hard to believe. If you're doubting my recollection, then perhaps you should ask Neely Kate."

"She's just going to corroborate your story."

I wanted to get angrier that he was questioning me, but the fact that I was meeting Darlene later and not telling him made it feel too hypocritical. "So call Dena, Joe," I said tightly. "You know she doesn't feel an ounce of loyalty to me or Neely Kate, yet she'll back me up."

He pinched the bridge of his nose. "Rose, I'm so sorry."

"I gave Darlene one of your cards and told her to call you, but I got the impression she wasn't going to." My irritation made me push it a step farther. "I'm discovering the citizens of Pickle Junction don't care much for the sheriff's department."

His lips pressed into a tight line before he said, "I'm tryin', Rose, but change doesn't happen overnight."

"Treating people with respect shouldn't be that hard," I countered. "And while I know you treat people that way, I can't say the same for some of your deputies."

He dropped his hand to his side and gave me a defeated look. "I won't be able to help you get the kids to church."

"We'll be fine," I said, my tone shorter than I'd intended.

"But you've got Daisy too."

"So we might be a little late to church," I said, softer this time. "It's not the end of the world."

Joe studied me as he took a step toward me, gauging if I was open to him giving me a hug. I held out my arms, and he pulled me into a tight embrace.

"I hate when we fight," he said into my hair.

"I hate it too." Especially since it didn't happen very often. Yet we'd had multiple disagreements in only a few days.

"I love you and the kids so much," he said, his voice breaking. "I don't want to lose any of you."

I leaned back to look up at him. "I'm not goin' anywhere, Joe." I gave him an ornery smile. "You can't get rid of me *that* easily."

He kissed me hard, and I could taste his apology and his fear. Was he afraid I'd leave him or that something would happen to me or the kids?

"I haven't brushed my teeth yet," I said as he pulled away. "My breath has to stink."

"I don't care," he said, giving me another kiss, this one gentler and lingering. "I miss you."

"I miss you too. The kids and I will be here when you get home, so go to work, and don't worry about us. We'll be just fine."

He gave me a long glance, then headed for the bedroom door.

"Joe?" I called after him.

He stopped in the doorway, his hair all askew as he turned back to me.

"Be careful."

Worry covered his face. "You too," he said and walked out the door.

Chapter Twenty-Two

I couldn't go back to sleep after Joe left, and I couldn't focus on work either. Instead, I grabbed my laptop and started a trial membership on an ancestry site. I wasn't sure how they worked, but I hoped I could get a better understanding of my family tree. I'd barely started when Liam woke up. I took him downstairs, and since we had plenty of time left before church, I made a breakfast casserole so there'd be warm food when the kids woke up.

The morning went more smoothly than I'd anticipated, and we were only five minutes late to church. Neely Kate called me while we were on our way, checking on Daisy. She met us in the parking lot and helped unload the kids and get them off to their Sunday school classes. I wasn't surprised Jed wasn't with her. He liked to joke he'd burst into flames if he ever walked into the church, to which Neely Kate said she'd carry a fire extinguisher with her to put out the flames. He still couldn't be persuaded, and she seemed to accept that.

"What are we going to do with the kids while we're at the store?" she asked as we headed to the church sanctuary.

Crap. With the craziness of the morning, I hadn't even considered it. "Maeve should be at church this morning. Maybe we can ask her to watch them."

"Good idea."

I stopped in the foyer and tugged her into a corner. "Neely Kate, Joe got called in early this morning." Surely that part was safe to tell. Neely Kate was intuitive. She'd figure out the rest.

She didn't disappoint. "Was there another murder?"

"I can neither confirm nor deny."

Her eyes widened. "They found the guy Austin saw murdered?"

"I don't know. Maybe." Dammit. I had to tell her more than that, but I felt guilty as sin telling her anything after I'd sworn to Joe he could trust my secrecy. "I'm not supposed to tell anyone, and I had to guilt it out of Joe, but they found a victim next to Shute Creek. He assured me it was a man and not a woman."

Worry filled her eyes. "That's good, I guess."

"I'm glad we're talking to Darlene. If we can find a connection between the victims, maybe we can put a stop to this before…" I couldn't bring myself to say it.

Neely Kate put her hand on my arm. "We'll save that woman from being murdered. I just know it."

My throat tightened. "I'm glad you do because I don't, Neely Kate."

She hugged me tightly. "Darlene is going to help us piece things together."

"I hope so." Then I added, "But you can't tell anyone what I just told you. Not even Jed. I feel guilty enough as it is."

She stared at me with a grave expression. "Then it will just be between the two of us." She looked into my eyes. "Do you want to try to have another vision?"

"Of the woman? I don't even know what to ask about. You weren't in the vision."

She held out her hand to me. "You can try anyway."

I frowned. "But I might see something about the baby."

She was quiet for a moment. "You won't, but if you do, then we'll deal with it."

My heart lurched. "Neely Kate."

"It's fine. Look. I want you to try." Then she took my hand and squeezed.

I closed my eyes and focused on the woman in my vision, not even asking a question. I came up with nothing, so I asked if Neely Kate knew the woman who had been murdered.

I opened my eyes. "Nothing." Then I relayed what I'd searched for.

"I'm sorry," she said, giving me a hug. "Now why don't you try to see if we get into trouble when we see Darlene?"

Still hugging her, I asked the same question of the universe. This time, an image of Darlene standing in the Piggly Wiggly appeared. Vision Rose was standing next to her, but the vision quickly faded.

"Darlene showed up," I said as I opened my eyes, the church foyer coming into view.

"Did she say anything?" Neely Kate asked, pulling back to look at me.

"No, but at least we know she'll come."

"Okay," she said. "Now we really need to find Maeve and see if she'll watch the kids."

Maeve was sitting in a pew with some of her friends. Neely Kate and I approached her and asked if she was busy after the service.

"Joe has to work this afternoon," I said, "and I usually grocery shop on the weekends. Neely Kate and Jed are busy, so I was wondering if you could watch the kids for about an hour? I'd take them all with me, but the last time I tried it, I nearly got banned from the Piggly Wiggly again."

Maeve laughed. "How many times would that be? Four or five?"

"Five," I said with a sheepish look, "but the last time wasn't my fault. Liam accidently pulled the toupee off of that poor man at the deli counter, and I tried to catch it before he tossed it into the slicing machine."

Neely Kate burst out laughing. "They were pulling plastic hair out of deli meat for weeks. Once the health department got involved, they had to shut down the deli for days."

"If they'd done a better job of cleaning it, it would have been contained," I protested. "In any case, I really hope to avoid a situation like that again, so if you're not busy, is there any way you could watch them, say around two?" I gave her a hopeful look.

She sighed. "Oh Rose, I would love to watch them, but the women's group is volunteering at Piney Rest this afternoon, and I'm in charge of the gift baskets." She paused, then her face brightened. "*But* I could take the older kids with me, and even Hope if you think Ashley and Mikey can help me corral her." She gave me an apologetic look. "I think Liam would be too much."

Some of the kids were better than none, and Liam wouldn't have any idea what was going on. Besides, he loved going to the store and riding in the cart. I'd just keep him away from older men's heads. I was meeting Darlene at the grocery store for heaven's sake. It wasn't like I was doing anything dangerous.

I glanced at Neely Kate, realizing I'd told Maeve that Neely Kate had other plans, so we couldn't very well ask her to watch Daisy. Not to mention, two three-year-olds would probably be too much.

Neely Kate patted my arm. "It's too bad Witt couldn't watch the other kids with Daisy too."

I wasn't sure if Witt was really watching my niece, but I was grateful Neely Kate was trying to relieve my concerns.

"We're meeting at the nursing home at 1:30," Maeve said. "Will that work with your schedule?"

"It works perfectly," I said. "I might come a little early so Mikey and Ashley can visit with Miss Mildred. She's a resident there now, and she doesn't seem to be adjusting well. I think she could use a visit from them."

"I gather that means she's meaner than ever," Maeve said. "Your heart has always been more forgiving than most people's."

"I definitely wouldn't say *that*," I assured her with a laugh. "I would still rather avoid her, but she and Violet had a special bond, and I know Miss Mildred loves her kids. If it helps the other residents tolerate her…" I shrugged.

"Don't worry about getting there early," Maeve said. "I'll make sure they drop in on Miss Mildred, and then you won't have to spend time with her."

"Maeve, you're the best," I said, giving her a hug. "I don't know what I'd do without you."

"Good thing you don't need to find out," she said with a chuckle, then turned back to her friends.

Neely Kate dragged me to the back of the church, and I asked, "Is Witt really watching Daisy?"

"As strange as it sounds, yes. He's been asking to babysit, and I figured this was as good a time as any to try it out." She shrugged. "She's a bright girl, and she's bossy—"

"Like her momma," I interjected.

"Okay, she comes by it naturally, but there's no harm in that. Especially since she'll likely tell Witt exactly how to take care of her." She slid into a pew, and I followed. "Part of me wants to say, 'What's the worst that can happen?', but I don't want to press my luck."

"Agreed."

After the service, I decided it wasn't worth going home for lunch, only to come back into town right afterward, so I took the kids to Big Bob's Burgers while Neely Kate ran Daisy home to eat lunch with Jed. The burger joint had recently added an indoor playground, and since it was still dreary and chilly outside, it was a way for the kids to burn off some energy before they went to the residential care center.

I was watching them play when my phone rang with a

number I didn't recognize. Since I got work calls on this phone too, I answered, "This is Rose."

"Are you one of the ladies from the landscapin' company askin' around about the buried box?" a woman asked.

I sat up straighter. "Yes."

"Was it dug up on Olive Street?"

"Yes," I said. "Do you know anything?"

"I'm pretty sure it belonged to a girl named Sarah. She used to live there with her sister and father."

"You knew her?"

"We were friends for a while when I was a teenager. My parents rented the house next door to her before they moved us. They didn't like me being friends with her. They thought she was a bad influence."

"Was she?" I asked before I could stop myself.

She laughed. "I didn't think so at the time, of course, but in hindsight, she probably was. Her father was an angry drunkard, and rumor had it he'd beaten her mother to death when the girls were younger, so it was just the three of them. Them and all the people who hung out there with their drugs and drinking. I had my first drink at Sarah's house. Tried pot there too."

"How old were you?"

"Fourteen," she said with a chuckle. "So now you can understand why my parents were upset."

"I get it," I said. "How old were Sarah and her sister?"

"Sarah was seventeen, and her sister was fifteen."

"So older bad influences," I teased.

She laughed. "Exactly."

"So what makes you think the box belonged to Sarah?"

"Sarah always called herself a secret keeper. She hid things in the walls of the house and in the floorboards. It wouldn't surprise me if she buried something in the ground. It definitely sounds like the kind of thing she'd do."

"And she was living there when you left?"

"Yeah. I don't know how much longer they lived there, but years later, I heard she'd died. I'm not sure how."

Which meant I couldn't talk to her.

"What about her sister?" I asked.

"Luna? I have no idea where she could be. She always said she was going out to California. I suspect you could find her there."

"Do you know if Sarah or Luna had a boyfriend or girlfriend with the initial J?"

She was quiet for a moment. "They were never serious about anyone, so I don't think so. Not that I remember anyway."

"Was their dad judgmental about their boyfriends?"

She laughed. "He didn't give a shit what they did or who they slept with."

That didn't fit with the note we'd found. J had said that S's father didn't approve. "Was there anyone that Sarah's father didn't approve of her hanging out with?" I asked. Especially someone with the initial J?"

"No, not really. Like I said, he didn't really care who they hung out with." Then she said, "Oh, wait! There *was* a guy, but I don't remember much about him."

"Oh?" I asked, trying to contain my excitement.

"Sarah would sometimes hang out with a boy from school named Jason. His father was a deputy sheriff. I don't think Sarah told her dad about him, and I never saw him at the house. I can see her dad not approving of her hanging out with someone whose father had the potential to arrest him."

"Did you know Jason at all? Would his parents have disapproved?" But it stood to reason that Jason's mother wouldn't have been happy about his relationship with the daughter of a drunkard drug user with a record.

"They were all so much older than me, and the upper classmen didn't hang out with freshman, so I can't really answer that question."

"That's okay," I said. "Do you happen to know any of their last names?"

"Can't help you there either. Even if I had remembered them, perimenopause would have wiped them right out of the memory bank. Gettin' older's a bitch."

"That's okay," I repeated. If the box was Sarah's, and she was dead, then we'd hit a dead end anyway. "Thank you for your help…I didn't catch your name."

"Dawn Kempner O'Reilly," she said. "I live up in Magnolia now. Sorry I couldn't be more help."

"You've been a tremendous help. Thank you."

I hung up and mulled over what Dawn had told me. It all fit, but what did we do now if Sarah was dead? First, we needed to confirm it, although that was hardly a priority with everything else going on.

I let the kids play a bit longer, then convinced them it was time to leave. Neely Kate had said she and Jed would meet me in the grocery store parking lot at 1:50.

We arrived at Piney Rest around 1:35. The older kids were excited to be somewhere new with Nana Maeve and barely paid attention to me once we walked through the doors. I was nervous about leaving Hope, but Maeve assured me she'd be fine. I reluctantly said goodbye, then headed to the Piggly Wiggly.

Jed and Neely Kate were already there, waiting in their car. Liam was sleeping when I pulled him out of his car seat, and he sagged against me as I propped him on my hip. I felt bad that I was blowing through his naptime, but it couldn't be helped. Jed and Neely Kate were in a heated discussion in their car as I started to approach, so I turned around and headed for the entrance of the store, texting them both that I'd gone inside and was going to start shopping.

I grabbed a cart, put Liam in the seat, and headed to the produce section. After checking the prices of some vegetables, I vowed to double the size of my garden and learn how to can. I told Liam my plans, but based on his droopy eyes, he was unimpressed.

I'd already put several items in my cart when Neely Kate approached with her own cart.

"You started shopping without me."

I laughed. "Grocery shopping doesn't seem like a team sport."

She laughed, but it was forced. "Dermot's not here. Jed said he got tied up with something else. He wouldn't say what."

I turned to look at her. "Is that what you were arguing about?"

Pushing out a sigh, she stopped and reached for a beet from the produce section. "No." She grabbed a plastic bag and started to put some more beets inside. "But Jed doesn't seem too worried that it's just him. He said he's only here as a precaution. In fact, he's on the phone in my pocket so he can listen in while hanging back. He's here if we need backup, but he plans to stay out of sight."

"Okay."

She grabbed a few produce items—fresh dill, pineapple, tomatoes, and potatoes—that made me question whether she'd resumed her obsession with the TV show *Chopped*, where chefs were given random ingredients to create a meal. Several years ago, she'd spent a month or so creating her own off-the-wall meals, but then I remembered she'd been pregnant with her twins during that time. Maybe she was doing it again with this pregnancy.

We finished with the produce aisle and moved on. Several minutes later, Neely Kate and I were heading down the baking aisle, where she was agonizing over which brand of coconut flakes to buy for her roast beef dinner—more proof she was into *Chopped* again—when I saw Darlene coming down the aisle toward us.

"This one says the coconuts were grown in India, and this

other bag says they're from Brazil." She made a face. "I suppose they both traveled by boat to get here."

"Neely Kate..."

"Maybe they flew in on a plane. Which one has a better carbon footprint?"

"Neely Kate," I said louder, catching her attention.

She glanced up and realized Darlene was standing in front of us.

"Do you prefer Indian or Brazilian coconuts?" Neely Kate asked her, holding the bags in both hands.

"Neither," Darlene said. "I hate coconut."

Neely Kate stuck out her bottom lip as she considered her statement, then put one bag back on the shelf and the other in the cart.

"Thanks for meeting us here," I said.

"Are we meetin' here so your husband doesn't find out?" she asked.

"One of multiple reasons," I said. "I don't plan on telling him we've met unless you give me permission." I gestured to the aisle. "How about we talk in the back of the store?"

"There's a couple of tables and chairs by the deli counter," Neely Kate said. "We could sit there."

The people at the deli counter weren't exactly fond of me, so I wasn't sure that was a good idea. Still, it would be awkward walking with three of us side by side in the aisle, not to mention we had two carts to manage.

Neely Kate led the way, and I parked my cart against a wall, pulling Liam out before I sat at one of the round tables with them, ignoring the dirty looks from the deli workers.

Obviously, they still held a grudge.

I set Liam sideways on my lap, and he leaned into me, closing his eyes. This was going to be a crappy nap for a second day in a row, but the poor baby was used to it by now with our busy weekends.

I leaned into the table and asked Darlene in a low voice, "Do you have any idea who killed your brother?"

"No," she said. "I'll admit that Harvey used drugs, but he wasn't your typical junkie. He was a casual user. He had a job. He had friends. People liked him."

"So no enemies?" I asked.

"None that I know about."

"Do you know where he got his drugs?" Neely Kate asked.

"He used to get them from a guy he went to high school with, Derby Sloan. But I heard Harvey was getting them from a new guy. When the sheriff's deputy told me he was dead, I thought maybe he'd overdosed or gotten a bad batch of drugs." Her chin quivered, and tears filled her eyes. "I never in a million years thought he'd be shot."

"Do you know who the new guy is?" I asked.

She shook her head. "No idea."

"Do you know how we can find out his name?" Neely Kate asked.

She shrugged. "I don't."

"Maybe you can give us the names of some of his friends," I said. "We can start there."

Darlene looked apprehensive but said, "Sure. I can do that."

"Has the sheriff's office given you any information?" Neely Kate asked. "What kind of questions have they asked?"

Darlene shot me a stern look. "Seems like *you're* the person who would know those things."

Liam shifted, and I adjusted him on my lap. "My husband doesn't share his work life with me, just like I don't share confidential stuff with him."

"And this is confidential?" she asked, sounding dubious.

"I already assured you that I won't tell my husband anything you don't want me to," I said. "But you have to believe me when I tell you that he'd want to help you. He's not your enemy, Darlene."

The irritated look on her face suggested she wasn't convinced.

"So what did the sheriff's detective ask you?" Neely Kate nudged.

"A big fat nothing," she said. "He showed up at my front door before the sun came up on Thursday morning and told me my brother was dead. Asked where he'd worked and lived, then said they'd be back to ask me more questions. I'm still waiting."

I stared at her in shock. "Who talked to you?"

"Not your husband," she said with a snort. "Some big guy who talked real slow and had an attitude."

I glanced over at Neely Kate and shook my head. I had no idea who she was talking about, but then again, I didn't know all the deputies in the department.

"And you don't know his name?" I asked.

"No," she said, sounding forlorn. "I was in too much shock to remember it. He told me right before he said Harvey had been shot and was dead. Then he asked those questions, and I gave him the answers, but I was pretty out of it. He left before I could get it together."

"Did he give you a card?" I asked.

"No."

"Did they talk to your parents?" I asked. "Maybe your other siblings, if you have them?"

"Our parents are deceased, and we don't have any siblings. It's just been me and Harvey for the past eight years."

And now she was alone.

"I'm so sorry," I said, my voice breaking.

She gave me a studied look, her attitude softening. "You meant it when you said you wanted to help me."

"I did," I said, then motioned to Neely Kate. "We both do."

She was quiet for several seconds as she mulled over my statement. I hoped she'd tell me she'd changed her mind about talking to Joe, but instead she said, "I love my brother." Her voice broke. "Loved." She dabbed her eyes. "I can't believe he's gone."

"We really are sorry," Neely Kate said. "We want to help you find out who did this. Right now, we're trying to determine if there's a connection between your brother and a couple of other people who were murdered this weekend too."

Darlene gasped. "There were others?"

I shot a glare at Neely Kate. As far as I knew, Joe hadn't released the ID of the second victim, but then again, we needed to find out if she knew of a connection. It would be difficult to do that without sharing some of what we knew.

"Unfortunately, yes," I said. "Although it's not public information. So I hope you'll keep this to yourself until they make it public."

Her head bobbed up and down. "Of course. If it helps find whoever killed my brother, I'll take it to my grave."

"Hopefully, it won't take that long," I said with an uncomfortable laugh. "We only know one of the other two victims' names—Noah Parker. Have you heard of him? Do you know if he knew your brother?"

Her eyes narrowed for a second or two before she shook her head. "No, but then again, I didn't know all his friends. Especially his weekend friends."

"Weekend friends?" Neely Kate asked.

Darlene sighed. "His partying friends."

"Noah Parker worked at Nimble's Lumberyard down in Sugar Creek," I said. "Do you know if Harvey ever went to that particular lumberyard?"

She released a short laugh. "I doubt Harvey had ever been to a lumberyard in his life."

"What were Harvey's hobbies?" Neely Kate asked.

"Besides partying?" she asked derisively, then ran her hand over her face. "Sorry. I'm not dealing with this very well."

"Of course you're not," Neely Kate said reassuringly. "How could you be?"

"You deal with all of this however you need to," I said. "And you're not obligated to answer any of our questions."

"If there's the slightest chance you can find out who murdered my brother, then I'll help you anyway I can."

"We appreciate that," I said. "Do you happen to know any of the people Harvey partied with or the locations?"

"He had a friend with a large garage south of Pickle Junction. A bunch of them would go down there."

"Do you know any names?"

"I know a few of the guys went to school with us," she said. "Like Scott Van de Camp and Hugo Dempsey."

"That's helpful," I said as Neely Kate typed the names into her phone. "Perhaps they'll know who your brother's new dealer was."

She shuddered and got a funny look. "Dealer makes it sound really bad."

"Dealers who provide drugs that can hurt people generally are," Neely Kate said. "They're self-centered assholes who only think of themselves."

Darlene looked down at her lap, biting her bottom lip as her chin quivered.

"Do you have an address for the garage where they met?" Neely Kate asked.

She shook her head. "No."

"What about a general location?" I asked. "That could help."

Darlene looked at me. I didn't think she was going to answer, but she finally said, "I've never been there, but Harvey said it was a big blue metal building off County Road 24, about ten miles south of the Pickle Junction city limits sign."

"That's good," Neely Kate said.

"Are you going to go down there?" Darlene asked, alarmed.

"We don't know yet," Neely Kate said. "We're working through this as we go."

"I hear it's kind of rough," Darlene said. "It didn't used to be, but Harvey said some new guys had moved in."

New guys. I resisted the urge to steal a glance in Neely Kate's direction. Was this further proof that a new criminal element might have moved into the county? Could it be affiliated with Hardshaw?

This was definitely something for Dermot to look into.

"Do you know two teenagers named Austin and Justin?" I asked.

She gave me a panicked look, then her eyes grew wide. "Oh, my God! Did someone kill two teenagers?"

"No," I assured her. "No, they're perfectly fine. But there might be a connection between them, your brother, and the other two victims."

"Do you have their last names?" she asked.

"Do you know teens with those first names?" I asked.

"No, but I thought their last names might jog my memory."

I didn't want to share that information, so I ignored her original question and moved on. "What about a woman named Selena?"

Her eyes narrowed again, but she shook her head. "No. I don't know anyone named Selena."

I nodded, feeling defeated. Sure, we'd gotten the names of a couple of Harvey's partying buddies and the semi-location of their frequent partying, but she hadn't given us any solid leads. Just bits and pieces.

I reminded myself this was how investigations worked—one piece at a time—but I kept seeing the woman in my vision, the bullet hole in the middle of her forehead. I wasn't content with pieces. I needed to save her, and I didn't know how much time I had left to do it.

"Is there anything else?" I asked. "Anything that you think is important or might be helpful?"

She hesitated. "Harvey was acting weird last week."

"How so?" Neely Kate asked.

Darlene made a face. "Kind of like he was anxious and paranoid."

"Do you think it was because of the drugs he was taking?" I asked.

"Maybe," Darlene admitted, "but he wasn't himself, and he didn't seem high."

"When was the last time you saw him?" I asked.

"Wednesday night. He came over for dinner."

"Was it just the two of you?" I asked.

"Yeah. I'm not seein' anyone right now, and neither was he. After he walked in, he glanced over his shoulder at the street, as though lookin' to see if someone had followed him. I told him he wasn't important enough for someone to follow. He laughed, but it sounded forced." Her chin quivered. "I should have paid better attention. If I'd pressed him for information, he might still be alive."

"You don't know that," I assured her. "You said the sheriff's deputy came to your house on Thursday morning?" She nodded, and I asked, "Did they mention what time he was killed?"

She shook her head, starting to cry. "No." A pleading look covered her face. "People will hear about the drugs and think, oh another drug user's off the street. Good riddance. But he wasn't a junkie. He was a productive member of society. He showed up to his shifts on time. He was rarely sick. He was reliable." Her shoulders shook, and she started to cry harder.

The deli workers gave me more disapproving glares, and her sobs made Liam stir.

She noticed and sat up straighter, then took a deep breath. "I didn't mean to disturb your baby. What's his name?"

The hair on my arms stood on end. Sure, she was probably harmless, but I wasn't willing to just give up his name. But what had I expected, bringing a baby to an investigative interview?

What in the world was I doing?

I abruptly stood. "Thank you for your help, Darlene. Neely Kate's gonna finish up."

Neely Kate stared up at me with wide eyes and an open mouth, but I didn't give either of them any more of an explanation. I turned and walked out of the store, leaving my cart against the wall. I desperately needed to see my kids.

Chapter Twenty-Three

Jed hurried over to me in the parking lot as I grabbed the door handle of my car.

"What happened?" he asked, his face pinched with worry. His phone was in his hand, and he was wearing one ear bud. I suspected he was still listening to Neely Kate through their call.

Liam had fallen asleep, and I held him tighter. "I just realized I shouldn't have dragged Liam into this." Tears stung my eyes. "What am I *doin'*, Jed? What kind of mother does that?"

He shoved his phone into his front jeans pocket and placed a hand on my shoulder. "I'm sorry, Rose. I should have had you leave Liam with me."

"If Joe finds out that I brought him here…" I choked back a sob.

"For what it's worth, I don't think meeting Darlene here was wrong. The chances of someone following her were slim, and she didn't seem dangerous. But I understand why you freaked out when she asked for Liam's name." He opened the back door and reached for my sleeping son. "Let's get him in his car seat."

I reluctantly handed him over and took a step back, trying to compose myself.

Liam stayed asleep while Jed placed him in his seat and got him strapped in. Jed shut the door and turned to face me.

"Are you gonna tell Joe about this?"

I pressed my lips together as I stared at my sleeping son through the car window. "No, because I told Darlene that I wouldn't, but it's just one more secret to add to a growing list." I hated it, but I didn't feel like I had a choice.

"I could hear most of the conversation. She gave us some decent information," Jed said. "I plan on checking some of it out after Neely Kate finishes. Dermot will look into things too."

"I'm worried that someone is movin' into the county." I looked up into his face. "Am I just being paranoid?"

He looked grim. "No. I'm worried about the same thing. I have a feeling Dermot is too."

My stomach churned. "Do you think these new people are interested in Lady? They were asking about her in my vision with Austin."

"I don't know, but I plan to find out."

"I need to tell Joe something, but what do I tell him without breaking Austin's and Darlene's confidence?"

"Gettin' these people to trust you is no small thing, Rose," he said. "Darlene wouldn't have told me or Dermot any of what she told you and Neely Kate. She sure as hell wouldn't have told Joe."

I rested my butt against the car and wrapped my arms over my chest. "I'm not scared for me, Jed. I'm scared for my kids. If someone hurt them…"

"No one's gonna hurt 'em, Rose," he said reassuringly. "I promise. Dermot and I are gonna find out who murdered those men…if Joe doesn't get to them first. We'll stop the woman in your vision from being murdered."

"They found a third victim by Shute Creek early this morning," I said.

He nodded, not looking surprised. Of course he knew.

How had I gotten sucked back into all of this?

Panic bubbled deep inside me, and all I could think about was hugging my kids.

"I'm gonna go get my kids at Piney Rest and head home," I said. "I'll just take off early tomorrow and grocery shop before I get the kids from daycare."

"That sounds like a good idea. If you're okay with it, I'm gonna have Neely Kate pick up Daisy and hang out with y'all at the farmhouse." He paused, then looked at Liam in the car before he turned back to me. "In fact, why don't you switch cars with her? She can drive Liam to pick up Daisy, and then you won't have to worry about waking him up when you pick up the kids. You can use Daisy's car seat for Hope, and there's a booster in the trunk that Neely Kate uses for Mikey when she has him."

Part of me wanted to say no. I didn't want to let Liam out of my sight right now, but my best friend would never let anything happen to him. I dug in my purse while Jed reached into his pocket, and we exchanged key fobs.

Jed offered me a reassuring smile. "We're gonna get to the bottom of this. I promise."

"I sure hope so." I walked over to Neely Kate's car and drove over to the nursing home, thankful I didn't have to wake up Liam to go inside. But I wasn't going to relax until I had all my kids locked inside our house.

When I walked into the nursing home, the kids weren't in the living room area where I'd dropped them off. My panic rose again, but I beat it back as I approached the reception desk. Voices and music floated from farther down the hall.

The woman sitting behind the desk greeted me with a smile. "Are you here to visit a Piney Rest resident, or are you with the church group?"

"The church group."

"They're down the hall." She laughed. "But the way you're already headed in that direction tells me you knew that."

I didn't run, but I wasn't strolling either as I headed toward the ruckus.

I stopped in the dining hall and saw quite a few Piney Rest residents sitting at tables, some in wheelchairs, each with a cupcake and small bowls of icing in front of them. It looked like the women's group was leading a cupcake-decorating class. One of the women from the lady's group at church stood at the back of the hall, giving directions, while other women were milling around, giving the residents assistance.

I started to freak out when I didn't see my kids, but then Hope called out, "That's so pwetty, Miss Midwed. Good job!"

I walked deeper into the room and saw Miss Mildred sitting at a round table in the back corner, surrounded by my children. Ashley sat on her right side with Mikey next to her, but my heart stopped at the sight of Hope sitting to Miss Mildred's left.

A new wave of panic set in. Miss Mildred had a vicious tongue, and Hope's feelings were easily hurt. I rarely questioned Maeve's judgment, but what had she been thinking by letting my baby sit next to Miss Mildred? Especially since she'd turned even meaner since moving here.

But as I hurried toward the table, I was shocked to see that Miss Mildred was smiling at my daughter with bright eyes, shining with happiness. She wasn't staring at Ashley or Mikey. She was grinning from ear to ear at *Hope*.

"Your cupcake is looking mighty fine too, Hope," Miss Mildred said encouragingly.

"What about mine, Miss Mildred?" Mikey asked, lifting his gaze to her. He gave her a big, toothy grin.

The elderly woman turned her attention to my nephew. "Why, it reminds me of dragon's nest of eggs."

"That's what I was tryin' to make!" Mikey exclaimed with excitement.

Miss Mildred actually winked at him. "Then good job."

I stepped behind a pole, then peeked around it, gawking in amazement. My ex-neighbor was acting like an entirely different person.

"I want to be an artist when I grow up," Mikey said, concentrating on his cupcake while he added what looked like sprinkles. "Aunt Rose says she's gonna get me art classes."

I cringed, prepared for her to slander me, but to my amazement, Miss Mildred said, "Of course she is. She knows talent when she sees it."

I had never heard the woman say a nice thing about me in my life, and while it wasn't entirely a compliment, I was still shocked.

"Rose!" Maeve said in surprise behind me. "I didn't expect to see you so soon."

"It's a long story," I said, making sure the kids hadn't heard us, but they were all focused on decorating their cupcakes. "Is it my imagination, or does Miss Mildred look *happy*?"

"You have no idea how excited she was to see the kids. It's like she's a completely different person."

"I was worried about how she'd treat Hope, but I heard her actually being sweet to her. And she even gave me a half-compliment to Mikey."

"How does someone give a half-compliment?" she asked with a laugh.

"Leave it to her to find a way."

She glanced at their table, then back at me. "Thank you so much for thinking of this visit. Mildred really needed it, and the children seem to be enjoying themselves as well." As if to punctuate her statement, a peal of laughter erupted from their table. She made a face. "Is there any way you could run another errand and come back in about forty-five minutes? I think they'd all enjoy a little more time."

"Oh."

I'd been dying to get back to them, terrified something would happen to them out of my sight. But I realized nothing was going to happen to them here. Maybe I could go finish my grocery shopping.

"Yeah," I said. "I can find something to do."

"Maybe you should take some time just for you," she suggested. "Grab a cup of coffee, and read a book."

"That's a great idea," I said, dying to do just that, but knowing I needed to do something more practical. I was going to finish my grocery shopping. "I'll be back in about forty-five minutes."

"Great."

I headed outside and pulled out my phone to call Neely Kate. She'd probably finished talking to Darlene, and I needed to touch base after the way I'd run out.

"Rose, are you okay?" she asked as soon as she answered.

"I'm fine. I just got freaked out when Darlene noticed Liam. It was stupid to leave like that. I'm sorry."

"It's okay, and I understand."

"Did she tell you anything after I left?"

"No, not really. I got the impression you're the one she was interested in talking to, and she seemed off after I asked about Harvey's drug dealer."

"I noticed that too. Do you think she's afraid of him? Maybe the reason she won't talk to Joe is because she's worried the dealer will find out and retaliate."

"Your guess is as good as mine."

"After I left and Jed convinced me to let you take Liam with you to get Daisy, I went to pick up the kids. When I walked into the dining hall, I found them all gathered around Miss Mildred, and she looked like she was having the time of her life. The kids were too."

"You're pullin' my leg."

"Nope. In any case, Maeve asked if I could come back in forty-five minutes, so I'm going to finish my grocery shopping really quick. Are you still at the store?"

"Nah. I checked out with what you and I had in the cart. Now Liam, who's still sound asleep, and I are on our way to get Daisy. We'll meet you at your house."

"You don't mind waiting?"

"Not at all. By the time I get home, gather up Daisy, and get back to your house, I suspect we'll get there at about the same time." If we didn't, she had a key and knew the code to the alarm system.

"Thank you, Neely Kate. You're the best."

"I know," she said with a laugh. "I don't intend to let you forget it."

I pulled into the Piggly Wiggly lot and headed toward the entrance when someone ran up behind me and grabbed my arm.

I spun around, ready to hit them with my purse, when I realized it was Darlene.

"Sorry!" she exclaimed, dropping her hold and lifting her hands in surrender. "I was just surprised to see you came back." A wary look crossed her face. "Where's your baby?"

My hair stood up on end. "He fell asleep, so I left him with a friend," I said, grateful I was telling the truth. "What are you doin' sneakin' up on me like that?"

"I didn't mean to scare you. Like I said, I was excited to see you came back."

"Why?" I said, stepping out of the way of an older couple who were walking into the store. "I thought you told us everything you had to say."

She made a face. "I may not have told you everything. I held some stuff back."

"Why?"

She glanced out into the parking lot. "I got scared. I saw that big guy hovering around, and I thought he was here to get me."

"Big guy?" Then I realized who she'd probably seen. "Close-cropped hair? Wearing jeans and a gray T-shirt?" When she nodded, I said, "That was Jed. Neely Kate's husband. He was worried about her meeting with you, so he was watching out for us."

"Oh." She pushed out a breath. "I suppose that makes sense, and it's actually kinda sweet." Tears filled her eyes. "The only person who would have done that for me was Harvey."

"I really am sorry about your brother," I said, my voice softening. "If you know more about what happened to him, I can tell my husband. I'll even tell him it's from an anonymous source."

Her eyes swam with tears. "What if it gets traced back to me?"

"Did you do something illegal? If you did, I'll figure out a way to protect you."

She smiled, but the corners of her mouth quivered. "I think you really are a nice person. Your friend too. I couldn't figure out why you'd want to help me, but it makes more sense now."

"We try to help people because people helped us when we needed it. We're just payin' it forward."

She nodded, looking nervous again.

"Do you want to go sit in my car?" I asked. "We can talk in there so we're not out in the open."

"Okay. That's probably a good idea."

I led her over to Neely Kate's car and pressed the key fob so the doors unlocked. She got into the passenger seat and glanced in the back.

"Only one car seat? I thought you had several younger kids."

My heart skipped a beat, and I decided I wasn't going to evade her questions or pretend they weren't making me nervous. "How do you know so much about my family?"

Surprise filled her eyes, then she turned in her seat to face me, holding up her hands. "Oh! I realize that must sound super creepy! I'm not a stalker or anything. I just looked you up after Neely Kate cornered me in the bathroom and offered your help."

"That makes sense," I said, but I was still going to be cautious. "I would have looked you up too."

"You didn't?" she asked, sounding surprised.

She had a point. We should have researched her more before coming to meet her, but I hadn't done this in three years. Heck, I wasn't trying to do it now.

"No, but things were a little chaotic last night and today." I drew a breath to calm my nerves. "You said you had more information that you held back."

She sat back in her seat as though she felt guilty for veering off track. "I think I might know of a connection between Harvey and the other guy, Noah Parker."

"Really? What?"

"My brother mentioned meeting a guy named Noah a few weeks ago. And I'm pretty sure he said he worked at the lumberyard."

"Where did they meet?"

She looked down at her hands in her lap.

"That's the part you didn't want to tell me."

Her gaze lifted, sorrow in her eyes.

"It's not yourself that you're trying to protect," I said softly. "It's your brother."

Tears streamed down her face as she nodded.

"What were he and Noah doing when they met?"

She swallowed, then took a breath before she said, "They were meeting with a guy about a new drug he was bringing to Fenton County."

I read between the lines. "He was recruiting them to sell drugs."

Her eyes widened suddenly. "Harvey swore it wasn't like that. He said it was to make a little money on the side while getting the drug for free. I told him he was insane, that selling drugs meant he was a dealer, and he needed to stop."

"So he started dealing drugs," I said not unkindly. It made sense why she'd clammed up after Neely Kate had called drug dealers selfish assholes. Darlene hadn't wanted us to judge her brother, just like she was worried Joe and his department would do if they found out.

She cringed but nodded. "I guess there's no way to pretty it up, is there?"

"Was Noah dealing for this new guy too?"

"Yeah, him and another guy. But last week, like I told you and Neely Kate earlier, Harvey seemed a little more paranoid than usual. He said someone was out to get him."

"Did he tell you who it was?"

"No. He wouldn't say, but after giving him the fifth degree, I figured out it was the guy he was selling for. He never confirmed it, but he didn't deny it either."

"Why would the dealer be out to get him?"

"I asked him the same thing, but the only thing he'd tell me was that his friends, Noah and another guy he didn't name, were also in trouble."

That fit with Austin's story. Was the other guy the man Austin had seen murdered? "Was the other guy at the meeting your brother had with the dealer?"

"I think so," she said. "He didn't give me many details, but I figured out he met this dealer guy at one of those parties. He brought his drug and shared it with them, then suggested they sell it to their friends so they could get their drugs for free."

I narrowed my eyes in confusion. "How big were these parties?" It didn't seem like three guys dealing at the same party was a very good business plan.

"Not that big, and I know where you're headed with your next question. How could all of them sell to the same group of people? Here's your answer: They couldn't."

"So you think their dealer killed them because they didn't sell enough?"

"I don't know."

I nearly asked her if we could search her brother's house, but that was dumb for several reasons. One, I couldn't go there. That was a line I wasn't willing to cross. Yet. But more importantly, I was certain several people had already searched. Joe and his men definitely would have gone there, and I suspected the drug dealer would have gotten there first.

"Why won't you tell my husband what you just told me?"

"And have Harvey's name plastered all over the news, labeling him a dirty drug dealer?" She shook her head adamantly. "No. No way. People will assume he was some drug den, homeless junkie, and he wasn't." She swallowed a sob. "He was a good person who made a really stupid decision."

I presumed his decision to sell drugs was the stupid decision she was referring to. I refrained from suggesting he'd made a few others. It wouldn't help anything, and it would only hurt her.

"So what do you want me to do with this information, Darlene?" I asked.

Her head jutted back in surprise. "I want you to find out who killed my brother."

"And if I find the person, what do you want to do then?"

Her eyes hardened. "Then I'll take care of him."

I shook my head. "No, I can't condone that." When she started to protest, I held up my hand and calmly said, "I won't be doing this on my own. When Neely Kate and I did this before, we weren't married, and we didn't have kids. But I have someone who will help—" I jutted my hand forward to prevent her from protesting. "I worked with him to take down Hardshaw, and he's not with law enforcement. I can't give you his name, but I promise he won't be turning over the information to them either. Once we find out who this person is, I'll let you know, and we'll all decide where to go from there."

"I want him to pay for killing my brother," she said through gritted teeth, anger burning in her eyes.

"I know you do, and I'll do my best to make sure he does."

She watched me for a moment, then wiped her cheeks and nodded. "Okay."

"Okay. Now I need more information about those parties and

who else might have attended." Were Selena and the woman from my vision part of the party group? Could the man in my vision be the drug dealer?

"I really did tell you almost everything I know," she said, her voice becoming steadier. "The parties were held at that garage south of Pickle Junction."

"You said these parties were on the weekends. Did they have them on Saturday and Sunday?"

She nodded. "Although I don't think as many people came on Sundays."

"Some people are better than none," I said. "Do you think Harvey's friends Scott or Hugo will be there tonight?"

"I don't know."

"What about his previous dealer? Derby Sloan. Did he attend the parties?"

"I don't know that either."

"Do you know if Harvey sold any of the drugs the dealer gave him?"

She shook her head. "If he did, not many. I'm pretty sure he took them himself."

"If a new guy was trying to break into the county, it would be stupid for him to kill his first dealers. Especially that soon after they started to work for him. Seems like he'd threaten them first because I doubt anyone's gonna want to work with him if he so trigger happy."

Darlene reached into her purse and pulled out an envelope. "Harvey left this at my house. I don't know if he intended to, or if he just forgot. It doesn't make sense though."

She handed it to me, and I took it, opening the flap and pulling out a piece of paper. A name, address, and a bunch of numbers were handwritten on the notebook page.

Thomas Benton
Dallas, Texas

00011458935

My blood ran cold.

Hardshaw had been based in Dallas.

I looked up at Darlene. "I take it you don't know anyone named Thomas Benton?"

"No, and I doubt Harvey knew anyone in Dallas. He'd never left the state, and all his friends were from high school or the county."

Could this be the "package" the murderers had been looking for?

"Do you think I could have a copy?" I asked.

She waved her hand toward me. "Keep it. I don't want it."

I refolded the paper and tucked it into my purse. "Do you have any phone numbers or addresses for Harvey's friends?"

"No. But I know Scott works at McDonald's. He's a manager there."

"Okay. We'll look into him. Anything else?"

She stared out the front windshield. "No. I just want to find who did this and make them pay." She turned to face me. "I don't have much money, but I'll pay you if you can tell me his name and where I can find him."

"We're not gonna take your money, Darlene. We want to find the culprit too."

"And you'll tell me who it is?"

"Yes." And I would. Just not before I told Dermot and Joe.

Tears flooded her eyes again. "Thank you."

"I'll let you know when we know something." I knew I should feel guilty for misleading her, but I didn't. Not if it protected her. I wasn't going to give her the chance to mete out her own vigilante justice. She was likelier to get killed herself.

Worried, I reached out and placed my hand on her arm, then asked the universe if Darlene was safe from Harvey's killers. A slightly fuzzy image popped up of a man holding a baby.

"We sure make cute kids," the man said.

"The cutest," Vision Darlene said.

I was back in the car blurting out, "You're gonna have a family."

Tears flooded her eyes. "Harvey was my family."

"You're gonna meet a sweet man and have babies. I promise."

She gave me a tight smile. "I really hope you're right." She reached for the door handle, then stopped. "If Scott won't talk to you, tell him I said if he doesn't cooperate, I'll tell the sheriff he set his house on fire for the insurance money." With that, she got out of the car.

Scott Van de Camp had committed insurance fraud? The secrets I was keeping from Joe were piling up.

I pulled out my phone to call Dermot. I needed to let him know what was going on, but I waited until Darlene got in her car and drove away before I pulled up his number and placed the call. It went straight to voicemail, so I left a message.

"Neely Kate and I talked to Darlene Smith, and then I spoke with her alone a little bit later. I have a few leads, so call me when you get a chance."

I considered my next move. I knew I really should go inside and get food for the week, but the pull to go to McDonald's and see if Scott Van de Camp was working won out.

And just like that, for better or worse, I was actively investigating.

Chapter Twenty-Four

I pulled into the McDonald's parking lot and hurried inside before I could talk myself out of it.

Since it was mid-afternoon, the restaurant wasn't that busy. There were a couple of cars in the drive-thru line, but no customers were in the dining room or waiting to place orders. I walked up to the counter, and a teenage girl greeted me with a bright smile. "Welcome to McDonald's. What can I get you today?"

"Actually, I was wondering if Scott Van de Camp was working today."

Her smile fell. "The manager? Did I do something wrong?"

"No, not at all," I assured her. "I need to speak to him about a mutual friend." Well, a mutual friend in a convoluted way.

"Oh," she said, still looking uncertain, but she took a step away from the register. "I'll go get him."

I gave her a big smile. "Thanks."

She disappeared in the back, then came back out with a man in his thirties.

He gave me a wary look as he approached. "I'm Scott. I hear you're lookin' for me?"

"Hi, Scott. I'm Rose. I just spoke with Darlene Smith. She

suggested that I talk to you about her brother, Harvey. Do you have a moment to talk?"

His face paled. "Are you with the cops?"

The girl at the register's eyes widened, and her mouth fell open in shock.

"No," I said with a short laugh. "Like I said, I'm a friend of Darlene's. I'm only trying to help her."

He glanced over at the girl and wiped his hands on his uniform pants. "Kylie, I'm gonna take a short break. Let everyone know not to bother me." He walked around the counter and headed toward me.

"Let's sit over by the window," he said, sounding nervous as he walked past me into the dining room.

I followed him into the unoccupied room and sat across from him at a four-top table.

"What did you say your name was again?" he asked, sweat breaking out on his forehead.

"Rose, and like I said, Darlene suggested I talk to you."

"What about?"

I took a breath as I folded my hands on the tabletop, deciding to keep my threat under wraps for the moment. "I'm sure you've heard the news about Harvey."

He swallowed hard, then nodded. "Yeah."

"I heard you two liked to hang out together on the weekends."

"Why exactly did Darlene suggest you talk to me?"

"I'm trying to help her figure out what happened to Harvey."

Fear filled his eyes. "Are you with the police?"

"No," I said with a short laugh. "Definitely not. I'm kind of like a private investigator." He seemed to relax a tiny bit, so I repeated my question. "So you and Harvey hung out on the weekends?"

He swallowed hard. "Yeah, we hung out sometimes."

"And had a good time doin' it," I said matter-of-factly.

He squirmed in his seat. "Why exactly are you talkin' to me?"

"What do you know about what happened to Harvey?"

His face paled. "I heard he got shot."

"Do you have any idea who would want Harvey dead?"

"You think I know a murderer?" he asked, looking like he was about to vomit.

I cocked an eyebrow. "I don't know, Scott. You would know better than me." I paused. "Most people are murdered by someone they know. Who wanted Harvey dead?"

"I didn't know him that well, so I don't know."

"Really?" I said, feigning surprise. "I heard you two go way back."

He swallowed again. "I'm not sure I should be talkin' to you."

"Why?"

"Because I don't want to end up like Harvey."

"Why did Harvey end up dead?" I pressed. "If you help find the person who did this, then they'll be arrested, and you'll be safe."

He studied me for a long moment, some of his color returning to his face. "I don't think you're with the police."

"I told you that I'm not, but I can take what I learn and hand it over anonymously, if you'd like." When he didn't respond, I said, "Have the police or sheriff's department questioned you?"

His eyes grew wide. "No. Why would they?"

What in the world had Joe and his department been doing? "Because you two were friends, and you hung out on the weekends."

"I wasn't lying when I said we weren't *close* friends. Sure, we hung out in the same place sometimes, but we weren't buddies, you know?"

"Yeah. But you obviously know something if you're this nervous talking to me."

"I don't know nothin'. I'm nervous because he and another guy who hung out at the garage were both murdered. That don't happen every day, you know?"

"I know, which is why I'm trying to get to the bottom of it. What was the other guy's name?"

"Noah something or other. We weren't friends either."

"How is it that all y'all were hanging out in a garage together on the weekends, but you weren't friends?"

He leaned back in his chair. "I don't have to talk to you, and I sure as hell don't need to be tellin' you shit that could get me killed."

Now I really needed to find out what he knew.

"I think you do want to talk to me," I said dryly. "Or the sheriff might be comin' by to ask you about a certain house fire."

He leaned forward, and cold sweat broke out on his forehead. "What?"

"Don't play dumb. A house fire? An insurance claim?"

"I don't know what you're talkin' about."

Except the way his entire body was shaking said differently.

"Okay then," I said, pushing my chair back. "I'm sure you'll have nothin' to worry about when the sheriff hauls you in for questioning."

I started to get up, but he called out a panicked "Wait!" while patting his hands toward me. "Wait," he repeated, sounding defeated. "I'll tell you what you want to know."

"So tell me more about the garage you hung out at."

He took several breaths before he said, "It's a bootleg bar. They don't have a liquor license, so it's kind of hush-hush. There's all kinds of illegal things goin' on. Gamblin', drugs." He swiped his hand across his forehead to wipe away the sweat. "You're not gonna tell the sheriff, are you?"

Crap. More secrets from Joe. "No," I said with a sigh. "As long as you tell me everything you know, I won't have a reason to go to law enforcement. But if you know something that can help catch Harvey's killer, then you really should talk to them."

"If Derby finds out I blabbed, he might kill me next."

"Derby Sloan?" I asked. "He's all y'all's drug dealer?"

He held up his hand and jutted his head back. "Now hold on there. I don't do any hard stuff. Just some weed to help me chill. Customer service is the shit, and then I'm managing teenagers all day. Harvey and Noah and a few others were into the harder stuff."

"And Derby supplied everyone with whatever they wanted?"

Scott hesitated, then nodded. "Derby owns the place. It's kind of an on-the-down-low-bar kind of place."

"Why doesn't he have a legit bar?"

"He's got some felonies and can't get a liquor license. Besides, with all the other stuff goin' on…"

Did Dermot know about this place? "Do you think Derby killed Harvey and Noah?"

He pushed out a long breath. "I don't know. I think Derby's capable of killin' someone, but as long you stay on his good side, he won't give you any trouble."

"What would it take to get on Derby's bad side?" I asked. "Maybe bringin' in drugs from an outside source?"

Fear flashed through his eyes. "Yeah, he wouldn't be too happy about that."

"I heard there was a new guy there offering a new kind of drug."

"Yep, and Derby kicked his ass out when he found out it was happenin'."

"I also heard that Harvey and Noah were dealing for the new guy. If Derby found out, could he have killed them?"

When he looked like he didn't want to answer. I asked, "Exactly how much money did you make off that fire?"

He swiped at his forehead. "He might have killed them."

I nodded. "Do you know the new guy's name?"

He shook his head. "I didn't have nothing to do with the guy when he came in. He mostly hung out with Harvey, Noah, and Huey."

"Do you know Huey's last name?"

"Dempsey."

Dempsey... "Is Huey also Hugo?" Could he be the third victim?

His eyes widened. "Yeah. How'd you know that?"

"Darlene told me about you and him."

He looked less spooked. "Huey, Harvey, and me all went to school together, but they were bigger stoners than me. I've tried the hard stuff, but I don't like how it makes me feel, so I stick to weed. But those other guys like the harder drugs."

"And Derby supplied both," I said, mulling it over in my head.

He wiped the corner of his mouth. "Yeah."

I could see how Derby Sloan could be pissed if someone was moving into his territory. And Scott believed he was capable of murder. Could this case really be this easy to solve?

"How long ago did this new guy talk to Harvey, Huey, and Noah?"

"Maybe a month ago? Then last weekend, the three of them were talkin' to everyone on the downlow about this new drug they were sellin'. Only no one was interested because no one else is stupid enough to cross Derby."

"Except for Huey, Harvey, and Noah," I said dryly.

"And two of them are dead."

Possibly all three, but I wasn't going to tell him that.

"Do you know where this new guy came from?"

"Rumor had it he was from Texas, but I don't know for sure."

Texas fit the name on the paper. It also fit the Hardshaw Group. I swallowed my fear and continued. "And you're sure you don't know his name? Maybe a snippet of something?"

He shook his head. "No. Nothing. They were huddled in the back corner, ignorin' the rest of us. And he was only in there one time."

"Did Harvey or any of the other guys mention his name after that?"

"Nope."

"Did they try to sell you any of their drugs?"

He released a bitter laugh. "No. They knew I wasn't into the hard stuff, so they wouldn't have wasted their time."

"Do you know anyone they might have tried to sell to?"

He stared at me, his lips pressed together. "Who are you gonna tell?"

"I told you I'm not gonna tell the sheriff."

"It ain't the sheriff I'm scared of."

"So who are you scared of?"

He remained silent.

I leaned closer and lowered my voice. "If you want me to protect you, I need to know who I'm protecting you from."

He swallowed again, looking like he was about to bolt. "How can *you* protect me?" he asked with a half-hearted sneer.

"I have powerful friends who can keep you safe. And I won't tell anyone of importance where I got this information." I leveled my gaze. "How many people go to this garage bar?"

"Maybe thirty or forty over the course of the weekend."

"That's a lot of people who could talk. How's the bar still a secret?"

"Because Derby would cut anyone who told down at the knees. Which is why he'll cut me down too."

"So far, what you've told me is too broad for anyone to trace it back to you, and I found out about the bar from Darlene." When he didn't respond, I said, "Do you think Harvey deserved to die?"

"What?" he practically shouted, then cringed. "No. Of course not. He was an idiot, but stupidity shouldn't get you killed."

"Then tell me anything that can help me find out who killed them."

"What if it was Derby?" he whispered. "The garage'll get shut down, and then where will we go?"

It took effort to stifle a groan of frustration. Funny, I remembered having more patience when Neely Kate and I had done this before. Maybe my impatience was because I needed to pick up my kids in fifteen minutes. "Let me get this straight. If Derby murdered those two men, you don't want him to get arrested because you're not sure where you'll get your pot," I said in an icy tone as I held his gaze.

His face flushed, and he had the good sense to look embarrassed. "Well, when you put it that way…"

Did Dermot sell pot? I supposed I should know what he did in the county. Then again, it was safer for all of us if I didn't. "I'm sure there are plenty of other pot sources if you look hard enough, and if worse comes to worst, you make a trip every other month or so to Missouri. It's legal there."

"But I don't have a reliable car," he whined, then gestured to the front counter. "Have you seen where I work?"

I forced a smile. "Someone will take his place. Nature abhors a vacuum, and something always takes its place." Part of me grew cold as I realized I was paraphrasing the exact same thing James Malcolm had told me years ago. Again, I had to wonder what role Dermot played in all of this.

Scott's face brightened. "You think?"

"I know." Sometimes for better. Sometimes for worse.

"I know they approached a few people, but no one bought anything from them."

"I need names, Scott."

He shook his head. "I want to help you, but I can't rat anyone else out. Sorry."

I could tell by the set of his jaw he wasn't budging, only it wasn't loyalty keeping his lips sealed. It was fear. I couldn't blame him for doubting my statement of knowing powerful people who could help him. I could use the Lady in Black card, but there was a chance he wouldn't know who she was. Not to mention, I still preferred to leave her in the closet buried in moth balls. I'd hand this information over to Dermot and let him see to the rest.

"Did Derby ever let teenagers into the bar?" I asked.

He blinked in surprise. "Yeah, sometimes."

"What's the youngest he'd allow?"

"Seventeen or so. He didn't like much younger because they didn't know how to keep their mouths shut."

"Good to know he had some scruples," I said sarcastically.

It went over his head, and he nodded agreeably.

"Any of them named Austin or Justin?"

He considered it a moment, then shook his head. "Not that I recall."

"You've only mentioned men, but I presume he lets women into the bar."

He laughed. "Half the guys wouldn't be there if he didn't."

"Did you ever meet a woman named Selena?"

He shook his head again. "No."

I pulled out my phone and showed him the image of the woman from my vision. "Did you ever see this woman there?"

He leaned closer. "No. Can't say that I have." He squinted, then glanced up at me. "Hey, she sort of looks like you. Is she your sister or somethin'?"

"No." I swiped to the next image. "What about him?"

He made a face and leaned back. "He looks like one mean bastard."

"He is. Ever seen him?"

"No."

I was equally relieved and disappointed. "You sure?"

"Trust me. I'd remember if I'd crossed paths with him."

"What about the guy who convinced Harvey and the other two to sell for him? Could this be him?"

He shook his head before lifting his gaze to mine. "That ain't no low-level lookin' guy, and anyone going into bootleg bars trying to get average guys to sell drugs for them is low level."

He had a point.

Did the guy from Texas work for the man in my vision?

Scott Van de Camp was filling in some of the blanks for me, but I didn't feel any closer to saving the woman in my vision.

"Can you think of anything else that might help me find Harvey's murderer?"

"No." He shook his head, looking sick. "I can't believe someone killed him."

I drew in a breath and sat back in my chair. "Well, thank you for your time, Scott. If you think of anything else, will you contact Darlene and have her let me know? She'll pass it on to me, and we can set up another time to meet."

"You ain't gonna give me your number?" he asked in confusion when I stood.

I stayed next to the table. "No." But if I were going to continue with this nonsense, then I'd have to get a burner phone.

What in the world was I thinking? I wasn't going to continue looking into this.

Maybe if I repeated it enough times in my head, I'd convince myself.

Chapter Twenty-Five

As soon as I got in the car, after a moment's hesitation, I called Dermot. He'd looked me in the eyes and told me he hadn't murdered those men. I had no reason to distrust him, even if I had some lingering doubts. The call went straight to voicemail again. Why was his phone turned off? That worried me more than a little.

"Hey, Dermot," I said after the beep. "I'm startin' to get a little concerned about you. I have more information, but I don't want to leave it in a voicemail. Call me back when you get this."

I hung up and headed to the nursing home, eager to see my children.

The kids were in the living room when I walked in, sitting around Miss Mildred, who was still basking in their attention. I wasn't sure I'd ever seen her this happy.

I hated that I was about to destroy that.

Hope saw me first and jumped out of her seat. "Momma! I made a cupcake with a bunny on top!"

I kneeled down and scooped her into my arms, hugging her. "That's so awesome! I can't wait to see it."

She hugged me back, then squirmed. "Why you huggin' me so tight?"

I kissed her cheek as I loosened my hold. Lifting a hand

to the side of her head, I smoothed back some of her dark brown waves. Her dark brown eyes studied me, and for a brief moment, I saw her biological father in her intense gaze. My heart tripped, but I plastered on a smile. "I missed you."

"I wasn't hewa vewy long, silly."

I laughed. "It doesn't matter how long or short I'm away. I *always* miss you."

Her mouth twisted to the side. "Will you be sad if I didn't miss you too?"

I laughed again. "No. I'm glad you had fun." The hug hadn't been enough to calm my nerves, but holding her any longer would look suspicious. Besides, Miss Mildred was staring at us, her smile gone.

I drew in a breath, girding myself for her sharp tongue.

Holding Hope's hand, I stood and turned my attention to Ashley and Mikey. "Did you guys have fun?"

"The mostest fun, Aunt Rose!" Mikey exclaimed. "I made a cupcake too, and it had dragon's eggs on top!"

"Oh my goodness!" I said, pretending to be shocked. "Where did you get dragon's eggs?"

Mikey started giggling, and Hope tugged on my hand.

When I glanced down at her, she said with a serious expression, "They awen't weal, Momma."

"What?"

"They just pwetend," she said, empathy on her face. "I'm sowwy if you'wa sad that they not weal."

I offered her a smile. "It's okay. But real dragon's eggs would be cool."

"The coolest!" Mikey said excitedly, then turned to Miss Mildred. "Right?"

"You'd be the only boy in the world with them, so that would definitely be cool," she said. Her smile was softer now, as though my presence had thrown a blanket over her happiness.

"Thanks for entertaining them, Miss Mildred," I said cautiously. "It looks like they had a wonderful afternoon."

"Somebody had to watch them," she said gruffly.

I quickly checked the kids' faces to see if her change in tone and demeanor had hurt them, but they were still beaming.

I glanced around the room. "I'm going to find Maeve and let her know I'm taking you guys home."

"Can we come back to see Miss Mildred again?" Ashley asked quietly.

"Of course," I said. "But you might not get to make cupcakes the next time. This was a special thing."

"I'll find something else for them to do," Miss Mildred said. "I got a copy of the key to the art supply room, so we can raid it when nobody's lookin'."

"Hey!" Mikey shouted. "I want to be an artist!"

"She knows," Ashley said with a sigh. "You told her and everyone else about twenty times."

"No harm in lettin' people know who you are," Miss Mildred said with an indulgent smile.

Ashley shrugged, then said to me, "Nana Maeve put our cupcakes on a table in the back. Can I go get them?"

"Sure, but do you know where Nana Maeve might be?"

"I think she's down there." She pointed down the hall by the front desk.

"Do you need help getting the cupcakes?"

She shook her head. "Nana Maeve put them in a box. I can carry it."

"Okay. I'll meet you back here in a minute."

I planned to take Hope with me to find Maeve, but she begged to stay with Miss Mildred so she could hear another of the older woman's funny stories. I'd never known Miss Mildred to tell a funny story in my life, but it didn't take much to entertain an almost three-year-old.

I headed down the hall, following Maeve's voice coming from

an open door. I stopped outside the entrance and peered in. Maeve was standing, speaking to a middle-aged woman sitting behind a desk. But when she saw me in the doorway, she cut herself off and smiled at me. "Rose! Back already?"

"I am. I found the kids in the living room, and Ashley is getting their cupcakes. Thank you so much for encouraging me to let them stay."

"Oh my!" Maeve said, excitement dancing in her eyes. "The residents *loved* having them here. The director and I are talking about bringing more children next time. Do you think you'd be open to the kids coming again?"

I leaned into the doorframe. "After seeing how much fun they had and how it changed Miss Mildred's attitude, *of course* they can come. I'm going to have to drag them out of here today."

I said goodbye, then found the kids assembled in front of Miss Mildred. She was talking to all three of them, holding Ashley's and Hope's hands while they stared at her intently.

"You be good for your momma," she said to Hope. Then she turned to Ashley and Mikey, "And your aunt. She ain't your momma, may she rest in peace, but your aunt loves you as much as Violet does." She swiped a tear from her cheek. "And if you're good, maybe she'll let you come back."

Miss Mildred's gaze drifted to mine, and for a split second, there was pleading in her eyes.

My chest tightened as I took a step toward them. "Well, here's some good news: Nana Maeve is making it so you can come at least once a month, and other kids are gonna come too."

"Awe they gonna steal Miss Midwed?" Hope asked. "She's ouws."

"Of course no one's stealing Miss Mildred, because she's a person and not a possession," I said. "And Miss Mildred can spend time with whomever she wants. So if she wants to spend time with you, then lucky you."

"Yay!" Mikey and Hope cried out in unison, while Ashley smiled.

"But now we have to head home because Aunt Neely Kate has Liam, and we're meeting her at our house."

"And we have to see Muffy," Hope said, her head bobbing. "She misses us."

"Yes, she does," I said.

We headed out to the parking lot. The kids were surprised and excited when I told them Neely Kate and I had traded cars. I got the booster for Mikey out of the back, clipped Hope into Daisy's car seat, and headed home.

My car wasn't parked in front when we pulled in front of the house, and a moment of longing for Liam filled me, but I tried to shake it off as we got out and went inside. The cooler weather had changed to the low seventies, so when we let Muffy out, we all stayed outside with her. The kids ran around the front yard, while I settled onto the porch swing, sipping a cup of tea. I was trying to decide if I should ease my fears and call Neely Kate when my phone rang. While I'd hoped to see her name on the screen, I was nearly as relieved to see Dermot's.

"What'd you find?" he asked straight away.

"Are you okay?" I asked as I scanned the yard for the kids' location. "It's unusual for your phone to go straight to voicemail."

"I had another interview with your husband."

My stomach dropped, then I thanked God that he'd turned his phone off. I had no idea how he had saved my name in his phone, but I could only imagine how it would look if my name had popped up on his screen during his interview.

"Do they think you're behind them?"

"No. I think it was another fishing expedition. They found a third body."

"I heard," I said. "Do you think it's the guy Austin saw murdered?"

"Possible. One of the detectives let it slip that the guy died from a head shot, but I'm reluctant to say it's the same guy. For all we know, it's a fourth murder."

"Agreed." Although I certainly hoped it wasn't.

"So what'd you learn?"

I told him about my conversations with Darlene and how I'd decided to stop by McDonald's and talk to Scott Van de Camp.

"Alone?" he grunted.

"He's the manager of a McDonald's," I said dismissively. "You think he's gonna do anything to me in front of his employees?"

"Still…"

"It was worth finding out what he told me." I paused. "What do you know about an illegal secret bar south of Pickle Junction? Some guy named Derby Sloan runs it on the downlow. He sells drugs and hosts gambling."

"I'm acquainted with Derby Sloan." His tone left me guessing what he thought of him.

"Derby Sloan provided drugs to Harvey, Noah, and a guy named Huey-slash-Hugo Dempsey."

"I talked to some of Noah Parker's coworkers," Dermot said with a grunt. "They never mentioned he was a drug addict."

"Darlene claims Harvey was a recreational user. That he held a job and was responsible and reliable. Of course, she's his sister, so she could have blinders on."

"That's what all of Parker's coworkers said as well. They didn't know of a connection with Harvey Smith. This Hugo Dempsey is someone Harvey went to school with?"

"Yeah, he and Scott Van de Camp." I took a breath, my gaze following the kids. "Scott says some dealer came into the bar about a month ago and gave them all some new drug. Then he convinced the three of them to deal for them."

"At Sloan's place?" he cursed under his breath. "Sloan don't tolerate that shit."

So Dermot *did* know about the bar. "I got the impression Scott thinks Sloan could have murdered them."

He was quiet for a moment. "That makes sense. Only there's a slight problem. Based on your vision and Austin's story, the murderer was looking for something. A package."

"About that…"

"You know what it is?" he asked in surprise.

"No, but Darlene found an envelope her brother left at her house. It has a name—Thomas Benton—then Dallas, Texas, and a long number that starts with a lot of zeros. It looks like it might be some kind of bank account. Darlene has no idea who Thomas Benton is and says Harvey had never been to Dallas, let alone left the state of Arkansas. Do you think the paper could be the package the guys were looking for?"

"Could be, but it's strange they'd call it a package."

"Agreed." Mikey and Ashley started kicking a soccer ball around, while Hope sat on the bottom porch step with Muffy.

"Where is it now?"

"Darlene gave it to me. She said she didn't want it."

"Can you take a photo of it and text me?"

"Sure. I'll do it as soon as we get off this call."

"Great. For now, just hang on to it."

"Okay." Hope let out a squeal as Muffy licked her face. "Do you think the outsider who convinced Harvey and the others to sell his drugs could have killed them?"

"Sloan seems likelier, but I'm not ruling out the new dealer. And Sloan's been around long enough to know about the Lady in Black, so his guys could have been in your vision of Austin being hunted down in the woods."

A chill ran down my back. "How dangerous is this guy?"

"Dangerous enough that I'm checking him out as soon as we get off this call." He took a breath. "Where are you now?"

"At the farm."

"If Sloan's behind this, you're safe. He's under my control, and I'll make sure he knows you're off limits, so I'm pulling my guys off you."

"You're sure it was Sloan?"

"I'd feel better if Jed or your husband were there, just in case I'm wrong, but I need those men for another job."

"Jed's not here, but Neely Kate is on her way. Between the two of us, I think we'll be okay," I said. "We can hold our own."

"You've done it more times than I probably even know about. I'm gonna go have a chat with Derby Sloan and see where he stands. I'll be in contact."

"Thanks, Dermot."

"Yeah." He cleared his throat, then asked, "What do you plan to tell your husband?"

My head began to pound. "This seems too big to keep from him, but the only way I can get these people to talk is if I promise not to tell Joe and his staff."

"Which puts you between a rock and a hard place."

"Yeah. I take it Austin hasn't changed his mind about talking to me?"

"Nope."

"Have *you* convinced him not to talk to me?" I asked bluntly.

Silence hung over the line for a moment before he said, "While I haven't discouraged him from taking the call, I haven't encouraged him either. You've done your part to protect him. The rest should be up to me."

That ticked me off, but I kept my temper under control to ask my next question. "I also take it you haven't found out anything about the man or woman from my vision? Scott said he'd never seen either one of them, and he doesn't know a Selena."

"I haven't found out anything either. I'll be sure to let you know when I do."

"Will you?" I countered.

"It sounds like your life may be on the line," he grunted, "even if you're not the woman in the vision, so you can bet your ass I'll let you know what I find."

My heart softened a little. "Thanks, Dermot."

He hung up without saying goodbye, and I wondered if I was on the verge of alienating him. I'd never challenged him like this before, but I refused to be a pushover.

Despite where we stood—or maybe because of it—I took a photo of Harvey's paper and texted it to him.

It had been at least ten minutes since we'd gotten home, and Neely Kate still hadn't shown up despite her lengthy head start. Worry kept winding more tightly around me. What if something happened to her, Liam, and Daisy? I decided to call her and relieve my anxiety.

Neely Kate answered, sounding breathless. "We're on our way! We had a few mishaps that delayed us, but we're about five minutes from the farmhouse."

"What kind of mishaps?" Was she trying to ease me into something big?

"Liam woke up and had a huge blowout in his diaper. He soaked the car seat cover and, of course, his clothes. So I gave him a bath and tossed the car seat cover into the washer. He's wearing the change of clothes you had in the car."

"Oh my goodness! I'm so sorry!"

"No worries. Witt helped. In fact, he's coming over too. Jed insisted."

"Have you heard whether Jed's found anything yet?"

"No, but I know he planned on talking to Noah's family and coworkers."

Dermot had already done that, but then again, Dermot may have gotten his information from Jed. "I have some new information, but I'll tell you when you get here."

"Have you been investigating without me?" she asked, sounding irritated.

"It kind of fell into my lap."

"Hmm."

"I'll tell you all about it when you get here," I repeated.

Several minutes later, Neely Kate pulled my car into our driveway, with Witt's pickup truck following behind her.

While they parked, I got up and started down the steps to get Liam. But by the time I got down there, Witt was already out and at the back door of my Suburban.

"Uncle Witt!" my kids cried out, running for him, then hugged his legs.

"You're gonna knock me and your baby brother down," he said through his laughter. "I'll play with you, but let me get Liam out first."

They let go of his legs but only backed up a few feet.

The kids all loved "Uncle" Witt. They called him uncle despite the fact he was Neely Kate's cousin. Daisy called him Uncle Witt too. Witt reveled in his role. He still hadn't found someone to settle down with, but once he did, I knew he was going to make an amazing husband and father.

He got Liam out of his seat, saying something to make him laugh, then set my giggling son down on the ground. "Okay. What are we playing today?"

"Soccer!" Mikey shouted. "I'm on a *real* team, Uncle Witt!"

"So I heard," Witt said good-naturedly. "I heard you scored some goals too. You must have learned those mad skills from me. I'm gonna have to come to a game to watch my prodigy. I'll make your mom tell me when you're playing your next one."

I froze, realizing Witt had called me Mikey's mom, but no one seemed to notice other than me. I pushed out a sigh of relief. Mikey likely wouldn't care, but I worried about Ashley's reaction. I tried my best not to take her mother's place, even though I was their mother in every way but title. But judging by the neutral look on her face, she'd let it slide by too.

Daisy came running around the car to join the group, and Witt started dividing the kids into teams.

Neely Kate carried a paper grocery bag as she walked around the front of the car. "Here's the groceries you left in the cart."

"Thanks. I'll pay you back however much it cost," I said.

Hope jumped up and down, Muffy dancing at her feet. "Can Muffy play, Uncle Witt?"

"Of course she can. I already decided she's on your team," Witt said. "You two are a pair."

Hope beamed, and Witt turned to me. "You look like you could use a break. I've got the kids. Why don't you head inside and get a glass of wine or a margarita."

"A margarita?" I asked with a laugh.

"Or whatever drink you like. Have Lipton Earl tea, for all I care. Just let me take over for a bit."

Neely Kate propped a hand on her hip. "It's either Lipton or Earl Gray."

"Do I look like a fancy tea drinkin' guy?" Witt asked, mimicking drinking a cup with his pinky extended.

The kids started to laugh.

"Get out of here already," he said, motioning for us to go inside.

I hesitated. "Okay, but I'll take Liam inside."

"And steal my star teammate?" Witt demanded in mock outrage. "I think not."

The kids laughed again, and I reluctantly went inside. I needed to tell Neely Kate about everything that had happened since I'd gone back to the grocery store, and while I'd talked to Dermot on the porch, Neely Kate and I could discuss everything more freely if we were inside.

Neely Kate put my few groceries away while I poured us each a glass of iced tea, then we sat at the kitchen table. I told her about Darlene and my meeting with Scott. She listened, asking a few questions. Then I told her about my short conversation with Dermot.

"So this Derby Sloan guy might have killed those men?"

"Maybe," I said, swiping at the condensation on my glass.

"Dermot was going to talk to Sloan as soon as we finished the call."

"But if it's Sloan, it really doesn't have anything to do with Lady," she said. "That's kind of an internal problem, right?"

"Internal to Dermot's organization, true. The question is, what were the guys who killed the guy at Adkins looking for? Was it the paper Harvey left with his sister?"

"But that doesn't really qualify as a package, does it?"

"Maybe Dermot or Jed will find out when they question Derby Sloan and find the out-of-town dealer."

"I sure hope so."

The kids came barreling through the front door a few minutes later, with Witt trailing behind.

"We're hungry!" Mikey called out.

"We have an appet and we hungwy bears," Hope said, then she and Daisy held up their hands, making claws and growling.

"I think you mean appetite," I said with a laugh. It was about an hour or so from dinnertime, but I wasn't even sure what I was making yet. "And, of course, y'all can have a snack." I grinned at Witt. "You too."

"Yay!" Witt shouted, like he was one of the kids.

My phone rang again, and I was surprised to see Joe's name on the screen. I held up my phone so Neely Kate could see the screen.

She made a shooing motion. "You go ahead and talk to him. Witt and I can get their snacks."

"Thanks," I said, already walking toward the front porch as I answered. "Hey, Joe. How are things goin'?"

"Hey, darlin'," he said, sounding exhausted. "Not the greatest. I feel like I'm chasing my tail."

"I'm sorry." My guilt ratcheted up several notches. I suspected I had information that would help him, yet I didn't feel right telling him.

How had I gotten here? *Again.*

Sure, if I told Joe what I knew, I would damage my reputation as Lady forever, but it wasn't like I wanted to be the Lady in Black again. I had enjoyed my peaceful life since I'd left the criminal world behind.

Right?

I settled onto the porch swing. "Do you know when you'll be home?" I asked with sudden desperation to see him.

"No." He sounded disappointed.

"I miss you," I said, my voice breaking. "The kids do too."

"I miss you and the kids too."

"When you come home, I'll tell you all about the kids visiting Miss Mildred this afternoon."

He released a short chuckle. "Anyone lose a limb?"

I laughed. "Everyone's appendages are intact. It went really well, actually. She was happy to see them and was even sweet to Hope."

"You're kiddin'?"

"Nope."

"So what are y'all doin' right now?" he asked wistfully.

"Neely Kate, Daisy, and Witt came over. Witt wore the kids out playin' soccer, and Neely Kate's getting them a snack."

"Where's Jed?" he asked, suspicion creeping into his voice.

I couldn't very well tell him, but at least I had a convenient excuse. "Considering how he and Neely Kate aren't exactly seein' eye-to-eye right now, I'm not sure." Not a lie. I had no idea where Jed was or what he was specifically doing.

"I forgot about that." He paused. "How's she doin'?"

"She seems to be fine. Not even much morning sickness. I'll feel better after her doctor's appointment on Tuesday, though."

"Me too."

We sat in silence for a few seconds before he said, "I wish I were there with you."

"Me too."

"I don't know how late I'll be."

"It's okay. We're doin' okay. We miss you, but your job is important."

"Thanks for understandin'."

I was about to hang up, but I blurted out, "Did you find a connection between Harvey Smith and Noah Parker?"

He was silent for several seconds. "How do you know the second victim's name?"

"Please," I said, trying to blow it off. "It's a badly kept secret."

He was silent again. "Do *you* know of a connection?"

I was relieved that he didn't sound angry. He sounded intrigued.

"Someone should really talk to Harvey's sister."

"Someone already has," he said, sounding irritated.

"Are you sure? Because she says the only contact she's had with the sheriff's department was when some unsympathetic asshat showed up at her door to inform her that her brother was dead."

"You've been in contact with her?"

"I told you I ran into her at Dena's Bakery. I can't help it if she wanted to chat with me and Neely Kate again."

He groaned. "I don't suppose you plan to tell me what she said."

"Someone should have given her a real, respectful interview, and you doggone know it, Joe Simmons," I said sternly. "Send someone who will actually listen to her and offer her some sympathy, and maybe she'll talk to them." Then I added, "But don't go yourself. That'll look too obvious. Just have someone tell her they realized they never got a proper interview with her. It's still gonna look suspicious, but not as suspicious as if you go."

"I'll send Randy."

"Good," I said, feeling relieved. "She's a sweet girl, and Harvey was the last family she had. She needs someone who's gonna be sweet to her. Randy will be perfect."

"Anything else I should know?" he asked, and again, I was grateful he didn't sound pissed.

"Nothin' I can tell you at the moment, but I think Randy talking to Darlene and acting like he really cares about her and her brother will get you headed in the right direction."

"Do you know who killed Harvey Smith and the others?"

"Others? Are there more than three?"

"You didn't answer the question," he said.

"No," I answered honestly, even though I had a suspect in mind. "I don't know who killed them."

"Hmm..." he said, then sighed. "I'll send Randy to talk to her. Thanks for the tip."

"Joe, before you go..."

He waited for me to continue.

"Do you have an ID on the third victim?"

"No, do *you* have one?"

"Maybe look for Hugo Dempsey." Then I added, "But you didn't hear that from me."

I was prepared for him to be aggravated, but he simply said, "I love you."

"You're not gonna ask me how I know that?"

"Are you gonna tell me?" When I didn't answer, he released a soft chuckle. "That's what I figured. And if you got it from Harvey Smith's sister, then you weren't interfering with our investigation, especially if Detective Wiseman really didn't interview her. And," he added, drawing out the word, "I trust you."

I felt close to crying. "Thank you."

"I love you, Rose. I hate when we fight."

"I love you and hate when we fight too. Now solve those murders and come home to us."

Chapter Twenty-Six

I hung up and went back into the kitchen. The kids were sitting around the table, eating yogurt, and each of them had one of the cookies we'd made the day before. They wanted to save the cupcakes so they could show Joe. Neely Kate got up from the table and met me by the entrance, lowering her voice so the kids couldn't overhear us. "Everything okay? Did Joe say when he'd be home?"

"He's still not sure," I said, watching Liam smear his yogurt on his tray like he was finger painting. It was also all over his face and partially in his hair. "I told him we were just fine and not to worry about us. He's going to have Randy go talk to Darlene."

"You told him to do that?" Neely Kate asked in surprise.

I made a face and turned to look at her. "I may have pointed out that we talked to her, and she mentioned no one from the sheriff's department had given her a proper interview."

Neely Kate frowned. "It's still going to look suspicious."

"There's nothing to be done about it, and I don't regret telling him. He would have figured it out on his own, but it may have taken another day or so. I told him to send someone kind and understanding because the first guy was an asshat, so he's sending Randy. Hopefully, he'll get something Joe can use."

"While Dermot's working off what she told you? What if they cross paths?"

"Dermot will be just fine." I had no doubts about that.

When the kids finished their snacks, I pulled Liam from his highchair and took him upstairs for another bath. Neely Kate kindly offered to clean up the mess, while Witt took the other kids outside again to keep them entertained until dinner.

After I got Liam bathed and dressed, I headed back downstairs to figure out what to make for dinner. I had spaghetti and jar sauce and some frozen meatballs and broccoli. Spaghetti it was again…even though I'd just given Liam a bath.

After I had dinner made, we'd just sat down to eat when my phone rang. Dermot's name popped up on the screen.

"It's Dermot," I said to Neely Kate as I got up from my chair. "I'm going to take this in the living room. Have you heard anything from Jed yet?"

Worry covered her face. "No."

I headed out of the room as I answered. "Hey, Dermot. Got any news?"

"Hugo Dempsey is alive and well."

I stopped in my tracks. "Wait. *What?*"

"I talked to the man myself just a few minutes ago. He isn't the third murdered man."

"So who is?"

"Hell if I know, but it's not Hugo. However, I *did* find out the identity of the man who recruited Hugo and his two friends. Hugo only knows him as Kramer. Don't know if it's a first name or a last. Supposedly, he's been staying at some residential hotel down in Sugar Branch. I'm about to go find him now."

"Did Hugo mention anyone else selling with them?"

"Nope. Just the three of them."

"But this Kramer could have recruited someone from somewhere else, right?"

"Very true, but it all seems kind of odd. He's gonna have a

devil of a time gettin' anyone to work for him if he's murderin' his hired help this early in the game."

He wasn't saying anything I hadn't thought of myself.

"So you don't think Kramer killed them?"

"My money's on Sloan, although that's pretty stupid too, and it doesn't account for the third murder. But if he's trying to send a message, Hugo Dempsey heard it loud and clear. He's been in hiding since he found out his buddies were dead."

"So do you plan to talk to Sloan next?"

"After I track down Kramer. He may not have killed those men, but I want to know where he came from and why he chose this county. He needs to know he's stompin' on my turf, and if he's plannin' on stayin', he needs to pay his dues like everyone else."

"Do you think he's with Hardshaw?"

"No. I think Hardshaw's six feet under, but it doesn't mean some other cartel might not be trying to move in. There's plenty to go around."

My stomach sank. "How would they know about the Lady in Black?"

"She's a legend, Rose. People talk."

"Three years later?"

"If a new cartel is moving in, and they know Hardshaw met its end here, it would be prudent to know who or what helped lead to their downfall."

My panic started to rise. "I didn't bring them down, Dermot."

"But you did inadvertently." He paused. "I take it your husband's not home yet."

"You think I'm in danger?"

"I didn't when I thought this was all Sloan, but now…"

"You are?" I pressed.

"I'm gonna send Jed to stay with you."

"Dermot, one more thing." I hesitated, feeling like I was betraying Joe's trust, but his concern over my well-being assured me I could trust him. "Joe's sending a deputy to talk to Darlene. The deputy he's sending is a really nice, caring guy."

"You think I'd be stupid enough to do something to a sheriff's deputy?" he asked with a chuckle.

"Of course not," I assured him. "I'm just saying there's a good chance she'll open up to him and tell him everything she told me. If that happens, you two might cross paths."

He paused. "Thanks for the info."

"You're welcome."

I hung up and went back into the kitchen, Neely Kate's gaze tracking me as I entered the room and took my seat. Everyone was still sitting at the table, eating their dinner. Liam was already covered in spaghetti sauce, and based on the sauce smeared on the floor, half his food had dropped there—where Muffy was sitting in wait.

"Jed's coming over soon," I said, picking up my fork.

"Uncle Jed's comin' to see us?" Hope asked, sounding excited.

"Hey!" Witt protested. "What am I? Chopped liver?"

"What's chopped liver?" Mikey asked, his face scrunched up.

"Something disgusting," Ashley said.

Hope's eyes widened. "I don't think youwa disgustin', Uncle Witt."

"Well, thank you, Hopey," he said with a laugh.

I turned to Neely Kate and said, "Dermot had a chat with Hugo Dempsey."

Her eyes grew round as she realized what that meant. "You're kiddin'."

"Nope, and Hugo gave Dermot the name of his new friend. Dermot's gonna pay him a visit."

"That's good news," she said, looking cautious. "But he's still sending Jed to come hang out with us?"

"Yeah."

I expected Witt to protest that he was all the muscle we

needed, but instead he engaged the kids in playful banter during the rest of dinner.

After we finished eating, Witt took the kids into the living room while Neely Kate and I cleaned up. Now that little ears weren't around, I told her more about Dermot's call. It had been nearly forty-five minutes since I'd talked to him, and the fact Jed wasn't here yet had us both worried. Even if Jed had been at the bottom of the county by the Louisiana border, he still should have been here by now. I was about to suggest she call to check on him, but my own phone rang. I was surprised to see Bruce Wayne's name on the screen.

"Neely Kate's here with me," I said when I answered. "I put you on speaker."

"Good," he said, sounding tense. "I'm glad you're both there. I got a notification that the alarm went off in the landscaping office, so I went to check it out." He paused. "Someone broke in and trashed the place. They didn't take the computers or anything of worth, but it's obvious they were lookin' for something. I just don't know what."

I gasped and stared at Neely Kate.

There was only one thing I could think of that they'd be looking for.

Neely Kate and I said it at the same time.

"The package."

Chapter Twenty-Seven

"What package?" Bruce Wayne asked in surprise.

"The kid who showed up at the job site saw someone murdered over a package," I said, realizing Austin had told us about the package in the truck—out of Bruce Wayne's earshot. "If they found out Austin came to someone at RBW Landscaping, maybe they think we have it."

"Shit," Bruce Wayne said.

"Agreed," Neely Kate said, looking pale.

"Do you know what this package is that they're lookin' for?" Bruce Wayne asked.

"I'm not entirely sure what it is," I said, which was true, but I suspected the envelope in my purse was part of it.

"What about that box you dug up?" Bruce Wayne asked.

"No," I said. "I don't see how it could be that." I told him what we'd found.

"You're right," he said. "That doesn't make sense."

My mind was racing. "I need to call Joe."

"The sheriff's department is here," Bruce Wayne said. "But I haven't seen Joe."

"We should go down there," Neely Kate said.

"We can't take the kids," I said. "And I don't feel right leaving them with Witt." I took a breath. "Neely Kate, why don't you go down and take a look, and I'll stay here with the kids."

"Are you sure?" she asked in surprise.

"Yeah. You can check to see if anything's missing, and I'll call Joe. I'll have him meet you there."

Uncertainty filled her eyes, but I put a hand on her arm for reassurance. "I have no interest in seeing our office torn apart right now. With everything else goin' on, it would be the straw that breaks the camel's back. You know?" I asked as tears stung my eyes. "You go, and let me know what you find."

She grabbed her purse, then found Daisy in the living room and told her she'd be staying with me and Witt while Momma went to check on something in her office. Daisy was too busy building Legos with her cousins to be upset.

Neely Kate gave me one last look, then headed out the door.

Witt moved close to me and said under his breath. "What's goin' on?"

"Someone broke into our office."

He looked startled. "What?"

"Bruce Wayne got notice that the alarm went off, so he went to check it out. He said the place was trashed, but it didn't look like they stole anything. She went to see if she could figure out if anything was missing."

His brow lifted. "What do you think they were lookin' for?"

"I'm not sure," I said, not willing to get into it. "I'm gonna go out to the front porch and call Joe."

He nodded. "Go. I've got the kids."

I headed out the door and sat on the porch swing as I pulled up Joe's name on my phone and placed the call. It rang several times before he answered.

"It's not a good time, Rose. Can I call you back?"

"Sure, but I wanted to let you know that someone broke into the landscaping office. Bruce Wayne is there with a few sheriff's deputies, and Neely Kate went to see if anything's missing. Bruce

Wayne says the computers are still there. The place just looks trashed."

"*What?* I had no idea. Are you okay? Are you home alone with the kids?" He sounded alarmed.

"Witt's still here, and so is Daisy."

"Just sit tight. I'll send Randy out to stay with you."

"Do you think that's necessary? No one's threatened me," I said, but in truth, I was nervous we *were* in danger.

"You've been asking questions. Do you think someone could be lookin' for something you found?"

I hesitated, then said, "They might be lookin' for the note."

"What note?"

"Did Randy talk to Darlene?"

"Oh, for heaven's sake, Rose," he snapped. "Your life might be in danger. I don't want to play guessing games. What note?"

"Her brother left an envelope with a note inside. It had a man's name on it—Thomas Benton—with Dallas, Texas, written underneath and a long number. It looks like it might be a bank account."

"And you didn't tell me? There was a time we were on the same side," he said, sounding defeated.

"Yeah, when you quit the sheriff's department," I snapped back, then immediately felt guilty. "I'm sorry. I didn't mean that."

"But it's true," he said softly. "Are you planning to get back into the criminal world?"

"I didn't ask for any of this, Joe," I protested vehemently. "It came to *me*."

"That's not what I asked, now is it?"

"I'm sorry." It was all I could say because I didn't have an answer.

He was quiet for a moment. "I'll send Randy to the house. In the meantime, I'll head over to your office and check it out. I take it you're in possession of the note?"

"Yes," I said, fighting tears. "I didn't ask for it. She insisted I take it, and for the record, I've only had it a few hours."

"I'd appreciate it if you'd take a photo and send it to me. Randy can collect it as evidence once he gets there."

"I love you, Joe."

"I love you too. Stay safe, and hug and kiss our babies for me." Then he hung up.

I sat on the swing for a few moments, guilt threatening to consume me, but I couldn't change what I'd done. And if I were honest with myself, I wasn't sure that I would. The Austins and Darlenes in this county needed to know they could talk to someone who had their best interests in mind. From what I knew of the underworld, Dermot was fair, but I suspected some people might be reluctant to approach him because he was so powerful. But now I worried I'd destroyed that by telling Joe about the note. Deep down, I knew he needed to know, but would Darlene trust me after this? Would anyone else?

I went back inside and finished cleaning up the kitchen, then started to get the kids ready for bed. Witt offered to get Mikey ready while I bathed Hope, Daisy, and Liam in my bathtub.

I'd just gotten them out and dressed in pajamas when Mikey yelled, "Aunt Rose! The police are here with flashing lights!"

I hurried to Ashley's bedroom, which overlooked the front of the house, with a diapered Liam on my hip. Joe's car pulled to a halt in the driveway, his lights flashing. He jumped out of his car and ran for the front door. I rushed to the top of the stairs as the door opened.

"Rose!" Joe cried in panic.

"Up here," I said, staring down at him. "What's wrong?"

"I've been calling you for the past half hour. Why didn't you answer?"

"I've been getting the kids ready for bed," I said. "With Witt's help. I must have left my phone somewhere." Which seemed pretty stupid considering everything going on. I descended a couple of steps. "I didn't mean to scare you. Why are you so freaked out?"

"Witt?" Joe called out as he came up the stairs.

Witt appeared in Mikey's doorway. "Here."

"Can you take Liam?" Joe asked as he reached me and wrapped an arm around my back. "I need to talk to Rose for a moment."

"Of course," Witt said, holding his arms out for the baby and taking him from me.

"Joe," I said under my breath, "you're scaring me." A sudden thought hit me. "Is Neely Kate okay?"

"She's fine. She's with Jed." He ushered me down the hall. "Let's talk in our room."

"Daddy!" Hope called out from her bedroom doorway. "Youwa home! I missed you!" She ran to him and hugged his legs.

He leaned down and wrapped an arm around her shoulders. "I need to talk to Momma for a minute, then I'll give you lots of hugs when we're done, okay?"

She looked up at him, her bottom lip sticking out in a pout. "But I have to go to bed."

"I won't be very long. You can wait up for me."

"Me too, Uncle Joe?" Mikey called from his bedroom doorway.

"Everyone gets to wait up, even Liam," Joe said, then took my hand. "We'll be out in a few minutes."

He tugged me down the hall to the bedroom, then shut the door behind us before leading me over to the bed. He sat on the edge, and I sat beside him.

"Joe, you're scarin' the crap out of me."

He took my hand and looked me in the eye. "We IDed the body we found by Shute Creek." He paused. "He was one of your employees."

My brain was scrambling as I tried to process what he'd just said. "*What?* Who?"

"Jeremiah Stone."

It took a second for the name to register. "He's one of Bruce Wayne's new hires."

"That's what Bruce Wayne said. He said he'd only been working for you for about three weeks." He paused again. "He had a record."

I nodded. I didn't know the specifics of what Jeremiah had done, but Bruce Wayne liked to give men on probation a chance. He said the second chance I'd given him had changed his life, and he wanted to pay it forward by helping other people find their way out of trouble. "Bruce Wayne won't take anyone with a history of any sort of violence." That was one of his hard and fast rules.

"Jeremiah Stone had some petty theft and drug convictions. He'd been in rehab a couple of times."

"Do you think he's tied to Harvey Smith's and Noah Parker's murders?"

"It seems the most logical explanation, but the break-in at your office worries me. Neely Kate says nothing appears to be missing. Whoever broke in was obviously lookin' for something, though, and I'm not sure it was the note Harvey left at his sister's house."

I ran through Austin's account of the murder he'd witnessed.

"Jeremiah's murderers were lookin' for some kind of package."

Joe's brow lifted, but he remained silent.

I closed my eyes and ran through my options. I wanted to keep Austin's secrets, but I could be at risk. My *kids* could be at risk. They had to come first. Always.

I opened my eyes, tears making his face fuzzy. "I think I know a witness to Jeremiah's murder."

Was it a freak coincidence that Austin had sought out the Lady in Black the day after Jeremiah's murder? Or that he'd asked to speak to Bruce Wayne, who'd been Jeremiah's direct supervisor?

"Like I told you, a kid showed up at one of our job sites, searching for Bruce Wayne because he thought Bruce Wayne had a connection to the Lady in Black. Bruce Wayne called me, and the kid said he had witnessed a murder. He was scared and wanted protection."

Joe's thumb slowly rubbed the back of my hand.

"The kid was belligerent at first, not that I was surprised. He was scared. He said the murderers saw him and tried to catch him, but he hid from them and walked back into town to find me."

"How'd he know where to go?"

"He said a friend told him to go to Lady for help, and he knew Lady had a connection to the landscaping company. The kid looked us up on Facebook and saw that our client that day had tagged the business."

Joe nodded but didn't look pleased.

"I already told you that I tried multiple times to get him to talk to you, but he refused, threatening to leave because he was scared of the treatment he'd get from the sheriff's department."

Joe's lips pursed. "Convenient story."

"Is it?" I countered, but without any heat. "Detective Wiseman lied to you about interviewing Darlene." I tilted my head. "Did *Randy* talk to her?"

"Yeah." He ran a hand through his hair. "The information she gave us would have been helpful a couple of days ago."

"See? He's not the only one who feels that way. So it's not so far-fetched that this boy was telling the truth."

"Maybe," Joe said, worry filling his eyes. "What happened to the kid?"

"Dermot took him to one of his safe houses. But we questioned him together at the jobsite, and with the information he gave us, Dermot confirmed that some kind of crime had taken place, even though there wasn't a body."

"Where'd this take place?"

"Adkins."

Joe released my hand and sat up straighter. "You think it was Jeremiah, and they moved the body."

"The kid said he saw them shoot the man in the head."

"And Jeremiah had a gunshot to the head."

I took a breath to settle my nerves. "The kid said they kept asking Jeremiah where the package was. He kept telling them he didn't know. Neely Kate and I don't think the paper Harvey left with his sister is what they were looking for. It's hard to call a paper a package."

"Maybe, maybe not," Joe said, getting a faraway look in his eyes. "It could be one piece of a larger whole."

"Do you think Jeremiah knew Harvey and Noah?" I asked.

Joe shook his head. "I have no idea. I had no idea there was a connection between Harvey and Noah until a few hours ago, after you steered me to Darlene. We just found out Jeremiah's name. I don't know anything about his personal life, and neither did Bruce Wayne." He took a deep breath and turned to face me, picking up my hand again. "I'm worried you and the kids are in danger. What if the guys who are looking for the kid think you have what they are looking for? They searched the office and didn't find it, so what if they come here next?'

I swallowed hard. I wanted to tell him he was wrong, but the break-in coming on the heels of Jeremiah's murder was too big of a coincidence. Still…Austin had only come to me *after* the murder.

"Do you think there's any chance this has something to do with the box Neely Kate and I found?"

He considered my question. "I don't see how. Harvey was murdered before you found the box." He made a face. "Maybe we should open it and see what's inside."

"We already did. There was a love letter from a guy to a girl, a goodbye letter, an empty locket, and about a quarter-carat solitaire engagement ring."

"Anything incriminating in the love letters?"

"Only that they were star-crossed lovers. Her dad and his mom didn't approve of their relationship, so he moved to Montana and told her to come find him."

"Any names we can track down?"

"There are only initials in the notes, but a woman called me this afternoon and told me she was friends with two teenage girls who lived in the house next door. The woman thinks one of the girls might have buried the box. Her name was Sarah, and her boyfriend was named Jason. She said Jason's dad was a sheriff's deputy. Sarah's father had several arrests. So it could fit."

"No last names?"

"She struggled to remember Jason's first name, let alone last ones."

"I'd sure love to track them down and have a chat."

"The woman said her parents moved them away because Sarah and her sister Luna were bad influences. But she says she heard years later that Sarah had died, and her sister had moved to California."

"Did she know how Sarah died?"

"No."

"So it could have been an accident or natural causes." He took a deep breath and pushed it out. "Again, it seems unlikely this has anything to do with the box, but I should probably take a look at it. But regardless of what these people are after, I'm worried you and the kids might be in danger."

"So what do we do? Do you want to put a deputy on guard duty?"

He squeezed my hand tighter. "No. I want to send y'all away for a while." He gave me a sad smile. "I want you to go stay with your Aunt Bessie and Uncle Albert in Lafayette County until this blows over."

"But Ashley and Mikey have school tomorrow."

"They're smart kids. They can miss a couple of days, and besides, with the issues Ash has been having lately, a few days away might do her some good."

"What about Neely Kate and Daisy? Neely Kate is as much a part of this as I am."

"I've already talked to Jed. He considered taking them somewhere himself, but he doesn't want to leave town. He wants to stick around and see this through, so we think it's best if they go with you."

I nodded, still trying to wrap my head around everything. "I need to call Aunt Bessie and make sure it's okay. We can leave in the morning."

"I already called her, and she's getting things ready for you now. I want you to go tonight."

"Tonight?"

"Jed and Neely Kate went to their house to pick up some things for the girls. Then they're heading over here. We're gonna take two cars, and then I'm gonna ride back with Jed."

"You're gonna take us?" I asked in surprise. "But you've got so much goin' on here."

He cupped my cheek. "Rose, you and the kids are the most important things in my life. You will always be my priority. I can be gone for a few hours."

"But you're exhausted."

"I'll catch some sleep on the ride back with Jed." He leaned closer and gave me a soft, lingering kiss. "I wish I could stay with you there…"

"You need to catch whoever is murderin' people," I said, my voice firm. "We'll be fine at Aunt Bessie's, but I don't want to worry the kids, so I think we should tell them we're taking a little mini vacation with their aunt."

"Ash isn't gonna totally buy it," he said, looking grim.

"She's too smart for her own good, so I'll feel my way with her."

"Okay."

I leaned back. "I have to pack. I haven't done laundry in days. I don't know if the kids have enough clean clothes."

"Good thing your aunt and uncle have a washing machine and dryer," Joe teased as he slid off the bed. He pulled me up and wrapped his arms around me, pulling my body flush to his. "I love you so damned much, Rose."

"You're not mad I kept all that from you?"

He held me tighter. "I wish you had told me sooner, but I understand. Thank you for trusting me enough to tell me now." He gave me another kiss, then dropped his hold on me and walked into the hall. "Okay, everybody!" he said. "I have an announcement!"

The kids quickly appeared in the hallway, their eyes shiny with anticipation. Witt stood in Liam's doorway, holding him on his hip.

"I have something exciting to tell you," Joe said, sounding like he was about to announce that we were headed to Disney World. "You have ten minutes to pack and get ready to go to Aunt Bessie and Uncle Albert's house! Mikey, pull out clothes for three days, and put them on your bed. Ashley, you can pack yourself. I'll pack for Hope, and Momma's gonna pack for herself."

"Can I go too, Uncle Joe?" Daisy asked, in her sweet little voice, standing next to Hope.

"Yep! Your momma's gettin' your clothes, then she's comin' with you."

"Can Muffy come?" Hope asked. Muffy, who sat at her feet, let out a forlorn little whine.

"Of course Muffy's comin'," I said. "We wouldn't dream of leaving her behind."

"But we're in our pajamas!" Mikey protested with a laugh.

"You don't need to change," Joe said. "You can go in your PJs."

"It's a pajama party!" I said, trying to make this impromptu trip fun and not scary.

"Yay!" the little girls called out in unison.

"So get packin'!" Joe said. "Now you have *nine* minutes."

The kids ran back into their rooms, although Ashley hesitated for a moment in the doorway before turning inside.

Joe turned to Witt. "Can you grab a bunch of stuff for Liam?"

Witt's forehead burrowed with concern, but he nodded. "Of course. Three days?"

"Hopefully that's enough."

Witt turned his back to the hallway and lowered his voice. "I take it that it's bad?"

"The third murder victim was someone on Bruce Wayne's landscape crew," Joe said.

Witt's eyes widened. "Shit. Are you stayin' with 'em at Rose's aunt's house?"

Pain crossed Joe's eyes, but he shook his head. "I wish I could, but I think I could serve them better by trying to catch the people who did this."

Witt nodded. "Then I'm goin'."

Joe studied him for a moment, his gaze flicking to our son, who was snuggled into Witt's side. He nodded. "Thank you."

Witt gave him a grim nod, then turned around and announced to Liam that he was going on vacation, and they needed to pack.

Joe turned to me, guilt filling his eyes.

"Don't look like that," I said, cupping his cheek. "You're doin' the right thing by staying."

"My head says I am, but my heart…"

"Daddy!" Hope called out. "Can I take my tutu?"

Joe released a chuckle. "Duty calls." But he still looked torn, like he could hardly bear looking away from me.

"Go pack clothes for our daughter that won't make my sister roll over in her grave," I said with a small laugh. "Meet you in *eight* minutes."

He gave me another kiss, then turned and walked away.

Chapter Thirty-Eight

After we got everyone packed and their luggage downstairs, I showed Joe the box in his office.

"See?" I said as he took out the contents and looked them over. "Nothing special."

"I agree. And it's not like they could have known you were going to dig up the box. It's just a coincidence." He put everything back inside and closed the lid. "But if you have that note that Harvey left with his sister, I'd like to take it to the station."

"Of course. It's in my purse."

I found my purse in the living room and handed the paper to him just as Jed and Neely Kate walked through the front door. Daisy ran to them, jumping up and down with excitement. "We're goin' on a trip! We get to go to a farm!"

"We sure do," Neely Kate said, trying to match her daughter's enthusiasm, but she shot me a worried glance over her daughter's head.

The guys grabbed the luggage and basket of dirty laundry and started to pack the car. The kids went out with them and began to pile in my Suburban.

"How bad was the office?" I asked Neely Kate.

"It's pretty ransacked. They were definitely looking for something."

"Joe thinks it was the package the killers were looking for when they shot the man at Adkins."

"You told him?" Neely Kate asked in surprise.

"Our kids' lives are at stake. I had to."

She nodded. "What about the box?"

"I told Joe we opened the box and showed him the contents. He doesn't think that's what they were lookin' for since Harvey was killed before we found it."

"Jed thinks the same thing." Then she added, "Joe doesn't want it for evidence?"

"He didn't say he did."

She nodded. "I need to go to the bathroom before we go. Pregnancy hormones."

I headed out to the car to help Joe get the kids buckled in, but he and Witt seemed to have the situation under control. Muffy settled in on the floor between Hope and Liam. After Neely Kate came out with her purse slung over her shoulder a few minutes later, Joe turned on the alarm and locked up the house. Once he was in the driver's seat of my Suburban, we took off. Jed followed, driving Neely Kate and Daisy, and Witt took up the rear in his own car.

The kids stayed awake during the hour and fifteen-minute drive. I was glad I wouldn't have to wake them and try to get them asleep again after we got to Aunt Bessie's, but it also meant that I wouldn't get any time for adult conversation with Joe. I'd hardly seen him for days, and the dark circles under his eyes worried me.

Aunt Bessie's farmhouse was lit up both inside and out when we got there. She must have been watching for us because she walked out the front door onto the porch as we pulled up. Uncle Albert was only steps behind her. They were both smiling, but I could see the worry in their eyes.

The kids were excited to be there and ran up the porch steps to give my aunt and uncle hugs. They hurried into the house after

Aunt Bessie told them she had some freshly baked cookies waiting in the kitchen.

Joe carried Liam up the stairs, while I greeted my aunt and uncle. "Thanks for letting us crash in on you like this," I said as I hugged my aunt.

"We're so happy to have you. It's just unfortunate it's under these circumstances." She gave Joe a questioning look.

"I'm working on it, Aunt Bessie," he said. "In the meantime, thank you for giving Rose and our kids a safe place to stay."

She gave him a curt nod, then turned back to me. "You're *always* welcome here. I don't have enough beds, but I figured you and Neely Kate can each get your own room, and the bigger kids can have the fourth room. I have some air mattresses the kids can sleep on in your rooms and the living room, if they like."

"I brought a Pack 'N Play for Liam," Joe said, "so you don't have to worry about him."

"Got it right here," Witt said, walking up from the back of the Suburban with the bed slung over his shoulder and a couple of duffel bags. "Just tell me where to put them, Miss Bessie."

"None of that Miss Bessie nonsense," my aunt said with a laugh. "How many times do I have to tell you it's either Bessie or Aunt Bessie?"

"Then it's Aunt Bessie," Witt said. "Because my granny would skin me alive if I called you by only your first name. Now, which room am I putting these in?"

"The room at the top of the stairs on the left," Aunt Bessie said. "It's slightly bigger, so I figured there'd be more room for the baby."

Witt gave her a wink, then headed inside.

"How many girlfriends has that boy been though?" my aunt asked with a chuckle.

"Surprisingly, fewer than you'd think," I said, watching him through the door. "By the way, he's staying too."

"Oh?"

"Just an added insurance," Joe said. "He can sleep on the sofa."

"Do you anticipate trouble?" Aunt Bessie asked, glancing nervously down the gravel drive to the main road.

Joe shook his head. "No. We weren't followed, and no one knows they're here. But Witt insisted, and I'm not gonna tell him no."

"Then we'll just have a houseful, and it will be *wonderful*," my aunt said, looking like she meant every word. "Come on in."

Joe handed Liam to me. "Rose, you go in and see if Witt got the crib set up, and I'll bring in the rest of the bags."

Witt was struggling to figure out Liam's portable bed, so I took over and put him in charge of getting the mattresses blown up.

Within twenty minutes, we'd figured out where everyone was sleeping, and the kids' teeth had been brushed again. They'd all missed Joe, so they talked his ear off with everything they'd been up to over the last couple of days. Daisy was sleeping with Neely Kate, so Joe and I got Mikey, Ashley, and Hope tucked into the kids' room. Liam fussed a bit about going to bed, but Joe began pacing with him in my bedroom and shooed me away. As I walked out, I heard Joe telling him that he and Daddy would have a day together soon. My heart swelled, ready to burst.

When I went downstairs, Aunt Bessie was making up a bed for Witt on the sofa, while he protested he could make it himself. Neely Kate and Jed were nowhere to be found, presumably spending some time together in Neely Kate's room.

There was no way I could sleep anytime soon, and I needed something to do, so I heated up some water for tea. Joe walked into the kitchen about five minutes later, just as I was pulling a tea bag from my cup.

"Want some tea?" I asked as I dumped the tea bag into the trash. "I heated up enough water."

He walked to me, took me into his arms, and pulled me close. "I love you so damn much, Rose Gardner Simmons."

I wrapped my arms around his back and held him tight. "I love you too. I'm sorry that my past has put us in danger."

He leaned back and stared down at me, shaking his head. "Your past is part of you, and I love every part. And that part of your past did a lot of good. We just need to figure out how it fits into the life we have now."

Tears stung my eyes. "Oh, Joe. I was so scared you wouldn't forgive me for putting us in danger."

"You didn't put us in danger. Whoever is murdering people put us in danger."

I placed my cheek on his chest. The steady thud of his heartbeat in my ear soothed something deep in my soul.

"Have you had any more visions of the woman being murdered?"

"No. Nothing. I even tried to have another vision with Neely Kate this morning."

"I wonder if you changed it."

"Maybe." But it felt like wishful thinking, especially since we still had no notion of who she was or who she might be connected to.

Joe kissed the top of my head. "I need to go soon. I don't want to, but…"

"I know," I said, pulling back and looking up at him. "I don't want you to go either, but I want you to stop this person."

"Thanks for the new information. I already have Randy lookin' into things."

"I don't suppose he had a chance to look up anything on Selena or find out anything more about the guy I saw in my vision?"

He gave me a squeeze. "No. I've had him workin' on other things, but we ran both drawings through a couple of databases and came up with nothing. There's not much else we can do."

I nodded. "That's okay. Like you said, I haven't had another vision. So maybe we did change things."

"But that doesn't mean I can't have Jed workin' on it."

I stared up at him with wide eyes. "What?"

"Jed's not part of my department, which means he can work on whatever he wants. That's why he's comin' back with me." He tilted his head. "Do you think he'd leave Neely Kate and Daisy if he didn't have a good reason?"

I knew Jed had been sleuthing, but I thought it had been to help Dermot. Maybe he was working with both of them.

"You two are a force to be reckoned with," I said. "You'll find who's responsible in no time."

"And now we have the added incentive of protecting the people we love more than anything in the world. There's no motivator more powerful than that."

I gave him a grim smile.

"Ready?" Jed said in a rough voice from the doorway into the kitchen.

"Walk me out?" Joe asked with a hopeful look in his eyes.

"Of course."

He took my hand, and we headed through the living room to the front door. Jed had already gone outside, and there was no sign of Witt until we walked onto the porch and found the two men huddled at the back of Neely Kate's car.

Joe cupped my cheek and tilted my head back, then gave me a kiss that expressed his love and fear.

"We'll be okay," I said when he lifted his head.

"I brought the shotgun. It's locked in a case in the garage. Don't hesitate to get it out if you feel threatened."

My stomach roiled. "Okay."

He kissed me again. "Keep your phone with you so I can check on you regularly."

"I will."

He nodded, dropped his hand, and walked down the steps. He

got into the car as Jed climbed into the driver's seat. Joe kept his eyes forward and didn't look back.

I watched the car travel the long gravel driveway, and as they turned onto the main road and their brake lights disappeared, I realized Joe hadn't said goodbye.

Chapter Twenty-Nine

The next morning was chaos. The kids had no idea what was going on and were excited to be somewhere new—especially on a school day. Uncle Albert told them he'd take them on a tractor ride after breakfast, so they wolfed down their scrambled eggs and bacon, took their plates to the sink, and met Uncle Albert at the barn. Witt said he wanted to see what the fuss was about and insisted on carrying Liam out with him. Liam was thrilled to be outside with everyone else.

Once the house cleared out, Neely Kate and I told Aunt Bessie that we had the kitchen cleanup covered, and she should go relax. She started to protest, then said she'd take her knitting out to the front porch and encouraged us to join her when we finished.

As I started rinsing dishes and putting them into the dishwasher, I realized I hadn't told Neely Kate what I'd learned about the box.

"I think I found out who buried the box."

She stopped in the middle of the kitchen, two plates in one hand and a syrup bottle in the other. Wide-eyed, she asked. "When? How?"

I told her about the call and the suspected identities of J and S.

Her face brightened with excitement. "So we just need to find Sarah."

I grimaced. "There's a problem with that. The woman said Sarah died a while back, and her sister Luna moved to California."

"How'd she die?"

"She didn't know. She'd heard it secondhand. But it sounds like maybe we've hit the end of the road."

She was quiet for a moment. "What about the boy? Jason? Maybe he'd want it back."

"Maybe," I agreed. "But we don't have any last names."

"If they went to school together, we could look up their names in old yearbooks."

"We could," I agreed. "Or we could just let it go. It might be too painful for Jason to get the letters and ring."

"Or maybe she's his long-lost love, and he would like to have a last piece of her."

I set a plate into the dishwasher. "Let's think about it. But I think this proves whoever broke into the office wasn't looking for the box. I mean, the person who broke in could have just told us it was theirs, and we would have willingly handed it over."

Scowling, she mumbled, "Maybe not so willingly, but yeah."

"When this is all done, we can look up the yearbooks," I said, hoping to cheer her up. "If we can figure out who Jason is, then we'll decide where to go from there."

"Okay," she said, sounding a little more encouraged. "Deal."

After we finished the cleanup, we joined Aunt Bessie on the porch. Uncle Albert had pulled his tractor out from behind the barn to give each of the kids a ride, while Witt kept the others corralled.

"Joe gave me a brief run-down of what was going on when he called," Aunt Bessie said as her knitting needles clacked in the quiet. "But I'd like to hear it from you."

I shot a glance at Neely Kate. Aunt Bessie had no idea about my Lady in Black history, so I told her that one of our employees had been murdered and our office had been ransacked. Since we had no idea why, Joe had thought it best if we left the county for a few days.

After I finished, she was silent for several seconds before she glanced up from her knitting and looked me in the eye. "I know there's more you're not telling me."

"Actually," Neely Kate said, "there is."

I shot her a warning look, but she said, "Rose has been having weird visions."

Aunt Bessie looked startled. "Weird visions? How so?"

I told her that two of them had been dreams that I'd been unable to reproduce with anyone. And I also mentioned I'd been completely alone when I'd had one of them.

"How did Rose's grandmother's visions work?" Neely Kate asked.

"Much like Rose's. She had to be with the person in the vision, but..." She paused her knitting and set it in her lap as she turned to face me. "There was one person she didn't have to be with to have a vison of."

Neely Kate leaned forward, her eyes bright with excitement. "Who?"

A troubled look crossed my aunt's face. "Her sister."

I shook my head. "Violet's dead, and I never had a vision of her when she was alive. At least, not one when I wasn't close to her."

"It was a rare thing, and it only happened twice." She paused and held my gaze. "Both times were when her sister was in danger."

Neely Kate gasped. "Oh my stars and garters! The woman in Rose's visions looked like her!"

Aunt Bessie's eyebrows rose.

"But I don't have another sister," I protested. "Or, at least, not a living one."

Neely Kate ignored me, focusing on my aunt. "Rose had a sketch made." She pulled her phone out of her pocket and swiped on the screen. "Look. It's obvious it's not her, but it definitively *looks* like her." She got out of her chair and reached over to hand the phone to my aunt.

Aunt Bessie took it and stared at the screen. "Rose, how old would you say this woman was?"

My heart sped up. "Do I have a cousin somewhere I don't know about?"

"She looks to be about twenty-five or twenty-six," Aunt Bessie murmured, studying the phone screen and then glancing up at me. "Does that sound about right?"

I swallowed the lump in my throat. "I suppose."

"What was her name?"

I shook my head. "I don't know. The woman I had the vision of was called Selena, and neither she nor the man called the murdered woman by name." Aunt Bessie's gaze dropped to the phone again.

"Aunt Bessie. This is crazy. I don't have another sister."

She took a deep breath and held out the phone to Neely Kate, who got up from her seat and took it. We both stared at my aunt in anticipation of her response.

Aunt Bessie reached for her glass of water and took a big swig before setting it down. "You might."

My head grew fuzzy, and I took a deep breath, hoping to clear it. "What are you talking about? This woman looked like she's younger than me."

Aunt Bessie nodded with a grave expression. "And she *would* be younger. By about three years."

I couldn't believe what I was hearing. "What? Daddy left Momma a *second* time?"

"No," she said, slowly shaking her head. "He didn't leave, but he stepped out on her when you were about two. Your momma never figured it out, but the woman he was seeing was crazier than a barn cat high on diesel fumes. She told your daddy she was pregnant, and if he didn't leave your mother and marry her, she was leavin' town, and he'd never see his child."

"So what happened?" Neely Kate asked.

Aunt Bessie sighed as she shrugged. "He stayed with Agnes, and the woman made good on her word and left town. Your father thought she was makin' the whole pregnancy story up, but about a year later, she sent a card with a photo of a baby that she claimed was his daughter. Your father came to me for advice. I told him he needed to man up and accept his responsibility in the matter. Although he wasn't happy with Agnes, he knew he didn't want to be with the momma of his third child. So in the end, he convinced himself the woman was lying and said it could be a picture of *anyone's* baby." Aunt Bessie's voice was shaking. "But I saw the resemblance to you and Violet. When I pointed that out, he got angry and said all children look alike and accused me of being unsupportive."

"What did the woman want?" I asked, finally finding my voice. "The mother of the baby?"

Aunt Bessie's eyes teared up. "She told him she was gonna give the baby up if he didn't send her five thousand dollars. And since he'd convinced himself she was lying, he ignored the letter."

"She gave the baby up for adoption?" Neely Kate asked in dismay.

Aunt Bessie shook her head. "I have no idea. We never heard from her again. Or, at least, if he did, he never told me."

"Did Momma ever find out?" I asked.

"No, your father was terrified she would and swore me to secrecy. I've never told another living soul—your uncle included—until now."

I couldn't believe what I was hearing. I'd been in shock at the news, but now I was overcome with anger. "Daddy knew he had another child, and he didn't *care?*"

"He said he didn't believe her, although I'm not sure if his denial was because he truly thought it was a lie or because he couldn't muster the strength to step forward."

I took a moment to let her news sink in. "So my father was a serial cheater, and he abandoned his child." Then again, he'd very nearly abandoned me after my birth mother had died. He couldn't handle his grief and had brought me to Aunt Bessie and Uncle Albert. The only reason I hadn't been raised by them was because Momma had convinced him to take her back, partly by swearing she'd raise me as her own. She'd lied, but then he hadn't seemed to care and had ignored her abuse.

Then a new thought hit me. "Did he cheat with other women?"

"I don't think so, but after my reaction to his dismissal of your younger sister, I doubt he would have come to me again to tell me about others." She sighed. "He only told me about this instance because she told him she was pregnant."

"Did the guy never hear about condoms?" Neely Kate muttered under her breath.

She had a point.

I suddenly realized what this meant. "So the woman I've seen murdered is *my sister*?" I asked in horror. "How do I save her? Do you remember her mother's name?"

"I only remember her first name—Stacy—and that the card came from Austin, Texas."

Texas? My panic began to swell, but I reminded myself that Texas was a huge state, and it was probably just a coincidence. "No last name?"

Aunt Bessie made a face. "Honestly, I don't know it. If it was on the card, I've since forgotten. I'm sorry."

"What about the baby's name?" Neely Kate asked.

"I think it was a flower name, but I've forgotten that too."

"So how do I save her, Aunt Bessie?" I asked, my voice breaking.

"Maybe you already did," she said. "Maybe that's why you haven't had any more visions."

"Or she's already dead." Because I hadn't done *anything* that could have saved her. I'd been looking for her in Fenton County, but she could be *anywhere*.

I'd just learned about my sister and possibly lost her at the same time.

"We don't know for sure that the woman in your visions is your sister," Neely Kate said. "This could be a total coincidence."

Sorrow overcame me as I turned to her and asked in disbelief, "You don't really believe that, do you?'

She made a face. "You truly believe you have a sister you never knew about?"

"*You* had a sister and a brother you didn't know anything about until a few years ago," I countered. "Why does this seem so far-fetched? How do you explain my visions?"

She sat back in her seat. "I don't know."

I didn't know either, and that was the problem.

"Have a vision," Neely Kate said, holding out her hand to me. "See if I ever meet her."

"*I* may never meet her, even if she's still alive," I said through my tears.

"You won't know unless you try. If you don't see anything, it won't mean she's dead, and if you *do* see something…" She smiled at me.

Nodding, I reached over and took her hand, asking the universe if I would ever meet my sister.

The vision was hazy, but I could see my face lit up with joy. "I found her, Neely Kate! I found her!"

Then I was back on the front porch, blurting out, "I found her" before I broke down into tears.

I had a sister, and she hadn't been killed. I had to trust that meant something had changed, and someday I would meet her.

UNCLE ALBERT AND WITT KEPT THE KIDS BUSY UNTIL LUNCH. They poured into the kitchen, filthy and happy. Even Ashley was having fun, and I was grateful she wasn't stewing over missing school and falling behind on her assignments. I assured her that I'd contacted the principal about her absence. He'd told me that Mrs. Pritchard was on leave until further notice, and the substitute would send Monday's assignments in an email later that day.

The kids had lunch, and we convinced the younger ones to take a short rest. Neely Kate was upstairs taking a nap, and Witt was doing who knew what with Uncle Albert outside. I felt like Ashley needed a little alone time with me and asked if she'd like to make bread with me in the kitchen, to which she eagerly agreed.

"Where did you learn to make bread, Aunt Rose?" Ashley asked as we added the ingredients together.

"Aunt Bessie taught me."

"Did she teach Momma too?"

"She did, but your momma wasn't terribly interested in baking bread. She much preferred making sweet things, like cookies and cake."

Ashley grew quiet as we took turns kneading the dough. Had I upset her by talking about Violet?

"Are you okay, Ash?" I finally asked as I stepped away from the dough to let her knead for a couple of minutes.

"Yeah." But she kept her gaze on the task in front of her.

"I know you're worried about missing school, but is there anything else you're worried about?" I paused. "Like the reason we came to visit Aunt Bessie and Uncle Albert?"

She glanced up at me with wide eyes.

I gave her a warm smile. "You're a smart girl. You would know this isn't an ordinary situation." When she didn't respond, I asked, "Do you have any questions about what's goin' on?"

She shrugged, her gaze still on the dough. "I know that some men were murdered and that one of them worked for you and Mr. Bruce Wayne. Uncle Joe thinks they might break into our house since they broke into your office, so that's why we're here."

She understood more than I'd expected, but again, she was an observant girl, and we hadn't been careful about some of it. "Yes. Uncle Joe thinks the bad men were lookin' for something, and for some reason, they think Neely Kate and I might have it. So Joe and Uncle Jed thought it would be better for us to stay at Aunt Bessie's until they catch the bad guys."

"Have they caught them yet?"

"No, but they're working really hard to do just that."

She was silent for a moment before she asked in a hushed voice. "Did my dad work for those bad men?"

My heart caught in my throat. I hated that she had to worry about that. "No, Ash. He worked for someone else, and those people are in prison too. I don't think they'll ever get out."

"But my daddy will."

"Yes. If he continues to be a model prisoner, there's a chance he might get out a year before you graduate from high school."

She was quiet again, the only sound the dough slapping against the counter. She looked up at me with tear-filled eyes. "Do Mikey and me have to live with him when he gets out?"

My jaw dropped, and I wasn't sure how to respond. Finally, I came to my senses. "You don't want to live with him?"

She slowly shook her head. "He scares me."

"Oh, Ash," I said, covering her hand with my own. "Your daddy would never, *ever* hurt you." I nearly told her that part of the reason he'd done what he'd done was to protect her and her brother, but she didn't need that burden.

"I just want to live with you and Uncle Joe."

"You and Mikey can live with us however long you want." I smiled through my tears. "You can live with us until you're forty-two, if you like."

Her nose wrinkled. "That's old."

"Not as old as you think," I said with a laugh. "But I want you and your brother to know that you are as important to us as Hope and Liam, and your home is with us for however long you want it to be. You may be my niece, but you're just like a daughter to me. I will never, *ever* take your momma's place, and I don't want to try, but I love you all the same."

She nodded slowly. "Do you think Momma would be mad if I called you Mom?"

My eyes and throat burned.

She hastily added. "It's weird that me and Mikey call you Aunt Rose and Uncle Joe, but Hope and Liam call you Momma and Daddy." She shrugged, trying to play it off. "It might be easier to say you're my mom instead of telling people I live with my aunt."

"I would be *honored* for you to call me Mom. And Joe would be thrilled for you to call him Dad. But just because you call us that doesn't mean your Momma isn't your Momma, and the same with your dad. Some people are lucky enough to have two moms and two dads."

She nodded. We finished kneading the dough, then placed it in an oiled bowl and covered it with a tea towel. After Ashley washed the flour and dough off her hands, she wrapped her arms around me and said, "I love you, Mom."

I choked back a sob and croaked out, "I love you too, Ash."

Then she hurried out of the room, carrying a piece of my heart with her.

Chapter Thirty

The kids were exhausted by dinnertime. With their late night the day before and Uncle Albert and Witt keeping them busy on the farm, despite their short respite in the afternoon, they were practically falling asleep on their dinner plates.

Neely Kate and I got everyone bathed and tucked into bed. Muffy claimed her usual spot with Hope. Aunt Bessie and Uncle Albert, who weren't used to all the excitement, called it an early night, leaving me, Neely Kate, and Witt to watch TV in the living room.

I'd been checking my phone all day, hoping to get updates from Joe, but he'd barely answered my texts throughout the day, except to send me mugshots of two men, asking if I'd seen them in any of my visions, specifically the one of Austin. They didn't look familiar, and I told him so.

Jed had been just as quiet with Neely Kate, but around ten p.m., he called her. She got up and started to walk out of the room as she answered, but then stopped. "Yeah, they're here. Hold on." She sat on the arm of the sofa and put her phone on speaker. "Okay, they're listening."

"Joe's about to make a couple of arrests," Jed said.

I sat up straighter. "What? Who?"

"Joe and I have been doing our individual digging, and all the evidence points to Derby Sloan and his right-hand man, John Ballister. Sloan owns a gun the same caliber as the one used in the murders. Joe should get the ballistics report within the next few days, but Sloan and his buddy don't have an alibi during the window when the forensic pathologist says the murders took place. In addition, Joe has witnesses that say Sloan was pissed at Harvey and Noah and had threatened to kill them."

"What about Jeremiah?" I asked.

"Joe hasn't directly tied Sloan to his murder yet, but with the other charges, that will give him time to build a case. We *do* know that Jeremiah had been to Sloan's bar, so there's every likelihood that the dealer roped him into his scheme too."

"Was Sloan lookin' for the paper Darlene gave Rose?" Neely Kate asked.

"Joe thinks so," Jed said. "He thinks the name on the paper has something to do with the dealer who roped the two guys in, and Jeremiah's friends said he'd recently started selling pot, so we think that's how he ties into this. Sloan was wanting revenge, and he wanted to eliminate the source of his competition. Only the men he murdered didn't know enough to help Sloan find the guy."

"Why did they call the paper a package?"

"Because the paper was only one part of what he was lookin' for. Harvey took the paper with the name and bank number, and Noah took a paper with the supplier's sources. Hugo had a third part that I can't tell you about, but he said he and the other two guys took them from the dealer's motel room after he started getting pissed at them. They thought they could use it as leverage."

"Sounds like it just got them killed," Witt said.

"Maybe, maybe not," Jed said. "Joe's hopin' to get Ballister to rat Sloan out to protect himself, so hopefully we'll find out how Jeremiah plays into this."

"So that means it's over?" Neely Kate asked in a hopeful tone.

"As soon as those two guys are in jail, y'all are free to come home." He paused. "You can even make your doctor's appointment tomorrow morning if you leave early enough."

Relief washed over Neely Kate's face, chased by worry.

"And Ashley can go to school," I said, hoping to change the subject in case Neely Kate was considering canceling. "I think she's worried she's going to fall behind."

"Like that could ever happen," Neely Kate said with a wave of her hand.

"Joe was heading out to make the arrests," Jed continued, "so I don't see why not. He's had eyes on Sloan for the past few hours while he was securing the search and arrest warrants. I'm sure he'll call you when he thinks it's safe."

"That's great news," Witt said. "Do you want me to drive with the girls and the kids tomorrow, or leave earlier to open the shop?"

"They should be fine goin' on their own," Jed said, "but I'll let you know if I hear otherwise."

I blew out a sigh of relief. My kids would be safe. The danger had passed.

"Is there anything else you need Rose and Witt to know?" Neely Kate asked. "Because if not, I'm going to take you off speaker and head to the front porch so we can talk privately."

"That's all," Jed said. "Other than *thank you, Witt*. I owe you for protectin' my family."

"Neely Kate's like a sister to me, and Daisy…" His voice broke, and he cleared his throat. "I would never let *anything* happen to them." He nodded to me. "Rose and her kids too."

"I know. There are very few people I'd trust with them. Just you and Joe. That's it."

Their exchange made me think of James. At one time, Jed would have trusted James with his family, but that had changed years ago, and I couldn't help thinking about how much James had lost. His lifelong friendship with Jed. His daughter. And, for a while, his freedom. As far as I knew, he was alone, and I couldn't help feeling sad for him. There was a part of him that wanted to be loved and needed, even if he refused to admit it to anyone. Despite everything that had happened, I hoped he would find that again someday.

"What about Dermot?" I asked, but Neely Kate had already taken him off speaker and was headed out the front door.

Witt sank back into the sofa cushions, relief washing over his face. "That's all good news."

"The best." But while my kids were safe, the sister I hadn't known I had might not be, and I had no idea what to do about it.

"As long as we get the all-clear before dawn, I'll take off early and probably won't be here when you get up," Witt said. "I need to go home and get a uniform before I open the shop at seven."

"Don't worry about us." I gave him a warm smile. "We'll be fine. Thank you for taking the day off to stand guard."

"Are you kiddin'? I had the best day," he said with a huge grin. "Your uncle was showing us everything about the farm. I think he wishes he had someone to pass it on to."

"I suppose we could keep it for Mikey or Ashley if they're interested in it one day," I said, my mind racing. "Uncle Albert did the same for my farm until I found out my birth mother had bequeathed it to me." I shook my head. "But what are we talkin' about? Uncle Albert's got years left in him."

"Maybe so, but he told me he's gettin' too old to run the farm on his own." But something in his gaze suggested there was more to it.

I cocked my head. "What aren't you sayin', Witt Rivers?"

"Uncle Albert asked if I'd be interested in taking over the farm." He held up his hands. "He's not giving it to me, so don't go worrying about that. I'd just run it for him, and if I love it, then he says he'll sell me part of it so I can have a farm of my own."

I stared at him in disbelief. "You don't know the first thing about farming. How do you know you'll even like it?"

"When I wasn't gettin' in trouble in my youth, I worked on the farm on the land adjacent to Granny's place," he said with a wicked grin. "I learned to do plenty."

"I stand corrected," I said, trying to wrap my head around it. "But what about the mechanic shop?"

"It's Jed's, and while I'm good at it, I don't love it, you know?" He paused. "I want to do something I love."

"I understand that," I said. "I feel the same way about my landscaping business. Violet was the one who wanted the nursery, and part of me did too, but my heart was in the landscaping." I looked him in the eyes. "I get it."

The corners of his mouth tilted up, and his eyes were glassy. "I knew you would."

"How do you think Neely Kate and Jed will react?"

"Jed won't love it, but he'll understand. Neely Kate, on the other hand…" He made a face.

"She might be upset at first, but she'll understand too. I know she will."

"I hope so." He paused. "She has Jed and Daisy, and this new baby they think I don't know about. They're doin' a piss-poor job of keepin' it secret." He released a chuckle. "She doesn't need me anymore."

It was then I realized that Witt had spent most of his adolescent and adult life being there for his cousin because after her mother had dumped her at her grandmother's house when she was twelve and had been surrounded by a passel of cousins, Witt and her granny had been her only true constants.

"She'll always need you to some extent," I said. "But you also no longer need to hold yourself back on her account."

He laughed. "Who's gonna play bodyguard when y'all get into trouble again?"

"Trust me," I said with a grin. "I'm gonna try hard to make sure we stay out of trouble."

His eyes twinkled with mischief. "I think that's like askin' a rooster not to crow."

"You could be right, but we'll be okay, Witt. Live your life. Neely Kate's gonna be okay."

He pressed his lips together and nodded.

"You've been takin' care of Neely Kate all this time," I said softly. "But who's been takin' care of you?"

His eyes widened with surprise, then he got to his feet. "I've been takin' care of myself for as long as I remember. At this point, I'm doin' just fine on my own."

He walked out of the room before I could respond. I'd watched him grow from an irresponsible kid into a dependable, honorable man. Witt deserved to be happy. I hoped he'd found that here, or wherever life took him.

I went upstairs and got ready for bed. Just as I was about to walk into my room, my phone vibrated with a call from Joe.

"Joe," I said in relief as I answered, grateful to hear his voice and hoping he had good news. "Tell me this is over."

"This is over, darlin'."

I sank my back against the hallway wall and closed my eyes. "Thank God."

"We arrested Derby Sloan and his muscle, John Ballister. They'll be arraigned tomorrow, but I doubt the judge will grant them bail. Or if he does, it will be so high, they won't be able to post it."

"So we can come home tomorrow?"

"You can come home tomorrow."

"Thank you," I said breathlessly. "I miss you."

"I miss you too, and I miss our kids. The house is too quiet without you. At least what little time I was there last night."

"Ashley will want to go to school, so we'll leave early enough that I can drop her and Mikey off. Then I'll take the kids to daycare and get to work cleaning up the office."

"We could hire a crew to do that," Joe said. "I hate that it hadn't occurred to me already."

"We can't afford it," I said. "Besides, Neely Kate and I have a system, and it'll be easier to do it on my own than try to tell someone else how to do it."

He chuckled. "If you say so."

We were silent for a moment before I asked, "Did you find the dealer who had recruited those men?"

"No, he'd already taken off before we got there. He was obviously spooked by the murders of his new hires. The hotel manager said he checked out on Saturday."

"Do you think he's still around?"

"No, I suspect he's on his way back to Texas."

"Speaking of Texas…" I let my voice trail off. The topic of my possible sister was a conversation best had in person. "I have something to tell you about my visions, but I'd rather do it face to face."

"Is it bad?" he asked, sounding concerned.

"No, it's just…" I paused. "It's about my father. Like I said, it'll be better done face to face."

He was silent for a moment. "Are you okay?"

My heart swelled with love. "I think so. I'll be more okay after we come home."

"Let me know when you leave tomorrow. Maybe I can drop by the office and spend a little time with you after the arraignment."

"Neely Kate has her appointment at 9:30, and who knows how long she'll be gone, so there's a chance we might even get some time alone."

"I like the sound of that," he said in a low, sexy voice.

"And you can watch me sort through files."

He laughed. "And maybe you'll even let me help sort through some of them."

"Maybe." He laughed again, and I said, "Will you be working much later tonight?"

"No. I have some paperwork that needs to be tackled, but I'm beat. I'm about to head home and get some sleep." He paused. "The bed's sure gonna be lonely without you."

"I'll make up for it tomorrow night," I said. "Maybe we can get the kids in bed early."

"Deal." That single word held a promise that made me tingle with anticipation.

Chapter Thirty-One

True to his word, Witt was gone by the time I was up at six and headed down to the kitchen to start a pot of coffee. His blanket and sheets were neatly folded and placed on top of his pillow.

Aunt Bessie came into the kitchen, wearing her beat-up robe, just as I was filling up the pot with water.

"Takin' over my job," she said with a chuckle as she walked through the door.

"Not on purpose," I assured her. "Joe called last night and said it's safe to come home."

Her face fell. "So you're leavin'."

"We are. Ashley's anxious about missing school, and Neely Kate and I need to clean up our trashed office." I poured the water into the coffeemaker, then pulled out the coffee.

"I hated the circumstances for *why* you were here," Aunt Bessie said, "but we've sure enjoyed having you. Albert hasn't looked this happy in years."

I started scooping coffee into the filter. "I hear he offered Witt a job workin' on the farm."

Her eyes widened. "He did? It's about time. It's all gettin' too much for 'im. Do you know if Witt accepted?"

"I don't think it's official, but yeah, I think he's gonna take it. He seems excited."

"Then he can live with us, of course," Aunt Bessie said, clapping her hands together. "We have all these empty rooms, and if he's here, the house won't feel so empty."

"I'll let y'all work that part out," I said, "but seeing as how he hasn't told Neely Kate yet, maybe keep it to yourself for now."

She mimicked inserting a key between her lips and turning it.

"Thank you so much for telling me about my sister," I said. "But I wish you'd told me sooner."

"I suppose I should have, but I had so little information, and it wasn't a definite thing. It still isn't."

"But you *do* believe she's Daddy's child?"

She nodded. "I do, and I confess I've spent more time dwelling on it than I probably should have."

"If you remember anything else about her or her mother, will you let me know?"

"Of course, Rose. I only wish I knew more."

"You could always try one of those family DNA tests," Neely Kate said, walking into the kitchen, stifling a yawn. "But it will only work if she does one too."

"True…" In truth, I was terrified of DNA tests because of Hope, but if there was a chance I could use one to find my sister, then it seemed like the prudent thing to do. Besides, it was Joe's DNA I needed to be worried about. His and Neely Kate's. James would never voluntarily give up his DNA, but his brother, who lived in the county, was an unknown.

"I guess it wouldn't hurt," I said. "Hopefully she's done one too." I swallowed the sudden fear that hit me. "But there might not be time. What if my vision comes true?"

"No," Neely Kate said firmly as she reached for a coffee mug in the cabinet. "We're gonna trust the vision you had about finding her."

"Neely Kate's right," Aunt Bessie said. "I think you'd know if she'd died."

Neely Kate grabbed the coffee pot, even though it was still filling with coffee.

"Should you be drinking that?" I asked.

She stopped mid-pour, shrugged, then filled the cup a half-inch from the top and handed it to me.

Aunt Bessie watched us but didn't say a word.

Hope and Daisy came running into the kitchen, barely stopping before they collided with a cabinet. "We want to ride the tractor!"

"Hey," I said. "Slow down before someone gets hurt. And you can't ride the tractor because we're going home this morning."

Hope made a pouty face. "We don't wanna go home. We like it hew."

"Yeah," Daisy said, making her own overexaggerated pout. "We like it here."

I squatted next to them. "And I love that you like it here, and so do Aunt Bessie and Uncle Albert, but we have to go home. Daddy misses us." I poked Daisy in the belly. "And your daddy misses you too."

Daisy giggled, and Hope complained that she didn't get poked, so I poked her too, and they both giggled.

"We'll need to leave pretty soon so we can get Ashley and Mikey to school on time," I said as I stood up.

"Come on, girls," Aunt Bessie said, taking each of their hands. "Let's go get you dressed and wake up the others."

I watched them walk out of the kitchen, feeling like a neglectful niece. I hadn't been to Aunt Bessie's house in nearly a year. "I need to make more of an effort to bring the kids to see my aunt and uncle. Not to mention, the kids had so much fun yesterday."

"Did you spend a lot of time here when you were a kid?" Neely Kate asked.

"I used to spend most of my summers here. Aunt Bessie was more of a mom to me than my mother was."

"Your mother wasn't a mother at all," Neely Kate said, her voice harsh.

"True."

"I suppose that makes you want to find your sister all the more. Aunt Bessie and Uncle Albert are all you have left."

I hadn't thought of it that way. "I don't feel like anything's missing in my life, you know?" She nodded. "But I'm sure *she* has questions. She's probably wondering who her family is."

"Or she may not be," Neely Kate said. "Some adopted people aren't curious at all. Daisy knows she's adopted, and we're leaving it up to her to ask questions or not. Her birth mother didn't want an open adoption, but if Daisy wants to meet her, we'll ask." She offered me a smile. "If you decide to search for her—and it sounds like you already have—just prepare yourself in case she says her life is good and she doesn't need you in it."

I nodded. "Yeah. Good point."

"It's going to be hard to find her since you really don't know anything, so I still think your best bet is DNA testing. Then you can contact her and warn her about your vision."

My heart sank. "If she hasn't already been killed."

"I think Aunt Bessie's right. I think you would know."

"Really?" I asked, realizing it sounded like a plea.

"Really." She gave me a hug, then reached for her phone. "I'll order one of those tests right now. I'll see if I can get a rush delivery."

"Thanks, Neely Kate. You're the best."

A grin spread across her face. "I know."

"I better get upstairs and get those kids ready to go." Then I realized we only had my car now, since Witt had already left. "Do you know if Jed left Daisy's car seat? We can fit it into the back row."

"He did, but Jed's gonna come get us," she said. "He wants to drive me to my appointment."

"I can take Daisy with me and drop her off at daycare with Hope and Liam," I said. "Then you two will have some alone time."

She considered it, and I thought she was going to say no, but then she pushed out a sigh. "Okay. Daisy would likely rather ride in your circus bus anyway."

"Circus bus?" I asked with a laugh.

"It's not an insult," she said. "I'm jealous of your circus bus." She put her hand on her belly. "Is it wrong that I want a circus bus of my own?"

"No, Neely Kate," I said softly. "I understand."

"I want this baby, Rose," she said, tears flooding her eyes.

"I know you do, honey. I'll do everything I can to help you get through this, but if the doctor says this could kill you…" A lump filled my throat. "I can't lose you, Neely Kate. And neither can Jed or Daisy or Joe. I'm going to be selfish and tell you that I may have a sister out there, but as far as I'm concerned, *you're* my sister. I need you."

She laughed through her tears. "I'm not goin' anywhere. I promise."

"But if the doctor says this could kill you, please consider the rest of us. What good is having a baby if you can't be your baby's mother?"

She nodded, tears flowing down her cheeks.

"But the doctor's gonna have good news," I said, forcing a smile. "We have to believe that."

"Yeah," she said, her head bobbing. "We have to believe it."

Loading everyone in the car felt like the circus Neely Kate had called us. Mikey and the younger kids didn't want to leave, while Ashley was getting upset that everyone else was taking too long. We finally got everyone and the luggage loaded, and I was about to get in when Neely Kate yelled, "Wait!"

"Do we get to *stay?*" Mikey asked hopefully.

"No!" Neely Kate and I said simultaneously.

Aunt Bessie, who was standing on the front porch, started to laugh.

"You're still leaving," Neely Kate said, "but I forgot something. Hold on." She ran up the steps and into the house. About half a minute later, she ran out holding the wooden box.

"How on earth did you get that?" I asked. "It was on Joe's desk."

"I grabbed it," she said. "In case those guys were actually after it. I want to give it to the person who buried it." Her face fell. "Which, I guess, is impossible now, but there's still Jason."

"Yeah." I walked around the back and opened the hatch. "I'll bring it to the office. Maybe in the next day or two, we can go to the library and look up those yearbooks."

She set the box in the back, and I closed the hatch.

"I'll see you after your appointment," I said, then gave her a hug. "Everything's going to be okay."

"I hope so," she said as she glanced at the back of my packed-to-the-gills SUV. "Good luck with the circus bus."

Laughing, I gave her another hug, then got into the car and headed back to Henryetta.

Chapter Thirty-Two

The kids were chatty on the way back, talking about their fun day at the farm and asking when we could go back to see my aunt and uncle. I told them I didn't know, but we'd talk to Daddy and figure out a weekend to make it happen.

I dropped Ashley and Mikey off at school first, but as we pulled up to the carpool drop-off lane, I realized we'd put their backpacks in the back. When it came time for them to get out, I ran around to the back and opened the hatch, while Mikey and Ashley climbed onto the sidewalk.

The woman in the car behind me leaned out her window and shouted. "Oh, come on!"

Ashley rounded the back of the car, her face red with embarrassment.

"Where did you get that cool box, Aunt Rose?" Mikey asked as he ran his hand over the carving.

"It's the box she and Neely Kate dug up," Ashley said, rolling her eyes.

I hadn't told her so, but she must have inferred it.

Mikey's face radiated with excitement. "Maybe it has a secret compartment like in the treasure book my teacher is reading. Maybe there's buried treasure inside!"

"Secret compartments and buried treasures aren't real," Ashley said with an exaggerated sigh as she grabbed her backpack. In her haste to make her escape, the wooden box fell out, landed on its side on the pavement, and shattered into multiple pieces.

She looked up at me in horror. "I'm sorry, Aunt Rose! I'm sorry!"

"It's okay," I assured her and bent down to pick up the pieces. Thankfully, the engagement ring was buried under several pieces of wood and hadn't rolled away. The necklace was there too. I picked up the envelopes and jewelry and tucked them into my oversized cardigan pocket.

The car behind me lay on the horn. "Ignore them," I said as Ashley and Mikey helped pick up the pieces. I grabbed a loose plastic Walmart bag that I kept in the back in case of accidents and held it out. "Let's put all the pieces in the bag, and I'll sort through it all later."

"What's this?" Mikey asked, holding up a very yellowed Ziploc bag that contained two yellow plastic squares.

It took me a second to realize what they were. "I think those are floppy disks."

Mikey scrunched his nose. "Floppy *what*?"

"Floppy disks. They used to go into computers." I wanted to ask where they had come from, but the obvious answer was staring me in the face.

He shook them. "They don't seem very floppy. How do you fit them in a computer?"

"Computers used to be a lot different," I said, taking the bag from him and setting it in the back of the trunk. "Those weren't in the box before." Had Neely Kate put them in there? But that seemed unlikely.

"I told you!" Mikey shouted excitedly. "It had a secret compartment!"

Was he right? As I considered it, I realized the inside of the box was a lot shallower than the outside. There was enough room to have at least an inch-thick hidden space at the bottom. How had we not figured that out before? "You're right, Mikey," I said. "I think it *did* have one."

"But not anymore," Ashley mumbled under her breath.

A boy who looked to be about Ashley's age lingered on the sidewalk near us. "Way to hold up the line, Ash-ley," he said with a sneer. "But then your daddy doesn't follow rules, so why would *you?*"

Oliver.

Ashley looked like she was about to burst into tears.

I had never yelled at a child who wasn't my own in my entire life, but I was close to doing just that.

The horn honked again, and I picked up the bag and stood, turning to face the woman. "We're doin' the best we can!"

Ashley tugged on my shirt sleeve. "That's Oliver's mom."

I glanced down at her. "The woman honking her horn?"

"Yeah."

I scowled. "That figures. She's just as rude as her son."

Mikey picked up more pieces and put them in the bag. "Can I go now, Aunt Rose?"

"Of course," I said, giving the woman a dirty look before I hugged them, wrapping an arm around each of them. "You two run off to class. I'll get the rest."

"Can I keep the floppy dishes?" Mikey asked as he picked them up out of the back and started waving them.

"That's floppy *disks*, and no." I took them from him. "I need to give those to Uncle Joe."

"Dad," he said quietly. "Ashley says we can call him Dad."

I blinked at him in surprise. "Joe would be thrilled for you to call him Dad, but only if you want to."

"I do."

I leaned over and kissed his cheek. "I love you, Mikey. Have a good day."

Beaming, he said, "You too, Mom." Then he spun around and ran toward the entrance.

Ashley turned toward Oliver, who was standing with a group of boys, and put her hands on her hips. "Turns out, my dad is actually the sheriff of Fenton County, and if you don't be nice, he'll come and arrest you."

"He's not your dad," he scoffed.

"He is *now*," Ashley said in a bossy tone. "Maybe I'll have him come visit our class tomorrow, and I'll show him who's been calling me names."

Oliver suddenly looked uncertain.

I knew I should correct her, but I couldn't bring myself to do it. Maybe I'd send Joe in for a visit myself.

Oliver's mom lay on her horn for several seconds, and instead of flipping her off like I wanted to, I gave her a pleasant wave, wiggling my fingers and giving her a mocking smile.

She pulled around my car, flipping me off herself as she drove away.

"Have a nice day!" I called after her. It was difficult to sound cheerful while grinding my teeth.

I finished picking up the rest of the pieces of the box and tossed them into the back of the Suburban, then pulled out of the school parking lot. I felt guilty about holding up the carpool line, but it couldn't be helped. Once I was on the street and headed to the daycare, I called Joe with my handsfree feature.

"Hey, Rose," he said when he answered, but his voice sounded strained. "Are you back in town?"

"I just dropped Ash and Mikey off at school. Oh, by the way, they want to call us Mom and Dad now, and Ashley just told Oliver that her new dad is the sheriff, and if he's not nicer, she'll have you come to school tomorrow and arrest him."

He was silent for a moment, then said, "That's a lot to unpack. When did this come about?"

"She told him off just a couple of minutes ago."

"I mean the calling us Mom and Dad?"

"Ashley asked me yesterday afternoon. She said it felt weird calling us Aunt Rose and Uncle Joe. I told her that we'd never replace her parents and that lots of kids have two moms and/or two dads."

"She really wants to call us Mom and Dad?"

"I about fell over when she asked. Then Mikey asked this morning if he could too. I told him yes, of course."

"Mom and Dad," he said in awe.

"But that's not why I called," I said. "Long story, but Neely Kate had brought the box to Aunt Bessie and Uncle Albert's and put it in the back of my car this morning. It fell out when we were getting the backpacks out of the trunk in the carpool lane, and the box broke into pieces."

"Oh no. I'm sorry."

"That's still not why I'm calling," I said, turning down the street toward the church. "There was an old, yellowed plastic bag with two floppy disks inside."

"Huh," he said. "I never saw any floppy disks in the box."

"Neither did I, but I think the box had a false bottom. After Mikey suggested it had a secret compartment, I realized the inside was shallower than the outside."

"Shit."

I turned into the church parking lot. "I know."

"Shit," Hope said cheerfully behind me.

"Shit," Daisy repeated, which sounded strange in her tiny princess voice.

Liam made a sound that was a pretty close approximation of the word.

"Did our children just say what I think they did?" Joe asked.

"Yep, and Daisy too. I'll let you explain it to Jed and Neely Kate."

"Shi—I mean crap."

"Cwappy doodles," Hope said with a grin.

I laughed.

"I really do have to go," Joe said reluctantly, "but I want to know about these floppy disks. Was there any writing on them?"

"Not that I remember. They're currently in the back of the car."

"Where are *you* now?"

"I'm dropping the three younger kids off at daycare, then I'm heading to the office."

"Okay, bring the disks in with you to the office. I was at the courthouse for the arraignment, but…" He hesitated, then said, "Can you take me off speaker?"

"Yeah," I said, starting to get worried. "I'm parking in a space right now. Give me a second." I parked the car and got the phone sorted, then held it up to my ear. "What's goin' on?"

"There isn't gonna be an arraignment today," he said solemnly.

"What?" I practically screeched. "Is the prosecutor dropping the charges?"

"No, Derby Sloan and his buddy were found hanging in their cells this morning."

"What?" I croaked out. "They—" I glanced back at the kids. got out of the car, and shut the door. "They hung themselves? *Both of them?*"

"That's the way it appears." But I could tell he wasn't buying it.

"Then what happened?"

"The video in their section of county lockup suddenly and conveniently went on the fritz," he said in disgust. "So God only knows."

"You think someone else is responsible?" I asked in shock.

"I have no proof, but yeah, I think this was staged."

I leaned my back against the car. "Are we still in danger?"

"If the person whom I suspect is behind it truly did it, then no."

"Wait," I said, realizing what he was suggesting. "You think *Dermot* arranged this?"

"I think Derby Sloan and his buddy knew too many things they could have used in a plea bargain."

I wasn't sure how to respond to that. I was still in a state of shock.

"I'm still supervising the investigation here at lock-up, but let me know when you get to the office so I can come see you."

"Okay," I said, struggling to wrap my head around what Joe had told me. "I'm about to head into the daycare now."

We hung up, and I opened the back door and unbuckled the kids. Once we were outside, I realized their bags were in the back too. I made the girls stay with me, holding hands, while I dug out their backpacks and Liam's diaper bag from the back. It took another ten minutes to get everyone settled in their classrooms.

I was pretty frazzled by the time I pulled up in front of the office. I sent Joe a quick text to let him know I had arrived. One peek through the window at the trashed interior sent me hurrying to the coffee shop a few doors down, in equal parts procrastination and the need for a caffeine boost. I considered locking myself in the office straightaway, but if Joe was right, Dermot wouldn't hurt me.

Was Dermot responsible? I was still trying to make it fit the man I knew, but then again, he was a crime lord. It made sense that he'd played a role in this mess.

The coffee shop was pretty busy for a Monday morning, so I had to wait several minutes before I could place my order.

"No crazy coffee order for Neely Kate today?" one of the baristas asked after I ordered my latte.

"Not today," I said as I paid for my order. "But I'm sure she'll want something tomorrow."

After my order was ready, I headed to the office and let myself inside, stopping in the doorway to take in the carnage. The place had been totally destroyed.

The desks were overturned. Papers were everywhere. Chairs had been flung around like toys. The table we used to meet with clients had been flipped over. The person or persons who had done this had not only been looking for something but had been pissed when they hadn't found it.

This was going to take forever to clean up.

My phone rang, and Dermot's name was on the screen. My heartbeat spiked. I shut the door behind me, wondering if I should answer. If Dermot was responsible for those men's murders, I needed to distance myself from him ASAP. But I didn't know that he was, and he'd always had my best interests in mind.

"Dermot."

"Tell me you're still out of town."

I stopped in my tracks. "Why?"

"I found out the name of that next-door neighbor you've been looking for."

It took me a second to figure out what he was talking about. "You mean the neighbor with the box?"

"One and the same. The guy's name was Clive Maxwell. He lived there for about a year and a half before he was arrested for manslaughter. He got out of prison a couple of years ago."

"Manslaughter? Who did he murder?"

"His daughter."

It took me a moment to recover from my shock. "Sarah?"

He hesitated. "You know her name?"

"An old neighbor called me Sunday afternoon. They were both teenagers at the time. She told me she thought Sarah buried the box, and I guess her boyfriend's name was Jason. The initials in the notes fit. She didn't know any last names, though. She told me she heard Sarah died years back, but she didn't know the details."

"Her father beat her to death," he said in disgust. "His younger daughter saw the whole thing and was a witness in her father's trial. The idiot turned down a plea bargain and thought he could convince his daughter to lie for him. Turned out, she was all too eager to put her daddy away for life."

"She saw it?" I asked in horror.

"Yep, and it wasn't pretty. I gathered hitting them wasn't an uncommon occurrence, but he was trying to get something out of her. The younger sister—"

"Luna," I said. "I heard her name was Luna."

"Luna said she wasn't sure what her father wanted, but her sister knew and refused to tell him, only saying she'd buried the box somewhere he'd never find it. She told him he had taken something important away from her, so she did the same to him."

"She was talking about her boyfriend," I said, my voice barely a whisper. The contents of the box had been sad before, but this was tragic.

"Yeah. Ol' Clive was beside himself with rage and beat the shit out of her. He even used a kitchen chair. When his rage ran out, he tried to get her to tell him where she'd buried it, but she was unconscious at that point. She died a few weeks later."

"Oh dear lord," I said, feeling lightheaded. "You said her father got out of prison a couple of years ago? Do you think he's the one looking for the box?"

"I'd bet money on it."

"How in the world did he find out about it?"

"Your employee—"

"Jeremiah."

"Jeremiah," he corrected, "knew him through mutual friends. He mentioned they were working on a property on Olive Street, and it was a pretty extensive excavation. Clive told the group that he used to live on that street. Then he figured out that he'd lived *next door* to the house your crew was working on. He told Jeremiah that his daughter had buried something important to him and asked him to let him know if y'all came across a wooden box."

"He knew she'd buried the wooden box?"

"It was the girls' mother's box. He'd kept it in his room, and the daughter—Sarah—had taken it."

"And put her things inside it."

"Appears so. I talked to a friend of Jeremiah's and he said Jerimiah planned to tell Clive that he'd found the box, but he was gonna make him pay to get it back. Based on what Austin said, Maxwell's muscle killed Jeremiah before he could tell him where to find it."

"The package."

"The package," he affirmed. "But damned if I know what it is."

"Floppy disks."

"What?"

"Long story short, but the box broke this morning, and an old Ziploc bag with two floppy disks fell out. They're in my purse now."

"Where are you?"

"I'm at my office."

"Does anyone else know you're back in town?"

I realized I hadn't told Dermot I'd gone to my aunt and uncle's house, but he likely knew from Jed. "No. I dropped the kids off at school and daycare and then came to work. I'm about to start trying to clean up this massive mess."

"Are Jed and Neely Kate with you?"

"No, they had a doctor's appointment."

"You're there alone? I don't like it. I don't have anyone available to go watch you. Can Joe spare a deputy?"

"I don't know. Joe's dealing with his own situation right now." I paused. "He's supposed to be at the arraignment for Sloan Derby and his right-hand man, but instead he's investigating their deaths."

He was silent for a moment. *"Excuse me?"*

"They were found dead in their cells this morning."

"What the fuck happened to them?" he demanded.

He sure didn't sound like he'd been responsible for their deaths. "I don't know," I fibbed. "Joe's lookin' into it now."

"Now I really don't like you bein' alone," he grunted. "Lock yourself inside the office, and call someone you know in the sheriff's department."

"I will." I stuffed down my fear as I hung up, spun around, and locked the door. How had Clive Maxwell found out we had the box? Then again, we hadn't been quiet about it. He would have just needed to hear it from the right—or wrong—people.

I quickly called Joe, but the call went to voicemail. "I'm at the office now, but I got word that Clive Maxwell was the father of the girl who probably buried that box. And he...he was convicted of murdering his daughter because she took something of his and buried it. I've locked myself in the office, but please come over when you hear this." I paused. "I love you."

I hung up and called Randy next, but his phone went to voicemail too. "Randy, I think I'm in trouble. The father of the girl who buried that box we've been looking for was convicted of murdering his daughter. I've locked myself in my office, but Joe's investigatin' two deaths at the county jail, and I'm here alone." I paused. "If you get this, call me back. I'm hoping Joe will be over soon."

I hung up and considered calling 911, but this wasn't a true emergency. Clive Maxwell wasn't here. I was safe.

I took a deep breath to settle my nerves. I wasn't leaving this office for a while, so I might as well start cleaning.

I took a sip of my coffee, and then set my things down on the staircase leading to the roof. It was the only place that hadn't been vandalized.

If Clive Maxwell had trashed our office looking for the box, then maybe he wouldn't be back. And he hadn't broken into the farmhouse because our alarm hadn't gone off. Not to mention, he had no idea when we'd be back here. My nerves began to settle. I was perfectly safe, and I needed to focus on getting the office cleaned up.

I stood at the back of the room and took in the damage. From this angle, it looked worse than from the front. Grief hit me hard, catching me by surprise. I told myself it was just an office, and they were just things, but I'd put my heart and soul into building this place. A lot of the furniture, décor, and rugs had been thrifted, but all combined, they'd made a cozy haven that had filled my heart with joy.

"It'll be like that again," I said with a heavy-hearted sigh. I just needed to get started, but it was such an overwhelming mess. I wasn't sure what to tackle first.

I decided to start with the papers. Once they were all cleaned up, I could determine what real damage had been caused.

We kept all our plans and invoices on our computers and in a cloud, but we often printed them out too. Maybe this was our sign to clean out the old paperwork.

I'd picked up several stacks and set them in a pile on the floor when a knock came from the front door. An older man with longer gray hair and a brown jacket stood there.

Was this Clive Maxwell?

I took a step back as I assessed the situation. I was standing behind a locked door, but it struck me that the front door had been locked when he'd broken in the first time. Funny how I hadn't thought of that before now. I pulled my phone from my back pocket and started to call 911, but then I realized he could be some random man who wanted to talk about landscape design. The Henryetta Police Department would be the ones responding to the call, and they'd give me grief if this turned out to be nothing.

I pointed to the sign in the front door and shouted, "Sorry! We're closed." Although now that I thought about it, the mess was a sure sign we weren't open for business.

I pulled up Joe's number and called him, but it went straight to voicemail again. "Joe. When you get this message, I need you to come to my office ASAP. I think the man who killed Jeremiah might be at the front door."

The man outside the door looked pissed when he saw the phone in my hand. He grabbed the door handle and began to shake it.

I was going to need help sooner than Joe was going to get here, so I sucked up my pride and dialed 911.

"911, what's your emergency?" the dispatcher asked.

"My name is Rose Gardner, and I'm in my landscaping office across the street from the courthouse. There's a man outside the front door who is trying to get in."

"Is he threatening you, ma'am?"

"He's shouting at me through the glass door."

"So why don't you let him in?"

I couldn't believe what I was hearing, but then again, it *was* the Henryetta PD. "My office is closed."

"Then if you tell him the situation, I'm sure he'll understand and come back when you open."

"You don't understand," I said in frustration. "He's now pounding on the glass with his fist!"

The man's face was flaming red as he beat the door. The heavy thuds echoed through the room.

"This doesn't sound like an emergency. It sounds like an eager customer, and in today's economy, you should be grateful," she said with an attitude, then sighed in exhaustion. "*But,* if you'd like, I'll send an officer out to see what's going on."

"Yes!" I practically shouted. "*Please!*"

"There's no need to get snippy, ma'am," she snapped as she hung up.

Clive wasn't about to give up on his quest to get inside, and I weighed my options. I could lock myself in the bathroom until someone showed up to help me, or I could go out the back door. The problem with the second option was my office was on the corner, and if he saw me going out the back door, he could round the corner and track me down in the alley.

Staying put seemed like the best option at the moment. But to be safe, I found my purse and pulled out my pepper spray. Too bad I didn't carry around my taser anymore. Or my gun.

Still, I couldn't just wait to see if he would give up or escalate his attempts to get in. I called Randy next and got his voicemail again. Instead of leaving a message, I pulled up the number for the sheriff's office and called Joe's assistant, Patty.

"Patty, this is Rose Gardner," I said in a rush when she answered.

"I'm afraid Sheriff Simmons isn't here right now, sweetheart," she said kindly. "He's at the county jail."

"I know, but I need *your* help."

"Oh," she said, sounding pleased. "I'm honored."

"There's a man outside my office door on the Henryetta Square, and he's trying to get in. Joe's not answering his phone."

"Oh, honey," she said, sounding concerned. "I'm afraid I can't help you. I don't even have a gun. You need to call 911."

"I already did that," I said. "But the Henryetta dispatcher said it wasn't an emergency. Can you please send a deputy out?"

"Of course, hon," she said. "I'll get on that right away. You stay safe now." Then she hung up.

"I'm trying to," I grumbled.

The man at the door looked even more pissed.

Then I realized I was out of time as he reached into his jacket and pulled out a handgun.

Time to go out the back door.

Crouching down, I hurried toward the back of the office, then squatted by the back door as shots rang out, followed by the sound of splintering glass.

My heart was hammering in my ears as I thought through my options again. But I didn't really have an option. I could either cower here and wait for him to come shoot me, or I could go out the back door.

I stood up and reached for the deadbolt.

Chapter Thirty-Three

I knew I was in danger of getting shot, but he'd already beaten his daughter to death and possibly killed Jeremiah, so I wasn't going to take my chances meeting him face to face.

I glanced toward the front door and saw that he'd shot out the glass and was now climbing inside.

Getting out the back door wasn't as smooth as I'd hoped. The dead bolt was stiff, and I had to put my weight into it to get it unlocked, wasting precious time. It felt like it took half a minute, but it was likely only a few seconds.

Still, it was long enough for Clive to reach me.

He grabbed my arm and gave me a vicious tug backward, throwing me into the closed bathroom door. My head hit the wood, and I saw stars, but I managed to keep the pepper spray gripped in my left hand.

"Where is it?" he asked from several feet away. Terror washed through me when I stared into his cold eyes. It was clear I was dealing with a hardcore killer.

While I suspected he was here for the floppy disks, I wasn't going to just hand them over. Maybe it was because I'd sworn to myself that I'd never grovel again, or maybe it was plain stupidity, but I found myself asking, "Where is what?"

He held up the gun and pointed it at my chest. "I want that goddamned box."

It would feel wrong to reward his murderous path of destruction by giving him what he wanted, not to mention, I was sure he'd kill me once he had them. I motioned to the door leading to the stairwell. "It's in there. In the Walmart bag."

Still training the gun on me, he backed up toward the stairwell door. "Who did you call?"

"My husband, the sheriff," I said with my back still pressed to the bathroom door. "He's across the street. He'll be here any second, so take the bag, and go before he shows up."

He reached behind him, still keeping his gaze on me. "I don't think so. Otherwise he'd be here already. Not to mention you made several other calls."

"That's right," I said. "I called 911, so the Henryetta police will be here any second."

He barked out a laugh. "So why aren't they here yet? The police department's only a block or two away."

"You know the Henryetta police," I said, trying to sound breezy to hide my panic. "You just never know when they're gonna show up."

His hand finally connected with the doorknob. He pulled the door open and snuck a glance down at the base of the stairs. Squatting, he reached down to grab the bag while still keeping an eye on me. Once he had the bag, he held it out toward me.

"What the hell is this?"

"The box," I said. "It fell and broke into pieces."

His mouth dropped open.

"Okay," I said. "You've got the box. Feel free to go." I motioned toward the back door. "I've already got it unlocked for you."

He reached for the bottom of the bag with the hand that held the gun, then dipped it over, dumping the wood pieces onto the floor. After a quick scan of the contents, his rage-filled eyes lifted to mine. "Where is it?"

"Your daughter's engagement ring? In my underwear drawer at home. I was holding onto it until I found her. At least until I realized she was closer than I realized, buried in the Henryetta Cemetery." That last part was a guess, but I figured I couldn't be far off.

"What engagement ring?" he demanded.

"You didn't know Jason proposed to her?" I asked. "That's what she buried in the box. That, a heart locket, and a few notes from her fiancé."

He looked momentarily shocked.

"You didn't know?" I asked. "She and Jason knew you and his mother would never approve, and for some reason, she refused to leave with him when he went to Montana."

"Who the hell is Jason?" he shouted.

I stared at him in shock, then started to laugh, my nervous energy needing to be expelled. "You didn't know?"

"I don't give a shit about some engagement ring and notes. I want the disks."

"What disks?" I asked, but even as I said it, I asked myself what I was doing. He'd killed two people when they hadn't given him what he wanted. There was every likelihood he'd kill me too.

But if I could stall him long enough, surely someone would show up and save me.

He lifted his arm, pointing the barrel of the gun at my face. "Don't play stupid with me. Either give me what I want, or I'll kill you where you stand."

"Like you killed Sarah?" I countered. "And Jeremiah when he wouldn't tell you where the box was?"

"I didn't kill Jeremiah," he grunted. "That stupid fool Emmett killed him. I told the boy he was no good to us dead, and then he goes and gets trigger happy."

"Maybe you didn't kill him, but you still tried to bury him."

His eyes widened in surprise. "You been talkin' to that boy

who was there?" Then he looked even more surprised. "Holy shit. You're her."

I kept silent because I was pretty sure it wasn't such a good thing that he knew I was the Lady in Black.

"You *are* her," he said, taking a step closer. An evil grin spread across his face, and he licked his upper lip. "You don't look so badass."

I didn't like the predatory look in his eyes, and waiting for someone to save me was no longer an option.

"I'm plenty badass," I said with a leer. "Why don't you come closer and find out for yourself."

He was still holding his gun on me, which made things dicey, but I was going to have to take the chance. It had been a long time since I'd practiced any self-defense moves, but I could press a button easily enough.

He began closing the distance between us, and when he was about three feet away, I lifted my left hand and sprayed his face.

Multiple gunshots echoed in the room, but I didn't wait to see if I'd been shot. Instead, I ran for the front door. While it was farther away, he stood between me and the back door. Not to mention, I'd rather run for my life on the public sidewalk than the back alley.

"You stupid bitch!" he shouted, then more gunshots rang out.

I didn't bother ducking. He was shooting blind, and I'd waste more time trying to crouch down than if I got outside quickly. Unfortunately for me, he'd realized I was trying to escape. He started stumbling after me, shooting wildly until his empty chamber clicked.

He was out of bullets.

There was a chance he had another gun, but I wasn't waiting to find out.

Sirens sounded in the distance, and I breathed a sigh of relief. I just needed to get out the front door, and I'd be safe.

But just as I bent down to duck through the broken glass, he threw himself into my legs, knocking me to the floor.

"Where is it?" he shouted. His eyes were barely cracked open, tears streaming down his red face. "Where are the disks?!" His meaty hands wrapped around my throat and started to squeeze.

I gasped for breath, realizing he was an utter idiot. Even if I planned to tell him, I wouldn't have been able to with my air supply cut off.

I knew I had seconds to break his hold before I passed out. I could try to pry his hands away, but I doubted that would work. Then out of the corner of my eye, I saw a three-inch-long pink crystal Neely Kate had bought about a year ago. She'd claimed it had healing properties and cleaned out negative energy. I stretched out my hand and clasped my fingers around it.

I was about to clean out some negative energy all right.

Using all the strength I could muster, I swung my hand up and smashed the crystal into the side of his head.

His hands loosened momentarily on my throat, and his mouth parted in surprise. His hands went slack, and he fell on top of me.

Well, crappy doodles.

It took a bit of shoving to get him off me, and just as I got him moved to the side, I saw Joe standing over me, panic on his face.

Relief washed through me, but I said with a hint of sass, "It's about darn time you showed up. I found Jeremiah's murderer for you."

Chapter Thirty-Four

I half worried I'd killed Clive Maxwell, but after the EMTs showed up, they declared that he was merely unconscious from a nasty concussion. He'd roused by the time they hauled him off to the Henryetta Hospital, handcuffed to his gurney, and he was spitting mad.

Randy showed up soon after the EMTs, and Joe had him take my statement. I told him that I knew Clive had killed his daughter looking for the floppy disks that had been hidden inside the box. But I didn't tell him how I knew Clive's history, and from the look Joe gave me, I knew he'd be asking questions later.

Apparently, the sheriff's department had been suspicious of Clive's buddy Emmett regarding a string of robberies, and they knew where he lived. Joe sent deputies out to pick him up while I was still giving my interview. They had him in custody within twenty minutes.

After I finished giving my statement, Joe wanted me to go to the ER to get checked out, but I insisted I was fine.

I just wanted to go home.

Joe announced he was taking the rest of the day off to spend with his wife, and he drove me home in the Suburban, leaving his car parked on the square.

We were both quiet on the drive home. When we got in, I let Muffy out to pee and sat on the front steps to watch her.

Muffy looked confused that it was just the two of us. She spun around and ran to the Suburban, probably searching for Hope. "Sorry, Muff," I told her. "It's just you, me, and Joe until the kids come home. Like old times."

"Speaking of old times," Joe said, sitting on the step beside me. He wrapped an arm around my back, and I leaned into him, resting my head on his shoulder.

"I didn't do anything to instigate that, Joe," I said defensively. "We were lookin' for the owner of the box. I told you I'd stop if it started to look dangerous, and I did. But Clive figured out we had the box and was determined to get it."

"For the floppy disks?" he asked.

"Yeah. Just like I told Randy."

He reached over and lifted my chin, staring into my eyes. "I'm sorry you feel like you have to explain yourself. I know you wouldn't unnecessarily put yourself or the kids in harm's way. I was out of line when I accused you of it a few days ago, and I'm really, really sorry."

"I know," I said, lifting a hand to his cheek. "And I'm sorry too."

"But if something like this happens in the future, we need to work out some kind of game plan so you're not keeping secrets that could help me with my investigations. We're on the same side here, right?"

"Next time?" I asked. "What makes you think there's gonna be a next time?" But then I remembered that Clive had figured out who I was. "We might have a problem, Joe."

"Whatever it is, we can work it out," he said, bending over to give me a soft kiss.

"It might be a big one," I said.

He sat back up and waited.

"Clive Maxwell figured out I'm the Lady in Black. Somehow, he knew Austin went to Lady for help."

He frowned. "It's not like it's a tightly held secret."

"True." Then I remembered something else. "Austin said something else when he came to me. He told me one of the guys shot Jeremiah, and the other said the big guy wouldn't be happy. I thought the big guy was Clive, but Clive was there when Jerimiah was shot."

Joe was quiet.

I pressed on. "Then I figured maybe Sloan was the big guy, but that doesn't feel right. Why would Sloan care about floppy disks from thirty years ago?"

"Good question," Joe said quietly.

"So if Sloan wasn't the big guy, who is?" I asked. I truly hoped it wasn't Dermot. He wasn't old enough to be around back then, but that didn't mean he hadn't heard about the disks or had some idea what was on them.

Joe pulled out his phone. "I don't know, but I plan on questioning Clive Maxwell and finding out." Then he put his phone back in his pocket. "But I'll question him later. It can keep. Right now, I'm right where I belong."

I snuggled into him, grateful to have him here, but somehow, I knew Clive wouldn't give him the answers we were looking for. Clive Maxwell was a stubborn jackass who would take the secret to his grave just to spite Joe and everyone else.

"Now that it's just you and me," he said, "tell me how you knew about Clive's history. It doesn't seem like something Clive would voluntarily spill."

"Dermot called me," I said. "Right as I got to the office. He told me he thought I was still in danger because he thought Clive killed Jeremiah looking for the box."

"Did Dermot know about the disks?" he asked, his voice tight.

"Yeah," I said looking up at him. "But not until he called me this morning and I told him I'd found them. Why?"

"Because the disks are missing."

"What? How? They were in my purse, and Clive was nowhere near it."

"I don't know, but there was a lot of commotion after the sheriff deputies and the Henryetta police showed up. If someone had a key to the back door, they could have come in and taken them."

My stomach dropped. "The back door was unlocked." I glanced up at him. "I got the deadbolt undone, but Clive reached me before I could get out."

"Giving Dermot or his men time to get the disks out of your purse while all the commotion was going on."

I started to contradict him, but he might have a point. Dermot was the only one who'd known where I'd hidden the disks.

"Dermot may not be the friend he used to be," Joe said softly. "So tread lightly."

Dermot had been there for me multiple times, and I hated that I had these doubts, but I wasn't stupid. Dermot was the head of the Fenton County crime world. I knew he got his hands messy. I just never asked how messy they got.

Muffy walked back over to us and climbed onto my lap. Joe and I sat there for several minutes in silence, and while I was grateful this was all over, part of me was worried it wasn't.

Would I spend the rest of my life feeling this way?

Joe and I made lunch, then decided to take advantage of our alone time. We went upstairs and spent some quality time in bed. Afterward, we took a shower. Joe pressed me against the shower wall and began to track kisses from my mouth and down my neck. It had been ages since we'd been able to take our time with each other.

"Oh my word!" I exclaimed.

He laughed, looking pleased with himself.

"Not that," I said quickly, then amended. "I mean, don't get me wrong. This is *great*, but I just realized I lost track of the time. We have to pick up the kids."

He continued kissing a trail down to my breasts. "Jed and Neely Kate are getting them."

"Oh!" Then I gasped as his tongue did things that made me tingle everywhere.

"You're surprised I arranged it?"

"That too."

He grinned up at me and continued pressing kisses along my abdomen and downward. "Do you know when they'll be home?" I asked, gasping again as he lifted my leg and placed my thigh on his shoulder.

"We have plenty of time for me to make you come again."

And then he proved we did.

AFTERWARD, WE GOT OUT, AND HE HELPED DRY ME OFF, HIS GAZE darkening as it landed on my neck. I turned to face the partly steamed mirror. Bruises in the shape of fingers had begun to appear on my neck.

"I'll wear turtlenecks and scarves for the next few days," I said. "I doubt makeup will cover them up, and I don't want to scare the kids."

Frowning, he placed a soft kiss on my neck, then stood upright, placing his hands on my shoulders. "I'm sorry I wasn't there when you needed me."

"You were there in time to help get him off me," I teased, then turned serious. "You showed up right on time, Joe. Don't doubt yourself because I'm not."

He nodded but didn't look convinced.

"Do you know how Neely Kate's appointment went?" I asked, feeling guilty for not having thought of it sooner.

He made a face. "I forgot to ask." He lifted his hand to my

cheek, delicately tracing under my cheekbone. "I was more concerned about you."

"I'm okay."

He looked dubious. "Are you sure? You were held at gunpoint, shot at, and nearly choked to death."

"Just a day in the life of the Lady in Black," I quipped before I could think better of it.

"That's what I'm afraid of," he said. "What about your visions of the woman being murdered? Have you had any more?"

"Actually, about that... I have something to tell you," I said softly. "I think I know who was murdered in the vision."

His eyes widened. "How? Did Clive tell you?"

"No. Aunt Bessie helped me figure it out." I paused. "You know how my grandmother had visions like me? Apparently, she had two visions when she wasn't with the person she had the vision of, which means it's possible for me to have visions if I'm not with the person. But there's a catch."

"And that is?" he prompted.

"When Grandma Gardner had the visions, they were of her sister. And both times, her sister was in danger."

Joe looked confused. "But that doesn't make sense. Violet is dead."

I bit my bottom lip, then said, "Aunt Bessie thinks I have a half-sister." I told him what she'd said about my father's fling and how the woman had threatened to put the baby up for adoption if he refused to pay her.

"And he didn't pay her?" Joe asked quietly.

"Aunt Bessie is sure that he didn't."

"So you have a half-sister somewhere?"

"Possibly in Texas."

We were quiet for several seconds before Joe asked, "Do you want to try to find her?"

"I'd like to, but I don't have any clue how to do it. All Aunt

Bessie knows is the mother's first name—Stacy—no last, and that she sent the letter from Austin." I looked up at him. "I was thinking about doing one of the DNA kits to see if she's done one too."

He was quiet for a moment, a serious expression covering his face as he nodded. "Good place to start."

"But I can't help thinking about Hope. So maybe I shouldn't do it."

He turned to look me in the eye.

"If Hope does it someday…"

He drew in a deep breath, then released it. "No sense borrowing trouble. We'll have to tell her eventually. We don't want her to find out on her own."

"You're her father, Joe," I insisted.

A soft smile lifted his lips, but sadness filled his eyes. "In every possible way that matters, I am and always be, but not in the way she was conceived. I made my peace with that before she was born. Hope is my daughter, and the fact that she doesn't carry half my DNA will never change that."

Tears stung my eyes, and I nodded.

"Hey," he said gently as he cupped my cheek and gazed into my eyes. "I wouldn't change a thing. Otherwise, we wouldn't have her. And I can't imagine life without her. She's a gift, Rose. We're damned lucky."

I nodded. "Yeah."

"But we *do* need to talk a little about your past." He waited a beat. "The Lady in Black name has been bandied about in the criminal world for the past couple of weeks. And I'm not just talking about Clive Maxwell knowing your identity."

My blood ran cold. "What does that mean?"

"People have been talking about her."

I shook my head. "In reference to what? The past or something current?"

"I'm not sure. Maybe both. Has Dermot said anything?"

Frowning, I said, "No. He seemed just as surprised as me when the boy showed up asking for protection from me."

"Are you sure he's tellin' the truth?"

I frowned. "Why wouldn't he be?"

Joe gave me a grim smile. "Exactly. What would he have to hide?"

But I couldn't help thinking about the missing floppy disks, and my anxiety began to rise. "Dermot cares about my well-being, Joe. And about our kids."

"I know, Rose," he said, pulling me back down, so I sank into his body. "Maybe I'm just being paranoid."

But was he?

The doorbell rang multiple times, and seconds later, Hope shouted from downstairs, "Momma!"

"Mom!" Mikey called out, and my heart bubbled from the warmth of hearing him call me Mom.

"We're home!" Ashley shouted.

Joe grinned at me. "I guess the kids are back."

I smiled, worry still churning in my gut. "I guess they are. Now we can find out how Neely Kate's appointment went."

"Coming!" Joe hollered out the door.

We quickly thew on our clothes and headed downstairs. Neely Kate and Jed were in the kitchen with all the kids getting a snack.

"Momma!" Liam shouted from his high chair.

"Why didn't you pick us up?" Ashley asked. "And why is Dad home too?"

Joe reached over and squeezed my hand. I knew what he was feeling. I loved that they wanted to call us Mom and Dad, although no small amount of guilt went with it.

"There was another break-in at the office," I told her. "And I was there. So I had to give a statement, and Dad came home with me." I shot a glance at Joe. Calling him that with her and Mikey was going to take some getting used to.

"Are you okay?" Ashley asked in alarm.

I instinctively reached a hand for my turtleneck-covered neck. "I'm fine."

Ashley got up and gave me a hug, holding me tight. "I'm glad you're okay, Mom."

A lump filled my throat. "Me too, Ash." I had to be more careful in the future. Ashley couldn't afford to lose another parent.

She released me, then sat back down. Neely Kate hugged me next. "I'm so sorry I left you alone. I should have been there with you. I was the one who insisted we look for the owners."

"Stop!" I chastised, pulling back to look at her. "You were exactly where you needed to be, and how were we to know it would turn into something dangerous?"

Her brow rose as she propped a hand on her hip.

"Okay," I conceded. "A lot of things we touch turn dangerous, but this seemed innocent enough, and I don't regret any of it. Now tell me what the doctor said."

She gave Jed a tentative smile then turned back to me. "I'm definitely pregnant. He said I'm eleven weeks and five days. Which means this baby is one-third of the way cooked."

Neely Kate was only a few days away from her second trimester.

I cast a glance at Jed, who was watching the children and not his wife. He obviously wasn't happy, but why? Had the doctor confirmed this pregnancy was too dangerous?

I turned back to Neely Kate. "And everything looked okay?"

"As well as could be expected," Jed said, still watching the kids.

"Jed just worries too much," Neely Kate said in exasperation, waving her hand toward him. "Everything looks fine."

"For now," Jed finished.

I nodded and glanced at Joe, who looked just as worried as I felt. "I guess we'll take it one day at a time," I said, trying to sound reassuring.

My phone vibrated in my pocket, and I almost ignored it, but then I wondered if it was my aunt checking on me. Or maybe Maeve had heard the news about what happened in my office. I wanted to reassure them both. But when I pulled it out of my pocket, my heart fell to my feet.

Mason Deveraux's name appeared on my screen.

My ex-boyfriend was now working for the Arkansas attorney general, and even though we had eventually parted on okay terms, I hadn't talked to him in a little over two years. Seeing his name on my phone after recent events shook me to my core.

I started to tell Joe and the others that I was going to take this call and would be right back, but Joe was focused on Liam, who had splashed yogurt on the wall, and Jed and Neely Kate were off in their own world. So I slipped into the living room and out the front door, taking up my perch on the porch swing as I answered.

"Hey, Mason, long time no see," I said, then I hastily added, "or I guess talk."

"I know," he said, sounding apologetic. "I've debated all weekend whether to call you with this piece of information. It could be nothing, but it could also be more than nothing. It only seemed fair to warn you."

"Warn me about what?" I asked, trying to hide my concern.

He paused. "A private investigator from Lone County, Arkansas, called my office on Thursday, wanting to speak to me about what I know about James Malcolm."

"I know he's living there now," I said, trying not to make too big a deal of the fact that I knew his location. "Has he gotten into some kind of trouble?" Last I heard, he'd been keeping a low profile.

"The sheriff there claims he's walking the straight and narrow, but we both know that men like him don't stick to it for long."

My stomach started to churn. I hoped and prayed James was

living a clean life. He'd been given a second chance when he was released from prison. I truly hoped he'd found peace and love, even if he didn't feel like he deserved either. But I knew that couldn't be the reason Mason had called. "I presume you're not just calling me to feed me some gossip?"

"No." He paused for several seconds. "The PI's name is Harper Adams. She used to be a detective with the Little Rock PD, but after she shot a teenager and was put on trial, she moved back to her hometown of Jackson Creek."

"That sounds vaguely familiar, but I've had my hands full the past year or so."

"I heard that Joe was elected sheriff," he said. "That must keep you busy since you have all the kids." He hastily added, "My mother loves you and your kids. She talks about them all the time."

"Oh."

"I'm not a stalker, I swear."

"I believe you."

"Good." He took a breath. "I wouldn't call just to tell you she asked about Malcolm. I've had the sheriff and the chief of Jackson Creek call me about Malcolm before, so that's not unusual. What *was* unusual about this request was that she also asked about *you*."

My heart skipped a beat. "Me?"

"She's curious about your connection to Malcolm."

It took my brain a couple of seconds to process what he'd said. "What did you tell her?"

"I called her back on Friday to see what she was fishing for, but she never called back. Turns out her mother died as the result of a single car accident. She drove off a bridge last week, and they fished her car out of the river last Thursday. Her mother's death is presumed an accidental drowning, pending the official autopsy report."

"Oh my word!" I gasped. "You don't think James had something to do with it, do you? It doesn't sound like something he would do."

It wasn't his style. He was more direct.

Part of me hated that I knew enough about him to make that deduction, while the rest of me felt guilty for defending him. But I knew the man. He wouldn't kill someone that way. Especially an older woman. In his own way, he was a man of principles. Or least he used to be.

"I don't know," he said without any animosity, "but I *do* know her call was made before they found her mother's car. The sheriff said she was looking into the disappearance of a businessman from the area that occurred about five years ago. The man's body happened to be found last week too, although someone else made the claim of discovering it."

"Did James have anything to do with the man's disappearance five years ago?"

"I don't see how," Mason said. "But the timing seems odd. Rumor had it that J.R. Simmons had some dealings in the county around that time, but nothing the state could prove."

"Joe's dad." But also James's old boss.

I'd been working for James as the Lady in Black five years ago. Surely, I would have known if James had been involved with the man's murder. Then again, I'd been his employee at that point. Not his friend or his lover.

But I knew James well enough to know he wouldn't have killed him without what he saw as just cause. And if the businessman had been working for J.R. Simmons, there very well may have been. The man had been evil incarnate.

"Joe's dad," he repeated. "Like I said, Ms. Adams never called me back, but if I do talk to her, I want to reassure you that I won't give her any information about you other than you were part of sting to bring J.R. down. The rest is in the report."

"And what do the reports say?" Funny how I'd never considered that before.

"Nothing too deep. You're safe."

"So why do you think she's askin' about me?"

"I don't know, but that's the part that has me worried. How and why did she make the connection to you?"

I drew in a shaky breath and released it, trying to calm my nerves. "I hear there've been some recent rumblings about the Lady in Black in the criminal world in Fenton County," I said, trying to hold it together. "A boy came looking for Lady last week looking for protection."

"Protection from what?" Mason asked, his voice sounding strained.

"He'd witnessed a murder and was scared to go to the sheriff. But he's seventeen, so he was pretty young when was I active as her. It just seemed odd he'd seek me out. And he claimed his seventeen-year-old friend was the one who suggested it."

"You're right. It does seem odd."

"Is another criminal group trying to move into this county, Mason?"

"Seems like Joe would be in a better position to answer that question," he countered.

"He doesn't think there is one, but all these coincidences…"

"Have you worried," he finished.

"Yeah."

"I confess, they have me worried too."

"Surprisingly, that makes me feel better."

"Not so surprising," he said softly. "You never were one to let things happen to you. You liked to take charge of your destiny. If a storm's coming, you want to have time to prepare."

"Do you think a storm's brewin', Mason?"

"Not yet, but don't be surprised if you'll need to batten down the hatches sooner rather than later."

That was exactly what I was afraid of.

Read a bonus scene on my website from Joe's POV a few days later.

ABOUT THE AUTHOR

Denise Grover Swank was born in Kansas City, Missouri and lived in the area until she was nineteen. Then she became a nomad, living in five cities, four states and ten houses over the course of ten years before she moved back to her roots. She speaks English and smattering of Spanish and Chinese which she learned through an intensive Nick Jr. immersion period. Her hobbies include witty Facebook comments (in own her mind) and dancing in her kitchen with her children. (Quite badly if you believe her offspring.) Hidden talents include the gift of justification and the ability to drink massive amounts of caffeine and still fall asleep within two minutes. Her lack of the sense of smell allows her to perform many unspeakable tasks. She has six children and hasn't lost her sanity. Or so she leads you to believe.

denisegroverswank.com

Don't miss out on Denise's newest releases! Join her mailing list.

Made in the USA
Middletown, DE
08 August 2024